Rebecca Winters lives in Salt Lake City, Utah. With canyons and high alpine meadows full of wildflowers, she never runs out of places to explore. They, plus her favourite vacation spots in Europe, often end up as backgrounds for her romance novels—because writing is her passion, along with her family and church. Rebecca loves to hear from readers. If you wish to email her, please visit her website at cleanromances.com.

The Billionaires' Club

REBECCA WINTERS

MILLS & BOON

First Published in Great Britain 2019
by Mills & Boon, an imprint of HarperCollins*Publishers*
1 London Bridge Street, London, SE1 9GF

ISBN: 978-0-263-27480-6

0319

RETURN OF HER ITALIAN DUKE

REBECCA WINTERS

To my darling daughter Dominique, a wonderful romance writer who has an editor's instinct and insight to keep her mother's writing on track and believable.

She too is a Dumas lover.
We're both Francophiles at heart.

CHAPTER ONE

Castello di Lombardi, ten years ago

AT TWO IN the morning, Vincenzo Gagliardi, newly turned eighteen, quickly dressed in jeans and a hoodie he pulled over his black hair. The long sleeves covered the bruises on his arms. He could feel the welts still smarting on his back and legs as he slid his pack over his shoulders. Then he looked around his room one more time, glancing at the bed.

A vision of Gemma, the woman who'd been entwined in his arms there the night before, wouldn't leave his mind. After the pleasure they'd given each other despite his wounds, and the plans he'd envisioned for their future, it killed him to think he had to leave her at all. But the difficulties with his father made his flight necessary. Worse, he couldn't tell her where he was going or why. It was for her own protection.

Once his father, the acting Duca di Lombardi, started looking for him, he'd interrogate everyone, including Gemma, and he would be able to tell if she was lying or not. If the girl he'd grown up with from earliest childhood knew nothing about his disappearance, then his father would sense it and have to believe her.

Arrivederci, Gemma, his heart moaned. *Ti amo.*

Making sure no one saw him, he hurried through the fourteenth-century *castello* to Dimi's room in the other tower. His cousin had left his bedroom door open. Closer than brothers, they'd been planning Vincenzo's disappearance for a year.

Dimi was waiting for him. "You're late and must go now! I've been watching from the parapet. The guard with the dog won't be walking past the entrance for another seven minutes."

"This is it, cousin. Remember—when I'm established in New York, I'll contact you. Look for the phone number through an ad in the help wanted of *Il Giorno*'s classified section. Be sure to call me on a throwaway phone."

Dimi nodded.

"It won't be long before you turn eighteen. I'll wire you money so you can join me. And as soon as I reach my destination, I'll phone our grandfather so he won't worry." Both boys were the grandsons of the cancer-stricken Emanuele Gagliardi, the old Duca di Lombardi, who no longer could function and verged on death.

His cousin's eyes teared up. "*Che Dio di benedica*, Vincenzo."

He tried to clear his throat. "God be with you, too, Dimi. Promise me you'll keep an eye on Gemma."

"You know I will."

Vincenzo hated this situation that took him away from her, but there was no going back. He thanked his cousin for his sacrifice, hating their gut-wrenching separation and the horrible position he'd been put in. But they both agreed the danger was too great to do anything else.

As they hugged hard, Vincenzo realized that he could barely see through the tears. The deep well of shame and pain because he hadn't been able to protect his mother was something he would have to carry for the rest of his life. Gemma was better off without him.

Because of Dimi's loyalty, no one would ever know where he'd gone. This was the way it had to be.

Now that Vincenzo had been forced to cut himself off from the world he knew, the need to make money had taken hold of his life and had become his raison d'être.

Gemma lay in bed, wide-awake, at six in the morning, reliving the moments she'd spent with Vincenzo the night before last. When she'd heard he'd suffered injuries from a fall off his horse, she hadn't been able to resist slipping up to his tower bedroom to see if he was all right.

Despite his physical pain, they'd tried to love each other until he'd told her she needed to get back to her room. Gemma had wanted to stay the entire night with him and couldn't understand why he'd been so insistent she leave. She'd wanted to lie in his arms forever.

It was painful to have to tear herself away from him. After making sure no guards were watching, she slipped down the winding staircase at the back of the *castello* to reach the rooms where she and her mother lived behind the kitchen.

Yesterday after school she hadn't seen him at all,

and she feared his injuries were worse. If she didn't spot him in the back courtyard today after she got home, she'd go up to his room again tonight to find out why.

He was such an expert rider, it was hard to believe he'd been hurt so badly. While she suffered over what had happened to him, she heard a knock on her bedroom door. "Gemma? Get up and get dressed, then come in the main room quickly!"

She didn't normally get up until six thirty to start getting ready for school. Alarmed by the concern in her mother's voice, Gemma did her bidding.

When she emerged from the small room, she saw a sight she'd never forget. Vincenzo's father, the acting Duca di Lombardi, stood there while three policemen searched their rooms off the *castello* kitchen.

He and Vincenzo bore a strong likeness to each other, but there was all the difference in the world between them. The *duca*'s stare at her was so menacing, she shuddered.

Her mother grabbed her hand. "The *duca* wishes to ask you a few questions, Gemma."

He'd never talked to her personally in her life. "Yes, Your Highness?"

"Where's my son?"

She blinked. "I—I don't know what you mean," she stammered.

"If you know anything, you must tell him, Gemma."

"I know nothing, Mamma."

The police reappeared, shaking their heads. The *duca* took a threatening step toward her. "My son is missing from the *castello*, and I believe *you* know where he's gone."

Gemma froze. Vincenzo was gone? "I swear on my faith in the Holy Virgin that I have no idea where he would be."

His face turned a ruddy color. He shot a fiery glance at Gemma's mother, who crossed herself. "She's lying! Since you can't get the truth from her, I insist you leave the premises immediately and take your baggage with you." Gemma flinched. "I'll make certain you're never able to get another job again!"

He wheeled around and left. The police followed and shut the door.

Gemma ran to her mother and hugged her hard. Both of them trembled. "I swear I don't know anything about Vincenzo. I swear it, Mamma."

"I believe you. Start packing your bag. I'll do the same. We have to get out of here as soon as possible in case he comes back. I'll call for a taxi from the kitchen. We'll leave for the train station and go back to Florence."

Fifteen minutes later they assembled in the kitchen. The other cook and her daughter, Bianca, Gemma's best friend, were there, too, with their bags. The *duca*'s fury knew no bounds. As they hurried out of the service entrance at the back of the *castello* to wait, the *duca*'s words rang in her ears.

She's lying! Since you can't get the truth from her, you must leave the premises immediately and take your baggage you. I'll make certain you're never able to get another job again!

When the taxi arrived, Gemma climbed inside feeling as dead as last winter's ashes.

New York City, six months ago

After Dimi had phoned Vincenzo during the night with news that had come close to sending him into shock, he made calls to his two best friends and asked them to come to his Manhattan penthouse above his office ASAP.

Once arrangements were made, he told his assistant he wouldn't be in the office today and didn't want to be disturbed for any reason. Within two hours they'd both shown up using his private elevator.

The ultra-contemporary apartment suited Vincenzo perfectly. He liked the modern art on the white walls and the floor-to-ceiling windows that let in the light. Up here there were no dark reminders of the past. Here, he could breathe. Or he'd thought he could, until Dimi's phone call.

"Thanks for coming so fast," he said in Italian. "I'm just thankful you were available."

Cesare nodded. "You made it sound like life or death."

"It is to me."

His friend Takis eyed him curiously. "What's going on, Vincenzo?"

"Something that will surprise you. I'll tell you over breakfast. Come to the dining room."

Once they sat down and started to eat, Vincenzo handed them each a photograph of the massive Castello di Lombardi. "You're looking at the former residence of the Gagliardi family. From that family, two hundred years ago, sprang the first illustrious Duca di Lombardi, an important political figure in that region of Italy."

They stared at the photo, then looked at him in confusion.

"Why am I showing you this?" He read their minds. "Because there's more to me than you know. What I'm about to tell you could cause you to distrust me. You would have every right to walk out of here and never look back."

"Tell us what?" Cesare asked in total bewilderment.

"I haven't been completely honest about myself. You know me as Vincenzo Nistri, but my full name is Vincenzo Nistri Gagliardi. Nistri was my mother's maiden name."

Takis blinked. "So you're full-fledged Italian? For some reason you remind me of one of my Macedonian friends."

"That's what I thought, too," Cesare said. "Maybe Eastern Europe."

"Is that so?" Vincenzo grinned, amused by their honesty. "Not that I know of. The *castello* you're looking at was my home for the first eighteen years of my life." *And the woman I left behind there so cruelly is still the only girl I ever loved, though there've been women since.* "If a great tragedy hadn't happened to my family—one that caused me to flee—I would have taken over as the next Duca di Lombardi upon my father's death."

There was no question that he'd stunned his friends. Neither of them said a word. They kept staring at him as if he were an alien being speaking an unknown language.

"Let me tell you a story so you'll understand everything. My father and uncle did very bad things, evil things. At one point I realized my life was in danger."

When he'd given them details, he said, "The old *duca*, my grandfather, died nine years ago, leaving the way open for my father and uncle to bring down the house of Gagliardi. To start paying their debts, they sold off family treasures, including other properties that had been in the family for hundreds of years. Inevitably they let go the staff who'd served our family faithfully.

"Then a month ago my father was riding his horse through the forest behind the *castello* in a drunken rage. The horse reared and my father fell, breaking his neck. That left my uncle, Alonzo in charge.

"He has just been sent to prison, where he's now serving a thirty-year sentence for manslaughter, drunkenness, embezzlement and debt in the millions of euros. The family has now disintegrated, and the authorities have closed up the *castello*."

His friends shook their heads. "How could such a thing happen to a powerful family like yours?" Takis asked.

"There's one word for it. Corruption. Absolute and truly terrible. The family coffers had been raided for so long there was nothing left but staggering debt they'd accrued. They were like two bad seeds.

"My maternal grandparents died two years ago, and the only remaining family members on my father's side besides my imprisoned uncle are my cousin Dimi, who is like a brother to me, and his mother, Consolata. They live in a small palazzo in Milan given to her by her grandmother before her marriage to my uncle."

It was the only piece of property that neither Alonzo nor Vincenzo's father had been able to lay his hands on at the end.

"Dimi lives there quietly with her because she's in a wheelchair, suffering from dementia, and needs care." He eyed them directly. "Can you forgive me for omitting all of this until now?"

"*Si*—" both men said in unison. Takis's brows met. "Your life was in grave danger."

"But that's in the past. Now I'm faced with something I hadn't imagined, and I wanted to discuss it with you."

Cesare's solemn gaze played over him. "Tell us."

"The *castello* is now in receivership. I swore to God I would never return to Italy, but the thought of my heritage being sold to some foreign potentate to help the slipping Italian economy is anathema to me.

"My cousin Dimi is particularly concerned. He has an eye on what's happening everywhere. Both Italy's Villa Giulia museum in Rome, built by Pope Julius III, and the nine-hundred-year-old Norman palace in Palermo, the seat of former kings, are soon to be on the list to be sold off by the government, too.

"In view of such a frightening prospect, I wondered if you might like to go into business with me. Dimi will assist behind the scenes. Not only will my cousin and I be able to preserve our own family heritage, we'll transform the *castello* into a glorious hotel with a restaurant that could be the toast of Europe. It would mean the three of us would have to put our assistants in charge of managing our businesses when we're not in the country."

After a pronounced silence, both men let out cries

of excitement. For the rest of the day the three of them brainstormed.

"Now that we've talked things out, there's one favor I must ask. I intend to be the silent business partner in this venture and prefer to remain anonymous because of the family scandals."

Their solemn acknowledgment of his request warmed him and he knew they'd honor his request.

"Now, you can imagine that when word gets out that the *castello* has been sold and turned into a resort by two businessmen from the US, the press will be all over it. Dimi will send me the necessary information and put you in touch with the contact person to get the ball rolling.

"If we do decide to go into business together, I'll expect you two to do the negotiating. Naturally I'll supply the money needed so we can get started on the renovations right away."

Cesare smiled. "The *duca*'s return."

"No, Cesare. I don't want my title mentioned. That's not for public consumption." He couldn't escape the title he'd inherited by being his father's son, but in time he intended to renounce it legally through the court system. *And I'll find Gemma if it kills me.* Over the last ten years, no search had turned up any evidence of her.

"Understood." Cesare eyed him seriously. "When we first met at university, I always knew there was a lot more to you, but I couldn't put my finger on it and didn't dare ask for fear of insulting you."

"Now it's all making sense," Takis admitted. "Your English is too perfect, and you're far more sophisticated and knowledgeable than anyone else I know."

"Your friendship has meant the world to me. Let's hope for success in our new venture."

Takis sat back in the chair. "Edmond Dantes had nothing on you, Vincenzo Gagliardi."

Florence, Italy, present day

The bulletin board of the Florentine Epicurean School of Hospitality and Culinary Arts listed the latest career openings across four continents for their recent graduates to investigate.

At twenty-seven years of age, Gemma had finally received her long-awaited certification with the much-coveted first-place blue ribbon, and she hurried down the corridor toward the office. Everyone wanted to apply for the most prestigious position posted. She didn't know what her chances were, but it didn't matter. Her hard, grueling years of schooling were over, and she would find a position that guaranteed her a new life so she could prove herself.

She wanted to pay back her mother's family, who'd taken them in after they'd been thrown out of the Castello di Lombardi. Her relationship with Vincenzo years ago had put her family in such dire straits, it had ruined her mother's career. Gemma felt the responsibility heavily, because she hadn't heeded her mother's warnings that a commoner didn't mingle with royalty. But those days were behind her.

With students gathered around the bulletin board, it was hard to get close enough to write down the information. Later the lists would be put online, but she was too impatient and took pictures of the various announcements with her cell phone.

Her best friend Filippa Gatti, who'd gone through pastry school with Gemma, had the same idea. They made plans to talk later before she hurried off. Gemma found a bench farther along the corridor and sat down to study everything but gave up because she couldn't concentrate with so much noise.

Once outside, she got in her old blue car and headed back to her aunt's apartment two miles away. Her mother's sister owned the hundred-year-old Bonucci family bakery and ran it with her married daughter. When Gemma and her mother had fled to Florence, her aunt had let them live in the apartment above the bakery.

Her aunt was goodness itself and had put her mother to work. She had also helped Gemma get a scholarship to attend cooking school, because her mother's funds were so low. Her cousin was wonderful, too, and they all got along.

Once she had started culinary school, Gemma had helped out in the bakery every day after classes. The culinary school required ten years of apprenticeship. After high school she'd begun her training there. Now that she'd graduated, it was important she start paying her aunt back for letting them live there and helping to get them on their feet after being kicked out of the *castello*.

Today she dashed up the back stairs to the door off the porch. Gemma couldn't wait to call her mom and aunt and tell them she'd been chosen the top graduate in her class. After they'd shown such faith in her, Gemma was thrilled that her hard work had paid off.

But of course, it would happen that her mother and aunt had just left to go on a well-deserved vacation to the United Kingdom with friends, their first in years. They wouldn't be back for three weeks, because their trip included England, Scotland, Wales and Ireland. Such good news from the school had filled Gemma with joy. She would have to phone her *mamma*, Mirella, immediately.

Now that she'd received her certification, she was anxious to find a fabulous job and move out. She planned for her mother to go with her. They'd find a small, affordable apartment. Her mother could stop working and enjoy her life while her daughter earned the living.

After grabbing her favorite fruit soda from the fridge, Gemma sank down on the chair at the small kitchen table and phoned her *mamma*. Frustrated when she got her voice mail, Gemma asked her to phone her back ASAP because she had exciting news.

Next, she scrolled through her photo gallery to the information she'd recorded on her cell. To her utmost disappointment, none of the eighteen openings for pastry chefs were in France, the place where she'd had her heart set on working.

Both the French and the Italians thought they produced the finest chefs. As her mother and aunt had told her, because she was a woman, she'd have an even harder time breaking into a top five-star restaurant in either country. Women chefs still struggled for equality. One day she would get a position on the Côte d'Azur. But for now she needed a job right away!

Trying to manage her disappointment, she studied each opening one at a time: five in Spain, three in England, one in Liechtenstein, two in Australia, three in Japan, three in Canada, one in Italy.

Since it couldn't be France, nothing else thrilled her, but she studied the requirements for the various openings.

It wasn't until she came to the last posting, from Italy, that Gemma was shaken to the core. She thought she'd read it wrong. The shock had her jumping up from the couch. She read the words again, attempting to quell the frantic pounding of her heart.

Location: Milan, Italy. Fourteenth-century castello and former estate of the deceased Duca di Lombardi, Salvatore Gagliardi. Grand opening of the five-star Castello Supremo Hotel and Ristorante di Lombardi, July 6.

July 6 was only four weeks away. She read on.

Résumés for executive chef and executive pastry chef are being accepted. See list of requirements. Only those with the proper credentials need apply.

Gemma came close to fainting when she thought of Vincenzo. The fact that he'd disappeared without even saying goodbye had caused an anger in her that, even now, she was still trying to suppress. He'd told her he was in love with her and that one day they'd find a way to be married.

After he'd vanished, she'd felt so used. What a fool she'd been to believe he could love the daughter of a cook! How naive of her to think the *duca*-to-be would consider an alliance with an underling like Gemma. In her dream world they'd been equals and anything was possible. But once Vincenzo's father had tossed her and her mother out like a heap of garbage, she'd received the wake-up call of her life. It had shaken her world forever.

As she read the announcement again, something twisted painfully inside her. The *castello*, an icon over the centuries that had been her home until the age of seventeen, had now been turned into a hotel and restaurant. She tried to understand how such a thing could have happened to the family with its succession of *duchi* for over two hundred years.

Gone was their birthright and traditions. Vincenzo had disappeared along with his family. Last year she'd heard on television that Vincenzo's father was dead. And soon after that Dimi's father had been sent to prison for fraud. Beyond that there'd been no more news.

Now she was horrified to think the *castello* had been put up and sold for its commercial value in an increasingly mercenary world. Gemma considered it a form of sacrilege.

No doubt every new graduate would apply there first, but they didn't have a prayer of being hired. Only the most famous chefs throughout Europe and elsewhere would be allowed an interview at such a magnificent and famous landmark. Many considered Italy to be the vortex of gastronomic delight in the world. The competition would be fierce.

Even so, she was going to apply.

After her failed relationship with Paolo, she realized she needed to draw a line under the past. Until she discovered what had happened to Vincenzo and why, she knew in her heart she'd never be able to move on with her life.

If by some miracle she only made it to the first interview before being rejected, maybe she'd be able to find out where Vincenzo had gone. What had caused the demise of the Gagliardi family? So much had been hushed up in the press.

Pushing those thoughts aside, for the rest of the day she emailed her prepared résumé to Milan, Valencia, Barcelona, London and Vaduz in Liechtenstein. For some reason she couldn't attach her picture, but it was too late to worry about that now.

Filippa called to tell her she'd applied for all three jobs in Canada. She would have preferred to go to the States, but Canada was the next closest place with openings. Gemma wished her luck and told her what she'd done. They promised to keep each other updated on what happened.

The next day she started receiving emails back and learned that the positions in Vaduz and Valencia had already been filled. Barcelona and London were still open. To her satisfaction, they'd sent her a specific day and time to report for a personal interview.

But it was the email that came after lunch from the *castello* that almost sent her into cardiac arrest. She was told to report there at noon tomorrow! And to please let them know immediately if she couldn't make it.

Gemma had thought, of course, that being a new graduate, she wouldn't have been considered. Something on her résumé must have caused them to give her an opportunity.

Thank heaven her mother wasn't in Italy right now.

Gemma needed to see this through before she told her parent anything. The last thing she wanted to do was hurt her *mamma*. But for Gemma's own emotional health and progress, she had to do this! It might be her only chance in this life to find out about Vincenzo. If she didn't follow through, she knew she'd always regret it.

With hands trembling, she sent an email to let them know she'd be there at the correct time. If she left Florence within the hour, she could drive to the village at the base of the *castello* today and find a room for the night. That would give her time tomorrow to get ready before the interview.

Gemma phoned her cousin to let her know that she was leaving for a day or two to go job hunting. She made no mention that her destination was the *castello*. Her cousin had been so hurt for Gemma and her mother, she would have tried to persuade her to avoid more pain and not go. But this was something she had to do.

Without wasting any time, she showered and packed a suitcase that included her laptop. After dressing in jeans and a blouse, she set off on the three-hour drive to Milan full of questions that might get answered after all this time. It would be a trip of agony and ecstasy, since she'd never once been back.

By seven in the evening, she'd arrived in the busy city and took the turnoff for the village of Sopri, where she'd gone to school with a few children of the other estate workers. Even after all this time, Gemma knew where to find a *pensione* with reasonable rates.

But sleep didn't come well. She tossed and turned

for hours. Memories of Vincenzo and the night they'd been together in his bedroom kept her awake. Lying in his arms she'd felt immortal, but he hadn't let her stay with him all night, something she'd never understood.

How she'd loved her life at the *castello* with him! For years since his disappearance she'd tried to discover his whereabouts, but he'd vanished as if into thin air. Over time it finally sank in that she hadn't been good enough for him. That's what her mother had been trying to tell her without putting the painful message into actual words. Gemma believed it now!

When she wasn't hating Vincenzo, she feared that something terrible had happened to him. The possibility that he might have died was insupportable to her. Combined with her pain over the loss of Vincenzo was her outrage for what his father had done to her and her beloved mother. The great, cruel Duca di Lombardi! There were times when the memory of that morning still tormented her.

Once they'd moved to Florence, she'd never heard anything about Vincenzo or Dimi. Where had his cousin gone? She'd once hoped that if she could even find Dimi, she'd get answers to all her questions. But it was as if the Gagliardi family had been erased from life. It was too strange… She missed Dimi. He'd been such a wonderful friend all those years ago.

Now she was going back to the place where she'd known such joy…and pain. What if by some stretch of the imagination she got the job? How would she feel? How would her mother feel to realize her daughter had graduated with honors from the top cooking school in Italy and was going to make it despite what the *duca* had done to them?

Wouldn't it be the height of deliciousness to be hired there, of all places on earth? Such sweet revenge after being kicked to the gutter.

Gemma was relieved when morning came. After washing her hair and showering, she dressed in a peach-colored two-piece suit, wanting to look her best. At ten she ate breakfast at a trattoria before leaving for the *castello* ten minutes away. She'd planned to get there early enough to look around and ask questions. Surely someone would be able to tell her about Vincenzo.

For him to disappear on her was a betrayal so awful, she hadn't been able to put her trust in another man for years. Even after she'd starting dating, the memory of that horrible time when it became clear he'd never be back still haunted her nights.

It had taken until a year ago for her to have her first serious relationship with a man. After a month of dating, Paolo wanted to sleep with her, but she couldn't. Her heart wasn't in it. She explained to him that in another eight months she'd be graduating and looking for a position, hopefully in France. There could be no future for them. She had to follow her own path.

After breakfast Gemma opened the car window and breathed in the warm June air as she drove past the familiar signposts, farms and villas toward the massive Castello di Lombardi.

The ocher-toned structure, with its towers and crenellated walls sprawled over a prominent hilltop, had its roots in ancient times. So many nights she and

Vincenzo had walked along those walls with their arms around each other, talking and laughing quietly so none of the family or guards would see or hear them.

Closer now, cypress trees bordered her on either side of the winding road. Memories came flooding back. Because of Vincenzo, she knew all about its history. The remains of a Romanesque church standing in the inner courtyard dated back to AD 875. But the *castello* itself had been built in the fourteenth century to protect the surrounding estate from invasions.

Many owners had possessed it, including the House of Savoy. By the mid–eighteen hundreds it had become the residence of the Gagliardi family. Although it was the first Duca di Lombardi who was considered illustrious, as far as Gemma was concerned that right would have belonged to Vincenzo. That was, until he'd plunged a dagger in her heart by disappearing.

The visitor parking beneath the four flights of zigzagging front steps held no cars. Her breath caught to see the profusion of flowers and landscaping done to beautify everything. New external lighting fixtures had been put in place. At night it would present a magnificent spectacle to guests arriving.

After taking it all in, she drove down a private road that wound around to the rear entrance where in the past the tradesmen used to come. Beyond it was a large parking area that she remembered had been used by the staff.

There were a dozen vans and trucks, plus some elegant cars, clustered in the enclosed area around the door. From the front of the *castello* the entire place had looked deserted, but that clearly wasn't the case.

Once she'd gotten out of her car to walk around, a male gardener planting flowers called to her. "The lady is lost, perhaps?" he asked in Italian.

She shook her head. *Anything but.* "I'm here for a job interview."

"Ah? Then you must go around to the front. The office is on the right of the entrance hall."

"Thank you." It seemed that the day room she remembered must have been converted into an office. She could never have imagined it. "Tell me—do you know why the *castello* was sold in the first place?"

He hunched his shoulders. "*No lo so.*"

With her hair swishing against her shoulders, Gemma nodded and walked back to her car, realizing she'd get nothing from him. Her watch said eleven forty-five. She might as well arrive a few minutes early to show she was punctual. She backed her car around, retracing her short trip back to the main parking lot, where she stopped the car and got out.

How many hundreds of times had she and her childhood friend Bianca—who'd had a crush on Dimi—bounded up these steps after getting off the school bus looking for Vincenzo and his cousin?

They would enter the *castello* through a private doorway west of the main entrance and hurry down the corridor to the kitchen. Once they'd checked in with their mothers, they'd run off to their hiding place in the back courtyard, where hopefully the two Gagliardis would be waiting.

To her surprise the old private entrance no longer existed. The filled-in stone wall looked like it had been there forever. Gemma felt shut out and could well believe she'd dreamed up a past life.

But when she entered through the main doors, she had to admit that whoever had undertaken to turn this into a world-class resort had done a superb job of maintaining its former beauty. Many of the paintings and tapestries she remembered still adorned the vaulted ceilings and walls on the right side of the hallway.

The biggest difference lay in the bank of floor-to-ceiling French doors on the left. They ran the length of the long hallway she used to run through on her way to the kitchen. Beyond the mullioned glass squares she could see a gorgeous dining room with huge chandeliers so elegant it robbed her of breath.

On the far side of the dining room were more French doors that no doubt opened on to a terrace for open-air dining. Gemma knew there was a rose garden on that side of the *castello*. And though she couldn't see it from here, there was a magnificent ballroom beyond the dining room to the south.

She was staggered by the changes, so exquisite in design she could only marvel. Whoever had taken over this place had superb taste in everything. Suddenly she realized it was noon and she swung around to report she was here.

The enormous former day room had been transformed into the foyer and front desk of the fabulous hotel, with a long counter, several computers and all the accoutrements essential for business. She sat down on one of the eighteenth-century sage-and-gold damask chairs with the Duca di Lombardi's royal crest and waited to see if someone would come.

Just as she was ready to call out if anyone was there, she saw movement behind the counter that revealed an attractive brown-haired male, probably six foot two and in his late twenties. Strong and lean, he wore trousers and shirtsleeves pushed up to the elbows. When his cobalt-blue eyes wandered over her, she knew he'd missed nothing.

"You must be Signora Bonucci."

CHAPTER TWO

GEMMA CORRECTED HIM. "I'm Signor*ina* Bonucci."

"Ah. I saw the ring."

"It was my grandmother's." Gemma's mother had given it to her on her twenty-first birthday. Her grandmother had also been a great cook, and the hope was that it would bring Gemma luck. Now Gemma wore it on her right hand in remembrance.

As for the name, Bonucci, that was another story. Once Gemma and her mother had left the *castello*, Mirella had insisted Gemma use her maiden name. She'd hoped to be able to find work if the *duca* couldn't trace them through her married name, Rizzo.

One corner of his mouth lifted in a smile. "Now that we have that straightened out, I'm Signor Donati, the one who's late for this meeting. Call me Cesare." With that accent the man was Sicilian down to his toenails. "Thank you for applying with us. Come around the counter and we'll talk in my office."

She got up and followed him down a hallway past several doors to his inner sanctum, modern and in a messy state. Everything about Cesare surprised Gemma, including the informality.

"Take a seat."

Gemma sat down on one of the leather chairs. “I have to admit I was surprised that you would even consider a new graduate.”

He perched on the corner of his desk. “I always keep an open mind. I had already chosen the finalists and the field was closed, but when your résumé showed up yesterday, it caught my eye.”

“Might I ask why?”

“It included something no one else’s did. You said you learned the art of pastry making from your mother. That was a dangerous admission and made me curious to know why you dared.” He was teasing her.

“It *was* dangerous, I know.” For more reasons than he was implying, but the *duca* was dead now. “To leave my mother from my résumé would make me ungrateful.”

She felt his gaze studying her. “For you to mention her means she wasn’t just an average cook in your eyes.”

“No. She came from a family of bakers. To me, her pastry will always be the best.” Gemma owed her mother everything after her sacrifices.

The man cocked his head. “It shows you’re willing to give credit where it’s due. But being the daughter of a cook doesn’t always make the daughter a cook, no matter the genes nor how many classes at school.”

“No one is more aware of that than I am, but I would be nothing without her. She helped me go to cooking school in Florence.”

He folded his arms. “The best in Italy, where you received the highest award during your ten year apprenticeship there. It’s a stringent education, but the most prestigious culinary schools require that much training to turn out the best cooks. She guided you well. Bravo."

A compliment from a man who knew the culinary business well enough to be in charge of staffing this new hotel came as a complete surprise.

"If I hadn't been born her daughter, I would never in this world have decided on a career that keeps you on your feet all day and night, that will never pay enough money and that is unfair to women chefs in general. In truth I'm shocked you allowed me this interview, even if you are exceptionally open-minded."

She shouldn't have said it, but she'd spoken without thinking. Incredibly he burst into laughter.

"Signorina, you're like a breath of fresh air and have won yourself one chance to prove if there's genius in you. Report to me at ten in the morning and I'll put you to work making what you do best."

Gemma stared hard at him. "You're serious..." Was it really possible?

His brows lifted. "When it comes to cooking, I'm always serious. You'll be sharing the kitchen with another applicant who is hoping to become the executive chef. All the ingredients you need will be provided, and you'll both have your own workspace. When you're finished, you will leave. Any questions?"

Yes. She had a big one, but now wasn't the moment. It had to be another test to see how well two different chefs got along under this kind of pressure. "None, Signor."

"*Bene.* When your pastry has been sampled by the people in charge tomorrow evening, an opinion will be made. The next day you'll be phoned and informed of their decision. Please see yourself out."

Now she was scared. She'd heard back from her mother last night and had been able to tell her about receiving the top marks for her certification. Her mother and aunt had been overjoyed. Gemma had told them she planned to apply at quite a few places for work, but she'd left out the position offered at the *castello*.

There was no need for her mother to know about it since Gemma had no real hope of getting it. Instead she'd asked them about their trip and they'd talked for a long time. Her mother had sounded so happy, Gemma hadn't wanted to say anything to take away from her enjoying the only trip she'd had in years.

Deep in painful thoughts, Vincenzo strode down the portrait-lined *castello* hallway toward his deceased grandfather's private dining room. Even after being back in Italy for a half year, it was still hard to believe this had once been his home.

All Vincenzo could think about was Gemma. Over the last ten years, he'd paid an Italian private investigator to look for her to no avail. For the six months he'd been in Lombardi, he'd doubled the search. Vincenzo's guilt over how his unexplained disappearance must have hurt Gemma beyond description had tortured him from the beginning. It matched his fear that he would never catch up to her again.

Though Dimi had promised to keep an eye on Gemma for him, fate had stepped in to change Dimi's life, too. The day that Vincenzo's father had gone on a rampage over his disappearance and had searched the countryside for him with the help of Dimi's father and the police, Dimi had realized the danger in staying at the *castello.* That very morning he'd left with his mother and taken her to her family's property in Milan, where they'd be safe and out of the way.

On his own, Dimi had searched for Gemma, but that path had led nowhere, either.

The thought filled Vincenzo with such profound sadness, gripping him to the point he couldn't throw it off. Echoes and whispers from a time when he'd known real happiness with Gemma haunted him and made his disconnect with the past even more heart wrenching.

His friends looked up when he entered. They must have heard his footsteps on the intricate pattern of inlaid wood flooring. Before he sat down at the oval table, Vincenzo's silvery-gray eyes—a trait of the Gagliardi men—glanced at the wood nymphs painted on the ornate ceiling.

Twenty-eight-year-old Vincenzo found them as fascinating now as he'd done as a little boy. One of them had always been of particular interest, because Gemma could have been the subject the artist had painted.

"*Mi dispiace essere in ritardo.* I was on the phone with Annette."

The savvy real estate woman he'd been involved with before leaving New York had wanted to plan her vacation to be with him for the opening. Deep down he knew she was hoping for a permanent arrangement. But since Vincenzo had stepped on Italian soil, memories of Gemma had had a stranglehold on him. He knew he wasn't ready to live with anyone, let alone get married.

Maybe after the opening he'd be able to relax and give it more thought. He enjoyed Annette more than any woman in a long time. But he had work to do and had told her he would call her back when he had more time to talk. The disappointment in her voice when he said he had to hang up because he was late for a business dinner spoke volumes. It was the truth.

Cesare smiled at him. "*Non c'e problema.*"

Greek-born Takis grunted. "Maybe not for you, Cesare, but I didn't eat lunch on purpose, and now I'm famished."

Vincenzo nodded. "I held back, too. Tonight is the night we make decisions that will spell the success or failure of our business venture. Let's get started."

"Just so you know, a fourth pastry chef applicant has created a sampling of desserts for us this evening."

"A fourth?" Vincenzo frowned. "I thought we were through with the vetting process."

"I thought so, too, but this one came in at the last minute yesterday with amazing credentials, and I decided to take a chance."

Takis groaned. "So we have to eat two sets of desserts?"

"That's right, so don't eat too much of any one thing," Cesare cautioned them.

On that note Vincenzo used his cell phone to ring for dinner. Tonight was the final night in their search to find the perfect executive chef and executive pastry chef for their adventure. The right choices would put them on the map as one of the most sought-after resorts in the world.

They'd narrowed the collection of applicants down to three in one category and now four in the other, but they were cutting it close. In one month they would be opening the doors and everything would have to be ready.

Their recently hired maître d', Cosimo, came up on the newly installed elevator and wheeled in a cart from the kitchen with their dinner. If tonight's food was anything like the other two nights, they were in for a very difficult time choosing the best of the best. The battle between the finalists was fierce.

For the next half hour they sampled and discussed the main course and made the decision that the French applicant would become their executive chef.

With that accomplished, Vincenzo rang for the desserts. Cosimo brought in the tray of delicious offerings from the third pastry chef.

"Remember," Cesare reminded them, "we have one more round of desserts from the fourth pastry chef to sample." He passed them a dish of water crackers. "Eat a few of these now so you'll be able to appreciate what's coming." They drank tea with the crackers to help cleanse their palates.

Cosimo wheeled in the last offerings of the night. As he placed the tray on the table, Vincenzo took one look at the desserts and thought he must be dreaming. *All* of them were Italian, and there were so many of them! They made up the parts of his childhood. He couldn't decide what to try first.

Unaware of his friends at this point, he started on *sfogliatelli*, his favorite dessert in the world, layered like sea shells with cream and cinnamon. When he'd eaten the whole thing he reached for the puffed dome of sweet panettone, the bread his family had eaten on holidays. When he couldn't swallow another bite, he lifted his head. His friends were staring at him like he'd lost his mind.

Takis nudged Cesare. "I believe we've found our executive pastry chef."

"But first we must get Vincenzo to a hospital. He's going to be sick."

Their smiles widened into grins, but he couldn't laugh. All these desserts were too good to be true and tasted like the ones prepared by Gemma's mother years ago. But that was impossible!

He eyed Cesare. "Who made these?"

"A graduate from the Florentine Epicurean culinary school."

Vincent shook his head. "I need to know more." At this juncture his heart was thumping with emotion.

Their smiles receded. Cesare looked worried. "What's wrong?"

"Tell me this person's name."

"Signorina Bonucci. I don't remember her first name. It's on her résumé in my office."

The name meant nothing to Vincenzo. "How old is she? Early sixties?" Had Mirella, Gemma's mother, seen the advertisement and applied for the position?

"No. She's young. In her midtwenties."

How could anyone reproduce desserts identical to Mirella's unless she knew her or had worked with her? If that were true, then perhaps she could tell him Gemma's whereabouts!

"What's going on, Vincenzo?"

For the next few minutes he told them about one of the cooks at the *castello* years ago. "Her pastry was out of this world. She had a daughter who was a year younger than me. We grew up together on her mother's sweets. She was my first love."

"Ah," they said in a collective voice, clearly surprised at another one of his admissions.

"I have no idea what happened to either of them. In fact, over the years I've spent a large sum of money trying to find them, with no success. I want to meet this applicant and find out how she happens to have produced the same desserts."

He jumped up from the chair and hurried out of the room to the elevator at the end of the hall. Once on the main floor, they walked through the lobby and congregated in Cesare's private office. His friend pulled up the résumé on his computer for Vincenzo, who stood next to him to read it.

Seeing her first name nearly gave him a heart attack.

Gemma Bonucci
Age: 27
Address: Bonucci Bakery, Florence Top student in the year's graduating class of pastry chefs.

He was incredulous. His search had come to an end. He'd found her!

Vincenzo had known her as Gemma Rizzo. So why Bonucci? So many questions were bombarding him, he felt like he'd been punched in the gut.

"This must be Mirella's daughter, but there's no picture of her."

"It wasn't attached to her application," Cesare explained, "but her cooking is absolutely superb."

"So was her mother's. I can't comprehend that she was in the kitchen earlier cooking our dessert."

"You look a little pale. Are you all right?"

Vincenzo eyed Cesare. "I will be as soon as I get over the shock. You don't know what these last ten years have been like, trying to find her and always coming to a dead end..."

"Do we agree she's our new executive pastry chef?" Takis asked.

Vincenzo looked at both men. "Don't let my overeating influence you in any way. I have a terrible Italian sweet tooth, but we need to consider the various preferences of all patrons who will come through our doors. I'm sorry that you haven't been able to vote your conscience because of my behavior."

"It wasn't your behavior that decided me," Cesare insisted. "That was the best tiramisu I've ever eaten."

"Don't forget the baba and the baby cannoli," Takis chimed in. "Every dessert was exquisite and presented like a painting. When the guests leave, they'll spread the word that the most divine Italian desserts were made right here."

"Amen." This from Cesare. "But Vincenzo, did you have to eat all the *sfogliatelli* before we could sample it? Cosimo had to bring us more. It was food for the gods."

It was. And the lips of the loving seventeen-year-old girl Vincenzo had once held in his arms and kissed had been as sweet and succulent as the cinnamon-sprinkled cream in the pastry she'd prepared for this evening.

"Takis will make the phone calls now and tell our two new chefs to come to the office at noon for an orientation meeting." Cesare's announcement jerked Vincenzo out of his hidden thoughts.

"I'm glad the decisions have been made. As long as I'm in your office, I'd like to see the résumés of the other pastry finalists." It was an excuse to take another look at Gemma's.

"Be my guest," Cesare murmured. "Those desserts finished me off. I may never eat again."

"You're not the only one. I'm going to my office to make the phone calls."

But for the stunning realization that tomorrow he would see Gemma—the chef who'd turned them all into gluttons—Vincenzo would have laughed.

He walked around the desk and sat down in front of the computer screen to look at it. Her training had been matchless. She held certificates in the culinary arts, baking and pastry, hospitality management, wine studies, enology, and molecular gastronomy. She'd won awards for jams, preserves, chocolate ice cream. Mirella's chocolate ice cream had been divine.

The statement she'd made to explain her desire to be an executive pastry chef stood out as if it had been illuminated. *I learned the art of pastry making from my mother and would like to honor her life's work with my own.*

His eyes smarted as he rang Cesare.

"*Ehi, come va*, Vincenzo?"

"Sorry to bother you. What was it about Signorina Bonucci's résumé that decided you on allowing her to compete? I'm curious."

"You know me. My *mamma*'s cooking is the best

in the world, and I never make a secret about it. When I read about her wanting to honor her *mamma*'s cooking, I decided it was worth giving her a chance. On a whim I told her to report to the *castello*. I did the right thing in your opinion, *non e vero*?"

He closed his eyes tightly. "You already know the answer to that question. If you'd ignored her application, I doubt I would ever have found her." His throat closed up with emotion. "*Grazie, amico.*"

"I'm beginning to think it was meant to be. Before I hang up, there's one thing you should know, Vincenzo."

"What's that?"

"I didn't tell you before because I didn't want you or Takis to think I was biased in picking her for personal reasons."

His pulse sped up. "Go on."

"The signorina is beautiful. Like the forest nymph on the dining room ceiling you were staring at tonight. You know, the one leaning against the tree?"

Yes. Vincenzo knew the one and felt his face go hot. One night when he'd been kissing Gemma, he'd told her she reminded him of that exact nymph painted in the room where Vincenzo had spent many happy times talking to his grandfather. Cesare had noticed the resemblance, too.

"*A domani*, Cesare."

"*Dormi bene.*"

Vincenzo turned off the lights and headed for his old bedroom in the tower. No renovations had been made here. Guests would never be allowed in this part of the *castello*. It was too full of dark memories to open to the public.

He removed his clothes and threw on a robe before walking out on the balcony overlooking Sopri at the foot of the hillside where he'd run away. Where was she sleeping tonight? Down below, near to where she'd once attended school? Or in Milan?

Vincenzo knew her deceased father's last name had been Rizzo. Everyone called her mother Mirella. He'd heard the story that her husband, who worked in the estate stables, had died of an infection in his leg. After that, Mirella moved up from the village where they'd lived before his death and was allowed rooms in the rear of the *castello* with her little girl, Gemma.

One of the cooks who'd lived there, too, had had a child of the same age, named Bianca. Vincenzo couldn't remember when he and his cousin Dimi had started playing with them on the grounds of the estate. They were probably four and five years old.

Strict lines between social classes were drawn to prevent them from being together, but like all children, they found a way. He remembered his eighth birthday, when Gemma entered the courtyard where he and Dimi had been practicing archery with his new bow. She gave him a little lemon ricotta cheesecake her mother had baked just for him. He'd never tasted anything so good in his life.

From that day on, Gemma found ways to slip sweets to him from the kitchen. They'd go to their hiding place at the top of the tower and sit outside, straddling the crenellated wall while they ate his favorite *sfogliatelli*. When he looked down from that same wall now, he realized they could have fallen to their deaths at any time.

An hour later he went to bed, but he couldn't turn

off his thoughts. When he'd had to leave Europe in the dead of night, he hadn't been able to tell Gemma why and hadn't dared make contact with her. Days, weeks, months and finally years went by, but she'd always lingered in his memory.

To think that while he'd been in New York buying and selling businesses and building new companies over the last decade, she'd been in Florence working heaven knew how many hours, day in and day out, before ending up back at the *castello* as executive pastry chef. *Incredibile!*

CHAPTER THREE

GEMMA HAD BEEN in a state of disbelief since last night. A Signor Manolis, the business manager, had called to tell her she'd been hired to be the executive pastry chef at the Castello Supremo Hotel and Ristorante di Lombardi! She was to report to him at noon today.

Things like this just didn't happen, not to a new culinary graduate. But it was, and it meant she didn't have to leave Italy. By some miracle she was going back to where she'd known years of happiness…being friends and falling in love with Vincenzo before that dreadful moment when she'd learned of his disappearance.

Don't think about that terrible morning when the duca *destroyed your life and your mother's. That part of your life was over a long time ago. Let the memories go...you're the new pastry chef. And now it's possible you can find out what happened to Vincenzo.* One of her new bosses had to have information.

But a huge new problem beset her.

How was she going to tell her mother about this? Her dear mother, who was in England and knew nothing yet.

Gemma flew around the room in a panic. How

would her *mamma* react to this after all the many sacrifices she'd made for her daughter over the years? Would it be like pouring acid on a wound? Or could Gemma make her see that this might just be the way to turn the ugliness around?

And what greater triumph than for Mirella's daughter to arrive at the *castello* as executive pastry chef? Gemma's mother had been hired by the old, beloved *duca*, Vincenzo's grandfather. Now Mirella's daughter would be following in her footsteps. Best of all, her mother wouldn't have to leave Italy and could stay in Florence if she wanted to. These thoughts and more filled her mind while she tried to convince herself this could work.

After showering, she decided to wear her other suit, consisting of a navy skirt and a short-sleeved white jacket with navy piping and buttons. Though she swept her wavy hair back with a clip when she cooked, today she left it to hang down to her shoulders from the side part.

Being five foot seven, she mostly wore comfortable flats for cooking. But on this special occasion she wanted to look her best and slipped on strappy navy heels. Tiny pearl studs were the only jewelry she wore besides her watch and her grandmother's ring she would always wear in remembrance of her.

Gemma didn't need blusher. Excitement had filled her cheeks with color. With a coating of frost-pink lipstick and some lemon-scented lotion, she was ready and walked out to her car without her feet touching the ground.

After stopping at the same trattoria for breakfast, she headed for the *castello*. Four days ago she'd been upset that she couldn't apply for a position in France. But she hadn't known what was awaiting her at the former ducal residence in Milan.

Yesterday she'd worked alongside another applicant who was hoping to be chosen executive head chef. The five-star hotel he'd come from in Paris was renowned throughout Europe. To be stolen to work here meant he was the best of the best.

Gemma had taken French and English all the years she'd ever gone to school. Her mother had insisted on it, which had turned out to be advantageous for her. Some of her classes at the culinary school had been taught by various French experts, and she'd been thankful she didn't have to struggle with the language.

After they'd been introduced, she wouldn't say Monsieur Troudeau was rude. If anything he treated her as if she were invisible. No chitchat. Naturally he was shocked that such a young woman was vying for the pastry chef position. She'd ignored him and had concentrated on the pastries she'd planned to make.

The newly renovated kitchen with state-of-the-art equipment had been a dream. If only her mother could have worked under such unparalleled conditions...but that was in the past. Perhaps her mother could come to the *castello* and see the way it had been renovated. And instead of the ducal staff and family, Gemma would now be making pastry for the jet set, royals, celebrities and dignitaries of the world. She still couldn't believe it.

This time when she drove up to the front of the *castello*, she saw a black Maserati parked there. Maybe it belonged to the business owner with the strong accent who'd phoned her. Gemma got out of her car and hurried up the steps. When she entered the lobby of the hotel, she saw a fit, dark blond man, maybe six foot one and thirtyish, waiting for her behind the counter. His hazel eyes swept over her.

"You must be Signorina Bonucci. I'm Takis Manolis."

"How do you do?" She shook his hand. The signor was another good-looking man, dressed more formally in a suit and tie. This one had rugged features and probably needed to shave often. He spoke passable Italian and reminded her of some of the guys she'd met at school, possibly Turkish or Greek.

"I'm still trying to come down from the clouds since your phone call."

He flashed her a quick smile. "Congratulations."

Her eyes smarted. "I'm so happy I could burst."

"We're happy, too. Now that we've found you, we can get going on the preparations for the grand opening. If you'll come back to my office, we'll start the paperwork and sort out all the little details to make this a happy working experience for you."

Once again she found herself walking around the counter and followed him to one of the offices down the hallway. He kept his room tidy and asked her to sit down while he took his place behind the desk.

When they'd finished, he told her to report for work the day after tomorrow at nine in the morning. All staff would be assembled in the grand ballroom off the dining room for an orientation meeting to meet the new owners. Throughout the day there would be sessions to discuss policies, after which she would meet with the newly hired kitchen staff. "Do you have any questions?"

"Just one, but it doesn't have anything to do with the position. Would you be able to tell me how it is that the Gagliardi family no longer lives here? I once lived here with my mother, who cooked for the old *duca*. I find it impossible to believe that this magnificent monument, if you will, has been turned into a hotel after centuries of being the ducal seat of the region."

He studied her for a moment, but it gave her a strange feeling. "You'll have to speak to the only man who can answer that question for you."

At last there was someone who knew something. "Do you have a phone number where I can reach him?"

"I can do better than that. If you'll wait here, I'll send him in to you." He got up from the chair and left the room.

Her heart began to thud while she waited. Maybe this man would be able to tell her where she could find Vincenzo. Perhaps this man could tell her where he'd gone that night or where Dimi was. It seemed impossible for a family to just vanish.

What if he's not alive? That question had haunted her for years. *No, no. Don't think that way.* By now he was probably married to a princess and had children he adored.

Gemma couldn't bear to think that he might have found someone else. *Oh, Gemma. You're still the same lovesick fool from years ago.*

Vincenzo was on the phone with Annette when Takis walked in on him. "She's in my office waiting for you," his friend whispered before leaving him alone.

His pulse sped up. Gemma was only a door away.

"Vince? Didn't you hear me?" Annette asked him.

He sucked in his breath. "Yes," he said in English, "but someone just came in and it's important. I promise to call you by this evening, my time."

"I hope you mean that."

"Of course."

"We haven't been together for five weeks. I miss you terribly."

He just couldn't tell her the same thing back. "I have to go. Talk to you later."

He rang off and got to his feet, dressed in trousers and a polo shirt. To see Gemma again meant facing demons he'd tried to repress for years. Too many emotions collided at the same time—anxiety, excitement, curiosity, pain, guilt. Terrible guilt.

She'd been with him the night he'd been at his most vulnerable. The night after that, he'd been forced to flee before more tragedy could befall the family. The two of them had only been seventeen and eighteen, yet the memory of those intense feelings was as fresh to him right now as it had been ten years ago.

Since he'd returned to Italy, thoughts of Gemma had come back full force. At times he'd been so preoccupied, the guys were probably ready to give up on him. To think that after all this time and searching for her, she was right here. Bracing himself, he took the few steps necessary to reach Takis's office.

With the door ajar he could see a polished-looking woman in a blue-and-white suit with dark honey-blond hair falling to her shoulders. She stood near the desk with her head bowed, so he couldn't yet see her profile.

Vincenzo swallowed hard to realize Gemma was no longer the teenager with short hair he used to spot when she came bounding up the stone steps of the *castello* from school wearing her uniform. She'd grown into a curvaceous woman.

"Gemma." He said her name, but it came out gravelly.

A sharp intake of breath reverberated in the office. She wheeled around. Those unforgettable brilliant green eyes with the darker green rims fastened on him. A stillness seemed to surround her. She grabbed hold of the desk.

"Vincenzo—I—I think I must be hallucinating."

"I'm in the same condition." His gaze fell on the lips he'd kissed that unforgettable night. Their shape hadn't changed, nor the lovely mold of her facial features.

She appeared to have trouble catching her breath. "What's going on? I don't understand."

"Please sit down and I'll tell you."

He could see she was trembling. When she didn't do his bidding, he said, "I have a better idea. Let's go for a ride in my car. It's parked out front. We'll drive to the lake at the back of the estate, where no one will bother us. Maybe by the time we reach it, your shock will have worn off enough to talk to me."

Hectic color spilled into her cheeks. "Surely you're joking. After ten years of silence, you suddenly show up here this morning, honestly thinking I would go anywhere with you?"

He'd imagined anger if he ever had the chance to see her again. But he'd never expected the withering ice in her tone. Her delivery had debilitated him.

"Four days ago I applied for a position at this new hotel. Yesterday I was told I'd been hired, and now you walk in here big as life. I feel like I'm in the middle of a bizarre dream where you're back from the dead."

That described his exact state of mind. "You're not the only one feeling disoriented," he murmured. He felt as if he'd been thrown back in time, but they were no longer teenagers, and she was breathtaking in her anger.

"How long have you been in Milan?"

"Over the last six months I've made many trips here from New York."

"New York," she whispered. A crushed expression broke out on her face.

"When Dimi told me the *castello* had gone into receivership, two of my friends in New York and I decided to go into business with Dimi and turn it into a hotel. We couldn't let our family home be seized by the government or sold off to a foreign entity."

"It's yours by right, surely, unless that was a lie, too."

"It *was* mine by right…once. But that's a long story."

She shook her head. "I tried to imagine where you'd gone. I'd supposed you had friends somewhere in Europe, but it never occurred to me you would leave for the States." Gemma rubbed her hands against her hips in a gesture of abject desolation.

Vincenzo pushed ahead with the story he'd decided to use as cover. "I'd turned eighteen and decided it was time I made my mark and proved myself by making my own money. But my father would never have approved, so I had to leave without his knowledge."

"Or mine," she whispered so forlornly it shattered him.

"I couldn't do it any other way." He didn't dare tell her the real circumstances. She'd suffered enough. Vincenzo's guilt was so great, he was more convinced than ever that she'd been better off without him and still needed protection from the hideous truth.

"Are you trying to tell me that there wasn't even one moment in ten years when you could send me as much as a postcard to let me know you were alive?" Her voice was shaking, partly with rage, partly pain. He could hear it because pain echoed in his heart, too.

"I didn't know where to write to you, let alone call you. Dimi didn't know where you'd gone and looked endlessly for you. You'll never know how I've suffered over that."

He heard another sharp intake of breath. "Are you honestly trying to tell me that you looked for me?"

The depth of her pain was worse than he'd imagined. "Over the last ten years I've had private investigators searching for you. I've never stopped."

"I don't believe you." It came out like a hiss. "Has Dimi been in New York with you, too?"

"No. He lives in Milan with Zia Consolata."

Her face paled, and a hand went to her throat. A nerve throbbed at the base where he'd kissed her many times.

"I've heard all I need to hear."

In the next breath, she moved toward the door. Before he could comprehend, she flung it open and raced down the hall to the lobby. He'd never seen her in high heels before. She moved fast on those long gorgeous legs of hers.

Vincenzo started after her, noticing her hair swish and shimmer in the sunshine with every movement. He didn't catch up until she'd reached her car. Too many questions about her life were battering him at once. He wanted to make up to her for all the pain he'd put her through by disappearing without a word. Vincenzo couldn't let her get away from him. Not now.

"Where do you think you're going?"

She ignored him and opened the car door. He was aware of a lemon scent coming from her that assailed his senses. Right this minute her fragrance and femininity wrapped around him like they had done years ago, and his desire for her was palpable.

Once seated, she slammed the car door. Through the open window he saw her put the key in the ignition.

"We have to talk, Gemma!"

Her cheeks had turned scarlet with anger. "That's how I felt for days, weeks, months, even years until the need was burned out of me."

"You don't mean that," he ground out.

"Let me explain it this way. Remember our discussion about one of the films of the *Count of Monte Cristo*? If you don't, I do. Mercedes had waited years for Edmond Dantes, the man she loved. But when he suddenly appeared years later, he'd changed beyond recognition and she said goodbye to him.

"I related totally to her feelings then and now. I celebrate your return to life and all the billions of dollars you've made in New York, Vincenzo Gagliardi. I wish you well. Please tell the business manager that

I've changed my mind and won't be taking the job after all. *Arrivederci*, signor."

Wild with pain, Gemma backed away and flew down the road leading to the town below. Her eyes stung. By the time she reached the *pensione*, she realized she'd lashed out for all the years she'd been crushed by his silence.

And for his being so damned gorgeous it hurt to look at him. In ten years he'd grown into a stunning man. Standing six foot three with hard muscles and hair black as midnight, he was the personification of male beauty in her eyes.

She could hardly breathe when he'd walked into Signor Manolis's office. No wonder she hadn't been able to go on seeing Paolo. The memory of Vincenzo had always stood in the way. *He* was the reason she hadn't been able to find happiness with another man.

When they'd been together for the last time, he'd imprinted himself on her. She'd read about such things in books of fiction, but the love she'd felt for him had been real and life changing.

To think she'd suffered ten years before learning that he'd left Italy with the sole desire to earn money! Being the *duca* apparent wasn't enough. All the time they'd been growing up, he'd never once shown signs of greed in his nature. But it turned out he was just like his father!

The moment he'd reached legal age, he'd disappeared like a rabbit down a hole to add more assets to the massive family fortune. Apparently if you were a Gagliardi with a title, you could never have enough!

She couldn't credit it. And no one had known where he'd gone except Dimi.

Because of Gemma's involvement with the *duca*'s son, her mother had paid a huge price the night he'd taken off without telling his father. Shame on her for believing in something that had been a piece of fiction in her mind and heart. How many times had her mother tried to pound it in her head that she and Vincenzo would always be worlds apart?

She could hear her mother's voice. She and Vincenzo hadn't just been two ordinary teenagers indulging in a romantic fantasy. She was from the lower class, while he was an aristocrat who would one day become the Duca di Lombardi.

Any woman he married would have to be a princess, like his aunt and his mother. Day in and day out, her mother had cautioned her against her attachment to Vincenzo, but Gemma hadn't listened, so sure she was of his love.

After she reached the *pensione*, her troubled cry resounded in the car's interior. If she hadn't applied for the position at the *castello*, they would never have seen each other again in this lifetime.

You simply can't let what he's done destroy your life.

For a few minutes she struggled for composure so the *padrona di casa* wouldn't know anything was wrong. Then Gemma went inside to gather her things before driving back to Florence. Her cousin wouldn't have to know what had gone on. Gemma could simply tell her she was still looking for a position but that it would take some time.

While she packed her toiletries in the bathroom,

there was a knock on the door. Gemma told the *padrona* to come in.

"*Scusi*, signorina." She shut the door. "There's a gentleman outside from the *castello* wishing to speak to you in private."

Her heart knocked against her chest, but she kept packing and tried to feign nonchalance. "Who is it?"

"Signorina—" She ran over to her with excitement. "I would never have believed it, but it's the dashing young Duca di Lombardi himself, all grown up."

She trembled. "Surely you're mistaken." What else could she say?

"No, years ago the police looked for him and circulated pictures." Gemma remembered those policemen. "I would know him anywhere. He has the Gagliardi eyes."

She moaned. Those silvery eyes were legendary. Had he decided to use his title with the *padrona* to get what he wanted? Gemma hadn't thought Vincenzo would go so far as to follow her here, but like his father, he did whatever he wanted. Well, he couldn't force her to work at the restaurant!

Now that Gemma had shown up on his radar, it seemed he'd decided it was all right to fulfill the role destined for him from birth. Though she wanted to ask the *padrona* to tell Vincenzo she wasn't available, she couldn't do that. The older woman wasn't a servant, and Gemma didn't want her involved.

"Thank you for telling me. I'm leaving now and going back to Florence. I've left your money on the table. You've been very kind."

Gemma picked up her bag and walked outside to find Vincenzo lounging against the front of her car with his strong arms folded. The *padrona* smiled at him one last time before disappearing back through the doors.

Gemma put her bag in the rear seat. "Why did you follow me? I thought I made it clear that I can't accept the position of pastry chef. You're crazy if you're trying to expunge your guilt this way. Perhaps not guilt, exactly… A *duca* doesn't suffer that emotion like normal people, right? Yet he's known to give payment to someone like the cook's daughter for past services rendered. However, I can assure you that it's wasted on me."

A little nerve throbbed at the side of his compelling mouth, a mouth she'd kissed over and over before he'd told her she had to leave. "Is that what I'm doing?" he fired in a wintry voice.

"Yes! I'm quite sure you didn't offer the new executive chef a room at the *castello*, but Signor Manolis was told to offer me one."

The brief silence on his part upset her even more, because he didn't deny it.

"I knew it! The truth is, I don't deserve this job. The offer was too good to be true. I sensed there had to be a catch somewhere. I just didn't realize *you* had everything to do with it."

"Would it be so terrible of me to want to do something for you after the way I left without telling you? Let me make this up to you."

"I don't want anything from you, Vincenzo."

"If you're worried about the bedroom at the *castello*, I promise it won't be the back room behind the kitchen where you and your mother once lived."

"It's a moot point, but I wouldn't mind if it were."

"Nevertheless, all of that area was renovated along with the kitchen. The offer for you to stay at the *castello* will always stand."

"Why aren't you listening to me? I was shattered that you didn't say goodbye, that you didn't even let me know you were alive, but as for the rest, you owe me nothing!"

"That's not true."

"Think back to that night! Because you were in too much physical pain from that terrible fall from your horse, we didn't make love, even if we came close. Let's not forget I was as eager as you. Those moments happen to teenagers all the time! I had the hots for you, as they say in the US."

He grimaced. "Where did you learn that expression?"

"I picked up some American slang from the students at culinary school. So forget trying to fix what can't be fixed. I don't want to be compensated with a position of this magnitude or the extra perks that come with it. I understand there are two other applicants you can choose from."

"Three, but that's not the issue here."

She hadn't known that. "Then there's no problem."

Lines darkened his striking features. "You're wrong, Gemma. As for your expertise as a chef, the desserts made by you overwhelmed the committee. You have to know the decision to hire you was unanimous."

"I'll never really know, will I?"

His chest rose and fell visibly. "What do I have to do to convince you? Both Takis and Cesare are connoisseurs of fine food and wine. They recognize what will bring heads of state, kings, princes and world celebrities to the hotel over and over again. They chose you."

"Does it matter? I have interviews with two restaurateurs in Barcelona and London. If one of them hires me, I'll know I got the job for my cooking ability, nothing else."

She climbed behind the wheel. At least he didn't try to stop her.

"Where are you going?"

"Back to Florence."

"To the Bonucci Bakery? I saw the address on your application."

"Yes."

He stood there with his legs slightly apart, piercing her with those fabulous eyes. "You'll be driving in heavy traffic."

Since when had that become a concern? For the last ten years he hadn't known if she were dead or alive. He'd been flying from New York to Milan for the last six months on business. Her temper flared again.

"Vincenzo—I haven't been a teenager for years and I love to drive." She started the engine.

He moved closer. "Before you leave, tell me about your mother. How is she?"

Her bitter laugh shook him to the core. "She's alive and well, not that you'd care or be the least bit interested. Now I really have to go."

To her profound relief, he stepped back so she could drive away. Through the rearview mirror she saw his incredibly male physique standing there until she rounded the next corner.

The irony of running away from him after looking for him all these years wasn't lost on her. She drove back to Florence feeling as if she'd jumped off a precipice into the void.

CHAPTER FOUR

VINCENZO REACHED FOR his phone and left a message for the guys to say that he wouldn't be back at the *castello* until late. There were other calls from his assistant and his attorney in New York on his voice mail. None of them sounded urgent. He would deal with them later. But Annette's latest message demanded his attention. Earlier that morning he'd promised to call her back.

After putting on his sunglasses, he climbed in his Maserati and followed Gemma to Florence. The satellite navigation would lead him to the Bonucci Bakery. There was no way he would let her turn things around and disappear on him. He needed the chance to talk to her. The depth of her pain had caused him to reel. This was worse than anything he'd imagined if he'd ever seen her again.

While he was en route, he phoned Annette.

"Is it possible you've found some time for me?" she teased, but he heard her underlying impatience and didn't blame her.

"I'm sorry, but I've had business that has taken priority."

"Vince, you seem different. What's wrong?"

There was no way to explain to her what was going on inside him right now. But Annette deserved to hear how he felt even if it was going to hurt her. "You've asked me before if there was a special woman in my life. I've told you no and would never lie to you about that. But in my youth I fell in love with an Italian girl I haven't seen or heard from in ten years. Today I met up with her by accident."

He was still trying to recover.

After an ominous quiet, she said, "So what are you saying? That after all this time you find you're still in love and don't want me to come for the opening?"

He took a deep breath. "I'm saying that a big portion of my past caught up with me today. To be frank, I'm reeling." It wouldn't have been fair to lie to her.

"I sensed there was someone else all this time. She must have a powerful hold on you for those feelings to have lasted over a decade."

"Annette, I can't honestly tell you where this is headed."

What he did know was that seeing Gemma again had stirred up longings in him more intense than he could ever have imagined. To find out that Gemma wasn't married yet was a miracle. But her anger had been so intense, he needed to talk to her about it.

"Neither can I," Annette murmured. "Under the circumstances, I don't intend to wait for calls from you that might not come."

"I haven't meant to hurt you."

"I realize that, but on my part I always felt something was holding you back. If you ever figure it out and find yourself whole of heart, you know where to find me."

Even deeply upset, she had a graciousness and maturity he had to admire. "I'm sorry, Annette. Give me some time and I'll get back to you."

"I won't be holding my breath, Vince."

He heard the click.

Though Vincenzo hadn't wanted to cause her pain, his sense of relief that he didn't have to pretend with her had removed a burden. He'd told her the only truth he knew, since he needed time to deal with his emotions.

The reality of seeing Gemma again, the incredible coincidence that she'd applied for the pastry chef position, had knocked the foundations from under him.

At ten after six, he entered Florence at the height of evening traffic and found the Bonucci pastry shop. After searching everywhere for her old Fiat, he drove around the corner into an alley. Her blue car sat beside a stairway leading to the second floor of the bakery.

He found another spot along the crowded one-way street. Once he'd parked his car at the rear of the *pasteria* next door, he took the steps two at a time to the little porch outside her door. To think all these years since leaving the *castello* this place had been her home. How could he or Dimi have known?

He knocked twice.

Soon he heard, "*Chi e?*"

He was glad she didn't automatically open the door. Anyone could be out here. "It's Vincenzo. I would have phoned you I was coming, but I wasn't sure you would answer."

There was a long silence. "Go away!"

"I can't. Surely you can see that," he fought back. "I never expected any of this to happen. Even if you refuse to come to work for us, how could you think I would just let you drive away?"

"I'm not going to open my door. Go back to your home, Vincenzo."

What home? He hadn't known that feeling in the ten years since he'd last been with her. He broke out in a cold sweat. So much damage had been done, he didn't know if he could repair any of it, even if he told her the real truth of everything.

"Would you deny your time to any other person you knew well in the past who wanted to get reacquainted after a long period of separation? Since I've come all this way and am starving, let's have dinner at the *pasteria* next door. We'll order some wine and reminisce over a time when life was wonderful for both of us."

"That would be a mistake."

"You don't recommend the food? If anyone would know whether it was good or not, you're the one."

"Be serious, Vincenzo," she snapped.

"I'm trying to be. You have no idea how isolated I've felt all these years. Dimi and I are the only ones left who can talk about that other life and relate. Our fathers kept us under virtual lock and key, with bodyguards controlling everything we did. You better than anyone know that they only allowed us to have a few friends they picked.

"But all these years there's been a huge hole, and you know why. Because that other life included you. I need a few hours with you, Gemma." His voice shook. "Will you grant me that much?"

He waited for her response. "You're not the person I thought you were, Vincenzo. Otherwise you wouldn't have left without so much as a goodbye. I was never good enough for you, we both know that. We've led separate lives since your disappearance, and we were never the same people growing up."

His eyes closed tightly, but her pain kept her talking.

"You're from one world and I'm from another. A little while ago the reminder came from the *padrona*, who said the Duca di Lombardi was standing outside waiting to see me. There's no need for us to talk or be with each other again, Vincenzo."

She knew where to thrust through to the gut. Her mother had done a sensational job of indoctrinating her over the nonsense of ancient class distinctions he couldn't abide.

"If I swear on my mother's soul to leave you strictly alone, will you accept the position at the *castello* to see us through the first three months? Takis and Cesare will be the ones working with you. I'll stay out of your way unless there's a professional reason why I have to talk to you about something."

Was she even listening?

"You can put me on probation, Gemma. If I make one mistake, you can leave immediately, no questions asked. If at the end of the three months you still want to leave, you'll receive impeccable recommendations and be given a generous severance package of your choosing."

"Why would you enter into an arrangement like that when you know how I feel?"

"Because your expertise as a pastry chef is unparalleled. My partners will be bitterly disappointed to learn that you've refused the position because you can't forgive me for my past sins."

"It's not a matter of forgiveness. The trust is gone."

Vincenzo couldn't take this much longer. "*They* trust me. You have to understand that I asked them to go into business with me. But for me they wouldn't be here. Not only my integrity, but their financial lives and reputations are on the line. Like me, they want our business venture to work."

"As you told me earlier, you have three other applicants eager to work there."

"My friends don't want anyone else and are convinced that with everything we've put in place including your cooking, we'll succeed beyond our wildest dreams. I *know* we will, because I grew up on your mother's delicacies that you've perfected. You have no equal, Gemma."

"Please leave."

"I only have one more thing to say. You don't have to make a decision this very minute. I'm on my way back to Milan." *I've got to stop and see Dimi.* He wasn't going to believe Gemma had been found.

"Gemma? If you don't show up for your first orientation meeting with rest of the staff the day after tomorrow, then I'll tell my partners you found you couldn't accept the position after all because of a family emergency at the bakery. Naturally we'll choose one of the other pastry chef finalists."

She still said nothing.

His pain had reached its zenith. "*Arrivederci, tesoro.*"

Gemma gasped. The night in his bedroom when they'd been wrapped in each other's arms, he'd called her his treasure. While her world spun in reaction to that endearment, she watched out the window. His car traveled down the street until she couldn't see him anymore.

Surely to accept his offer would mean that she had no self-control, that all he had to do was summon her in his inimitable, seductive way and she'd come running.

What else could she expect when Vincenzo's immoral father and uncle had been his role models? He might not think he could ever behave as they'd done, but the precedent had been set for decades. Once he married a princess and had children, the need for distraction would come.

With business enterprises on either side of the Atlantic, he'd have ample opportunities to be with women his wife wouldn't know about. Or would pretend not to know about. Who better than the adoring daughter of the former cook to fill the position as one of his mistresses and provide him amusement during secret getaways when he was in Italy?

Gemma, unmarried and childless, wouldn't have a life while she waited for those moments of rapture with him. Little by little his need for her would grow more infrequent while she went on getting older and more unfulfilled. Over the centuries, women of the lower class had done as much in order to be with the titled men they'd loved, but Gemma refused to be one of them!

She'd been afraid he'd break her down with words like this. Somehow he was succeeding despite her determination not to listen or be moved. Tears dripped from her eyes while she called Filippa, who'd just come out of a bad relationship.

Her friend knew Gemma's history. When she heard Vincenzo was back in Gemma's life, she cried out in shock. For the next hour Gemma told her everything.

Before they hung up, Filippa asked her one salient question. "Did he ever do anything in his past that caused you not to trust him until the day when you learned he had disappeared?"

"No. But we're grown up now, and he's the *duca.* I can't see our lives together in any way, shape or form."

"From what you've told me, he hasn't asked for more than a three-month probationary period to help him get their restaurant off the ground. He wants you to have this position because you were the top applicant. Naturally he wants to make it up to you for leaving without an explanation."

"I know."

"Remember that he said he needed to make money and couldn't let his father find out his plans. That sounds like a strong reason for what he did. And don't forget he said he looked for you over all these years. So what more can he do to make you feel any better? You *did* sign on with them in good faith, and they did, too."

Gemma sniffed. Put that way, there was no argument. "You're right."

"If I were you, I'd agree to his offer. He promised to leave you alone away from work, and he would be a fool if he reneges. Just think, Gemma—the opportunity to be the head pastry chef there will give you entrée anywhere in the world when you leave. With a five-star recommendation, you'll have carte blanche with whichever wonderful restaurant in France you'd like and you could realize your dream."

Filippa made it sound possible, even easy. But she'd never met Vincenzo Gagliardi and had no comprehension of the man Gemma had always loved. Every day of those three months she worked at the *castello*, she'd be in agony thinking about him, desiring him. Was he on the premises, or was he in New York? How soon would the media reveal breaking news about the fiercely handsome, dashing Duca di Lombardi coming back home? Which gorgeous princess would be the one to catch his eye and become his bride and the mother of his children?

"Gemma? Are you still there?"

She blinked away the moisture. "Yes, of course. I was deep in thought. Sorry."

"So what are you going to do?"

"I'm not sure, but I love you for listening to me and helping me sort through my pain."

"You've done the same thing for me too many times to count. I've got to go right now. Let me know what you finally decide."

"I will. Ciao, Filippa."

"Ciao, *amica*."

While Gemma fixed herself an omelet, she reran their conversation over in her mind. By the time she went to bed, her pragmatic side had taken over. She needed a job and had been offered one that would make her the envy of everyone at her school. There was no way she could turn down his offer.

When she gave her mother the news, she'd tell her it was only for a three-month period. But she'd wait to tell her *mamma* anything until Mirella got back from her vacation. By then Gemma would have lined up another job so that when the three months were up, they'd leave Lombardi and the *castello* behind.

With a top recommendation, she would be set up to find a great restaurant in the South of France that would hire her. In time she could accrue enough savings to put down roots.

Gemma had dreamed of buying a little villa in Vence or Grasse with a garden and some fruit trees overlooking the Mediterranean. She'd won an award for her jam. Since her mother would be living with her, maybe they'd make their own and sell it locally. Anything could happen. Filippa had made her see that.

For now she would have to trust Vincenzo to keep their bargain. As she'd told her friend, she'd trusted Vincenzo in the past. It would be her own fault if she couldn't remain strong and stay away from him.

Grateful for her friend's advice, she woke up early the next morning and got busy house cleaning. When her mother and aunt returned from England, they'd find the place spotless. At four that afternoon, she left with her large suitcase and went down the steps to her car parked in the alley. It was best her cousin didn't know where she was going until Gemma had told her mother everything first.

When she reached Sopri, she called on the *padrona di casa* and told her she would like to stay at the *pensione* for a three-month period because she'd be working at the new hotel. Would that be possible?

The older woman couldn't have been more delighted and they settled on a good price. "You'll be working for the *duca*. Any arrangement you want is fine." On that note she let Gemma into the room she'd had before with a huge smile. Such was Vincenzo's effect on every female, young or old.

Gemma got settled in and pulled out her laptop. She needed to send emails to London and Barcelona and thank them for setting up appointments with her. In her note she told them she was sorry but she'd found another position. If by any chance it didn't work out at the *castello*, she wondered if they would allow her to reapply?

Once that was done, she got ready for bed and lay back against the pillows. Tomorrow morning she'd be meeting with Signor Donati at nine for the orientation meeting. The newly hired kitchen staff would also be present. Being part of a hotel, the restaurant would serve meals throughout the day and evening as well as provide room service. Such organization required a genius at the head.

Vincenzo.

Because he was the one who'd masterminded everything, he would always have input. She expected that. Naturally they'd see each other coming and going, much the same as they'd done ten years earlier. But this time everything would be different. In order to survive, she was forced to put on her armor and leave the sweet innocence of their youthful love in the past.

After confiding in Dimi the evening before, Vincenzo had worked through the night on his personal business affairs here in Italy. Establishing Nistri Technologies in the south of the country consumed a lot of his spare time, but that was good. He existed on coffee, trying not to think about what would happen if Gemma didn't show up today. He hadn't told the guys anything, not wanting to alarm them.

His cousin didn't have great hopes where Gemma was concerned. She was an unknown entity at this point. Vincenzo didn't like hearing Dimi's opinion but appreciated that his was the voice of reason.

After a shower and shave, he put on a business suit and tie before leaving his tower room to go downstairs. His watch said it was ten to nine, and already the ballroom appeared full. But as he looked around, his worst nightmare was confirmed, because Gemma was nowhere in sight.

His fear that she'd left Florence and he'd never see her again came close to paralyzing him, but for the guys' sake, he had to pull himself together. He'd wanted to hire security to keep an eye on her but had resisted the impulse. That's what his father had done to him and Dimi. He knew Gemma had already accused him in her heart of being like his father. He didn't dare make that mistake.

At their first break in the morning schedule, Vincenzo would take his partners aside and give them the bad news. While they ran the next segment without him, he would have to go to his office and contact their other applicants. If none of them were available, there was more work to do.

A blackness had descended on Vincenzo as he joined Takis in front of their awaiting audience. He was on the verge of asking him about Cesare when the Sicilian entered through the tall double doors.

Gemma followed him in. At the first sight of her, Vincenzo's heart kicked him in the ribs so hard he almost moaned aloud. Somehow she'd managed to put aside her hurt and anger enough to accept his proposition.

She'd come dressed in a fabulous peach-colored suit. It was a miracle he had any breath left. He couldn't take his eyes off her as she found a chair on the end of a row halfway toward the front. Vincenzo was still in a state of shock when Takis stood up with the microphone in hand.

"Welcome, everyone! Take a look around. The success of the new Castello Supremo Hotel and Ristorante di Lombardi is in your hands. By the end of the day it's our hope you'll feel like family. It's the only way our enterprise will work."

Vincenzo had hoped everyone they'd hired would feel like family. After all the work he and his partners had done over the last six months, he couldn't help but be proud of what they'd accomplished so far.

He was happy that he'd asked the guys to employ as many local staff as possible, especially those who hadn't been able to find work lately. It was a way to give back to the community that had been harmed because his father and uncle had been such bad people.

For a long time he'd been worried that he'd involved his friends in a project that could have professional as well as personal repercussions if things didn't go well. But Gemma's appearance a minute go went a long way to help calm some of those fears. With both of them together again in the same room, he felt an odd sense of rightness.

"At your interviews, you were given a small history of the *castello*. For as long as you work here, guests will ask you repeatedly about this iconic hundred-years-old structure. As you've learned, it was the home of the first Duca di Lombardi of the house of Gagliardi in the eighteen hundreds.

"Today I'm honored to introduce one of the owners and chief operating officer for the estate, security and publicity, Vincenzo Nistri Gagliardi, seated on my right."

A collective sound of surprise was followed by resounding applause that filled the room. With the media calling for information at this point, Vincenzo had given Takis permission to offer public disclosure of their three-owner enterprise. He'd felt it was time he embraced his name again. But there'd be no mention of the family title.

"I'm Takis Manolis, one of the owners and general manager of the hotel. On my left is Cesare Donati, the other owner and general manager for the restaurant." More clapping ensued.

Takis finished talking and handed Vincenzo the mic.

Vincenzo only intended to say a few words that would put the floating rumors to rest. "Some of you may know this was my home for the first eighteen years of my life. Though I've spent the last ten years in New York City, my roots are here."

The girl who made it my own private heaven is seated among you.

"My business partners and I hope this will become a desired destination for locals and tourists from around the globe. If we all work together, I know it will be a great success. Thank you."

This time everyone got to their feet and kept clapping. He handed the mic to Cesare and sat down.

His friend took over the reins. When the noise subsided, he introduced their head chef, Monsieur Maurice Troudeau. Then he turned to Gemma.

"In the words of Schiaparelli, 'a good cook is like a sorceress who dispenses happiness.' That would describe the Italian desserts of our executive pastry chef, Gemma Bonucci Rizzo. Please stand, signorina."

There was more applause.

Vincenzo's pride in her accomplishments brought a lump to his throat. At the same time he couldn't stop his eyes from fastening on the lines of her beautiful figure.

Cesare continued to introduce the entire kitchen staff that also included the sous chefs, dishwashers, and front of house staff. Takis followed by introducing the front desk group, the head of housekeeping and the laundry staff. Then it was Vincenzo's turn once more to present the estate manager and gardeners. The security men made their own presentation.

After a ten-minute break, his partners met with the employees under them to get down to specifics on the job, including the hours they would work. That left Vincenzo to circulate.

He visited Takis's group first and added a few words. Then he walked to the kitchen, where Cesare laid out the hours for each shift and their duties, which included room service and the dining room. Vincenzo refused to look at Gemma. After saying a few more words of greeting, he made certain he stayed on the far side of the room away from her.

Gemma and Maurice had been asked to make out a day's worth of sample menus for the three meals they'd serve the day of the grand opening. Cesare looked them over before passing them to Vincenzo for his opinion. Since he didn't want to give Gemma any fuel to leave and never come back, he took the menus and walked to his office.

After sitting at his desk for a few minutes, he realized that having to distance himself from her was going to be the hardest thing he would ever have to do in his life. The key was to focus on work.

He spent the next few minutes studying her dessert choices, including the rolls, breads, preserves and jams she'd suggested to accompany Maurice's entrées and specialty dishes. They were both masters at what they did. He put his seal of approval on them.

But thoughts of Gemma made it impossible for him to stand his own company any longer. He walked to Cesare's office to give him the menus. His friend wasn't around. Vincenzo left them on his desk and went in search of Takis, who was still in the ballroom directing some of the newly hired staff to put the chairs away.

He waved. "*Ehi*, Vincenzo—all in all, I think it went well."

"I agree." But it would have been a disaster if Gemma hadn't shown up.

"Want to have drinks on the east patio later?"

"Sounds good, but I'll see. I have to run an errand, but I should be back soon."

Vincenzo hurried out of the *castello* to his car, too restless to stay put. After getting behind the wheel, he took off and drove aimlessly. He had a hunch Gemma had spent last night at the same *pensione* as before. If he returned by way of Sopri later, he assumed he'd see her car parked in front. But much as he wanted to find out where she was staying, he didn't dare.

Instead he ended up in the little village of Cisliano, only three miles from Sopri. He passed in front of the Rho Bistro. The owners had had the unique idea of waiting for all the customers to arrive. Then they started cooking the same menu for everyone and served it at one time.

Vincenzo had eaten there several times in his youth after a bike ride with Dimi, always being followed by a guard his father had hired. On his eighteenth birthday, he and Dimi had slipped away from their tutor and the guard. They'd arranged to meet Gemma and Bianca here.

He remembered that Friday as if it had been yesterday. Bianca's mother had taken pity on him and his cousin. She'd dropped the girls off and come back for them two hours later without telling Gemma's mother, who would have been upset.

The memory of that red-letter day had taken hold of him. Wanting to relive it, he decided to go in, but parking was difficult. He ended up driving around the corner to find a spot. For the moment all he cared about was soaking up those moments when he knew they'd been crazy in love with each other.

As usual, he discovered the noisy, unpretentious place was filled with summer customers at the dinner hour. There was one empty table in the corner partially separate from the others, probably available for any overflow. He grabbed it and was served coffee while everyone waited to be served.

CHAPTER FIVE

AFTER HER LAST meeting for the day, Gemma left the *castello* experiencing so many emotions, she didn't know where to go with all her feelings. Cesare's comments about her in front of the whole assembly had been very touching. She'd enjoyed the various sessions and had gotten on well with Maurice. But overriding everything was the realization that Vincenzo was back in Lombardi.

Along with his partners, they'd turned the *castello* into a hotel and restaurant that would definitely be the envy of other resorts in Italy. She'd felt the camaraderie among the people hired and had heard their praise for the new owners. The favorable whispers about Vincenzo would have pleased him.

Part of her had wanted to go to his office and thank him for this opportunity, but it was too difficult for her to be in such close proximity to him. She feared she wouldn't be able to fight her attraction to him. But the other part of her would always struggle, because he hadn't felt she was good enough to confide in before he'd disappeared. He'd created a deep wound that would never heal.

Where was the Vincenzo she would have done

anything for? On his eighteenth birthday, she'd dared to eat a meal with him at a restaurant outside the *castello*, even knowing they could both get into terrible trouble.

Caught up in the memory, she drove to Cisliano and found a parking place at the end of the street near the Rho Bistro. She and Bianca had spent two divine hours here with Vincenzo and Dimi. The need to recapture that moment took her inside, but the place was packed. As she looked around, her gaze suddenly collided with a pair of silver eyes staring at her between black lashes.

Vincenzo—her heart knocked against her ribs. He was here?

She watched as he got to his feet and walked over to her. "It appears you and I had the same idea this evening. As you can see, the whole world is here. You're welcome to join me at my table. I think I have the only free one left."

Gemma couldn't believe this had happened, but to turn him down would be churlish at this point.

"Thank you. I have to admit I'm starving."

No sooner had he held a chair for her to sit down than the waiters started bringing the food. The menu included antipasto, risotto, sautéed mushrooms, roasted polenta and potatoes, with a dessert of *limoncello* and iced cookies.

After a few bites she said, "I had no idea you were here."

"That works both ways." He sipped his coffee. "Seeing you again has made me nostalgic for my happy past, and I found myself driving here. The meal we enjoyed on my birthday will always stand out in my mind."

"Truthfully, I'll never forget it, either," she confessed. "On the way back to my flat, I decided to drive by and see if this place still existed. We were fed so much food, I didn't think I would ever eat again."

"You're not the only one."

"I was frightened someone from the *castello* would find out and word would get back to my mother. She would have grounded me forever."

"Three weeks after my birthday, I was in New York, ending our one and only over-the-*castello*-wall experience."

Over the wall was right! But Gemma didn't want to think about the past and changed the subject.

"After the last meeting in the kitchen, Cesare told us to go home and get a good sleep before we report in the morning ready to dig in. I didn't expect to see you here, but since we have bumped into each other, I'd like to thank you for giving me the opportunity to be the pastry chef. It *is* the chance of a lifetime."

"If anyone should be doing the thanking, it's me," he came back unexpectedly. "When I saw you walk into the ballroom this morning, I was able to breathe again. Later in my office I started looking over the menus. You and Maurice stimulate the brilliance in each other. There's no doubt in my mind the food at the Castello Supremo Ristorante will bring the world to our door."

"Coming from you, that's a great compliment." But Gemma wished he'd stop being so…so nice and charming the way he'd been years ago, the way he'd been today during the orientation meeting.

He kept talking. "Cesare is the true expert. The light in his eyes after he'd studied the menus and handed them to me told me all I needed to know about how excited he is about our new chefs." He drank more coffee.

"That's very gratifying to hear."

He flashed her a penetrating glance. "I can't believe you aren't married."

She drank her *limoncello* too quickly and started coughing. Had he been hoping she'd found a man? Would it make him feel less guilty for disappearing from her life? Why not turn things around on him?

"What about you, Vincenzo? You've been in New York all this time. I don't see a ring on your finger."

His mouth tautened. "I've been too busy conducting business to think about getting married."

No woman could resist him, so he couldn't have suffered in that department. But there probably weren't that many available princesses on the East Coast of the US to consider marrying. For that, he'd have to return to Europe. No doubt there'd been a short list compiled years ago for Vincenzo to consider.

She cleared her throat. "Labor-intensive work *does* have a way of interfering. Being an apprentice at the school hasn't allowed me the time to consider marriage. They require nine to ten years from you. That doesn't give you a spare moment to breathe." Except for that one month with Paolo, which was a mistake.

"Understood. As long as we're together, would you be willing to answer a question for me? Your last name is Rizzo, yet you used Bonucci on your application. Why?"

They were wading into dangerous waters now. "That's a long story."

"Is there some secret?"

Her eyes closed tightly. If he only knew.

"Bonucci is mother's maiden name. When we moved to the apartment above my aunt's bakery, Mamma told me to put Bonucci on my application. That way when I attended pastry school, it would be an easy identification with her family's bakery."

"Mirella was an intelligent woman and was always very kind to me and Dimi."

Just hearing him say her mother's name made her eyes smart. She nodded. "People love her. I love her terribly."

"Gemma," he murmured. "Don't you know I've missed that old life more than you can imagine? I know she's your whole world and you are hers. Interesting that after you left the *castello*, no one knew you as Gemma Rizzo. That's why neither Dimi nor I could find you."

Oh, no. She clenched her fists beneath the table. "Mamma would have done or said anything she could to—" Gemma stumbled "—to increase my chance to succeed."

She knew by the flicker in his eyes that he'd caught her correction. Vincenzo was a shrewd, brilliant businessman, and she was afraid he wouldn't let it go. "Your *mamma* got her wish. My colleagues have been praising your expertise." Heat crept into her cheeks again, but this time anger wasn't the culprit.

"That's very nice to hear. Now I've got to go so I'll be fresh for tomorrow."

"Gemma," he whispered. "What aren't you telling me?"

The tone in his voice reminded her of the old Vincenzo. Slowly, steadily, he was breaking her down. His magic was getting to her. *Damn, damn, damn.* Her heart pounded so hard, she was certain he could hear it. "I don't know what you mean."

"You forget I've known you since you were four years old. When you're nervous or afraid, your voice falters. You did it just now. You said that your mother would have done or said anything to…to what, Gemma? You left out something of vital importance. What was it?"

She felt sick inside. "You're wrong."

"Now your cheeks are red. They always fill with color when you're not telling the truth." He wouldn't stop until he'd wrung it out of her.

Vincenzo, Vincenzo. "Mamma said I had to say my last name was Bonucci in order to…protect me."

His handsome face darkened with forbidding lines. "From whom?"

"I—it was a long time ago and doesn't matter."

He let out an oath, and his brows formed a black bar above his eyes. "Did you get into trouble that night after you left my room? I still had to stay in bed the next day, so I didn't see you."

Gemma was thrown by the haunted sound in his voice. "No," she answered honestly.

"Why don't I believe you?"

"Vincenzo, I promise. After looking out the door that night, I snuck down the back staircase when I knew a guard wouldn't be there. No one saw me."

"Do you swear before God?" A vein stood out in his neck.

She sensed an unfathomable depth of anxiety here. It wasn't something he could hide. "Why have you asked me that?"

His body tensed. "Because if I thought my father had been waiting in the hall and did anything to you..."

"No one saw me." It was her turn to shudder at the degree of his concern. "I swear, nothing happened to me, Vincenzo."

"Keep talking to me, Gemma. There's still something else you haven't told me."

She stirred restlessly. Now was her chance to reveal every single cruel thing his father had done to her and her mother. But looking into his eyes and seeing the pain, she found she couldn't.

"Did you get questioned after my father found out I'd gone missing?" he demanded.

Give him some of the truth so he'll be satisfied.

"He and the police commissioner interrogated everyone at the *castello*, one at a time. No one knew anything about your disappearance. At that point they looked elsewhere for answers."

"Grazie a Dio."

She heard the tremendous relief in his voice, but by the way he was staring at her, she could tell he was far from finished with her, and she started to be afraid.

"When were you let go at the *castello*?"

Her pulse raced. "Does it matter? It's all in the past."

He shook his dark head. "Did it happen after my *nonno* died?"

"Yes," she said quietly, because with that question Gemma realized he really didn't know anything that had happened. Neither did Dimi, otherwise his cousin would have told him.

His sharp intake of breath was alarming. "You're lying to me again."

She jumped up from the chair. "I can't do this anymore. Thank you for letting me eat with you. Now I have to leave."

He looked up at her. "Where are you going?"

"Back to the *pensione*."

"If you leave now, you'll never know the true reason behind my sudden disappearance and why it had to be carried out in complete secrecy."

Stunned by what he'd just said, Gemma clung to the back of the chair. *The true reason?*

"On the strength of the years you and I spent together as children and teenagers who fell in love, isn't learning the whole truth worth something to you?"

"I thought you said you left to make your own fortune and name."

"That was a by-product of the real reason I left, but I didn't tell you the truth in order to spare you more grief. I can see now that I've been wrong to do that."

Along with everything he was saying, his confession that he'd been in love with her a long time ago was almost too much to bear. Gemma couldn't talk, couldn't think.

"I don't ever remember you running out of words before, so I'm following you home." He put some bills on the table. "We need privacy because we're not finished talking, but we can't do it here. People are watching."

"You made a promise."

"I would have kept it, but you've just told me another lie. If you don't want to work at the *castello* then I'll have to live with it, but I need the truth from you first. Let's go."

With her heart in her mouth, Gemma left the restaurant and walked to the end of the street to reach her car. She started the engine and pulled into traffic. Soon she was headed for Sopri.

Through the rearview mirror she could see the Maserati following closely behind. Adrenaline gushed through her veins. Finally she would know what had happened all those years ago. It didn't take long to reach the *pensione*. Vincenzo pulled up behind her and parked his car.

Without looking at him, she went inside, leaving the door open. He followed, closing it behind him.

"Come in and sit down. Take your pick of one of the chairs or the love seat."

Vincenzo did neither. First he looked around at the small, well-furnished flat. From the living room he could see part of the bedroom. Then he walked into the kitchen, where she was clinging to the counter.

This evening, the fear that he was losing his grip on Gemma had made him realize he had to tell her the painful truth about his disappearance if he ever hoped to have a chance of keeping her in his life. All the guilt and the shame would have to come out. He'd wanted to protect her, but it was too late for that now.

But first he needed to hear what had happened to her after he'd left. He sucked in his breath. "The truth,

Gemma. All of it! How soon after I disappeared did you and your mother leave the *castello*?"

She was trembling. "The second your father learned you were missing, he came with the chief of police and guards to our rooms at six that morning, demanding to know where you were. I told him I knew nothing. They searched our rooms before the police chief said he believed me.

"Your father told my mother to get out and take her baggage with her—meaning me, of course. Your father's outrage was frightening. The idea that his son, who would one day become the Duca di Lombardi, was enjoying life below the stairs with one of the cooks' daughters put him into a frenzy.

"He vowed to make certain she never got a job anywhere else. He threw Bianca and her mother out that same morning before he left with the police to start searching the countryside for you. That's why Mamma made me use the Bonucci name, so he couldn't find us."

Vincenzo's pain bordered on fury. He fought to stay in control. "What he did was inhuman. You should never have been forced to live through such a nightmare, and all because of me. I can never hope to make this up to you."

"It's over, and he was a sick man."

His jaw hardened. "More than sick. You don't know what a frenzy is until you've seen him raging drunk. My uncle was the same. Dimi had to get away, too."

She swallowed hard. "You said he lives in Milan with his mother."

He nodded. "They left the same day as you and

your mother did, while my father was out with the police hunting for me."

"When I first met your aunt Consolata, she was in a wheelchair. I always worried about her."

"I know you did. She always spoke of you with fondness, but she isn't well and has lost her memory."

"That's so sad."

This was the girl he'd remembered and dreamed about. She'd always had a sweetness and kindness that made her stand out from any woman he'd ever known.

"Did you ever hear how she ended up in her wheelchair?"

"Mamma told me she had a disease."

"No, Gemma," he ground out. "That was a story the family made up to cover the truth. My father and my uncle Alonzo were the ones with the disease."

"What do you mean?"

"They are alcoholics. Alonzo drove Dimi's mother home from a party when he was drunk out of his mind. She begged for someone else to drive her, but he became enraged and dragged her to the car. En route home, there was a terrible crash. The man in the other car was killed and Dimi's mother was paralyzed from the waist down, unable to walk again. But as usual, my father had it hushed up to protect the family honor."

Tears splashed down her cheeks.

"Just know that since my uncle has been imprisoned, Dimi and my aunt have been able to live in peace. But there's a lot more you need to hear in order for you to understand my sudden disappearance."

"A lot more?"

His fear for what his father might have done to her

triggered other thoughts. "The night we almost made love, you thought I'd been recovering from a fall after I'd been out horseback riding."

She nodded. "That's what they had been gossiping about down in the kitchen. I snuck upstairs that night to see how bad your injuries were."

"My bruises and welts weren't because of an accident, Gemma."

A cry escaped her lips. She looked ill. "Your *father* was responsible?"

"*Si.* He beat me almost to a pulp." Gemma winced. "But he did worse to my *mamma*, and she died because of it."

"Oh, Vincenzo—no—" Hot tears spurted from her eyes. "Why would he do that? She was a wonderful person."

"My parents' marriage was a political arrangement with a lot of money and land entailed. But my grandfather Count Nistri, the one who lived in Padua, didn't trust his new son-in-law. Even back then my father had a reputation for drinking and gambling. But he came from a family of great wealth and was a business wizard.

"To make certain his daughter, Arianna, my mother, always had security, he'd put a fortune in a Swiss bank account for her alone."

"He sounds like a loving man and father."

"He was, but my father resented me having any association with him. Still, he couldn't stop me from visiting him from time to time. My grandfather had the foresight and the means to help me get away when the time came."

"How did he do it?"

"Through a secret source, he learned my father had been badgering my mother for her money. At that point he gave her the information to access it and passports for both of us so we could escape."

Another gasp flew out of her.

"During the last year before she died, my father started hitting her when he couldn't get at her money. She couldn't withstand all those beatings." His eyes stung with tears. "Do you have any idea what I went through, hearing her cries while I was held back by the guards so I couldn't help her?"

Gemma covered her mouth in horror.

"I was helpless. He was the acting *duca*. He was the law. No one questioned him or his authority. If I'd sent for the police, they wouldn't have stopped him. Mamma needed me, but I failed her as her son."

"Of course you didn't!" Gemma cried. "Don't say that! Don't even think it!"

"For a long time she'd begged me to take the money and escape because she feared for my life. That's when I started to plan my disappearance, but I would never have left her behind. As far as escaping, I had to be an adult and couldn't go anywhere until I was of age.

"My uncle had no reason to stop his brother, since he was in worse trouble financially and was fighting to stay out of prison. To escape my father, I had to get as far away from Italy as possible. The US suited my plan perfectly."

She shook her head. "What plan?"

"The one Dimi and I devised a year before I left."

"A whole year, and you never once told me?" Her voice shook with pain.

"I didn't dare until I knew it was safe for you. But when that time came, you were nowhere to be found in Italy. Dimi hunted endlessly for you, too. When I escaped, our family had been unraveling at the speed of sound, Gemma, but until I turned eighteen and Mamma passed away, I couldn't do anything about it. If my father had gotten wind of anything, that would have been the end of me.

"Worse, if he'd found out that you knew where I'd gone, there's no telling what price you might have had to pay. As it was, your mother paid dearly for my disappearance. Thank heaven you got away without him beating you, too."

"This is a horror story."

"After Mamma's funeral, my father followed me to my room. He'd been drinking heavily. This time he beat me with his horse whip after I'd gone to bed."

At this point Gemma was quietly sobbing.

"He thought he could force the truth from me and get his hands on Mamma's fortune. As you know, he was a tall, powerful man. He would have succeeded in killing me if he hadn't been so drunk.

"Somehow I held him off. The next night was when you came up to my room looking for me. Your loving comfort and kisses held me together. But I was afraid my father would be back. That's why I couldn't let you stay the whole night with me. I was afraid if he found us, I wouldn't have the strength to protect you."

She'd buried her face in her hands. "I understand now."

"I'll always be in hell because I couldn't protect my mother."

She lifted her head. "Thank heaven you got out of

there alive. I remember the menacing look in your father's eyes. No wonder you were running for your life."

"The night after we were together, I made my getaway with Dimi's help. But leaving you without telling you anything was the hardest thing I'd ever had to do in my life. My cousin had to take the brunt of everything, and I asked him keep me informed about you. He was frantic because he didn't know where to look for you."

"I was so hurt and angry at you, I didn't even try to say goodbye to him. I'm so sorry now. He didn't have any way of knowing where we'd gone."

Without conscious thought Vincenzo wrapped her in his arms, and they clung while she sobbed. He wept in silence with her. After her tears subsided, she said, "Tell me what happened the night you left. I want to hear everything from the moment you left your room that night."

CHAPTER SIX

A MIRACLE HAD HAPPENED, because Gemma wanted to keep talking. Vincenzo kissed her hair and forehead.

"Let's go in the other room, where we can be comfortable." He walked her trembling body to the love seat, where she sat down, then he pulled the chair closer to be face-to-face with her.

"After I got up and dressed, I snuck to Dimi's tower room at two in the morning. We hugged and then I stole down the back staircase and through the old passage no longer used to reach the outside."

"I remember it."

"Knowing the guard wouldn't be able to see me yet, I raced through the gardens to reach the forest on the estate property without problem. The family cemetery plot was a good spot to rest. Then I ran past the lake and stables to the farthest edge of the property and hid up high in a tree until another guard had passed around the perimeter and disappeared."

"The dog didn't give you away?"

"It wasn't with him. That was another miracle. I stayed free of detection for twenty more minutes before climbing the fence. You should have seen me. I ran like hell down the hillside."

A little laugh escaped. "I can just see you!"

"My destination was a farm, where I waited behind a truck for the sun to come up."

"That must have been so scary."

"Not as scary as worrying that I'd be spotted before I jumped the perimeter fence. When I saw more activity on the road, I started walking to the village."

"Did anyone recognize you?"

"I put on a baseball cap and sunglasses."

She smiled. "I would have loved to see that."

"It did the trick. A half hour's walk and I reached the bus stop that took me into central Milan, where I got off near the main train station. After buying a one-way ticket to Geneva, I boarded a second-class car and found a group of German backpackers to sit by."

"Naturally you struck up a conversation with them. I know your royal tutors taught you four different languages, including German."

"My education came in handy during that four-hour train ride to Switzerland."

"Weren't you worried someone would recognize you?"

"I was lucky and made it to Geneva without problem."

"Thank heaven."

"Around three in the afternoon, the train arrived in Geneva. I said goodbye to the other backpackers and took a taxi to the Credit Suisse bank in the town center. I'd planned every step with Dimi and only withdrew enough cash to fly to the States and get settled."

"I often wondered about those secret meetings you had when Bianca and I weren't included."

"Now you know why. After showing the banker

my passport and the letter from my grandfather verifying the origin of the funds in my account, I took a taxi to the airport."

Her eyes lit up. "You really were free at last."

"Except that you weren't with me."

"Let's not talk about that. Tell me what happened next."

"I bought a one-way ticket to New York. As it took off, I saw the jet-d'eau at the end of Lake Geneva and the Alps in the distance. You know I'd traveled through Europe before and had been to Switzerland on several vacations. But this time everything was different."

Shadows marred her classic features. "I can't imagine it."

His body tautened. "That's when I realized I had left you behind for good. You wouldn't be able to come to me, nor I to go to you. My ache for you turned into excruciating pain." Hot tears stung his eyes. "Gemma—I swear I didn't know how I was going to be able to handle the separation."

Hers filled with tears, too, revealing the degree of her pain.

"You and I had grown up together and lived through everything. I was tortured by the knowledge that until the situation within my own family changed, our separation would have to be permanent."

"When I first heard you'd gone, I thought I was going to die."

He reached for her hand, enclosing it in his. "I would have given anything to spare you that pain. There was no way to know how soon we'd ever be able to see each other again."

She gave his hand a little squeeze before removing hers.

"You can't imagine my panic. I feared you would hate me forever for my inexplicable cruelty in telling you nothing. There'd be no way you could forgive me. But I didn't know how else to keep you safe from my father's wrath. To my sorrow, you didn't escape it entirely."

"You know what hurts the most, Vincenzo? To realize our teenage love wasn't strong enough in your mind to handle telling me the truth before you ever left Italy."

"I thought I was protecting you."

"I realize that now, but why did you lie to me again the other day about your reasons for leaving?"

"Again, I wanted to shield you from so much ugliness."

"Did you think I'm not strong enough to handle it?"

"I know you are, Gemma. Forgive me."

"Of course I do," she cried. "Finish telling me about New York."

"It was a different world. I checked into a hotel and called my grandfather Emanuele to let him know where I was, knowing he wouldn't tell my father. After talking with him, I phoned my grandfather in Padua to thank him for all he'd done for me…all he'd tried to do for my mother."

"He must have been so thrilled to hear from you."

"When he knew I had escaped, you should have heard him weep."

"Oh, Vincenzo. To think he'd lost his daughter at your father's hands. It's so terrible."

He could feel her grief. “It was over a long time ago, Gemma. Later I placed an ad in *Il Giorno*, needing to talk to Dimi. Four days later the call came. The first thing I demanded was to hear news of you!”

She’d buried her face in her hands. “What did he tell you?”

“Dimi couldn’t give me any information. He said that while an intensive search of the countryside had been going on for me, he’d arranged to leave the *castello* that morning with Zia Consolata. He realized that if he didn’t get them out of there, he would be my father’s next victim.”

“I can’t bear it, Vincenzo.”

“The news was devastating to me. He’d promised to watch out for you. Instead you were gone, and he had to leave, too.”

“I’m so sad that you and your cousin will always carry those scars.”

He took a deep breath. “I cringed to realize the suffering my disappearance had brought on everyone. And worse, knowing I couldn’t comfort you. Neither could Dimi. He tried looking for you.”

She dashed the tears from her eyes. “I can hardly stand to think about that time, but I have to know more. How *did* you survive when you got to New York? You’d never been there before.”

Her interest thrilled him, because until he’d told her the truth, she’d refused to listen to anything.

“Don’t forget I’d been making plans for a whole year. As soon as I arrived, I checked into a hotel Dimi and I had picked out, then had my funds electronically transferred from Switzerland to a bank in New

York. Two days later I applied to take the SAT college entrance test."

"You're kidding—"

His brows lifted. "You can't go to college without sending in the results."

He felt her eyes play over his features. "With your education, you must have been a top candidate."

"Let's just say I did well enough to get into NYU, but I didn't receive the results for eight weeks. During that waiting period, I purchased a town house in Greenwich Village."

"What was it like?"

"The architecture is nineteenth-century Greek Revival, with three bedrooms. I wanted to have enough room for Dimi when he was able to join me. But of course that never happened because he didn't want to move my aunt, who preferred being in her own palazzo."

"Of course. I'm so sorry. Tell me about the university. What courses did you take?"

"Business and finance classes. Thanks to my grandfather Nistri, who was my business model growing up, I started buying failing companies with his money and turning them around to sell for profit."

She let out a cry. "Nistri Technologies is your corporation!"

"One of them. My *nonno* was brilliant and taught me everything he knew. Little by little I started to build my own fortune and planned to pay him back every penny once I'd made the necessary money. But he died too soon for that to happen."

"You're a remarkable man." Her voice shook.

"No, Gemma. Just a lucky one to have had a

mother and grandfather like mine. He had a contact at NYU who taught an elite seminar for serious business students. This revered economics professor formed a think tank for his most ambitious followers and told us to visualize our greatest dreams."

"Is that where you met your friends?"

"*Si.* For different reasons, Takis and Cesare came to the States from Greece and Sicily to study and work. Like me, they wanted to make a lot of money. This seminar that brought us together was a complete revelation to the three of us. We grew close, and they went on to become wealthy, highly successful hotel and restaurant entrepreneurs."

"As did you. Why was this professor so effective?"

"No particular reason except he was brilliant. We learned it wasn't good enough to want to make money. You've got to know how to get it, how to deal with brokers, renovate, assess the value of property, how to buy, sell and secure a mortgage. He sounded just like my grandfather."

"Was that period of your life good for you?"

"Very good in some ways. Our mentor drummed into our heads how to cut costs, decide how much risk to assume in investments and balance our portfolios in order to impress anyone. His final rule was ingrained on my psyche. 'You must find out if your friends can be loyal.'"

"You and your partners must be very close."

"I trust them implicitly. That means everything. When I brought them together with my idea to buy the *castello*, I hadn't seen either of them in at least two months and had missed them. They got excited when I showed them pictures."

"There's no place like it." Her eyes glistened with unshed tears. "After the pain you and Dimi endured at the hands of your fathers, I'm glad you've found friends like that."

"So am I."

"When I met them, I didn't know they were owners and your partners. Both of them have made me feel comfortable. Some of the people in the culinary world are hard to deal with, but your friends aren't stuffy or full of themselves."

"So you like them?"

"I do. They have a lot of charm and sophistication. Before I knew what was going on, I thought that whoever owned this hotel knew what they were doing to employ them."

"They're the best, and they'll be pleased when I pass on what you said."

She cocked her head. "Do you mind answering another question for me?"

"Ask away."

"You may not be married yet, but is there someone waiting for you to return to New York?"

Vincenzo was in a mood to tell her the whole truth. "Yes and no."

He saw her swallow. "What do you mean?"

"I've been away from Annette five weeks this time. Yesterday on the phone she told me I sounded different. She wanted to know why. I told her about the Italian girl I fell in love with in my youth, the girl I hadn't seen or heard from in ten years until two days ago."

If he wasn't mistaken, he heard a moan pass her lips.

"I explained that meeting you was a complete accident. Annette wanted to know more. All I could tell her was that a big portion of my past had just caught up with me and I was still reeling. I know she wanted more reassurance, but I couldn't give it to her."

She averted her eyes.

"What about you, Gemma? There has to be someone in your life." He braced himself for what might be coming.

"I dated a little after moving to Florence. But the only important relationship I had with a man was a year ago."

The blood pounded in his ears. "Did you love him?"

"I tried. My feelings for Paolo were different than those for you, but I felt an attraction. He was a writer for *Buon Appetito*, a nationwide food magazine, and had covered the school for an article. His interview with me turned into a date, and we started seeing each other.

"After a month he wanted me to sleep with him. I thought about it, hoping it would help me forget you, but in the end I couldn't do it. He was very upset, so I told him I couldn't go out with him anymore because it wouldn't be fair to him. He accused me of loving someone else even though I'd told him there'd been no important man in my life for years."

Vincenzo's breath caught. He'd hoped for honesty from her and her confession brought out his most tender feelings. He now had his answer to why she'd come to this particular restaurant tonight. Her ache for him had grown worse, too. They suffered from the same pain.

"Paolo said he wanted to marry me, but I told him

no because I didn't love him the way he needed to be loved. I couldn't even sleep with him. For both our sakes, I knew we had to stop seeing each other and get on with our separate lives. I'd lost my heart to the man I'd grown up with."

"Gemma..."

"After this long, it had to be unbearable to relive the ugly truth of your family's tragedy to me tonight, Vincenzo. Thank you for your courage, for forcing me to listen to the last page in the book. You were right. I needed to hear the ending so I can let go of my anger. Now I can close it."

This intimacy with Gemma, the knowledge that all the secrets were out, had changed his world forever. They'd been brought together again, and he loved her with every fiber of his being. The rush of knowing she'd been the constant heart in their relationship filled every empty space in his soul.

He grasped both her hands, ignited by the desire to be her everything. "Since we're past the age of eighteen, I have a simple solution to our problem that has been out there for the last ten years."

"What are you saying?"

"Marry me, Gemma."

With those words, everything changed in an instant.

A stillness seemed to envelope the room. Her complexion took on a distinct pallor that revealed more than she would ever know.

"A *duca* doesn't wed the cook."

Somehow he hadn't expected that response. He'd thought that because a miracle had brought them together at last, they'd gotten past every obstacle. After baring his soul to her, Vincenzo couldn't sit there any longer knowing she was more entrenched in that old world than he would have believed. She still saw him as the son of the evil *duca*. Like father, like son?

Cut to the quick, he let go of her hands and got to his feet. "This *duca* won't be a *duca* much longer. Enjoy the rest of your evening, *bellissima*."

He flew out of her flat to his car. As he accelerated down the road, he could hear her calling to him in the distance, but he didn't stop. After believing that telling her the truth would make them free to love each other as man and wife, the opposite had happened.

A duca *doesn't wed the cook.* The words that came out of her had been so cold, it frightened him. He felt as if the bottom had dropped out of his world once more. But by the time he'd pulled up to the front of the *castello*, his sanity had returned.

Vincenzo should have been ready for that automatic response—after all, Gemma had learned it from her mother at a very early age. He'd known how Mirella had always tried to guide Gemma and put distance between them because they were from different classes. But tonight his heart had been so full, he couldn't take the answer she'd thrown back at him.

The class divide was a more serious obstacle to a future with her than anything else. He planned to deal with that issue soon, but first he needed to leave for New York and take care of vital business. When he returned, he'd be able to concentrate on Gemma and their future. Because they *were* going to have one!

No sooner had Vincenzo gone than Gemma's phone rang. But she was so fragmented after her conversation with him, she ran into the other room and flung herself across the bed. Great heaving sobs poured out of her.

Something was wrong with her. Since the moment he'd entered Takis's office, appearing like a revenant, she seemed to have turned into a different person, one she didn't know. Nothing she'd said had come out right. Every conversation after that had ended in disaster. Either she ran out on him or he walked out on her.

Marry me, Gemma.

That's what he'd asked her moments ago. And what did she do? Throw his proposal back in his incredibly handsome face! *That's because you've been on the defensive from the moment he came back into your life, Gemma Rizzo!*

No wonder he'd walked out on her. Why wouldn't he? Didn't he know she loved him with all her heart and soul? But he was a *duca*. And that made a marriage between them out of the question, even though it was what she wanted more than anything in the world. While he'd been holding her hands, her body had throbbed with desire for him.

Gemma lay there out of her mind with a new kind of grief. All these years she'd misjudged him so terribly. Now the truth of his revelations burned hot inside her. At this point she knew she was more in love with him than ever.

But the woman who owned the *pensione* had recognized Vincenzo as the new Duca di Lombardi. That revelation was the coup de grâce for Gemma. His title created a chasm between them that could never be bridged. His marriage proposal thrilled her heart, but she couldn't marry him. In fact, everything was much worse.

While she worked at the *castello*, she would have to keep her distance from him. That she'd been crazy in love with him and they'd grown up spending as much time together as possible made it all the more difficult.

He had a potent charisma she found irresistible. Gemma didn't trust herself around him. Vincenzo had a way of crooking his finger and she'd come running no matter how hard she fought against it.

But she couldn't allow things to end this way. It was up to her to repair the damage and reason with him so he would understand. She hadn't told him that her mother didn't know about her new job yet. If Mirella had any idea he'd asked Gemma to marry him, there'd be even more grief, and Gemma didn't want to think about that.

Unfortunately it was too late to see him tonight. Tomorrow after work she'd find him and ask him if they could go somewhere private and talk this situation out.

After she'd cried until there were no tears left, she went to the bathroom to get ready for bed, then she returned Filippa's phone call. Her friend was excited because she'd received an affirmative response from one of the restaurants in Ottawa. "I'm flying to Canada tomorrow for the interview."

"That's wonderful." Gemma was thrilled for her. "Call me when you get there and tell me everything. Just think. You'll be closer to New York."

"It's very exciting. Now tell me, what's the situation on your end?"

"You don't want to know and I don't want to burden you when you're so happy."

"Let me be the judge of that."

Gemma spent the next while telling her all the shocking truths Vincenzo had revealed. "Although I've forgiven him, and I do understand, I'm still hurt he couldn't tell me the truth before."

"He was only eighteen, remember? And tonight he finally told you the whole truth."

"But you haven't heard it all yet. He's asked me to marry him."

"What?"

"Yes, and because I know a marriage to him is so impossible, I told him a *duca* doesn't marry the cook!"

"Oh, Gemma…you didn't! No wonder you're a mess."

"I am. During those early years we never had trouble communicating. Not ever."

"But you want something that isn't possible, because you're not teenagers anymore."

"I was more sane as a teenager than I am now. Forgive me for not making any sense tonight."

"You've been in shock since his return. I'm pretty sure he's in the same condition. Give it all time to sink in."

"I don't have another choice. Promise to call me from Canada and tell me everything."

"Don't worry. Now try to get a good sleep."

"I don't know if I can. Be safe, Filippa, and good luck!"

"Thanks. Be nice to Vincenzo. He could use it. Ciao."

Those words couldn't have made Gemma feel

guiltier, but she knew her friend hadn't intended anything hurtful. Quite the opposite, in fact. Filippa always made good sense. With a plan in mind to talk to Vincenzo tomorrow, Gemma got ready for bed and was surprised she didn't have trouble falling asleep.

The next morning, she got up and ready for the day. With the formal meetings with the owners and staff out of the way, she dressed for regular work in a short-sleeved top and pleated pants rather than a skirt. Before she left Sopri, she would buy a few groceries to put in the mini fridge for future meals. In fact, while she was shopping, she'd buy a pool lounger to take out to the lake behind the *castello*.

Until the opening of the hotel, she and Maurice would be working midmorning hours on menus and ordering the staples. But for a few more weeks there'd be free time in the afternoons before the intense work began and she earned her keep.

In the past there was nothing she'd enjoyed more than watching the swans, especially when Vincenzo had joined her. She assumed the water fowl were still there and would be an attraction for hotel guests. For now, she could lie in the sun and read a good thriller before leaving to drive back to the *pensione*. Maybe she could ask Vincenzo to meet her out there later in the day so they could really talk.

Though she followed through with her plans, she discovered that Vincenzo had flown to New York and wouldn't be back for a while. The news made her ill. She kept busy, but inside she was dying. He could have left Italy for personal as well as legitimate business reasons. She'd never know and speculation didn't get her anywhere.

Four days later she was in the depths of despair when she overheard Cesare and Takis talking in the kitchen. Vincenzo would be arriving at the airport at eight thirty that evening. She hugged the information to herself, trying not to react to her joy so anyone would notice.

After she finished the day's work with Maurice, she drove back to the *pensione* and kept busy until evening. Once she'd showered and changed into a sundress, she drove back to the *castello*. To her relief she saw the Maserati parked in front. Thankful Vincenzo was back safely, she hurried up the steps to find him.

One of the security men, Fortino, let her in the front entrance. This was the first time in ten years that she'd been here at night. The place was quiet as a tomb. Maybe because it was a Friday night and Vincenzo's partners had gone out. It was too early for anyone to be in bed. Gemma had no idea about their personal lives, though she remembered Vincenzo telling her that they were both single.

She wished she had his cell phone number, but he hadn't given it to her. If he wasn't in the kitchen, he might be out with Takis and Cesare. Then again, he was probably exhausted after his long flight and could be up in his tower room.

A long, long time ago, she'd gone looking for him there after hearing he'd suffered a terrible fall from his horse, or so she'd been told at the time. Desperate to make certain he was all right, she'd made her way to his aerie at the top of the *castello*, afraid one of his father's guards would see her. His door had been ajar and she'd heard him moan.

Summoning her courage tonight, she stole through the massive structure and made the same trek as before up the stone staircase at the rear. It wound round and round until she arrived at the forbidding-looking medieval iron door. This time it was closed. She held her breath while she listened for any sound.

Nothing came through except the pounding of her own heart.

Gemma knocked. "Vincenzo? Are you in there?" She waited.

Still no response.

It was here—away from everyone, away from any help—that Vincenzo's father had attacked him. A little sob escaped her lips to think something so terrible had happened to him. Yet he'd survived. She loved him desperately.

Desolate because he wasn't there, she turned to go back down when she heard the heavy door open behind her and whirled around.

"Gemma—" His deep male voice infiltrated her body. "What are you doing up here?" He was half-hidden by the door.

"I heard you were back from New York and I've been waiting to talk to you in private. I know it's late, but I need to apologize for my cruelty to you the last time we were together."

"Growing up I memorized your mother's views on class distinctions like a catechism. Your answer to my marriage proposal shouldn't have come as a surprise, although I'd hoped for a different response."

She bit her lip. “That’s why I came up here. To talk about this like an adult.”

“My problem is, I’m in an adult mood. If you cross over my threshold, I won’t be accountable for my behavior. Is that honest enough for you?”

Thump, thump went her heart. “Vincenzo—I’m so sorry—”

“For what?”

“For throwing your proposal back in your face like I did.”

“Are you saying you didn’t mean it?”

“Yes—no—I mean—”

“You can’t have it both ways,” he broke in on her.

“This isn’t a black-and-white situation.”

“So you admit there’s some gray area where we can negotiate?”

She let out a troubled sigh. “I shouldn’t have come up here.”

“Are you saying good-night, then? I can assure you I’d much rather you came in my room the way you did a long time ago, but the decision is up to you.”

Close to a faint from wanting to be with him, she turned to go back down the stairs. The next thing she knew, Vincenzo had caught her around the waist with his strong arms. “*Oh*—”

“Is this what you want, Gemma? Yes or no?”

Heaven help her. “Yes—”

CHAPTER SEVEN

VINCENZO PULLED HER into his room so her back was crushed against his chest.

"After our troubled reunion days ago, I didn't expect a welcome home like this. I love this dress, by the way. You're not so covered up." He kissed her neck, sending curls of delight through her body.

There was a playful side to him that seduced her. Though he was still dressed in trousers, Gemma could tell he was shirtless. His male scent and the faint aroma of the soap he used were intoxicating. She struggled for breath. "I didn't know if you were up here or not."

"I'd barely arrived and was getting ready to drive to the *pensione* to find you." He buried his face in her hair like he'd done so many times in the past. "You have no idea how beautiful you are. I couldn't get back fast enough. When did you let this profusion of silk grow out?"

"Mamma liked it short, but I got tired of the style."

"It's breathtaking and smells divine."

He'd always said wonderful things to her. "I don't remember your voice being this deep."

His low chuckle excited her. "Yours is the same."

"I think you're taller than you once were."

"So are you, in high heels. I don't think I ever told you how much I love your long legs." He turned her around so he could look into her eyes. "Do you think we're through growing up?"

In the dim glow of a lamp she saw a glimmer of a smile hover at the corners of his compelling mouth.

"I don't know. You're still the tease I remember."

"And you still blush. Give me your mouth, Gemma, so I'll know not everything has changed."

She put her hands against his chest with its dusting of black hair. "Please don't kiss me again, Vincenzo. I was simply trying to find you so I could explain what I meant the other night after you followed me to the *pensione* to talk. Everything came out wrong. I'll go downstairs while you finish getting dressed and meet you in the lobby, where we can have the conversation we should have had."

Gemma tried to pull away from him, but he held her firmly in his grasp. "The last time you came to this room, I had to let you go too soon because I was afraid you could be in danger. That's not the case anymore, and I've waited too long for this moment."

He lowered his mouth to hers and began kissing her. A kiss here, a kiss there, then one so long and deep her legs started to give way. Vincenzo picked her up in his arms and carried her past the square hunting table in front of the fireplace to the hand-carved bed.

The suite had been redecorated in nineteenth-century decor with every accoutrement befitting his title. But Gemma wasn't aware of anything except this man who was kissing her senseless. No longer the eighteen-year-old she'd adored, he was a man already making her feel immortal.

When she'd come to his bed ten years ago, he'd been suffering, in pain, and they'd had to be so careful how they kissed and held each other. Not wanting to make it worse, Gemma had had to be the one to make it easier for him to get close to her and caress her.

Tonight that wasn't their problem. With one kiss Vincenzo had swept her away to a different place, exciting her in ways she hadn't thought possible. He rolled her over so he could look down at her. His hands roamed her hips and arms as if memorizing her.

"I could eat you alive, *bellissima*." He kissed every feature of her face before capturing her mouth again and again. One kiss turned into another, drowning her in desire. Vincenzo was such a gorgeous man, she couldn't believe he was loving her like this. "I know this is what you want, too. You can't deny it. You're in my blood and my heart, Gemma."

"You're in mine," she cried softly. "I can't remember a moment when you weren't a part of me."

"I want you with me. It's past time we were together."

She cupped his striking face in her hands. "That's what you say now."

He kissed the tips of her fingers. "What kind of a comment is that? You think I'm going to change? Wouldn't I have already done that over the years we've been apart? I've already asked you to marry me. What more proof do you need? That's a commitment to last forever." He plundered her mouth with another heart-stopping kiss.

Gemma moaned. "All lovers say that. If you were a normal man, I could believe it."

He raised up on one elbow, tracing the outline of her lips. "You don't think I'm normal? We've been apart too long. Spend the night with me and you'll find out the truth."

"I don't mean that kind of normal, and you know it."

"With you lying here in my arms, your lambent green eyes as alive with desire as your body, I'm in the mood to humor you. I hunger for you, Gemma."

"You're not thinking clearly, Vincenzo." She fought tears. "I can't marry you."

Lines marred his arresting features. "Of course you can. A *duca* can do whatever he likes, choose whatever woman he wants, just like any other man."

"I know," she whispered, turning her head away. Oh, how well she knew after learning the dark secrets inside the walls of the *castello*. His father's and uncle's proclivities for other women had been one of the great scandals in all Lombardi.

He caught her chin so she had to look at him. "Let's get something straight once and for all. I have despised the class system all my life and fought against it growing up. The idea of finding the right princess to marry in order to gain more power and money is revolting to me. Your love sustained me growing up. It means more to me than any riches or possessions."

She eased away from him and sat up, smoothing the hair off her forehead. "You say that now."

"I'll say it now and until the end of our days together."

"Vincenzo—" A sob escaped. "You just don't understand."

"Then help me." He tugged on her hand so she couldn't get off the bed. She'd never heard him sound so dark.

"You're the most wonderful, remarkable man I've ever known. But you were born with a special destiny."

"No. I happened to be born the son of a *duca*. That's not destiny. It's an accident of birth."

"Please listen. I'm going to tell you something you never knew. One time when your grandfather was out in the back courtyard in his wheelchair, I was sent out to take him a sweet. He loved Mamma's zeppole. I gave them to him.

"After he thanked me, I started to hurry away, but he called to me. 'Come back here, *piccola*,' he said and reached for my hand. 'I've seen you with my grandson. You've been a good friend to him and I can tell you like him. And I know why. Can you keep a secret?' I nodded.

"'There's a reason everyone likes him. One day he'll grow up to be the finest *duca* of us all. With his princess he'll raise future *duchi*, who will have a wonderful father to look up to. But I'm afraid I won't live to see it.' He kept hold of my hand and wept.

"Even though I was young, I realized that he was letting me know how lucky I was to be in your company. When I ran back to Mamma and told her, she said it was a sign from heaven that I should always respect my friendship with you. To think of wanting anything more would be sacrilege."

* * *

"*Santa Madre di Dio!*" Vincenzo got off the bed, putting his hands on his hips in a totally male stance. "So *that's* the reason for all this talk! Gemma—if it will ease your mind, I've heard your opinion on the subject before. Your mother shared her beliefs because she loves you and wants to protect you."

"Still, my temper sometimes gets the best of me."

"I remember," he murmured. "That time you and Bianca went swimming in the lake without your clothes. You thought Dimi and I had been spying on you and had taken them. I confess we did spy with my binoculars from a tree at the edge of the forest."

"Vincenzo—"

"But it turned out we weren't the culprits. The dog of one of the guards ran off with your clothes. We chased it down and brought your things back to you, but I don't recall you thanking us."

She shook her head. "We were too embarrassed to talk. That was so humiliating, you can't imagine."

"You were our wood nymphs come to life. Dimi and I thought it was the most wonderful day we'd ever spent."

"You would!" But even across the expanse separating them he detected a half smile.

"I'll tell you another secret. My mother was very fond of you. But because she was a princess, she believed any feelings I had for you would come to grief. Like your mother, Mamma had also been raised in a different world of rigidity within the titled class."

Gemma sat on the edge of the bed. "Her words were prophetic."

"Not completely. Dimi and I broke rules all over

the place. It's a new world now. Because of a reaction to the misuse of noble titles in our country, you'll notice a trend among legitimate aristocracy in this last decade to refrain from making use of their titles."

"I didn't realize."

"What's important is that you and I have found each other again and I'm no longer in danger from my father or uncle. The powers that be are gone."

"Thank heaven for that, Vincenzo. But what did you mean when you said you wouldn't be a *duca* much longer?"

He hadn't meant to tell her this soon, but right now he was desperate to get closer to her. "Since my return to Italy, there are men in the government who know of my business interests in the US and here. I'm not blind. Because of my title they want me to get on board with them to play an economic role in the region's future. It's all political, Gemma. The title corrupted my father and uncle. It turned their souls dark. I refuse to let that happen to me."

"You don't know if the title did that to them, Vincenzo. I watched you grow up titled, remember? I never once saw you do an unkind thing in your whole life." She stared hard at him. "You can't change who you are."

"Oh, but I can."

"How?"

"By renouncing my title. Once that's done, it's permanent. If I have a son or sons, they won't inherit it, and any daughters I might have can't inherit it anyway. The beauty of it is that an Italian title of nobility cannot be sold or transferred. In other words, the abuse stops with me. My male children and their children and the children after them won't be burdened."

Her eyes widened. "If you do that, won't the title fall on Dimi through his father?"

"Yes, but he's taking the same steps."

"You'd both stop the title from progressing after centuries of succession?"

Vincenzo nodded. "There are so many dreadful things my father and uncle did in the name of that title, seen not only in the scars that Dimi and I carry. You know the head gardener who was introduced at the orientation meeting?"

"Yes. I met him out in back the first day."

"Years ago, my father got angry at him for planting some flowers Mamma wanted. He told him to get out and never come back. He didn't give him a reference or any severance pay. While Dimi and I were looking up old employees, we found him.

"That's just one of a hundred stories I could tell you of my father's cruelty. If he and my uncle hadn't been born to a *duca*, they wouldn't have felt they had the right to treat people like animals. The only way to end the corruption is to rid ourselves of the title and restore the honor of those noble Gagliardis from the past by preserving the *castello*."

"*That's* why you turned it into a resort," she whispered.

"What better way to make restitution than by allowing the public to enjoy its heritage, thereby giving back something good and decent to the region."

Her features sobered. "You loved your grandfather Emanuele. He was a great *duca*. How would he feel about this?"

"I can't speak for him, but if he's looking down on us now, he couldn't be pleased with what his sons did while he was dying. Being born with a title gives some men dangerous ideas."

"But not you, Vincenzo. Emanuele adored you. I don't think he'd want you to do this."

He frowned and got to his feet. "For someone who came close to bearing the brunt of my father's dark side, I'm surprised to hear this coming from you. I thought you of all people would be happy to see this kind of inequality come to an end."

"But you're a different breed of man and shouldn't have to give up what is part of you."

"I'm a man, pure and simple. Don't endow me with anything else. This isn't an idea I just came up with on a whim. When I was five, maybe six, I saw my father kick one of the young stable hands to the ground because he didn't call him Your Highness. It sickened me. That was the day my plan was born. Now I can see it through to fruition."

The way she shook her head filled him with consternation. What could he say to get through to her?

"Years ago I told you I'd find a way for us to be married. A few days ago I asked you to be my wife because there'd be no barrier between us. But there *is* one. It goes so much deeper than I realized."

His words caused her to flinch, alarming him.

"When you said you and I weren't the same people growing up, I didn't understand how fully you meant it." His chest felt tight. "It's clear you don't love me the same way I love you, no matter what I do. I can tell you would rather I keep the title, the very thing you think prevents us from ever getting married."

He started pacing in frustration, then stopped. "Is this because of what my *nonno* said? It's no wonder you don't think you can marry me."

"I didn't mean to upset you. I thought if I told you about that experience, you would begin to see."

"I see, all right," he muttered. "Mirella deliberately interpreted it so you would only worship me from afar. She didn't want you getting any ideas about a real relationship with the future *duca*. After all this time, it's still working."

"You can scoff about this all you want, Vincenzo, but it was very serious to me. He was a prayerful man. I saw him go to Mass in the private *castello* chapel every day before I left for school."

"He wasn't a priest destined to be cardinal one day, Gemma. Who do you think administered the Mass to him every morning?"

"You don't have to be a priest to be a godly person. Everyone felt that way about the old *duca*. I know you loved him."

"That's beside the point. He knew he was dying. All he was doing that day was expressing his sentiment about me to a sweet girl who'd brought him his favorite dessert baked by the best cook around. But to see that as a sign from above..." He shook his head.

Gemma slid off the bed. "My mother was raised in a good Catholic family."

He raked a hand through his midnight-black hair. "Heaven help me, so were you."

"That's why she honored the traditions here."

"You're right, but she went too far. Without giving me any voice at all, she made me out as the untouchable one, the future *duca* whose word was law.

It's that old divine right of kings business and it disgusts me."

No one could confuse her like he could with his logic.

"It's time to put the past *in* the past, where it belongs. There's no room in the modern world for it. I'm a normal guy, Gemma. Warts and all."

"You don't have any."

Vincenzo leaned against the door with his strong arms folded. "Of course I have flaws and imperfections, like every other man. Think about it—until I called my friends together about buying the *castello*, they didn't know my last name or the fact that I inherited a title. Do you see them treating me any differently? Have they once shown me a special kind of deference?"

"Actually, no," she said with her innate honesty.

"Good. Maybe that will convince you. Please hear me out. We need to be spending time together as adults, not as those teenagers from the past having to live by ridiculous rules that constantly divided us in your mind. It's important—in fact, it's *vital*—that you throw away the blinders while we explore the world we're living in now as equals in all things and ways."

Gemma could hear what he was saying, but it was so hard to silence her mother's warnings after all these years. It meant throwing off old fears and conceptions that had dominated her thoughts forever.

"I'm in love with you. Isn't it worth it to you to find out if you can see me as a typical man you've met and want to get to know better?"

Vincenzo was the most atypical man she'd ever

known, but he couldn't see it. He wasn't a woman. She hugged her arms to her waist. "You already know what's in my heart."

"I do?" he quipped, making her smile. "Then prove it. Here's what we're going to do."

She recognized that no-nonsense tone in his voice. When he went after something, he was impossible to stop. Gemma knew she had to get away from him. "There's nothing to do, Vincenzo. I have to leave."

With a few long strides, he stood in the front of the doorway so she couldn't walk out. He was such a breathtaking male, her legs turned to mush.

"The second I learned you didn't have a husband, I planned for us to take a vacation together. That's why I left that night for New York. There were loose ends I needed to tie up first so we wouldn't have anything standing in our way."

"That's a fantasy you need to let go of. For one thing, you just employed me. I can't take a vacation."

"There's still enough time before the grand opening for us to be gone a couple of weeks. My partners will handle everything, and you've already done the most important work with Maurice. When was the last time you went off on a real trip anywhere? Be honest."

Her eyes closed tightly. "I don't remember."

"That's what I thought. I need a holiday badly, too, but I never felt like taking one because the woman I wanted with me wasn't available. My fear that you were happily married and living somewhere in Italy with your husband and children tortured me more nights than you'll ever know."

Gemma had battled the same fears about him and had suffered endlessly for years.

"We'll leave in the morning. Go home and get packed. I'll come by the *pensione* at eight. We'll drive to the airport and have breakfast on the plane."

He was serious. It frightened and thrilled her at the same time. She moistened her lips. "Aren't you too tired to go anywhere after coming back from New York?"

"When we get to the beach, we'll sleep, relax and play in the water to our hearts' content."

It did sound out of this world.

"If—if we go," she stammered, "I don't want us to sleep together. When we're in each other's arms we communicate as a man and woman, but—"

"We certainly do."

Heat filled her cheeks. "You know what I mean. I didn't think of you as the *duca* while we were on the bed, but at other times—"

"I get where you're going with this," he broke in. "You want to see us as that man and woman no matter what else we're doing."

She nodded.

"So do I, so I'll try to keep my hands off you. But I'll warn you now, it's not going to be easy." He walked over to the massive dresser and pulled out a knit shirt he put on. "I thought I'd better cover up before I walk you out to your car. Fortino's a man and would understand, but I don't want him to get the wrong idea about you."

"Thank you."

His deep chuckle reverberated through her body as he caught her face between his hands, kissing her long and hard. Like old times, they wrapped their arms around each other and started down the winding staircase. Vincenzo stopped every so often to give her another kiss. She didn't think they'd ever reach the bottom and didn't care.

They crossed through the *castello* to the front entrance. "It feels like we're the only two people on earth."

"Don't I wish," he whispered against her throat. They nodded to Fortino and went down to her car. "Let's exchange phones so we can put in our numbers. I want you to call me the second you reach the *pensione*."

She nodded. When that was done, he crushed her against him. "*Ci vediamo domattina.*"

If she wasn't dreaming, then she would be seeing him in the morning. Taking the initiative, she pressed a kiss to his lips and climbed in the car. "Tomorrow."

Vincenzo packed a bag, then phoned his cousin before getting in bed. "Dimi?"

"Are you back from New York?"

"Yes, and I'm going away again, but I wanted to call you first. How's Zia Consolata?"

"Failing a little more each day."

"I'm so sorry. When I get back from this trip, I'll come and spend a few days with her to give you some relief."

"Where are you going?"

"I've had a breakthrough with Gemma." He'd always told his cousin everything. For the next little while he explained what had gone on this evening.

The part about her conversation with their grandfather Emanuele came as a shock to him.

"You're right. That gave Mirella more ammunition. But I'm worried. You sound too excited, Vincenzo. The zebra doesn't lose its stripes."

Vincenzo didn't want to hear that. "But she has agreed to go on vacation with me."

"Just be warned. You've been in hell for years. Two weeks with her might still not be enough to make her see the light."

His breath caught. "Thanks for your optimism."

"I just don't want you to end up in more pain that could last for the rest of your life."

He didn't want that, either, and worried about his cousin. Vincenzo wished there was more he could do for him. Dimi had relationships with various women, but his prime concern was to take care of his mother.

"I love you for caring, Dimi. Talk to you soon. Ciao."

CHAPTER EIGHT

WHEN MORNING CAME Vincenzo dressed in chinos and a sport shirt, then met early with Cesare and Takis to tell them his plans. With everything settled, he phoned Gemma to say that he was on his way to Sopri in one of the hotel service vehicles. He'd parked his Maserati around the back of the *castello*.

When he pulled up in front, she came out with her suitcase. His heart rate picked up speed. She looked fabulous in white sailor pants and a sleeveless white top. He wondered how long it would be before the sight of her didn't send adrenaline pounding through his blood.

He jumped out of the car to help her in and put her case in the back. Those luscious lips of coral were too much of an enticement. By the time he'd finished kissing her, there was no more lipstick left.

"The *padrona* was watching out her window."

"Are you ever going to stop worrying about being with me?"

Her chest heaved. "I promise to try not to let my fears get the best of me."

"That's all I can ask." He tucked some strands of honey-blond hair behind her ear.

"Where are we going?"

"First we'll fly to someplace I haven't been before. Have you ever traveled to Bari along the Adriatic?"

"No."

"Good. I want to explore the coast."

"Ooh. That sounds exciting. Are we taking the ducal private jet?"

"No. We're flying commercial, like two ordinary people."

Her head turned toward him. "Are you teasing me?"

"Does that mean you're disappointed?"

She blushed. "Of course not."

"We're simply two people on holiday together, doing whatever we feel like."

By two in the afternoon, they'd arrived at Bari international airport and rented a car. Vincenzo was starting to feel in the holiday mood. They stopped at a deli to buy some wine and a bag of Italian sausage and egg pies.

He looked over at her. "Having a good time?"

"This is the best. Can you imagine how much fun we would have had if you'd been able to drive us around years ago?"

"I've tried hard not to imagine what joy that would have been. In truth, if I'd driven off in a car with you, no one would have seen us again. My father knew that if I got behind the wheel of any car, I'd disappear."

"No, you wouldn't have. Like you told me, you'd never leave your mother."

He squeezed her thigh. She remembered everything.

"When did you learn to drive?"

"After I got to New York and bought my first car."

"What kind?"

"A white Sentra, perfect for a college guy. I have pictures I'll show you."

"I want to see and know everything that happened to you."

"We've got the rest of our lives, Gemma."

She didn't respond, but he wasn't worried. She'd come with him and today was only the first day. They whizzed along, chatting and eating. They explored Puglia before coming to the medieval town of Polignano a Mare, scattered with white buildings.

"Oh, look, Vincenzo. This whole area is built on sheer cliffs."

"This is where we're staying tonight. Years ago the guys told me about this place. I've been anxious to see it ever since." He turned in to the Grotta Palazzese Hotel built from the local stone. "We can't see it from here, but there's a cave restaurant below where we're going to eat tonight."

"I've heard about it. I can't wait to see it! A real cave."

"Yes. Seventy or so feet above the water. Let's check in and get our room, then walk around some of those narrow streets until we get hungry."

Gemma's heart raced when Vincenzo asked the concierge for a key to their room. Except for the night she'd crept up to his room all those years ago, and last night, she'd never been in another man's bedroom.

There were several couples checking in. She wished she could be nonchalant about their situation. After they reached their room and closed the door, Vincenzo put their bags down and pulled her into his arms. They kissed hungrily.

"Relax. It'll get easier." He knew everything going on inside her. "Go ahead and freshen up." She passed the queen-size bed on the way to the bathroom. This was all so new to her, she had to pinch herself.

Before long he took her out to play tourist. She had the time of her life as they meandered through the ancient streets hand in hand. No woman they passed could take their eyes off Vincenzo. One of the clerks in a tourist shop fell all over herself to get his attention.

But he'd fastened his attention on Gemma. He constantly teased and kissed her all the way back to the hotel, where they dressed for dinner. In their youth they'd had to plan every move to be together so no one would find out. It had been as if they were caged. Little could she have imagined a night like this with him. To be free and open to show their love was intoxicating.

A cry escaped her lips when they went down the steps to the limestone cave restaurant below. In the twilight, the individual tables had been lit with candles. The whole ambience had a surreal feeling with the warm evening breeze coming off the Adriatic.

They were shown to a table for two and served an exquisite meal of prawns and swordfish. She looked into his silvery eyes. "You can hear the water lapping beneath us. This is an enchanting place."

"The guys were right. You can't find a more romantic spot anywhere in Italy."

"I agree. A restaurant without walls. It's incredible." Near the end of their meal, the waiter came over. "No more wine for me," she said. "One glass is all I can handle."

Vincenzo declined a second glass, too. "Shall we take a little walk before going to bed?"

The thought of being with him all night sent a wave of delight through her body. "I'd love it."

An hour later they returned to the hotel and headed for their room. Vincenzo waited for her to get ready for bed. While he was in the bathroom, she climbed under the covers, dressed in the only long nightgown she owned. She wasn't quite as full now, but the food had stimulated her. She doubted she'd be able to sleep at all lying next to him.

He entered the darkened room in his robe and opened the window to let in the sea air. When he got into bed, he turned on his side toward her and drew her around so she faced him.

"Do you know that since we've been together again, all we've done is concentrate on me? I want to talk about you. I want to hear everything that happened to you from the morning you had to leave the *castello*."

She tucked her hands beneath her pillow so she wouldn't be tempted to throw them around his neck. "That was the worst moment of our lives. Mamma was so quiet I was frightened. We left with Bianca and her mother in a taxi early in the morning. At the train station in Milan, we all said goodbye. They were going back to Bellinzona in Switzerland, where their family came from."

He let out a groan. "So that's why Dimi couldn't find her, either."

"I cried for days. Bianca and I promised to write,

but it didn't last very long, because they moved again and one of my letters came back saying *return to sender*."

Vincenzo stroked her hair with his free hand.

"As for Mamma, she at least had her sister and niece in Florence. They offered us a home over the bakery. I loved them and we were very blessed, really. She was able to work in the bakery immediately to start earning money."

"Thank heaven your aunt was so good to you. I'd give anything to make it up to your mother for the pain. Not only couldn't I protect my own mother, I couldn't do a thing for yours."

Gemma heard the tears in his voice. "Please don't worry about it. My aunt knew Mamma had to use the Bonucci name so your father couldn't track her down. Everything worked out.

"On our first weekend there, Mamma took me to the cemetery to see my *papà*'s grave. I never knew him, so all I could feel was sadness for that. But for the first time in years, I watched her break down sobbing. I'd been so fixated on my own problems, I never realized how much she'd suffered after losing my father.

"Their married life had been cut short and she didn't have any more babies to love. My selfishness had caught up to me and I determined to be a better daughter to her from then on."

"You were the best, Gemma! I was always impressed by how close you were to her. How did you end up going to cooking school? You never talked about it to me. I didn't know that's what you wanted to do."

"I didn't, either. I assumed I'd to go college. One time when you and I were together, I told you as much in order to impress you."

"After I went to New York, I'd hoped that was what you would do."

"The trouble was, I didn't know what I wanted to study. Two weeks after we got to Florence, the family sat me down. I sensed they were worried about me, and they said they thought I might have been suffering from depression."

Vincenzo reached for one of her hands and kissed the palm.

"They told me I should attend cooking school. If I didn't like it, I didn't have to keep going. But since I'd already learned how to cook by watching Mamma, I'd be way ahead of the other students applying there.

"It sounded horrible to me, but everything sounded horrible back then." Her eyes stung with tears. "I'd lost all my friends."

"That's exactly how I felt when I arrived in New York," he whispered.

"Oh, Vincenzo—" She tried not to cry. "Over the years Mamma had saved a little money, but not enough to go toward my schooling. Yet I never felt deprived."

"You were loved, and that kind of wise frugality puts the sins my father and uncle committed to shame. Now keep telling me how you became a cook."

"So my aunt who runs the bakery knew someone in the administration at the Epicurean School, and I was given a scholarship. When she said that it was close enough for me to take the bus there, I realized they were all telling me I had to go and try it. I knew it was what my mother wanted. She'd sacrificed everything for me, so I did it."

"Did you hate it in the beginning?"

"No."

He smiled. "That's interesting."

"It was a surprise to my family, too. On the first day I met a girl named Filippa Gatti, who was from Florence. She reminded me of Bianca, and we became friends right away. She said she was tired of academic studies and wanted to do something different. After buying an expensive slice of ricotta cheese pie that tasted nasty, she thought, 'Why not be a pastry cook? Anyone could cook better than this!'"

"Why not?" Vincenzo laughed.

"With so many classes together, we hit it off, hating some of the teachers, loving others."

"You mean the same way Dimi and I felt about our tutors."

"Exactly."

"I'd like to meet her one day."

"She'd pass out if she ever met you."

"Ouch."

Gemma chuckled. "You know what I mean. There's no man like you around anywhere." He kissed her again. "She helped me deal with my pain over losing you, and our friendship got me through those nine years as an apprentice."

"I'm glad you have her in your life."

"So am I. You'd love her. She's darling, with black hair like yours and the most amazing sapphire-blue eyes. She's fun and *so* smart. After work we'd go to movies and eat dinner out and shop. Sometimes we took little trips along the Ligurian coastline. We'd visit lots of restaurants and check out the food."

He grinned. "Were there any good ones?"

"I found out you can't get a bad meal in Italy, but we determined to invent some fabulous dishes that would become famous someday. The truth is, Mamma was the creator in our family, better than my aunt or my grandmother and great-grandmother, who started the bakery. All I could do was try to match her expertise."

"You've succeeded, Gemma. Is Filippa as good a cook as you?"

"Much better, and that's the truth. She's innovative, you know?"

"I saw your résumé. You were named the top student in your class."

"That's because Signora Gallo, the woman on the board, loved my aunt and knew it would make her happy to give her niece the top ranking. It should have been Filippa."

"Where is she now?"

"In Canada, applying for a pastry chef position in Ottawa."

"Could you have applied there?"

"Yes, but I wanted a position in France. That is, until I saw the opening advertised at the *castello*."

"It was our luck we got you first. Finders, keepers. Cesare believes you applied for the position because it was meant to be. But I hope your friend gets what she wants."

"Me too. She always wanted to work at a restaurant in New York City and be written up in some glossy magazine as Italy's greatest cooking sensation. I'm kidding. She never said that, but I know she wanted to work in New York. In time I know she will, and I hope she becomes famous."

"I could put in a good word for her with Cesare. He owns an excellent restaurant chain."

She put her fingers to his lips. "No favors. We're going to be ordinary people right now, remember? But thank you for being so kind and generous."

"Gemma…an ordinary person can recommend someone for a job without being a *duca*."

"You don't know Filippa. She's intensely proud. The only way she would take a job would be for her to prove she's the very best at what she does. To be given a chance through a friend wouldn't go down with her at all."

"Sounds like your soul mate."

"Vincenzo—"

"Does she have a boyfriend who's going to miss her?"

"She *had* one. He let her down in a big way, but she's over the worst of it now."

"That's good. Now come here and let me kiss you the way I've been wanting to. We've talked long enough."

"I don't dare."

"Then will you do me a favor and turn on your other side? I can't promise not to reach out for you during the night. I have no idea what I do in my sleep."

"Then we're both in trouble. *Buonanotte*, Vincenzo. I've had the most wonderful day of my life."

"Guess what? We have two weeks of wonderful

days and nights ahead. Tomorrow I thought we'd fly to the island of Mykonos."

"You're joking. Aren't you?"

"Is that excitement I hear in your voice?"

"Yes! I've never been to Greece."

"Neither have I. Ironic, isn't it? I've traveled all over North and South America, parts of Asia. I've been to many of the states in the US—Hawaii, Alaska—and I know New York City like the back of my hand. But the rest of my education is still lacking."

"So is mine," Gemma murmured after she'd taken in what he'd just told her about his travels.

"Both Takis and Cesare say I have to see the Greek islands. Once you go there, you'll never want to travel anywhere else. I've arranged for us to stay at a small hotel with a restaurant, Gemma. It's on a white sandy beach where the waters are blue and crystal clear. You step right out of the room onto the beach. If you want, you can walk to town from there."

She let out a long sigh, picturing the white Greek architecture. "In my opinion, to live and be surrounded by water is true paradise. That's the one thing missing in Milan and Florence. They're both landlocked. Eating by the sea tonight inside that grotto was sheer enchantment. No other restaurant could compare."

"Being with you made it magical. Tomorrow morning we'll fly straight from Bari to Paxos. Sleep well, *il mio adorabile cuoca*." He leaned over to give her a tender kiss, then rolled on his other side.

Vincenzo had just called her his adorable cook.

"You're too good to me, you know. I haven't done anything for you but cause you trouble."

"If you want to make it up to me, all you have to say are four little words besides *I love you*."

I know.

"We're doing fine, aren't we? We're a man and a woman enjoying life together, right?"

"Yes." Her voice wobbled.

"You sound like you're going to cry."

"How do you know me so well?"

"Maybe because we met from the moment we were out of the cradle. You're as familiar to me as Dimi. No one else was in my world. I saw you in every mood and circumstance, just as you saw me."

"Our deep friendship is unique. On the strength of it, will you tell me the truth about something? When you went back to New York this time, did you see Annette?"

"Yes. We went to dinner and I told her she wouldn't be seeing me again because I was so madly in love with you, it was as if we'd never been apart."

"But—"

"No buts, Gemma. I can read your mind. If you can't commit to me by the end of our vacation, my feelings for Annette won't be resurrected. I can't imagine being a good husband to any woman when my heart has been yours from the age of five."

Now the tears started.

"Maybe that was the problem with my father and my uncle. Both of their marriages were arranged. They didn't have the luxury of already being in love with the women chosen for them. Our poor mothers had no choice, either."

"But they had you and Dimi to love."

"Still, what a shame they weren't lucky enough

to have grown up with the sweetest little girl on the planet. If I had to look for a reason for their notorious philandering, that might be one of them. I'd have fought dragons for you."

"I would have nursed your wounds." Her words came out ragged.

"That's what you did the night you came to my room. I ought to be thankful for what my father did to me. Though you didn't know he was the reason I was hurt, the news brought you to me."

"I still can't believe what he was capable of."

"It's over, and we were able to have that precious time together before I had to leave the country. The memory of that night was the only thing that has gotten me through the years—and Dimi, of course."

"Has he met a woman he loves?"

"He's had girlfriends, but no one special. My uncle is still alive and in prison. Work is Dimi's panacea to stave off the demons. With his contacts and resources, he's helped us put the details of the *castello* transaction together. He and the guys have developed a strong friendship already."

"You can't help but love Dimi. I've missed him terribly. Does he ever go to see his father?"

"Not yet. He's does a lot of his business at home to be with my aunt. She has several health care workers who provide relief for him. He says her doctor doesn't give her much longer to live."

"How hard for him. How hard for you. Forgive me for talking my head off."

"It's music I'll never grow tired of, Gemma. We were parted by too many years of silence. I'm greedy for all the time I can get with you."

She lay there bombarded by shock waves of feelings and emotions. Gemma didn't need any more time to know she wanted to be his wife. She'd always wanted to belong to him. What she had to do now was believe that even if he was the *duca*, he would stay this normal man who made her feel so complete she could die of happiness.

In that regard every woman wanted to believe that about the man she married. She wanted proof that he would always love her and never change. But no power on earth could give you proof like that. Her faith in him had to be enough. She *did* have faith in this man. Since she'd been with him again, it had been restored to new heights.

He's back now, Gemma.

He's back now, so what are you going to do about it?

Ten days playing on the beach beneath the Grecian sun had turned both of them into bronzed facsimiles of themselves. The shiny hair on Vincenzo's wood nymph reflected golden highlights that hadn't been visible before their trip. He never tired of watching Gemma or the voluptuous mold of her body.

She lay in the late-afternoon light on a lounger by the pool wearing a new turquoise-and-blue bikini.

"We've invented a new phrase, Gemma. Beach potatoes."

She lowered the thriller she was reading and broke into serious laughter, the kind he remembered from long ago. The nervous, worried woman he'd started out with on their flight to Bari was no longer visible. He loved this new Gemma, who seemed carefree and relaxed.

But she hadn't broken down, letting him know she wanted him to make love to her. The signs that she was ready to give him the answer he was waiting for hadn't come.

The zebra doesn't lose its stripes. Dimi's warning had haunted him throughout the night.

He'd decided to speak his mind now. There was no sense in putting it off, especially since the phone call he'd just received from Dimi.

Their loungers were placed side by side. She turned her head toward him. "I can see that look on your face."

"What look is that?"

"The one that says you've got something important to say."

"I can't hide much from you, can I?"

"Do you want to?" Her anxious question startled him. Well, well…beneath her calm facade she wasn't calm at all.

"No, Gemma. I was teasing. What I wanted to tell you was that while you were out in the sea a few minutes ago, Dimi phoned me."

"I didn't realize." She looked alarmed. "Is your aunt worse?"

"No. He called me because he just got word that my uncle died of liver failure in prison last night. They rushed him to the hospital, but it was too late."

Gemma sat up and slid her feet to the patio. "I hardly know what to say."

"That makes two of us."

"I'm sure he needs you right now."

Vincenzo nodded. “I’ve already made the flight arrangements for morning. When we reach Milan, we’ll drive to his villa.”

“In that case I’d better start getting packed.”

“Wait—before you go in the room, there’s something else I must tell you. I’ve been hoping you’d break down and talk to me about the thing I want most to hear. Since you haven’t, I’ve decided you need another nudge.”

“I don’t understand,” she cried softly.

“I’m renouncing the title right away. My uncle’s death convinces me even more it’s the right thing to do. Now Dimi and I can wipe the slate clean and be done with it. Even your mother would approve and give you her blessing. I’m looking forward to talking to her.”

A gasp escaped her lips.

“Why the consternation? It’s what you’ve always wanted so we could be together. Deep down it’s what I’ve wanted, too. These days with you have been the happiest of my life. I’m not going to let anything change that now.”

He got up from the lounger to pick up the towels and carry them into the room. She followed with the sunscreen and her book, but when he looked at her, she reminded him of a person suffering from shellshock. Good! The situation couldn’t go on this way any longer.

“While I’m at the front desk making arrangements for an early-morning drive to the airport, why don’t you decide where you want to go for dinner? I’ll be back in a little while.”

"To be honest, I'm not hungry. We had a late lunch."

"Then I'll stop at the deli for some snacks in case you change your mind later." He put on a sport shirt and left the room.

Gemma put her book down and sat on the bed, alarmed.

Vincenzo was going to renounce his title! He honestly believed that by getting rid of it, he'd be freed of the curse and Gemma would be happy. Her poor darling Vincenzo believed it would open up the way for her mother's blessing on their marriage.

But Gemma wasn't happy. Not at all.

She didn't want him to give up something that was part of him. He was already proving to be a wonderful *duca* through his vision of the *castello* and by all the great things he'd done to this point to restore the family's good name.

Unfortunately, until he could accept the whole of himself—until he could trust himself the way she trusted him—how could they be married? How could she live with herself knowing he was tearing himself and the fabric of his life apart just to be with her?

Gemma couldn't let him renounce the title, she just couldn't. She wouldn't let him. Somehow she had to find a way to stop him.

Oh, help! Her mother wasn't even home from her trip yet. She didn't know Vincenzo was back in Gemma's life! Gemma hadn't told Mirella about the job at the *castello* yet, either. She thought Gemma and Filippa were out together looking for jobs.

Propelled by anxiety, she headed to the bathroom

for a quick shower. Then she started packing, trying to sort out her thoughts. She wouldn't be able to work on Vincenzo tonight, not when he had Dimi's family on his mind. In a few days she would find the right time to beg him to listen to her, but it couldn't be right now.

As for her mother, Gemma would wait until she returned from England before she told her the news that would shake her *mamma*'s world once more.

An hour later Vincenzo returned and could see Gemma had showered. Her bags were basically packed and now she was in bed looking a beautiful golden honey blond. Though she'd opened the same book she'd been reading earlier, the page never turned.

Before they'd come on this trip, she'd claimed to be all mixed up. But these days in Greece had proved to him they were divinely happy doing the kinds of things other couples did on vacation. So why had the announcement she'd wanted to hear caused her to lose her concentration? Whatever was going on, he intended to get to the bottom of it.

She looked up at him with those dazzling green eyes. "Hi."

"*Buonasera.* I bought a few spinach rolls in case you want them."

"Thank you. Maybe I'll try one in a little while. Vincenzo? When you talk of marriage, do you even know where you'd want to live? You have a huge business empire in New York and are building one here. Once the resort is running smoothly, do you intend to go back and forth to the States? Are you and your friends going to put other people in charge at the *castello*? Don't they have to get back to New York, too?"

He unbuttoned his shirt before getting ready to shower and flashed her a piercing glance. "Don't you think I need an answer to *my* question first? The most important one I'll ever ask?"

Without waiting for a response, he went into the bathroom. When he came out later wearing his bathrobe, he discovered her, white-faced, sitting on the side of the bed in her nightgown, waiting for him.

"Vincenzo—I *can't* answer your question."

They'd been through this before. He shuddered. "Why not?"

"Because I've thought long and hard about it, and I don't want you to renounce your title. Not for me. I couldn't live with it."

"I'm not doing it for you. I thought you understood me. Isn't that what our whole trip has been about? Enjoying life like normal people?"

She got to her feet. "But you're not an ordinary man."

He shook his head. "Thank you for your nonanswer. I finally understand the meaning of déjà vu." After shutting off the lights, he climbed in his side of the bed. "I'm tired, Gemma. We have an early-morning call."

So saying, he turned away from her, unable to deal with this right now. Dimi's words were screaming in his head.

Just be warned. You've been in hell for years. Two weeks with her might still not be enough to make her see the light.

CHAPTER NINE

GEMMA HADN'T SLEPT at all and was numb with pain. Vincenzo's rare show of sarcasm last night, followed by his silence, was worse than any visible anger.

On Friday morning he rented a car at the airport in Milan and drove them to an area off the Duomo with a few secluded properties of the wealthy. She wasn't surprised when he pulled into the courtyard of a small, exquisite nineteenth-century palazzo. This represented the world he intended to give up.

After what he'd told her last night, she believed him. Her opinion *didn't* enter into his decision to give up the title. He'd hated it all his life and didn't want anything to do with it, period!

But in her heart she felt it was wrong, because he was the best thing that had happened to the Gagliardi family in two hundred years. Though she couldn't convince him of this, maybe Dimi would listen before it was too late.

Vincenzo helped her out of the car and walked her to the front entrance. To her surprise the double doors opened and his black-haired cousin stood there, almost as tall as Vincenzo. In trousers and an open-necked white shirt, he'd turned into one of the most attractive Italian men she'd ever seen. He too had the Gagliardi build and silver eyes, though his features were his mother's.

"Dimi!" she cried. The world stopped for a moment as a myriad of memories from their youth passed through her mind. He held out his arms and she ran into them. After he'd swung her around at least three times, she cried for him to put her down. "You look so wonderful!"

He wiped his eyes. "I swear I never thought to see you again in this life. Come with me." She felt his arm go around her shoulders. "We'll go out to the garden to talk."

"I'll look in on Zia Consolata while you two get reacquainted."

"*Perfetto*, Vincenzo."

Together they walked through a palazzo filled with treasures, leaving Vincenzo behind.

"How beautiful!" she exclaimed when they reached the sunroom that led to the outside patio. The rose beds were in full bloom. Dimi sat down beside her next to the wrought-iron table with an umbrella to shield them from the hot sun.

"Mamma loves it out here."

"Of course she does."

He hadn't lost that sweet smile. "Let me take a good look at you." His eyes played over her. "Short or long hair, you're a vision, Gemma. That's an extraordinary tan you and Vincenzo acquired in Greece. Your body was so white that day at the lake when—"

"Don't you dare say another word!"

Dimi burst into laughter. The sound took her back years. "I see my cousin told you about that."

"I'd rather not think about it." She reached over and grasped his hand. "He's told me all about your mother…and now your father."

His features sobered. "To be honest, I'm surprised his diseased liver held out as long as it did."

She squeezed his fingers before letting him go. "I understand your mother isn't aware of what has happened."

"No. Besides Alzheimer's, she has developed bradycardia, a slow heartbeat. The doctor inserted a pacemaker, but her body has rejected it. She's close to death now and never leaves her room."

"Would it be possible for me to talk to her?"

"That wouldn't be a good idea. She gets agitated by anyone who comes. But you're welcome to look in on her before you leave."

"Thank you." A lump had lodged in her throat. "Dimi, how can we help you with your father's funeral? Vincenzo couldn't get here soon enough."

"That's the way it has always been between us. If you want to know the truth, there's little to be done. My cousin and I are planning on the priest giving a blessing at the grave site tomorrow morning behind the *castello*. That's where all the Gagliardis are buried. No one will be invited."

"Not even me?" she asked in a small voice.

Gemma knew the location well. It was located in a special section deep in the forest. Vincenzo had met her there several times and had given her a history of the Gagliardi line. There was one spectacular monument among the headstones where the first Duca di Lombardi was buried. But she hadn't visited the family cemetery since coming to the *castello*. Duca Emanuele would be buried there now.

A strange sound came out of Dimi. "He doesn't deserve anyone as kind and loving as you being with us to say goodbye."

"Your father gave you life." Tears filled her eyes. "I can't imagine my youth without you. For that, I'm grateful to him. Something in his brain had been wired wrong, but look how you've turned out. You've been the greatest blessing to your mother, who has always adored you."

Dimi got out of the chair and paced for a few minutes, reminding her so much of Vincenzo when he had something painful on his mind. She stood up and walked over to him, putting her hands on his arms.

"You and Vincenzo are the greatest of all the Gagliardi men. I know, because I grew up with you for seventeen years and never saw anything but goodness in either of you."

He shook his head.

"I beg you to listen to me, Dimi. Don't let the actions of your fathers stain your lives and prevent you from doing the extraordinary things you were meant to do. You've both risen above the evil and corruption that entrapped them. Can't you see it's within your power to restore the good name you inherited?"

His features hardened, just like Vincenzo's did. It was uncanny. "That's a tall order, Gemma."

"Of course it isn't! Look at me." He lifted his eyes to her. "Vincenzo doesn't believe in destiny. He says your titles came as an accident of birth. Does that matter? You could raise the bar above everyone else. In fact, you've already started."

"What do you mean?"

"I've heard Vincenzo's partners talking. The two of you have hired dozens and dozens of local workers who've been unemployed to help restore the *castello* and grounds. Vincenzo started Nistri Technologies in southern Italy, putting over five hundred people to work. And Cosimo told me in private that you've started a huge new charity for Alzheimer's victims in honor of your *mamma*.

"You've done amazing things and opened doors only you could with your money and your positions as leaders. Please promise me you'll think about it and talk to him before he makes a mistake I can't bear for either of you to make."

He stared at her through narrowed eyes. "What happened to the girl who couldn't see past the title that divided you?"

She drew in a deep breath. "She grew up and is standing in front of you with no more blinders on. On this trip Vincenzo has shown me he can be a *duca* and the most wonderful man who ever lived, all at the same time. I'm so proud of both of you and all you've accomplished. It's made me see clearly at last. But he needs to believe it, too. You both do."

Gemma couldn't tell if she was getting through to Dimi or not. "Will you let me do something for you?"

"What would that be?"

"Stay with your *mamma* while you bury your father? It will be my way of showing my respect. She was a lovely woman and so kind to me. I realize she won't know me, but I can be in the room while you and Vincenzo do your part in the morning. In a small way it will make me feel connected again. If my mother weren't away on her trip, she'd want to be with the *principessa* at a time like this, too. Everyone loved her."

A mournful sigh escaped before Dimi drew her into his arms. He rocked her for a long time without saying anything. Suddenly Vincenzo's shadow fell over them.

"Zia Consolata is asleep. I'm going to run Gemma to her *pensione* right now, but I'll be back."

Dimi let her go. "I haven't even offered you something to eat or drink."

"We ate on the plane. See you soon."

Gemma waited for Dimi's answer, but he didn't say anything as he escorted her and Vincenzo through the palazzo to the front entrance. Dimi's eyes locked with Gemma's. "You have no idea what it meant to see you today."

"I feel the same way. *Piu tardi*, Dimi." She kissed his cheek and hurried out to the car. Vincenzo joined her for the twenty-minute drive to Sopri.

"Is Consolata as bad as Dimi said?"

"Worse. I can't see her lasting long now. We may have another funeral before long."

"Thank you for taking me with you to see him. I love him."

"That was quite a hug he gave you."

Within a few minutes Vincenzo pulled up to the *pensione* and helped her take in her bags. She stood at the door. "I told him I'd like to stay with Consolata in the morning. Will you let me know if he'd like that?"

His lips had formed a thin line. "I'll call you later after I've talked to him."

Gemma bit her lip as he walked back to the car and drove away. No sooner had she shut the door than her phone rang. Hoping he had regretted his hasty departure, she clicked on without checking the caller ID. Her heart was thudding. "Vincenzo?"

"No. It's Filippa."

The world spun for a moment and then settled back just as quickly. "It's great to hear your voice. Did you get the job?"

"No, I'm no longer in Canada. Instead of returning to Florence, I flew straight to Milan to see you. Do you mind if I come by the *castello* to talk? I've rented a car."

"I just got home from a trip with Vincenzo and am at the *pensione* alone. By all means, come!" Gemma knew in her heart Vincenzo wouldn't be by again today, and she needed her friend. "We'll eat lunch here and catch up."

"Thank you. You'll be saving my life."

"Let me give you instructions how to get here. My car will be out in front."

"I'll find you."

Half an hour later her darling friend came running to the door and they hugged.

"Come and sit down on the love seat. You're the last person I expected to see for a long time." She sat on the chair across from her friend, whose shoulders were shaking while she tried to hold back tears. "Talk to me, Filippa."

"Oh, Gemma—"

"I can't believe you didn't get the position."

"I did get it—but I was so homesick, I knew I

couldn't live there. If I'd had a chance to work in New York, I know it would have affected me the same way. All this time I thought I wanted to go to someplace new in the world and make my mark. By the time my orientation was over, I had to tell the owner I couldn't take the job."

Little did she know Gemma had told Vincenzo she couldn't accept the position. Twice, in fact! But not for the same reason.

"I felt terrible about it, but he was very nice. Do you know what's funny? He'd moved there from Hong Kong to start a new restaurant that's very successful."

That *was* funny, but Gemma didn't laugh and moved over to put an arm around her. "I'm so sorry."

"I'm okay, but I'm embarrassed to go home and tell the family their daughter who's never going to get married is a great big baby."

"No, you're not. Vincenzo and I have spent the last nine days in Paxos on a beach. If I thought I had to go there alone, beautiful as it is, and cook at a restaurant with no friends or family for thousands of miles, I couldn't do it."

"That's not true."

"I wouldn't lie about something like that."

Her brows lifted. "This trip you took. Does it mean—"

"No. We haven't been together like that. I'm not sure we ever will be now, but I'll talk to you about it later. Let's concentrate on you. You're welcome to stay with me on the couch for as long as you want."

"I wouldn't do that to you, but if you're willing to put me up for one night, I'll leave for home tomorrow."

"You've got to stay a couple of days at least. I don't have to be to work until Monday."

"You always make me feel good."

"Ditto. To be truthful, you couldn't have shown up at a better time for me. Vincenzo and I had to come home early from our vacation. His uncle died and he has to be with Dimi to plan the funeral. Come in the kitchen. I made a salad for us."

"Oh, it's so great to see you! What on earth was I thinking to go off, when the world I love is right here?"

"That's what I'm trying to convince Vincenzo of. He's planning to renounce his title, something that's part of him. I don't want him to do that, not for me nor for himself.

"Filippa—he doesn't think he's a whole man because of it. Somehow he's got to develop faith in himself that he can be a good man and a good *duca* at the same time. I couldn't marry him knowing he was giving it up partly because of me. The problem is, I've agreed to stay on at the *castello* for three months no matter what happens. I'm praying that in that amount of time he'll begin to see what I see."

They ate and later went to a movie. After they got back around nine, her phone rang. It was Vincenzo. With her hand shaking, she picked up and said hello.

"Gemma? I've been busy making arrangements for the burial and haven't talked to Dimi yet. If you haven't heard from him by now, then I would imagine he has decided against your staying with my aunt. I'll see you at the *castello* on Monday. Takis is calling a meeting."

She pressed a hand to her heart. "I'll be there." She

fought the tremor in her voice. "Thank you again for the trip of a lifetime, Vincenzo."

"I'm glad you enjoyed it. *Buonanotte.*"

Click.

Gemma made up a bed for Filippa on the couch, then pulled back the covers to get into her own bed. There'd been no life in Vincenzo's voice. Her grief had gone way beyond tears.

As she slid beneath the bedding, her phone rang again. This time the caller ID reflected an unknown number. She answered it with a frown. "*Pronto?*"

"Gemma? It's Dimi." She couldn't believe it. "I've decided I would like you to be here with Mamma while I'm gone. I called the *castello* for your address and phone number." *Not Vincenzo?* "I'll be by for you at eight o'clock in the morning."

Joy. "I'm honored and I'll be ready."

After she got off the phone, she ran into the living room and told Filippa. "I want you to stay. I won't be gone for more than a couple of hours."

"All right."

Like the night before, Gemma didn't get much sleep. The next morning she showered early and put on the one black dress she had in her wardrobe. It had capped sleeves and a slim skirt. Nothing fancy, but she felt it was appropriate.

Her friend had gotten busy in the kitchen and fixed them a delicious breakfast. When Dimi came for her, she didn't know who looked more surprised, him or Filippa.

It was very interesting to feel the aura that surrounded two stunned, beautiful people before Gemma introduced them. Dimi wore a black mourning suit. Filippa had put on a summer dress in a small blue-and-white print, bringing out the intensity of her blue eyes.

When Gemma explained why Filippa was there, he turned to her friend. "Please come with us so Gemma doesn't have to sit alone."

"I don't want to intrude in such a private matter."

"You're her best friend. We have no secrets and it's no intrusion. If you're ready, let's go."

They walked out to the black limousine with the insignia and coat of arms of the Duca di Lombardi. When they got in the back, Dimi placed himself across from them with his long legs crossed at the ankles. All the way to the palazzo, Gemma sat there in wonder as he and Filippa talked quietly, sharing small confidences so naturally, it surprised her.

By the time they reached their destination, Gemma was convinced something of consequence was happening between them. Dimi's eyes never left her face. As for Filippa, her expression had to have mimicked Gemma's the first time she'd seen the dashing, grown-up Vincenzo in the office at the *castello*. If any man ran a close second to Vincenzo, it was his cousin.

He led them inside his mother's bedroom. A health care worker sat beside the bed. Dimi showed the two of them to comfortable upholstered chairs in a corner of the room. He made arrangements for food and drinks to be brought to the small table if they wanted them.

Gemma squeezed his hand. "God bless you today, Dimi."

He kissed her cheek. "Thank you for doing this."

His eyes swerved to Filippa. The look he gave her friend was a revelation. "Thank you for coming with her. I won't be long."

A cloudy sky above the opening in the forest didn't allow the sunlight to shine on the casket. Vincenzo and Dimi stood side by side holding long-stemmed yellow roses while Father Janos delivered the funeral prayer.

"Here we have gathered in memory of Alonzo Trussardi Gagliardi, second in line to the Duca di Lombardi, so that we may together perform one final duty of love. As an act of remembrance, we have gathered to place his remains here in this sacred resting spot. In so doing, we trust that somehow what was best in his life will not be lost, but will rejoin the great web of creation.

"May the truth that sets us free, and the hope that never dies, and the love that casts out fear be with us now until dayspring breaks and the shadows flee away. We have been blessed by life—go in peace. Amen." He made the sign of the cross.

Dimi placed his rose on the casket, then Vincenzo. They both thanked the priest and had just started to walk away when Dimi said, "Let's go over to your father's grave before we drive back to the palazzo." He pulled two more long-stemmed roses from a planter vase for them.

Vincenzo hadn't visited it since he'd been back in Italy. He hadn't ever planned to take a last look, but something fundamental had changed in him since he'd been with Gemma. All their long talks about the past had forced him to delve deep inside himself for the first time in ten years. Perhaps it was time.

His father's grave was behind a nearby tree. They looked at the writing on the headstone. Was it possible that all the evil had been buried with him and hadn't been handed down to Vincenzo? He wanted to believe it. He wanted to believe Gemma, whose soul had been in her eyes when she'd begged him to keep the title and do great things with it. If he thought he could…

Dimi turned to him. "Gemma gave me a piece of advice earlier."

Gemma again, Vincenzo mused. She'd had a profound effect on both of them.

"She said not to let our fathers' misdeeds stain our lives. Though my father was never the *duca*, he'd always hoped to be one day. But no matter what, being the offspring of the old duca didn't make him or your father who they were. It was a flaw in them. She was right, you know?"

With those words he placed his rose at the base of the stone. Clearly Dimi had forgiven both their fathers.

Gemma had forgiven them, too. She'd seen the example of the old *duca* and she believed in Vincenzo. That belief caused an epiphany in him.

As he stood there, he realized his faith in himself had been restored. Stunned and humbled, he put his own rose by the headstone. Then they walked back to the limousine. Vincenzo had come to the cemetery in his car parked behind the limo.

"I'll follow you to the palazzo, Dimi. I don't want you to be alone today."

His cousin eyed him oddly. "I won't be. Gemma

and her friend are there. I picked them up early this morning so they could sit with Mamma."

Vincenzo reeled from the news. "What friend?"

"Filippa. I'm sure she's told you about her."

"Yes, but I thought she was in Canada interviewing for a pastry chef position."

"It seems it didn't work out and she came back last evening."

"A lot has gone on since I dropped Gemma off yesterday."

Dimi nodded. "I told you we talked while you were with Mamma. Something she said, plus what Father Janos said today, has decided me against renouncing the title."

Vincenzo knew the line he was talking about. It had struck a chord with Vincenzo, too.

"Remember the part, 'We trust that somehow what was best in his life will not be lost, but will rejoin the great web of creation'? Gemma convinced me there's a lot you and I can do if we keep our titles to create something really good to repair the damage. In my soul I know she's right." He opened the rear door. "I'll see you back at the palazzo, cousin."

Vincenzo stood there for a few minutes pondering everything. Little did Dimi know he'd been preaching to the converted. In time he broke free of his thoughts long enough to jump in his car. He took off behind Dimi, intending to talk to Gemma as soon as possible.

Dimi was waiting for him in the courtyard when he pulled in. "Have you ever met Gemma's friend?" Dimi asked as they went inside.

Vincenzo hadn't expected that question. His cousin's decision not to renounce his title had been superseded by something else—like the fact that Dimi had a woman on his mind when they'd just laid his uncle to rest.

"Not yet."

Once they entered the palazzo, he followed him through the house to his aunt's bedroom. There he found Gemma and her friend talking quietly to one of the health care workers.

The older woman said Consolata had been resting comfortably all morning, which was a relief. Vincenzo tore his gaze from a pair of green eyes to a pair of blue ones. He had to agree with Gemma's assessment—with that coloring, Filippa was a knockout. Dimi told them to come to the sunroom. When they stood up, he noticed Signorina Gatti was a little shorter than Gemma, but just as curvaceous.

Outside in the garden, formal introductions were made. The maid served them iced tea and sandwiches. Dimi wasn't inclined to talk about the funeral service. If anything he seemed intrigued by Filippa and asked her about her trip to Canada.

Vincenzo took advantage of the moment to get Gemma alone. "We need to talk. How long is your friend going to be with you?"

"She's driving back to Florence tomorrow."

"I'll take the two of you to your place as soon as you're ready to leave. Hopefully we'll find time to be alone tomorrow after she's gone."

Before he could hear her answer, Dimi had walked over. "I've told Filippa I'd like to drive her back to the *pensione* later. What are your plans?"

This day wasn't going the way Vincenzo had imagined at all. He'd thought he might be able to console his cousin, but it didn't look like he needed it. Under the circumstances, nothing could have suited Vincenzo better than to get Gemma alone without offending her friend. He had something vital to tell her.

Gemma gave Filippa the key to the *pensione*. They all said goodbye and Vincenzo walked out to his car with Gemma. But when they left the heart of the city, he turned onto the A8 motorway.

Her head jerked around. "Where are we going? This isn't the way to Sopri."

"First you need to answer a question for me. What magic did you weave on Dimi that has caused him to want to keep his title? He has spent a lifetime telling me he despised it."

"I'm glad he feels that way." She sounded overjoyed.

He gripped the steering wheel tighter. "Was that your plan? To get him on your side so he'd try to influence me?"

"I'd do *anything* to get you on my side! I've finally realized why you don't want to keep the title. You think you can't be a whole person unless you renounce that part that has pained you. But don't you see? You've already done so many things for the community, for your country since you've come back. You're an extraordinary man by being exactly who you are. I don't want you diminished in any way, shape or form. I love you, Vincenzo, title and all."

He didn't know where to go with his emotions. It seemed he didn't have to explain how his feelings had changed about the title and the good he could do with it. "I'm glad you feel that way, because I've decided to keep it. Does that mean you'll marry me?" This was the last time he was going to ask.

"Yes, yes, *yes*!"

CHAPTER TEN

JOY ROCKED VINCENZO'S WORLD, but he groaned aloud. "*Gemma*—what a time to tell me! I'm driving and can't pull over right now. The summer traffic will be bumper to bumper like this all the way to Lake Como."

"That's where we're going?"

"If we can ever get there. Everyone's trying to leave Milan at the same time."

An infectious giggle came out of her, a happy sound he hadn't heard in years. "We've practiced self-control for the last few weeks. Another hour won't kill us."

"You mean *two*. It's *killing* me, you beautiful witch." He reached for her hand and clung to it.

"I want to marry you, Vincenzo. I'm crazy, madly, terrifyingly in love with you. I'm sorry it's taken me so long to get my head on straight. Please—while you can't touch me and I can't make love to you—tell me where we're going to live. I want to know everything. Will we fly back and forth from here to New York every few months? The suspense is killing me."

"One answer at a time. We're going to live here permanently."

"You really mean it?" That was pure happiness he heard in her voice. "Where is here, exactly?"

"That's what I want to show you."

"You mean at Lake Como?"

"The first night in Greece, when we were on the beach, you said that to live surrounded by water would be paradise. I've always wanted to live by water, too. There's a place I've had my eye on for the last six months, never dreaming I'd find you again. And it's not too far from the *castello*."

"I've never been to Lake Como. Have you already bought it?"

"No. The Realtor has been holding it for me, but my time is almost up."

"What town is it in?"

"Cernobbio, in the foothills of the Alps, where the scenery truly is magnificent."

"Is it as fantastic as I'm imagining it is?"

"You'll have to wait and see. I'm sure your mother will love it. She'll be living with us, wherever we are. When the traffic is light, it's only a little over an hour's drive from Milan. There's a private dock on the lake, so we'll have to buy a boat."

"She doesn't know about us yet."

"I didn't think she did. When will she be back from her trip?"

"Tomorrow."

"That's perfect. We'll drive to Florence tomorrow and tell her we're getting married. She loves you enough to want what you want. I'll spend the rest of my life proving to her our marriage will work. But the ceremony has to happen before the grand opening, so we only have a few days left to plan it."

"I'm so happy, I feel like I'm going burst!"

"Don't do that while we're still in this traffic."

She grabbed onto his arm. "When we're married, if the traffic is too horrible to drive home, we can always go upstairs to the tower room, and we'll hibernate while I feed you *sfogliatelli.* No one will know where we are."

Vincenzo didn't know how much longer he could last without pulling Gemma onto his lap. "The one thing we won't have at Lake Como is a beach. Almost no property has beachfront."

"There's only one beach I want. It's in Greece. You've spoiled me. I know I'm dreaming. Do you care if I keep working?"

"I want you to be happy, whatever it takes."

"Will you be happy living away from New York?"

"I have a confession to make. I was never happy there."

"Honestly?"

"I'm an Italian. I was homesick."

Gemma let out a cry. "Filippa said the same thing. That's why she's back."

"Good for her. Where would you like to get married, *bellissima*?"

"I think that should be up to you."

"Then I say we ask the priest to marry us in the *castello* chapel."

"That would make me the happiest woman on earth." Tears ran down her tanned cheeks. "It is so beautiful. I remember looking inside when your grandfather was in there. I thought it was the closest place to heaven."

"Have you considered what he was trying to tell

you that day out in the courtyard might have had a different meaning? My belief is that he knew you were my soul's delight and saw you as the princess I would marry one day."

"Do you really think that?"

"Yes. I'm going to tell your mother that. She'll have to be happy for us."

Gemma's eyes filled with tears. "I'll treasure what you've said all my life."

"You're *my* treasure, Gemma."

"Oh, I can't wait until we get there."

Another few minutes and they passed through Como. Cernobbio was only a little farther up the lake. When they reached it, Gemma gasped. "I didn't know scenery like this existed on earth. There are dozens of incredible villas!"

He wound around until they came to one that jutted out into the lake. At the sign—Villa Gagliardi—he slowed to a stop on the private road.

Gemma took it in with disbelieving eyes before she turned to Vincenzo. "This villa belonged to your family?"

He nodded. "Until my father gambled it away. I've negotiated to buy it back. It's ours if you want it."

"If I *want* it?" She launched herself at him, throwing her arms around his bronzed neck. "I want you forever, any way I can have you. I'll take anything that comes with you."

For the next little while, they tried without success to show each other how much they loved and wanted each other. It was impossible within the confines of his Maserati.

"How can you do this to me?" he whispered against

her lips. “For nine days you held me off. Now you’re giving yourself to me and I can’t do a thing about it until we find a place to be alone.”

“I know. I’m sorry, but I promise I’ll make it up to you.”

“Let’s get married the day after tomorrow. No man ever needed a wedding night more than I do.”

She buried her face in his neck. “How can we do that? Wouldn’t you have to get a special license?”

“Yes. But I’m the Duca di Lombardi. I’m the person who makes these things happen.” His smile melted her bones.

“I presume Father Janos will perform the ceremony whenever you say.”

He nodded.

“Won’t he think it’s too soon after the funeral?”

“Not at all. He’ll be happy we’re making a dream come true in the midst of so much sadness.”

She kissed every feature of his face. “Is there anything you can’t do?”

“No.”

“Vincenzo—” She hugged him harder. “Be serious. You want to get married the day after tomorrow?”

“Don’t you? With your mother coming back tomorrow, there’s no reason to delay it a second longer.”

“I love you, *il mio amore*.”

“Then we need to drive back to Milan immediately and make all the arrangements. Besides your mother, I want Dimi and my partners there.”

“I’ll tell Filippa she can’t leave for Florence until after the ceremony. She can stay at the *pensione* until then.”

"Kiss me one more time, Gemma, so I know I'm not hallucinating."

"I plan to kiss the daylights out of you after we say 'I do.' But since I shouldn't be bothering you while you're driving, I'm going to call Mamma right now and tell her everything. She can think about it on her flight back to Florence."

He squeezed her arm. "I'll talk to her, too, and tell her we've just come from the home where we want her to live with us."

Gemma was euphoric as she pulled out her phone to reach her mother. No matter her parent's first reaction, Gemma would talk her down, because there was no one like Vincenzo. She planned to be his wife, and her mother had to understand that.

The phone rang a few times until Mirella picked up. "Oh, Gemma—I'm so glad it's you. I'm tired of traveling around and am anxious to come home."

"I can't wait for you to get here, but please don't be too tired, Mamma."

"Ah? What's wrong?"

"Everything is so right, I don't know where to start."

"You must have gotten a wonderful job."

"Oh, I did!"

After a pause, her mother said, "I haven't heard you this happy since…"

"Since we once lived at the *castello*?" she answered for her.

"Gemma? What's going on?"

"Vincenzo is back in my life! That's what's going on." She smiled into his eyes of molten silver. "You're not going to believe why he really disappeared or why he's back now. We're going to be married the day after tomorrow."

"But he's a *duca*!"

She smiled at Vincenzo through her happy tears. "Yes, and I'm going to be his *duchessa*. That's why you can't be too tired. Tomorrow we have to buy me a wedding dress and a beautiful dress for you. Filippa will need one, too. The ceremony is going to take place in the *castello* chapel by Father Janos. You remember him?"

"Lentamente, mia bambina—"

"I'm too excited to slow down. Tomorrow I'll tell you all the details while we're looking for dresses."

Vincenzo took the phone from her. "Mirella? We want your blessing. No one knows better than you how much I love your daughter. The day you made that little lemon ricotta cheesecake for me when I was eight was the day I fell in love with you, too. Here's Gemma back."

Tears were rolling down her cheeks as she took the phone from him. "Mamma? Did you hear what Vincenzo said?"

"I did," she answered in a croaky voice. "Tell him that if I hadn't loved him, too, I wouldn't have made it for him."

Gemma could hardly breathe. "I'll tell him. I love you, Mamma. See you tomorrow. Fly home safe."

The minute she heard the click, she told him what her mother had said. His eyes filled with tears before she broke down sobbing for joy.

When Dimi arrived at the *pensione* in the ducal limousine at three o'clock, Gemma walked outside with

Filippa, leaving the place in a complete mess. She wore the white wedding dress her mother and her friend had helped her pick out in one of the shops in Milan earlier that morning.

The skirt was a filmy chiffon that fell from the waist and floated around her legs. Lace made up the bodice and short sleeves. Instead of a veil or a bouquet, she wore a garland of white roses and a single strand of pearls with matching earrings that had been delivered that morning by courier. Vincenzo's prewedding gift.

Filippa had helped her put them on and handed her the enclosed card.

Ti amo, squisita.

You are my treasure.

The little makeup she wore was ruined by her tears, and she had to rush to repair the damage.

Gemma had wanted a simple wedding outfit that would still look bridal. If they'd been getting married in front of several hundred people, she would have chosen a long dress with a train and veil. But she was happy with their perfect little wedding.

Dimi took pictures with his camera first. Gemma insisted on taking some of him. Within minutes he helped her into the back of the limousine, where her mother was waiting in an ivory lace suit and pearls. Then he assisted Filippa.

He looked marvelous in a dark blue suit with a white rose in the lapel. Her friend wore a pale pink silk sheath with a corsage of pink roses and looked stunning.

As the limousine drove away, Gemma looked across at Dimi. She squeezed her mother's hand. "I've been thinking back through the years when we were just little children."

"Now you're all grown up." Mirella smiled at them.

"I can't believe this is really happening, Mamma."

Dimi grinned. "Neither can my cousin. He's been waiting for this day for so long, I hope he's still holding it together. I told his friends to do whatever was necessary to help him make it through to the four o'clock ceremony. It's your fault he's in this state, Gemma."

"I've been in a state since I applied for a job at the *castello*, battling my old demons."

"Vincenzo and I know all about those. But yours are gone, right?"

Filippa spoke for her. "I can promise you that my dear Gemma is the most divinely happy woman on the planet. I ought to know. For the last nine years I've listened to her pain over losing Vincenzo."

"Oh—" Mirella threw her hands in the air. "I prayed every night the pain would stop."

Gemma's friend chuckled. "The minute I heard he was alive and back at the *castello*, I actually sent up a special prayer of thanksgiving."

Dimi nodded. "I did the same thing when he told me you'd applied for the pastry chef position. It was your recipes, Mirella, that put Gemma over the top with Vincenzo's partners. Do you know that from the moment he arrived in New York, I've heard nothing but grief from him where Gemma was concerned?

Today I'm the happiest man on the planet to know that this torturefest is about to be over."

The four of them laughed.

"I love Vincenzo so much. When he walked in the office, I almost fainted."

Dimi leaned forward and patted her hand. "When you two met, we couldn't have been more than four or five. Even then it was as if no one else existed. He followed you around like a puppy dog. You teased him and provoked him, but he just kept coming."

"He teased me back constantly. His growls were terrifying when he chased me around the old ruins. I laughed until I fell down and couldn't catch my breath. Every day when I woke up, I knew I was going to see him and there'd be a new adventure. Nothing else mattered.

"But I want you to know something, Dimi. I loved you, too. So did Bianca. I don't think there were four happier children anywhere."

"I agree. What I want to know is, are you ready to be chased around the *castello*'s secret corridors and chambers for the rest of your life?"

"Yes. I can't wait!"

"Gemma!" Mirella cried, but she knew her mother was only pretending to be shocked.

"I'm warning you. He hasn't outgrown certain tendencies." His wicked smile reminded her of the old Dimi.

"Neither have I, but don't you dare tell him."

When she looked out the tinted windows, she realized the limousine had pulled up in front of the *castello* steps. She gripped her mother's hand. "This is it."

Dimi got out and held the door open for the three of them. "Be sure you want to go inside, Gemma," he teased. "Because when you do, you'll never be the same again."

"I know." She gave him a hug. "I'll be Signora Gagliardi. Don't have a heart attack, Mamma."

Her mother only laughed, the most wonderful sound Gemma had ever heard from her parent. eh.

"Well, here goes!" She took off alone and rushed up the steps, breathless to find Vincenzo, who was inside waiting for her. Never had there been a bride as eager as she to seal her fate.

Cesare stood at the entrance in a becoming tan suit. He too wore a white rose in his lapel. "Your husband-to-be has asked me to do the honors and escort you to the chapel." He kissed her on both cheeks.

"Thank you so much."

He gave her his arm and they walked through several long corridors to reach that part of the *castello*. "I had no idea when I interviewed you that you were the person who ruined every woman for Vincenzo all those years ago."

"That's not quite true. I know of one special woman, very recently in fact."

He shook his head. "No, no. If she'd been the one, he would have brought her with him. Did you know he wanted you to stay in the tower room of the former *principessa*?"

Warmth traveled up her neck to her cheeks. That had been her favorite room in the whole *castello*. "He was only joking."

Cesare laughed. "Denial becomes you."

They reached the closed chapel doors, where Takis

stood, dressed in a beige suit, also wearing a white rose. He hugged her before Dimi introduced Filippa and Gemma's mother to the other men.

Cesare gave her a special smile. "So you're the *mamma* responsible for raising our new executive pastry chef. She gave all the credit to you on her résumé. I understand why. The pastry she made for us was beyond compare. I'm honored to meet you." So saying, he gave her a kiss on both cheeks. Gemma loved him for showing her mother such deference.

Dimi turned to Filippa. "This is where I leave you to join Vincenzo, but Takis will take good care of you." Dimi's gaze swerved to Gemma's. "You're sure you want to go through with this?"

"*Dimi*—" she cried softly in exasperation.

"Just checking."

He took more pictures of all of them, then folded her mother's arm over his and they moved inside the chapel.

Gemma looked at Takis. "Have you seen Vincenzo? Is he in there?"

"*Si.*"

"And Father Janos?"

"*Si.*" With a poker face, he added, "In case you can't tell them apart, Vincenzo is the tall guy wearing the gray suit and white rose. The short, portly father is wearing...well...let's just say he's dressed in splendid robes for this once-in-a-lifetime celebration of your marriage."

Her eyes smarted. "Thank you for being his dear friends. Your friendship saved him at the darkest moment of his life."

Takis cocked his head. "Someday we'll tell you

just how dark our lives were when we arrived in the States. Meeting Vincenzo was the best thing that ever happened to us. Isn't that right, Cesare?"

The Sicilian nodded and lent her his arm. "It's four o'clock. Time to begin."

Takis opened the doors and walked Filippa down the aisle. Gemma followed with Cesare. For such a small chapel, the interior was breathtaking, with wall and ceiling frescoes still vibrant with color.

This was where she'd seen Vincenzo's grandfather worship. Now Emanuele's two grandsons stood on either side of Father Janos, waiting for Gemma. She feared her heartbeat could be heard throughout the incense-sweet interior. With each step that took her closer to Vincenzo, it seemed to grow louder.

Except for the absence of the father she'd never known, Gemma couldn't imagine a more perfect setting for their intimate wedding. The most important people in the world were here in attendance.

Cesare walked her to the front, where Vincenzo reached for her hands. Beneath his black wavy hair, the bronzed features of his striking face stood out against the frescoes. The candles beneath the shrine cast flickering shadows, revealing to Gemma the impossibility of his male beauty.

They both whispered, "*Ti amo...*" at the same time.

Father Janos bestowed a thoughtful smile on them. "I understand this moment has been in the making for many years."

She nodded. Vincenzo must have told him everything.

"That is a good long time for you to have loved each other and should give you the faith that your union will be blessed by the Almighty. Vincenzo? Take her right hand in your left and repeat after me. 'I, Vincenzo Nistri Gagliardi, Duca di Lombardi, take Gemma Bonucci Rizzo for my beloved wife. I will love her, cherish her, protect her for the rest of my life.'"

Gemma heard him repeat the words in that deep, thrilling voice of his.

"Now, Gemma. Repeat these words."

She looked into Vincenzo's eyes. Between the dark lashes they gleamed pure silver. "I, Gemma Bonucci Rizzo, take Vincenzo Nistri Gagliardi, Duca de Lombardi, for my beloved husband, who has always been beloved to me." The last part of the sentence was her own addition. It brought a smile to Vincenzo's lips.

"I will love him, cherish him, support him and honor him for the rest of my life." The honor part was another deviation from the script, but she wanted him to know how complete was her commitment to him.

"Because you have taken these vows, I pronounce you man and wife. In the name of the Father, the Son and the Holy Spirit. Amen. Vincenzo? Do you have a ring?"

"I do."

"You may present it to your wife.

She was his wife!

His fingers were sure as he pushed home a diamond in a gold band on her ring finger.

"Do you have a ring, Gemma?"

"She does," Dimi said and came forward. He handed her the gold band she'd picked out for Vincenzo during their shopping spree with her mother.

"You may present it to your husband."

Vincenzo helped her put it on, then pulled her into his arms and kissed her. It went on for a long, long time. Gemma forgot everything and everyone. Somehow she'd been given her heart's desire, and nothing mattered but to pledge her heart and soul to him in the most intimate way she knew how.

"I love you, Gemma. You just don't know how much."

"But I do, *amore mio*."

They kissed each other once more. When he finally lifted his mouth from hers, she realized they were the only ones left in the chapel. "Oh, no—even the priest has gone."

He gave her that white smile to die for. "Father Janos was a man before he wore the robes. That should answer your question."

"There's no one like you. It was a perfect wedding."

Vincenzo wrapped his arms around her. "There's more. Much as I want to take you upstairs, our friends are waiting in my grandfather's small dining room to celebrate with us. I'm excited, because Cesare's contribution has been to make the meal for us. He learned to cook from his mother, just the way you did. It'll be an all-Sicilian menu tonight."

She put her arms around his neck. "I love your friends. I adore Dimi, and I love my dear friend Filippa. I've decided her timing in coming back to Italy was meant to be, as was Mamma's. Now I guess we'd better not keep them all waiting."

He kissed her eyes, nose and mouth. "They understand and will enjoy the vintage Sicilian wine until we get there. One more kiss, *sposa mia*."

Twenty minutes later they walked arm in arm to the second floor. When they entered the dining room, Gemma could smell the beef fillet in brandy before she saw the paintings of wood nymphs, all in a serious state of undress. Her face turned scarlet.

Everyone clapped. Vincenzo walked her to the table and sat down next to her, putting his hand on her thigh beneath the table. Heat coursed through her body.

Dimi raised his glass. "To my cousin and his wife. To Mirella. None of you have any idea how long I've wanted to say that. I don't know when I've ever been this happy." His eyes were smiling. So were Filippa's.

Cosimo waited on them, bringing one delicious dish after another. Caponata...*arancini*...pasta with urchin sauce.

When the meal concluded, Gemma got to her feet. "This is joy beyond measure to be surrounded by our friends and my beloved mother. What can I say about our bridal feast? The six-star award goes to Cesare for the best meal I've ever eaten in my life. *Grazie* with all my heart."

Cesare beamed. "*Di niente.*"

Vincenzo stood up and put his arm around Gemma's waist. "I can't improve on anything my bride said. And now I must tell you we have a pressing engagement elsewhere and ask to be excused, but we know you will understand."

The men's deep laughter filled the room while Filippa and Gemma exchanged a secret smile. With her friend planning to stay at the *pensione* for a few more days, everything was working out perfectly. On a whim, Gemma removed her garland of roses and tossed it to Filippa, then tossed her mother a kiss. She would be staying in the tower room of the *principessa* until after the hotel's grand opening. Vincenzo couldn't do enough for her.

"Come with me," her husband whispered.

She needed no urging. Her desire for him had reached a flashpoint.

Vincenzo rushed her through the hallways to the back of the *castello*. When they came to the winding steps, he picked her up in his arms and carried her to the tower room. His strength astounded her. When they'd reached the bedroom, he wasn't even out of breath.

"I've dreamed of doing that for years. Help me, Gemma. I want you so much I'm shaking."

While he was helping her out of her dress, she was trying to take off his suit jacket. Somehow they managed and kissed their way to the bed. He lay down with her and crushed her in his arms, entwining his legs with hers. After suppressing their needs for the last two weeks, the freedom to love each other made her delirious with longing.

Each touch and caress ignited their passion. Vincenzo had lit her on fire. The right to show her husband everything she felt and wanted was a heady experience too marvelous to contain. They drank deeply from each other's mouths, thrilling in the wonder of being together like this.

Far into the night, they gave and took pleasure with no thought but the happiness and joy they found in each other. Gemma hadn't known the physical side of their lovemaking could be this overwhelming. Her rapture was so great that at times she cried afterward and clung to him.

When morning came he began the age-old ritual all over again. They'd suffered for so long, they thoroughly enjoyed becoming one flesh, one heart.

Toward noon, they lay side by side, awake again. Vincenzo smiled at her. "I feel like I've just been reborn."

"I know. I've had those same feelings."

He suddenly pulled her on top of him. "I'm too happy, Gemma."

"Can there be too much happiness?"

"I don't know. Promise me it will always be like this."

She searched his eyes. "My love for you just keeps growing."

Rolling her over, he kissed her fiercely. "I want to make love to you all over again, but I know you must be hungry. Are you?"

"Yes. For you!"

"I'm serious."

"So am I."

"Cesare told me yesterday he'd have food brought up to us. I'm pretty sure it's outside the door now."

"Then we'd better eat it. I don't want to hurt his feelings." Her darling Vincenzo. He was starving, but he didn't want to admit it. She loved this man beyond description. "Why don't you go look and see?"

He pressed a kiss to her throat. "I'll be right back. Don't go away."

"Where would I go?"

"Never disappear on me, Gemma. I couldn't take it." Lines had darkened his face.

She couldn't understand it and pulled him back. "Someone once said, 'Don't give in to your fears. If you do, you won't be able to talk to your heart.'"

"That was Paulo Coelho."

Gemma caught his handsome face in her hands. "You're disgustingly intelligent, my love, but you need to take his advice. Don't you know I plan to cling to you forever?"

"I'm besotted with you, Gemma." He hurried to the door in his robe and came back with a tray of food that smelled divine. "Cesare has really outdone himself."

She took it from him and put it on the bed. "Let's eat fast so I can love you all over again."

His smile melted her bones. "I'm planning to keep you locked up here forever."

She leaned across to kiss his jaw. He needed a shave. "That's fine as long as you let me out in time for the grand opening. It'll be here in a few days. I was hired to cook, remember?"

Those silvery eyes blazed with fire for her. "Do you think I can ever forget anything since you came back into my life?"

He ate his cheese-and-ham strata in record time, displaying the appetite she always associated with him. Then he put the tray on the floor. After taking her in his arms again, he buried his face in her neck.

"We were meant to be together from the beginning. Love me, *sposa squisita.* I was hooked from the first time I saw the cutest little honey-blonde girl on earth come running out to the ruins to play hide and go seek. Her eyes were greener than the grass and her smile was like sunshine. My five-year-old heart quivered, and that has never changed."

"*Vincenzo—*"

EPILOGUE

THE MORNING OF the day before the grand opening, Gemma worked with her team as they prepared everything. While she was supervising the tiramisu desserts, Cesare walked in the kitchen and came over to her.

"*Per favore*, will you stop what you're doing and come out in the hall? This will only take a minute."

"Of course." She washed her hands and wiped them on her apron as she hurried after him. Once through the doors she came to a full stop. *Paolo!*

Cesare said, "I understand you two know each other."

"Yes. It's good to see you, Paolo."

He gave her a slight nod. "I understand you're Signora Gagliardi now. I get why it didn't work out for us. The Duca di Lombardi was the man you could never forget."

"You're right."

"Congratulations on your marriage."

"Thank you."

"*Buon Appetito* magazine has sent me out to cover the grand opening of the restaurant tomorrow and write up my opinion. Knowing that *you're* the new executive pastry chef has blown me away. Signor Donati told me I could say hello to you if I waited out here. I realize how busy you must be, so I won't keep you. *Buona fortuna*, Gemma."

She felt his sincerity, though that didn't mean he wouldn't be brutal if her food didn't measure up to his idea of five-star dining. "To you, too, Paolo. *Grazie*."

Two mornings later

While Gemma lay wrapped in her husband's arms, both still exhausted from all the work of the grand opening, she heard a knock.

"Vincenzo, get up and see what I've slipped under your door."

At the sound of Cesare's voice, both of them came awake. *The reviews!*

"Grazie!"

"Stay there, *caro*." Gemma bounded out of bed first and grabbed her husband's robe to put on. Half a dozen computer printouts had been pushed through. She reached for them and ran back to the bed.

By now Vincenzo was fully awake. He threw his arm around her shoulders while they read the glowing reviews. Then his cell phone rang. He saw the caller ID and picked up, holding the phone so Gemma could hear, too.

"Dimi?"

"Have you read everything yet?" His cousin sounded ecstatic.

"Almost."

"Our cup has run over today."

"I agree."

"I'm bringing Filippa to the *castello* with me later on today and we'll celebrate."

"That sounds perfect. Ciao."

He hung up and they began to read Paolo's article.

A new star is born in Lombardi!

Ring out the bells for the Castello Supremo Hotel and Ristorante di Lombardi. From its hundred-years-old ducal past has emerged a triumph of divine ambience and cuisine so exquisite to the palate, this critic can't find enough superlatives. One could live forever on the slow-cooked boeuf bourguignon and the *sfogliatelli* Mirella dessert alone. This critic thought he'd died and gone to heaven.

It deserves six stars. Bravo!

Gemma put it down and threw her arms around Vincenzo's neck. "You and Dimi and your partners did it, *amante*! You did it!" She broke down crying for joy.

"We all did it, including your wonderful *mamma*."

"Was it your idea to name the dessert after her?"

He studied her features before kissing her passionately. "It was Cesare's. An Italian loves his mother. After hearing your story, he knew your *mamma* deserved the credit on the souvenir menu commemorating the opening."

"That's so sweet of him. When Mamma sees this, she'll die."

"I have a better idea. Let's frame it, along with a menu, and give them to her for a special present. Cesare was touched that you loved your mother so much you talked about her on your application. I already know how sweet you are.

"The day you came running outside with the lemon ricotta cheesecake she made for my birthday, you ran straight into my heart and never left. You'll always be there. *Ti amo*, Signora Gagliardi."

"*Ti amo*, Your Highness."

"Don't call me that."

"It's the highest honor I can give you, Vincenzo. You're the greatest Gagliardi of them all."

* * * * *

BOUND TO HER GREEK BILLIONAIRE

REBECCA WINTERS

To my first editor and friend, Paula Eykelhof,
who believed in my writing and helped me find
a happy home at Mills & Boon Romance.
I've been there ever since.
How blessed could an author be?

CHAPTER ONE

LYS THERON ARRIVED ahead of time for her appointment with the detective at the prefecture in Heraklion, Crete. The officer at the desk looked her over in a way she found insulting and hurtful.

From her early teens she'd had to get used to men young and old staring at her. But his scrutiny was different because the unexpected and unexplained death a month ago of Nassos Rodino, the Greek multimillionaire hotelier on Crete, continued to be under police investigation and she was one of several people still being questioned.

The well-known, forty-nine-year-old owner of the Rodino Luxury Hotel and Resort in Heraklion had died too young. Nassos had always been an object of fascination in the news. But since the divorce from his wife, Danae, four months ago, there'd been rumors that he'd been having an affair with twenty-six-year-old Lys, his former ward who'd lived in their household since the age of seventeen.

While Lys struggled with her grief over his death, and many people lamented his demise, the media had done their best to sensationalize it, developing a story that had played every night in the television news cycle. Had Lys conducted a secret affair with the famous hotelier for several years? Questions had been raised as to what had actually caused the divorce and his ultimate death.

Without answers, speculation grew that foul play might have been involved. Rumor that Lys might have caused his death to gain access to part of his money had caught hold. Though the detective conducting the investigation hadn't put the blame on anyone, the reason for Nassos's death still hadn't been declared and a cloud hung over her. Lys's heart shuddered over the cruel gossip. Nassos was the man she'd loved like a father since childhood.

At seventeen, her millionaire Greek father, Kristos Theron, owner of a successful hotel in New York City, had been killed in a small plane accident. He'd left a will with a legal stipulation. If he died before she was of age, his best friend and former business partner, Nassos Rodino, would become her legal guardian.

Nassos had come to New York often throughout her early childhood and she had seen him as part of her extended family. When her father died, it was no hardship to travel to Greece with him.

But the moment Nassos had brought her to his home, she'd discovered that he and his wife had been living in a troublesome marriage.

Lys had never known the reason for their struggles, but it grieved her because she'd sensed that deep down they loved each other. It was all very complicated and she'd tried not to add to their problems. But in that regard she felt she'd failed when she'd started dating men neither of them approved of.

Nassos called them rich men's playboy sons.

Danae saw them as opportunists with no substance, adding to Lys's insecurity that somehow she didn't have the ability to attract the right kind of man. None of her relationships developed into anything serious because she sensed her adoptive parents' disapproval.

Since coming to live with them, the paparazzi had followed her around, never missing a chance to exploit her private life by filming her accompanied by any rich man she may have been seen with in public. Unfortunately in her work at Nassos's exclusive hotel chain, wealthy people made up her world. She'd never known anything else.

If she'd met and fallen in love with a poor fisherman, would they have approved of her choice? She didn't have an answer to that question, nor to the many others that she often thought of as Lys suffered from a lack of confidence. Having lost her mother at the age of nine hadn't helped.

Their disapproval hurt her terribly because she'd loved Nassos and his wife so much and wanted their acceptance. Lys's father had entrusted her to Nassos. Right now she felt like she'd let down three of the most important people in her life, but not on purpose.

Though he and Danae had suffered marital difficulties, they'd been wonderful to Lys and had made life beautiful at their villa on Kasos Island while she'd dealt with her sorrow. They'd helped her through those difficult years and had made it possible for her to go to college on the mainland.

Nassos was the kindest, dearest man Lys had ever known in her life next to her own father. The two men had been born on Kasos and had always been best friends. Early in their lives they'd gone into the fishing business together and had slowly amassed their fortunes. Kristos had ended up in New York, while Nassos stayed on Heraklion and had eventually married.

For Lys, the underlying strife during their divorce had been devastating. Since then she and Danae had been estranged. It tore her heart out. At this point Lys didn't know how to overcome her pain except to pour herself into work at the hotel, and avoid the press as much as possible.

Deep in tortured thoughts, she heard a voice. "Kyria Theron?" She lifted her head to see another officer in the doorway. "Thank you for coming. Detective Vlassis will see you now."

Hopefully this meeting would provide the answer that let her out of proverbial jail and allowed the funeral to take place. She walked inside.

"Sit down, Kyria Theron."

Lys found a chair opposite his desk.

"Coffee? Tea?"

"Neither, thank you."

The somber detective sat back in his chair tapping the tips of his long fingers together. "I have good news for you. The medical examiner has turned over his findings to my office. We know the truth and foul play has been ruled out."

"You're serious?" Her voice shook. The rumor that she might have poisoned Nassos with some invisible drug in his penthouse apartment in order for her to get a portion of his money had been devastating for her.

"It's been determined he died of a subarachnoid hemorrhage probably caused from an earlier head injury."

"Why did it take so long?" she cried.

"Unfortunately the bleeding went undetected. The reason it was difficult to find the first time was because it's not unusual for SAH to be initially misdiagnosed as a migraine."

"So the doctor didn't catch it."

"Not at first. A human mistake. It caused a delay in obtaining a CT scan."

A small gasp escaped her lips. "After he'd hit his head on the kitchen cupboard several months ago, I thought he must have suffered a concussion. I told him I wanted to talk to his doctor about it, but Nassos told me to stop fussing because the pain went away. That must be why he had a stroke." Tears rolled down her cheeks. "Thank heaven he can now be laid to rest."

"This has been a very stressful time for you, but it's over. The press has been informed. I'm sorry for your loss and wish you well in the future."

Another miracle. "Thank you. Have you told his ex-wife?"

"Yes."

"Good." Now Danae could make the funeral arrangements. "You'll never know what this means to me."

Lys jumped up from the chair. "Thank you." She couldn't leave the police station fast enough and rushed past the officer posted at the front desk without glancing at him. She couldn't endure one more smirk.

Once outside, Lys hurried to her car, running past the usual news people stalking her movements to take pictures. She got into her car and drove back to the

Rodino Luxury Hotel where she had her own suite. She'd been living there and working in the accounts department for Nassos since graduating from business college in Heraklion four years ago.

The moment she reached her room on the third floor, she flung herself across the bed and sobbed. It was over at last. But with Nassos's death and Lys's unwanted estrangement with his ex-wife, there was no one to pick up the emotional pieces.

The couple's tragic divorce had fragmented Lys. If they'd been going to end their marriage, why hadn't it happened years before now? She simply didn't understand. And then had come the shocking news of his death… The loss was almost more than she could bear.

They'd worked together at the hotel. He'd taught her everything about the business. He'd been her friend, confidant, mentor. How was she going to be able to go on without him?

For Nassos not to be there anymore was killing her and she missed Danae terribly. Until the police had closed the case, Lys had been in limbo, trying to do her usual job, but her mind and heart hadn't been there. When she did have to leave the hotel for any reason, she'd felt accusatory stares coming in all directions and avoided any publicity if she could help it.

Thankfully this was over and there'd be an end to the malicious talk that he'd been murdered. Hopefully everything would die down, but where did she go from here? Lys felt like she'd been driving her car when the steering wheel had suddenly disappeared, leaving her to plunge over a cliff. She was so heartbroken she could hardly think.

While in this state, the phone rang. Lys turned over to look at the caller ID. It was Xander Pappas, Nassos's attorney. She picked up and learned that he'd be in Nassos's private office at the hotel in a half hour to talk to her. The detective had already been in touch with him.

"I have something important to give you."

She sat up in surprise. "Will Danae be meeting with us?" Lys longed to talk to her.

"No. We've already spoken and I've read her the will. She'll be calling you about the funeral."

"I see."

Stabbed with fresh pain, Lys thanked him and hung up. If there hadn't been a divorce, she and Danae would have planned his funeral together. Now everything had changed. More tears gushed down her cheeks before she got off the bed to freshen up.

Of course she hadn't expected to be present at the reading of the will and hadn't wanted to be. Danae had been married to Nassos for twenty-four years. That business was between the two of them.

A few minutes later she left for the corporate office downstairs. On the way, she couldn't help but wonder what Xander wanted to give her. Nassos couldn't have known when he would die, so she couldn't imagine what it was.

After nodding to Giorgos, the annoying general manager of the hotel, she walked in to Nassos's private office. The attorney greeted her and told her to sit down.

"I have two items to give you. Both envelopes are sealed. You'll know what to do after you open the envelope marked Letter first. Nassos wrote to you at the time he divorced Danae." He put both envelopes on the desk.

She swallowed hard. Nassos had written something that recently? "Have you read it?"

"No. He gave me instructions to give them both to you upon his death, whenever that would be. Who would have imagined he'd die this early in his life? I'll miss him too and am so sorry since I know how close you two were. I'll leave now. If you have any questions, call me at my office."

After he left the room, Lys reached for the envelope and pulled out the letter with a trembling hand. She knew Nassos's handwriting. He wrote with a certain panache that was unmistakable.

My dearest little Lysette,

Immediately her eyes filled with more tears.

I'll always think of you that way, no matter how old you are when you read this letter. You're the daughter I never had. Danae and I couldn't have children. The problem was mine. I found out early in our marriage that I was infertile. It came as a great shock, but I'd dreamed of having children, so I wanted to adopt. She didn't, and I could never talk her into it. I decided she didn't love me enough or she would have agreed to try because I wanted children more than anything.

Six months ago, Xander let me know that he knew of a baby we could adopt. I went to Danae and begged her. It could be our last chance, but she still said no. In my anger I divorced the woman I loved and always will. Now I'm paying for it dearly because I don't believe she'll forgive me.

You need to know that you were never the reason for our marital troubles. I ruined things at the beginning of our marriage by making an issue that she stay at home. I insisted she quit her job because I was raised with old-fashioned ideas. I was wrong to impose them on Danae. She's very much a modern woman and a part of me resented the fact that she couldn't be happy at home.

Please realize that your coming to us helped keep our marriage together and deep down she knows it. I'm afraid it was because of my damnable pride—my greatest flaw—nothing more, that made me divorce her, so never ever blame yourself. If I was hard on you because of the men you dated, it was only because of my desperate fear you might end up in a bad marriage with a man who didn't value you enough. Danae felt the same way.

Forgive us if we hurt you in any way.

"Oh, Nassos—" Lys cried out in relief and anguish.

You have a massive inheritance from your father that will be given to you on your twenty-seventh birthday. He dictated that specific time in his will to make sure you'd be mature enough when you came into your money.

Lys was incredulous. She'd thought it had all been incorporated into the Rodino empire. Nassos would have deserved every euro of it.

> Again, I have no idea how old you are now that I'm dead. I suspect you're a very wealthy woman, hopefully married with children, maybe even grandchildren. And happy!
>
> As you will have found out from Danae, she inherited everything with one exception…the hotel is your inheritance from me to own and run as you will.

Lys reeled physically and clung to the arms of the chair.

No. It wasn't possible. The hotel should have been given to Danae, who understood the hotel business very well. It was Nassos who'd hired her away from another hotelier to come and work for him twenty-four years ago. How sad that even after his death, Nassos couldn't allow her to continue in a career she'd enjoyed.

Lys's eyes closed tightly for a moment.

Danae hadn't contacted Lys yet. There hadn't been time. How could Nassos have done this to the woman he'd loved? Wiping her eyes, she went on reading.

> But you're not the sole owner, Lys.

What? The shocks just kept coming.

> Before you take possession, you must give the sealed envelope to Takis Manolis. You've

heard me and Danae talk about him often enough. When he came to Crete periodically, we'd discuss business on my yacht where we could be private. I never did believe in mixing my business matters with my personal life. The two don't go together.

You'll know where to find him when the time comes. The two of you will share ownership for six months. After that time period, you'll both be free to make any decisions you want.

By the time you read this, he's probably married with children and grandchildren too. I've thought of him as the son I never had.

It was my thrill and privilege to be your guardian, friend and adoptive father for the child of my best friend Kristos.

Love always,

Nassos.

You can't go home again.

Whoever coined the phrase was wrong. Yes, you could go home again.

In the last eleven years, Takis Manolis had made four trips a year to Crete and nothing had changed… Not the pain, not the landscape, not his family.

Naturally they were all a little older each time he flew here from New York and later from Italy, but everything had stayed the same if you looked at the inner vessel.

The village of Tylissos where he'd been born was still situated on the northeastern mountainside of Psiloritis near the sea. Time hadn't altered it a whit.

Nor had it altered the views of Takis's father or his elder brother, Lukios, who helped their father run the old ten-room hotel.

His family followed the philotimo creed for all Cretans to maintain their unflappable dignity even if their existence bordered on poverty when the hotel didn't fill. They respected the rich and didn't try to become something greater than they were. Takis was baffled that they didn't mind being poor and accepted it as their lot in life.

Until recent years there'd been very little inherited wealth in Greece. Most of the Greek millionaires were self-made, but envy wasn't part of his brother's or his father's makeup.

Takis's older sister, Kori, married to a cook at one of the village restaurants where she worked, didn't have to tell him that she and her husband, Deimos, struggled to make a decent living.

They had a little girl, Cassia, now three years old, who'd been in and out of the hospital after her birth because of chronic asthma and needed a lot of medical care. He was thankful that at least Kori kept the cash he'd given her for a belated birthday present, knowing she'd use it for bills.

Though the family accepted the gifts he brought whenever he came, pride prevented his father from taking any monetary help. Lukios was the same. Being a married man with a wife and two children, who were now four and five, he would never look to Takis for assistance to make life a little easier for his family and in-laws.

This centuries-old pride thwarted Takis's heartfelt need and desire to shower his family with all the things of which they'd been deprived and caused him deep grief.

Early in life he'd known he was different from the rest of them, never going along with their family's status quo. Though he'd never openly fought with his father or brother, he'd struggled to conform.

His mother knew how he felt, but all she could do was urge Takis to keep the peace. When he'd told her of his dreams to go to college to better himself, she'd said it was impossible. They didn't have the money. None of the Manolis family had ever gone for a higher education.

Takis just couldn't understand why neither his father nor brother didn't want to expand and grow the small hotel that had been handed down from an earlier generation. He could see nothing wrong with trying to build it into something bigger and better. To be ambitious didn't make you dishonorable, but his father and brother weren't risk takers and refused to change their ways.

There were times when he wondered if he really was his parents' birth child. Except that his physical features and build proclaimed him a Manolis through and through.

By his midteens, Takis had feared that if he stayed on Crete, he would turn into his brother, who was a clone of the Manolis men before him, each having so little to show for all their hard work. More and more his ideas clashed with his father's over how to bring in more clients and build another couple of floors on the hotel.

Takis had worked out all his ideas in detail. One day he'd approached his father in all seriousness, wanting to talk to him man-to-man. But when he made his proposals, his father said something that stopped him cold.

Your ideas do you credit, my son, but they don't reflect my vision for our family business. One day you'll be a man and you'll understand.

Understand what?

Pierced by his father's comment, Takis took it to mean his ideas weren't good enough and never would be, even when he became a man.

At that moment something snapped inside Takis. He determined to go to college despite what his mother had said.

So he bought a secondhand bike and after helping his father during the week on a regular basis, he rode the few kilometers to his second job at the famous Rodino hotel and resort in Heraklion on weekends to earn extra money. The manager was soon impressed with Takis's drive. In time he introduced him to the owner of the hotel, Nassos Rodino, who had several talks with Takis about his financial situation.

One day the unimaginable had happened. Kyrie Rodino called him to his office and helped him apply for a work visa and permit to travel to New York. His best friend, Kristos Theron, the owner of a successful hotel in New York City, would let Takis work for him. He could make a lot more money there and go to the kind of college that would help him get ahead in the business world. He'd improve his English too.

Takis couldn't believe anyone would do something so fantastic for him and returned home to tell his parents about the opportunity.

His mother kept quiet. As for his father, he listened

and nodded. *If this is what you want to do, then you must do it.*

But how do you feel about it, Baba*?* Takis had still wanted his father's approval.

His father shrugged his shoulders. *Does it matter? You're eighteen years old now and are in charge of your own destiny. At eighteen a man can leave his father and make his own way.*

That isn't the answer I was hoping for. His father hadn't given him his blessing and probably resented Nassos Rodino for making any of this possible.

If you're a man, then you don't need an answer.

Takis had felt rebuked. His mother remained silent as he left the room with a hurt too deep to express. After the talk with his father, he'd had the feeling his parent had already felt abandoned before he'd even approached him.

Combined with the pain of having recently lost his girlfriend, who'd been killed in a bus accident, he finally made the decision to leave home. She'd been the one he could confide in about his dreams.

After all their talks, she'd known he'd been afraid to leave his family in case they thought he was letting them down. But she'd encouraged him and told him to spread his wings. They'd talked about her joining him in New York at a later date.

With her gone, he'd had no one who understood everything going on inside him. Her compassion had made her such an exceptional person, and he'd never found that incredible quality in the women he'd met since leaving Crete.

In the end, he'd made the decision to go after the opportunity that would enrich his life and he vowed, one day, that he would return and help his family in every capacity possible.

That was a long time ago.

On this cool March day, he held in the tears as he embraced his mother one more time. On this trip he noticed she'd aged and hadn't exhibited her usual energy. That troubled him. "I promise I'll be back soon."

"Why don't you come home to live? You can afford it. We miss you so much." Her tears tugged at his heart.

His father didn't weep, but Takis detected a new sorrow in his eyes. Why was it there? Why didn't his parent speak the words of love and acceptance he longed to hear?

"Do what you have to do." Those were similar to the words he'd said to Takis before he'd left for New York eleven years ago. "Be safe, my son."

But his father still hadn't been the one to ask him to come home or tell him he'd like him to work at the hotel with the family again. Had Takis done irreparable damage to their relationship?

"You too, *Baba.*" His throat had swollen with emotion. "Stay well."

He turned to his mother once more. Was the sorrow he'd seen in his father's eyes over concern for his wife? Was there something wrong with her? With his father? Something no one in the family was telling him?

This visit had troubled him with thoughts he didn't want to entertain. He hugged everyone and kissed his nieces and nephews. Then he climbed into the taxi in front of the family-owned hotel that needed refurbishing. Heaven knew it needed everything. *They* needed everything.

His eyes clung to his mother's once more. *Had she been trying to tell him something?* He blew her a kiss.

The flight to Athens would be leaving from Heraklion airport in four hours. First he would attend the funeral services for Nassos Rodino at the Greek Orthodox church in the heart of Heraklion. The recently divorced hotel owner, rumored to have a mistress, had suffered a stroke in the prime of his life—a stroke that had preceded his death. This had shocked Takis, who'd met with the man, who had given him so much, on his yacht to talk business when Takis had last come to Crete.

Most important to Takis was that he owed the hotelier a debt that bordered on love. His gratitude to the older man knew no bounds.

In truth he couldn't think of another successful man who would have gone to such lengths to give Takis the chance to better himself, even to go as far as sponsoring him in the United States.

Once the funeral was over, he'd fly to Athens. From there he'd take another flight to Milan, Italy, where he was part owner, and manager of the five-star Castello Supremo Hotel and Ristorante di Lombardi.

But all the way to the church his mother's words rang in his ears. *Why don't you come home to live. You can afford it.* His mother had never been so outspoken in her thoughts before.

Yes, he could afford it. In the eleven years he'd been away, he'd made millions while his family continued to eke out their existence.

Was she telling him something without coming

right out and saying it? Was she ill? Or his father? Death with dignity? Never saying a word? *Damn that pride of theirs if it was true!*

Neither Kori nor Lukios had said anything, but maybe his siblings had been kept in the dark. Then again maybe nothing was wrong and his mother, who was getting older, was simply letting him know how much they'd missed him.

He missed them too. Of course he'd come back in an instant if they needed him. But to come home for good? Even if his two business partners were in agreement and bought him out—even if he sold his hotel chain in New York, would his father allow him to work alongside him? What if he refused Takis's help? What would Takis do for the rest of his life? Build a new hotel conglomerate on Crete?

His eyes closed tightly. He could never do that to his father and use the Manolis name. A son honored his father and showed him respect by never taking anything away from him.

Two years ago Takis had built a children's hospital in his hometown village of Tylissos on Crete in order that his niece Cassia would get the kind of skilled medical help she needed. The hospital gave free medical care with no child turned away.

He'd kept his dealings anonymous, using local people who had no idea Takis had funded everything including the doctors' salaries. It helped him to know he was doing something for his family, even if they weren't aware of it.

Long ago Takis had lost hope that one day his father might be proud of him for trying to make something of his life in order to help them. His parent had never been anything but kind to him, but deep in his heart lived the fear that his family had always compared him to their ever faithful Lukios and would never see Takis in the same light.

In his pain he needed to get back to Italy and ask advice from his partners, who were as close to him as brothers.

"Kyrie?" The taxi driver broke in on his tormented thoughts by telling him they'd arrived at the corner of the square.

Takis had been in a daze. "If you'll wait here, I'll be back in an hour." He handed him some bills and got out to join a crowd of people entering the church, where the covered coffin faced east.

Once he found a seat, he listened to the white-robed priest who conducted the service. After leading them in hymns and scriptures, the priest asked God to give Nassos rest and forgive all his sins. As far as Takis was concerned, the man had no sins. Because of him, Takis had been given a precious gift that had changed his life completely. But at what price?

Soon the bereaved, dressed in black, started down the aisle to go to the cemetery. One dark-haired woman in a black veil appeared particularly overcome with sorrow. Nassos's ex-wife? Takis had never met her. Nassos had kept their few meetings totally private.

Because he'd arrived late, he'd taken a seat on the aisle at the back. While he waited for everyone to pass, his gaze happened to fasten on probably the most gorgeous young dark-blonde woman he'd ever seen in his life.

Her two-piece black suit provided the perfect foil

for her stunning classic features only rivaled by violet eyes. Their color reminded him of the Chaste plant belonging to the verbena family that grew all over Crete. They peered out of dark lashes that took his breath. But he could see she was grief stricken. Who *was* she?

He turned his head to watch her walk out the rear of the church. If he weren't going to be late to catch his flight, he'd drive to the cemetery and find out her name. Hers was a face and figure he would never forget, not in a lifetime.

CHAPTER TWO

Five days after the funeral, Lys left Giorgos, the manager of the Rodino Hotel, in charge. The paparazzi took pictures as she climbed in the limo taking her to the airport for her flight to Athens. It connected to another flight to Milan, Italy. Her destination was the Castello Supremo Hotel and Ristorante di Lombardi.

In the year before her father's death, she'd heard her father and Nassos talking about a new employee at her father's hotel named Takis Manolis. Nassos had made it possible for the younger man from Crete to get a work visa and go to college in the United States while working at her father's hotel in New York. Lys's understanding was that he was exceptional and showed real promise in the hotel industry.

Their interest had piqued *her* interest, but she'd never met him since she and her father had lived in their own home in the city. She'd rarely gone to the hotel for any reason.

After her father's death, and the move to Crete to Nassos and Danae's villa on Kasos, the name of Takis came up again. Nassos spoke fondly of him and she learned more about him. The Manolis teen had come from Tylissos and had needed help to escape a life that was close to the poverty line.

When Lys asked Nassos why he cared so much, he'd told her the young man had reminded him of himself at that age. Nassos, who'd gotten little help from his ailing grandfather, had to fish from a row boat and sell his catch at the market to support them. Lys's father, Kristos, also dirt-poor, started fishing with him.

Both men had wanted more out of life and had gone after it. In time they built businesses that grew until Kristos decided to travel to New York and take over a hotel there.

Nassos was able to buy property in Heraklion and build a hotel on Crete. He'd made it into a huge success story. Nassos had seen that same hunger in Takis, who he said was brilliant and had vision in a way that separated him from the masses. Both men wanted Takis to realize his dream. That's why Nassos had made it possible for Takis to travel to New York and work at the hotel Lys's father had owned. Their hunch had paid off in a huge way.

Later on, through Nassos, Lys learned more about the enterprising Takis. His chain of hotels and stock market investments had turned him into a billionaire. She found herself fantasizing about him, and loved Nassos for his goodness. He was a saint who'd become the father she'd lost. Imagine making such a thing possible for the younger man, who was a home-grown Cretan like himself!

Though she couldn't imagine how Takis Manolis would feel when he heard the news that he was the new half owner of the Rodino Hotel, she was excited to be able to carry out Nassos's final wish. In truth she couldn't wait to meet this twenty-nine-year-old man she'd heard talked about for so long.

She'd endowed him with her idea of what the perfect Cretan man looked like. It was very silly of her, but she couldn't help it. Both her father and Nassos had made him out to be someone so unique and fascinating, she'd wouldn't be human if her imagination hadn't taken over.

As for her being the other half owner, she didn't know how she felt about it yet. Everything depended on today's meeting.

It was midmorning as Lys left her hotel in Milan dressed in a heavy black Ralph Lauren shirt dress she could wear without a coat. After setting out on her mission, she gave the limo driver directions to the *castello* outside the city. Then she sat back to take in the fabulous scenery of farms and villas lined with the tall narrow cypress trees indigenous to the region.

Mid-March felt like Heraklion, a cool fifty-eight degrees under cloudy skies. The only difference was that Milan wasn't by the sea. According to Nassos, this refurbished Italian monument built on top of a hill in the thirteen hundreds—originally the home of the first Duc di Lombardi—was a triumph that Takis shared with two business partners. It had become the showplace of Europe.

Lys had come to Italy without letting anyone know where she was going, or why, only that she'd be out of the country for an indefinite period. It was heaven to escape Crete for a little while where few people would recognize her. If anyone knew her reason for coming here, it would make more headlines she didn't want and would do anything to avoid.

Hopefully the press would leave her alone from now on. Though sorrow weighed her down, she intended to ignore any further publicity and carry on as Nassos had expected her to do.

The driver let her out at the base of steps leading to the front entrance. During her climb, she marveled at the trees and flowers surrounding the building. This was a magnificent edifice, high up where she could see the landscape in the far distance. No wonder the Duc di Lombardi found this the perfect place to rule his kingdom.

Inside the entry she was struck by the palatial grandeur with its sweeping corridor of glass doors and chandeliers. The exquisite furniture and paintings of a former time created a matchless tapestry of beauty in the Italian tradition.

A few hotel guests came out of the dining room area. Others walked down the hallway toward the front desk. A lovely woman at the counter, maybe thirty, smiled at her. "May I help you?" she asked in Italian.

Lys answered in English because she could only speak a few words in Italian. "I'm here to see Mr. Manolis, if that's possible."

"Do you have an appointment?" Her switch to excellent English was impressive.

"No. I just flew in to Milan. If he's not available, I'll make an appointment and come back because this is vitally important to me."

"Are you a tour guide?"

"No."

The woman studied her briefly before she said, "What's your name?"

"Ms. Theron."

"If you'll take a seat, I'll see if I can locate him."

Wonderful. He was here somewhere. She'd been prepared to fly to New York to see him if necessary. By coming here first, she'd saved herself a long overseas flight.

This close now to meeting the man her father and Nassos had cared so much about, she felt an attachment to him difficult to explain. Apparently if she'd met this Takis in Heraklion and had started dating him, Nassos would have given his wholehearted approval.

Lys was dying to know what he looked like. As Nassos had explained in his letter to her, he never liked mixing business with his personal life, so she could only guess. Neither he nor Danae had ever mentioned that aspect of him. With a heightened sense of excitement, she turned and sat on one of the beautiful upholstered chairs with the distinctive Duc di Lombardi logo. Her heart pounded hard while she waited to meet Takis.

Midmorning Takis sat with his partners in the private dining room on the second floor of the *castello*. This was the first time he'd had a chance to speak to them after returning from Crete. So far he was no closer to knowing what to do about his worry over his parents and he wanted their opinions. Vincenzo had asked that breakfast be brought up from the kitchen, but Takis had lost his appetite and only wanted coffee.

"You don't have to make any kind of a rash decision right now," his friend counseled. "Rather than just a weekend visit, why don't you simply go back to Tylissos for a couple of weeks? We'll be fine without you. Stay with your family, see what you can do to help out. Surely if there's something wrong with either of your parents, you'll pick up on it and go from there."

As usual, Vincenzo, the present-day Duc di Lombardi, made sense.

Cesare Donati, whose oversight of the restaurant had turned the hotel into *the* place to dine in all of Europe, eyed him over his cup of coffee. "What would be wrong by going home and asking them outright if there's a problem they don't want you to know about? Do it in front of the whole family so if anyone squirms, you'll see it."

That was good advice too. Cesare wasn't one to hold back. He acted on instincts, thus the reason he was the best restaurateur on five continents.

"I'm listening, guys, and am taking both ideas under consideration." Two weeks with his family would give him enough time to get the truth out of them. While he was there he could also track down the woman he'd seen at the funeral whose image wouldn't leave his mind.

While he was deep in thought, his phone rang. Takis checked the caller ID. It was the front desk. He clicked on. "Yes, Sofia?" The woman was Swiss-born and spoke six languages.

"Sorry to bother you when I know you're in a meeting, but a woman I don't recognize has flown to Milan and come to the *castello* to see you. She's not a tour guide and says it's of vital importance, but she didn't explain the nature of her business. She had no card. Her last name is something like Tierrun."

"What's her nationality?"

"She sounds American to me." Maybe she'd been sent from his headquarters in New York for a special reason, but Takis found it strange that his assistant hadn't said anything. "Do you wish to meet with her, or shall I make an appointment?"

Takis had no idea what this was all about, but he might as well take care of it now. "I'll be right there. Take her back to my office." He rang off and glanced at his friends. "I've got to meet someone downstairs. Thanks for the much needed advice. I'll talk to you later."

Lys followed the concierge down a hall lined with several doors. She opened the one on the right. "Mr. Takis will be with you in a minute. Make yourself comfortable. Would you care for coffee or tea while you wait?"

"Nothing, thank you."

After the woman left, Lys sat down near the desk. On the top of it were several little framed snapshots of what she assumed were family photos. Some she surmised were of his parents, some were his siblings and small children. Along with those pictures was a small statue of King Minos, the mythological leader of the great Minoan civilization on Crete, who was clothed in mythology.

As she continued to look around the uncluttered room, a cry escaped her lips. Hanging on the wall across from her was a large framed picture of a younger Nassos with a lot of black hair, standing on the deck of his yacht in a sport shirt and trousers. Takis must have taken it with a camera and had sent the photo to be enlarged. There were no other pictures.

With pounding heart she jumped up from the chair and walked over to get a closer look. Nassos's signature was in the bottom right hand corner. He'd personalized it. *Bravo, Takis.* He signed everything with a flourish.

Seeing him so alive and vital in the picture brought tears to her eyes. He would be thrilled if he knew his autographed photo hung in the office of his unofficial protégé in the most prominent spot. The fact that this man had honored Nassos this way told her a lot about his character and she knew he was deserving of the gift he was about to receive.

Lys heard a little rap on the open door and whirled around.

She hadn't known what she'd expected to see. Only her imagination could have provided that. But it wasn't the tall, hard-muscled male so striking in a rugged way who'd just walked in his office...an olive-complexioned man come to life from ancient Crete though he was dressed in a stone-colored business suit and tie.

"Oh—" she cried softly because the sight of him caused her thoughts to reel.

Those penetrating hazel eyes of his put her in mind of one of those heroic dark-blond warriors depicted in frescos on the walls of temples and museums. She studied his arresting features, remembering one prince who could have been his double. The five o'clock shadow on his firm jaw gave him a sensual appeal she hadn't been prepared for.

While she continued to stare at him, she realized he'd been examining her the way someone did who couldn't believe what he was seeing. He gave her a slight nod. "The woman at the desk thought you were American, but didn't quite get your name." The man spoke English with a heavy accent she found exciting.

"I'm Lys Theron," she said in Greek.

A look of astonishment crossed over his face. "Wait," he said, as if sorting out a puzzle. "Theron… Kristos Theron. He was *your* father?"

"Yes."

Clearly her answer shocked him.

"He was a wonderful man. It came as a terrible blow when I heard about the plane crash. He'd been very kind to me. I'm so sorry you lost him."

"So am I."

The second she'd spoken, silence enveloped the room's interior. His eyes seemed to go dark from some unnamed emotion. A hand went to the back of his neck, as if he were questioning what he'd just heard. "I saw you at Nassos's funeral last weekend," he murmured in Greek.

His admission shook her to the core. "You were there?"

"That's right. I wouldn't have missed it. Aside from my father, Nassos Rodino was the finest man I ever knew. His death came as a great shock to me."

He'd been at the church! No wonder he'd stared so hard at her, but she hadn't seen him. Her pain had been too great.

She took a deep breath. "To know you flew to

Heraklion to honor him, and that you have his photograph hanging in this office, would have meant the world to him."

A strange sound came out of him. "You're a relation of his?"

"I was seventeen when my father died. Nassos was his best friend and became my guardian. He took me back to Crete where I lived with him and his wife."

He shook his head. "I can't credit it. You and I never met, yet your father and Nassos are the reason I have a life here."

"I've heard about you for years and have been wanting to meet you. You're the brilliant son of Nikanor Manolis from Tylissos. Nassos's belief in you was clearly deserved."

His chest rose and fell visibly. "His support was nothing short of a miracle," he whispered.

"A miracle couldn't work if the seeds of greatness weren't already there."

Another unearthly quiet emanated from him, prompting her to speak. "I was sixteen when I first learned about you. Nassos came to visit often and asked my father if he'd give you a job at the hotel in New York. I thought it was so wonderful that they wanted to help you so you could go to college. They really believed in you!"

He moved closer. "Your father's close friendship with Nassos made it possible for me to work and go to school. He was very good to me."

"To me too." She smiled. "It was hard to lose him when I did."

She felt his compassionate gaze. "I can only imagine your feelings right now. I'm sorry you've suffered so many losses."

"Death comes to us all at some point." She sucked in her breath, still dazed by his striking looks, in fact by the whole situation. "To be honest, I've always wanted to meet the famous Takis Manolis. The last time Nassos spoke of you, he said you were already a living legend before you were thirty."

His dark brows furrowed as if in utter disbelief over those words, revealing a humility she found admirable.

"Please. Sit down." While she did his bidding, he paced the floor looking shaken, then he stopped. "Can I get you anything? Have you had breakfast?"

"Thank you, but I ate before I left the hotel in Milan several hours ago. I should have contacted you for an appointment ahead of time, but decided to take my chances and fly here first. I haven't taken a real trip in a long time. I love getting away from everything for a little while."

"I don't blame you. I saw what was written about you in the paper while I was in Crete. The press manages to find a way if they're looking for a story." By the tone of disgust in his voice, she imagined he'd had to deal with his share of unwanted invasions. She could relate to his feelings, making it easier to confide in him.

"Nassos's unexplained, unexpected death wasn't solved until a week ago when the medical examiner said he'd died from a subarachnoid hemorrhage. Over the last month while everything was up in the air, the press labeled me everything from a murderer who'd poisoned him, to an opportunistic floozy. You could add adulteress, narcissistic liar and evil spawn of Satan in some of the more sordid tabloids. The list goes on and on."

Their eyes met. "Is that all?" he teased unexpectedly, catching her off guard. His bone-melting charm, not to mention his refreshing humor was so welcome, she felt a great release and laughter bubbled out of her.

She could easily understand why Nassos had found him an extraordinary human being in ways other than his business acumen. After reading Nassos's letter, she knew Nassos hadn't talked to him about her or Danae. Nassos had always been a very private person.

"I came to see you for a very specific reason, but if this isn't a good time to talk, please say so. I can return to Milan and wait until I hear from you. Or I'll fly back to Crete and come another time when it's more convenient."

His eyes narrowed on her features. "The daughter whom Nassos helped raise for his best friend has my full, undivided attention. Tell me what's on your mind. Obviously it's very important to you, otherwise you wouldn't have flown all this distance during your bereavement. I'd do anything for him, so that translates I'd do anything for you. Just name it."

Lys felt his sincerity sink deep into her psyche. "Thank you for saying that. I guess I don't have to tell you what this means to me."

Takis sat on the corner of his desk. "How can I help you?" he asked in a quiet tone, drawing her attention to his powerful legs beneath his trousers. She couldn't stop noticing every exciting male trait about him.

"It concerns the hotel in Heraklion."

One of his brows lifted in query. "Go on."

She got up from the chair, struggling with how to approach him. "In his will, every possession and asset of his *except* the hotel was left to his ex-wife, Danae."

The man listening to her didn't move a muscle, but she saw a quickening in his eyes, not knowing what it meant.

"That was as it should be," she continued. "Danae was his devoted wife for twenty-four years. When they divorced, he left her with everything she would need. Now that she has received the full inheritance he left her, I know she'll be well provided for all of her life."

"So I'm presuming the hotel is now yours."

Lys shook her head. "I only have half ownership and didn't want the half he left me."

Lines marred his features before he got to his feet. "That's very strange, but what does any of it have to do with me?" Confusion was written all over his handsome face.

Lys had tried to present this the right way, but she wasn't getting through to him. Taking a deep breath, she said, "Nassos hoped to leave a lasting legacy. Since none of us knows when we're going to die, he took precautions early to preserve that legacy when the time came, whenever that was."

"I still can't believe he's gone." His mournful comment touched her heart.

"Neither can I. Because he didn't have children, it meant putting the hotel in the hands of someone who understands and shares his vision."

Takis was listening. "That was you."

She took a deep breath. "I worked for him, yes. But I think this decision was made because he'd been my guardian and was always protective of me. He probably felt I needed someone to share the responsibility so I wouldn't make a serious mistake."

His brows dipped. "Mistake?"

"Yes. He loved the myth of King Minos, who forgot to rule wisely. Because of his mistake, he was killed by the daughters of King Cocalus, who poured boiling water over him while he was taking a bath. I notice you have a little statue of him."

"The story of King Minos intrigued me as a youth too."

Lys smiled sadly. "It proves you and Nassos had minds that thought alike. More than ever I'm convinced there was only one other person he could think of who would honor what he'd built."

She opened her handbag and pulled out the sealed envelope she handed to him. "That person is you, Kyrie Manolis. His attorney instructed me to give this to you. Any explanations are inside. I don't know the contents."

If Nassos had another flaw besides his pride, it was his secrecy, which had left Lys at a loss.

After clearing her throat she said, "In case you're not aware, it made Nassos happier than you could ever imagine to know that the little help he gave you in the beginning was the only thing you needed to go all the way. It means a lot to me to have met you after all this time. Not everyone could accomplish what you've done in so short a time. I'm truly impressed."

She moved to the door while he stood there in a trancelike state. "I have to get back to Crete. Please don't take long to let me know your plans. I wrote my private cell phone number on the back of that envelope. I live at the hotel and will meet with you at your convenience. Now I must get going. My limo is waiting in the front courtyard. *Kalimera.*"

She hurried down the hall. To stay in that room with him any longer wasn't a good idea. They'd only just met, yet she'd felt a strong, immediate attraction to Takis that had rocked her world. It had gotten its start in the long-ago conversations between her father and Nassos, and the impression she'd created of the younger man who'd been hungry to better his life.

She knew she had to get away from him and leave the *castello* before she didn't want to leave. Lys had never felt these kinds of initial feelings about any man in her life.

Those playboys who'd passed in and out of her life couldn't touch this extraordinary man, who'd earned the highest praise from her father and Nassos. The intense way he was looking at her, the emotions he'd aroused, had caused her bones to melt.

CHAPTER THREE

TAKIS KNEW HE HADN'T dreamed up this meeting with the woman Nassos had helped raise. When she left his office, her flowery fragrance lingered, providing proof she'd been in here.

He'd seen tears in her eyes when she'd heard him enter the room. She'd just been looking at Nassos's picture. The exquisite woman who'd walked down the aisle at the funeral had been his ward at one time. Shame on Takis for wondering if she could have been the mistress talked about in the news.

How old was Lys Theron? Twenty-five, twenty-six? And now she was half owner of the hotel, with Takis owning the other half.

Several emotions bombarded him, not the least of which was the attraction to her he'd felt at the funeral. He looked at the envelope his hand had squeezed without his being aware of it. According to her, this was Nassos's gift to him.

Utterly incredulous, he opened it and pulled out a letter and a deed. To his shock it was official all right, signed with Nassos's distinctive signature, stamped and dated. There it was in bold letters.

Takis Manolis, half owner of the Rodino Hotel
in Heraklion.

The letter indicated he should get in touch with the attorney Xander as soon as possible. Once Takis returned to Heraklion, he could sign the deed in front of witnesses so it could be recorded and filed for the court.

He read more. Neither owner would be free to do what they wanted with the hotel until six months had passed.

Aghast, he shook his head. What on earth had possessed Nassos to do such a thing?

Once Takis's hotels in New York had started making money, he'd paid the older hotelier for the help he'd given him. No amount could really be enough. How did you assign goodness a monetary value? He'd tried, but to his chagrin Nassos was now gone and there'd be no last time to thank him for everything.

This unimaginable development had thrown him.

For Nassos to turn around and simply give him half the hotel in Heraklion made no sense whatsoever. Takis didn't want the hotel! He'd paid him back generously.

What in the hell was Nassos thinking? Now that he'd passed away, there was no way to confront him about this. The inconceivable gesture made him feel as if he'd always be the boy who'd come from near poverty. The thought hurt him in a way that went soul deep.

To add to the hurt, this deed had been delivered by special messenger in the form of Nassos's beautiful former ward. Why would he force Takis's hand by making him a co-owner with her?

She was *too* damn beautiful. The kind of woman he never imagined to meet. Didn't want to meet. Only one other woman had touched his heart and she'd died. He didn't want to experience those kinds of feelings again. Yet a few minutes with this woman and a fire had been lit.

How did *she* feel about being half owner with a stranger, even if she knew a lot about him from Nassos and her father?

His thoughts centered on what she'd told him about the way the press had labeled her in the cruelest of ways. With her kind of unforgettable looks, she was an easy target. Was Nassos's divorce the result of his taking on Kristos's lovely teenage daughter to raise?

What business is it of yours to care, Manolis?

Unfortunately it *was* his business until he could fly to Crete and clear up this whole mess with the attorney of record.

Adrenaline surged through his veins. He wished to hell none of this had happened. He still couldn't believe Nassos was gone. Worse, he didn't want to know anything about *her*. Takis wished he'd never laid eyes on her. He didn't want this kind of a complication in his life. Loving a woman made you vulnerable.

A violent epithet flew from his lips. In his rage he tossed the deed across the room. It hit Cesare in the chest as he walked inside Takis's office.

With great calm his friend picked it up and put it on the desk. He shot Takis a questioning glance. "I take it this had something to do with the drop-dead-gorgeous woman I saw leaving the hotel a minute ago. Where on earth did *she* come from?"

Takis had trouble getting his emotions under control. "You don't want to know."

"Yes I do. You've been with several women over the years, but I've never seen you turned inside out by one before."

"It's not just the woman. It's everything!" His voice shook. "I feel like my world has been blown to smithereens and I don't know where I am anymore."

Takis should never have left his parents' home. He should have stayed on Crete and worked alongside his brother. He'd been so certain he'd had all the answers to help his family. But in the end he'd accepted the help of a wealthy man.

The thought of the deeded gift sickened him. That kind of gift might be given to a son, but Takis hadn't been Nassos's son. He was the son of Nikanor, who after all these years still didn't want his money. Neither did his brother. Worse, one of his parents was probably ill and Takis didn't have a clue because he'd been living out of the country for years. He was the ingrate of all time.

"What's the point of anything, Cesare?"

Worry lines darkened the features of his Italian friend. "Hold on, Takis. Come with me. We're going for a ride. My car is parked in the rear lot of the *castello*."

"You don't want to be with me."

"Well, I refuse to leave you here alone. It wouldn't do for Sofia to find you in this condition." Cesare was right about that. He didn't want his assistant privy to his personal life. "Whatever trouble you're in, we're going to talk about it. Let's go."

Takis grabbed the papers and stuffed them inside his suit jacket. They walked swiftly through the corridors past some of the guests to the outside. Cesare started up his sports car. He followed the road around from the back of the *castello* and they drove down the hill to the little village of Sopri. Before long he parked in front of a sports bar on the outskirts that didn't look crowded this time of day.

They went inside and found a quiet spot in a corner. Cesare ordered appetizers and their favorite Peroni, a pale lager from the brewery that had been founded in Lombardi. Once they'd been served rolls along with a hot plate of *grigliata mista di carne,* he eyed Takis.

"You didn't eat breakfast, which might explain the state you were in. You need lunch, *amico*, and you've got me for an audience. Now start talking and don't stop."

Cesare knew Takis's weakness for their grilled sausage, lamb and steak mix. Combined with the lager, it did taste good and he could feel his strength returning.

He pulled the deed out of his pocket and pushed it toward Cesare. "As you know, I attended Nassos Rodino's funeral while I was in Crete. Would you believe in his will he gave half the Hotel Rodino in Heraklion to me as a gift? The other half was given to that woman you saw. She was the courier who delivered it."

His friend studied it. "Who is she?"

"Lys Theron, the daughter of Kristos Theron, the

hotel owner in New York who gave me my first job after I reached the States. You remember me talking about him. When he died, his best friend, Nassos, Rodino became her guardian and brought her back to Crete to raise."

A low whistle came out of Cesare. But Takis didn't want to talk about the beautiful woman who'd robbed him of breath the moment he'd laid eyes on her. She was another problem altogether.

"I thought the money I sent to Nassos for his help had changed his image of me as the poverty-stricken teen from Tylissos." He swallowed part of his lager. "But I was wrong. In his mind's eye I would always be the poor son of poor Nikanor Manolis, humbly scraping out a living day after day.

"I never wanted anything from Nassos. His kindness gave me a new life, but I paid him back. To be handed a deed to part ownership of a property that isn't mine, that I never earned, is worse than a stiletto to the gut."

Cesare shot forward in his seat. "You couldn't be more wrong. It's his tribute to your raving success."

"You think?"

"Of course."

Takis shook his head. "Maybe the problem lies inside me. Maybe I've been too proud wanting to make a success of my life. Nassos's gift of the hotel takes me back to the time when I was eighteen. He approached me about furthering my education, not the other way around, Cesare.

"The hotel manager I worked for arranged for me to meet Nassos. I never asked for his help. When I finally accepted it and left for New York, I started paying him back as soon as I could. But being given half ownership of his hotel now doesn't feel right and has made me feel…guilty all over again."

"What's gotten into you, Takis? Guilty for what? Help me understand."

"That I've failed my family."

"In what way?"

"I left them to do something purely selfish. I accepted a rich man's help. My father couldn't give me that kind of help or encourage me. If I'd been any kind of a man, I would have stayed home and helped him."

"That's crazy talk, Takis. I left home too in order to pursue a dream and accepted a lot of help along the way."

"This is different, Cesare. You're not a Cretan."

"So what? I'm a Sicilian. What's the difference? My pride is no less fierce than yours."

Takis had no answer for that. "You don't understand. My brother stayed behind to work with my father. He never failed him. But that wasn't the case with his second-born son. What did I do? I took off. When I think about it now, I cringe to realize how deeply I must have disgraced him."

"Disgraced?" Cesare sounded angry. "You don't know any such thing. He must be bursting with pride over you. When was the last time you had a real heart-to-heart talk with him?"

"Before I left for New York, we talked. I went to him with ideas for what we could do with the hotel. He looked me in the eye and told me my plans for the family hotel didn't fit his vision, and that one day when I was a man, I'd understand. That was it! End of conversation. It shut me down. After eleven years I'm afraid I still don't understand."

"Then you need to force another conversation with him and find out what he meant."

"My father isn't easy to talk to."

"Then it's time you faced him so you won't stay in that hellhole you're digging for yourself. Let me ask you a question. Do you think *me* selfish? Or Vincenzo?"

Takis didn't have to voice the easy *no* that came to his mind.

"Come on and finish your food. Then we're going back to the *castello* to talk to Vincenzo before he leaves for Lake Como with Gemma. You're not the only one who has known the pain of separation from family. Don't forget that he *ran* from his father as fast as he could and hid out in New York under a different name for over ten years."

Takis had forgotten nothing. The three of them would never have met if they hadn't left their homes and their countries and gone to New York. He couldn't imagine what his life would have been like if he hadn't met Cesare and Vincenzo. The friendship they'd forged in college had changed his entire world.

All because Nassos made it possible for you, Manolis, said a voice in his head, sending him into worse turmoil.

Cesare paid the bill and got to his feet. "Are you ready?"

Once Lys had received the return phone call from Danae at noon, she walked out the door of the penthouse foyer to the elevator off the small hallway to await her arrival. The penthouse in Crete had been Nassos's domain, and a decision had to be made about the furnishings.

After being back a week from Milan, Lys still hadn't heard a word from Takis Manolis. But she'd daydreamed about him and what it would be like to go out with him. Since meeting him, she couldn't imagine ever being attracted to another man. She'd hoped to know his plans before telling Danae the latest state of affairs, but no such luck.

The doors of the elevator opened. Lys greeted the dark-haired beauty and walked back in the penthouse with her. Dressed in mourning clothes, she looked particularly elegant in a Kasper color-blocked black Jacquard jacket and skirt. Danae had always been a fashion plate and was the true love of Nassos's life.

No matter what he'd told Lys in his letter to her, she feared Danae might still blame her for their divorce. The pain of that would never leave her. No olive branch offered could ever change the past.

If Lys had known what would happen after Nassos had insisted she leave New York and come to live with him and Danae, she would have run away rather than have stepped foot on Crete. Hindsight was a wonderful thing, but it came far too late.

"Thank you for coming, Danae. I'm sure you hoped we'd seen the last of each other at the funeral, but I'm carrying out one last thing Nassos would have wanted done, even if it wasn't in the will. Come in the living room and sit down—I'd like to explain a few things."

The older woman followed her and found a seat on one of the upholstered chairs. Danae's natural olive complexion had paled. "I can't imagine what would have been so important you had to see me in person."

"Maybe you'll think it isn't important when I tell you, but I have to do it. As you know, Nassos left me half the hotel and nothing else. That means everything in this penthouse is yours. He lived up here after he left the villa. I happen to know you are the one who designed it and put it all together years ago. You're a real artist in many ways. All this furniture you picked out, the paintings… You know he would have wanted you to have everything."

She jumped to her feet, visibly disturbed. "I don't want anything," she bit out too fast, revealing her pain.

Lys could understand that and her heart went out to her. "If you don't want any of it, then you need to make arrangements for it to be sold or given away, or whatever you think is best. Otherwise I'll ask the co-owner of the hotel to do with it as he or she wishes."

"Who is it?"

"Would it surprise you to know its Takis Manolis?"

Danae's head reared. "Actually it doesn't. Nassos liked him very much."

Lys was glad she'd told her the truth. "I don't know if he wants it. But until he signs and files the official document with the court, it's still up in the air. On Xander's instructions I flew to Italy, handed him the documents and left."

"So you met him."

"Yes."

"What's he like?"

She took a deep breath. "Very attractive, but I haven't heard from him. Maybe he's trying to find a way to get out of it and possibly designate a person from his New York chain. That could be the reason there's been no word yet.

"Xander will have to be the one to keep us informed. I just thought you might like to have the movers come before anything else happens."

No sound came out of Danae. Lys could tell she was in a bad way and she wanted to comfort her.

"Nassos's death came as a painful shock to both of us." The anguished look on Danae's face prompted Lys to reveal something she'd held back since the divorce. "I'd like to talk frankly with you. When my father died, I was afraid to come to Crete, where I didn't know anyone. But I was underage and as you know, Nassos made a promise to my father to take care of me in case he died. I realize that my arrival was probably your worst nightmare, but it was something I had no control over."

Danae lowered her eyes.

"You were so wonderful to me, I got over a lot of my pain and started to be happy with you. In time I learned to adore you. But you must know that *you* were the great passion of Nassos's life."

The other woman started to tremble.

"I have something to show you." Lys pulled the letter from Nassos out of her purse and handed it to her. Nassos hadn't meant anyone else to read it, but Lys couldn't keep it from Danae, who deserved to know the truth.

"So you won't think I'm holding anything back, I want you to read this. Xander gave it to me after reading the contents of the will to you."

She watched as the older woman took in the contents. Soon her shoulders shook.

"As you've read, Nassos wanted children and I happened to fill a hole in his heart for a while as the daughter you two never had."

Danae looked crushed and put a hand to her throat. "I—I was afraid I wouldn't be able to love a child that wasn't mine. That's why I didn't want to adopt."

"I can understand that. I'm sure a lot of childless parents worry about the same thing when they adopt. But you showed me so much love, perhaps it was just that Nassos had more faith in your parenting abilities than you did. When he moved to the penthouse after your divorce, he was a ruined man."

"Why didn't he tell me all these things?" she cried in agony.

"His pride. What about yours? Would you have listened?"

She shook her dark head. "I don't know. I don't know. I harbored a lot of resentment over the years because he didn't want me to work. When he begged me to consider adoption, I felt anger because of the many times I'd begged him to let me try even part-time work. We were both so hardheaded."

"I'm so sorry, Danae." As they stared at each other, Lys reached for the letter she put back in her purse. "I hope you'll listen to me now because there's something else I've wanted to tell you since your separation from him." Her throat swelled with emotion.

"I love you. You were kind and loving and helped me so much. The two of you had a beautiful marriage in so many ways. For what it's worth, you would have made a wonderful mother. Maybe there's a man out there who could fulfill that dream for you. Many women have babies at your age. It's not too late if you decide to get married again. You're a very beautiful woman."

A long silence ensued before Danae jumped up from the chair and hugged her hard. "Thank you for saying that to me. I love you too, Lys. You have no idea how much I've missed you."

With those words, Lys's pain was lifted. "I feel the same." She finally let go of Danae, and wiped her eyes. "Tell me something else. Would you have liked to inherit the hotel and run it?"

Danae shook her head. "It doesn't matter what I would have liked. He wanted a stay-at-home wife and didn't want me working at the hotel after we were married. Now I'm not interested."

"But you could read between the lines in his letter to me. He admitted he was wrong about divorcing you, and he was wrong not to have let you work alongside him after you were married."

She grasped Lys's hands. "You're very sweet, but it's too late for that."

"Are you sure? You could talk to Xander and fight for it. I'd step aside in an instant if I knew it was what you wanted."

"It isn't. Truly. But I'll take your advice and get movers in here to ship everything back to the villa."

"I'm glad about that!" Lys hugged her again, then headed for the foyer.

Danae followed. "Where are you going?"

"Back to my room. I need to return Anita's call. You remember my mother's friend? She came to Nassos's funeral."

"Of course. It was wonderful of her to come."

"I know. I couldn't believe she'd fly all this way from New York." Lys pressed the button that opened the elevator doors, then turned to Danae. "If you need anything, just phone me."

"I want you to come to the villa as soon as you can. It's so empty now."

"I promise to visit you all the time."

"You mean it?"

"Of course I do. I love you, Danae. *Yassou.*"

Lys rode the private elevator six floors to the lobby, then took the main elevator back to the third floor. She needed to make a phone call to Anita on Long Island. They'd stayed in close touch over the years.

Anita had invited Lys to stay with her and her husband, Bob, for a time. Maybe a little vacation would be a good thing. Maybe not. She just didn't know.

The limo pulled up to the Rodino Hotel in Heraklion. For the moment he had business to take care of here. Lys Theron had no idea he'd flown to Heraklion two days ago to stay with his family. Now he was ready to talk to her, but he wanted the element of surprise on his side.

Before he'd left for New York, Takis had done every job there was to do there at the hotel for that year. He'd often escorted VIPs to the penthouse Nassos used for business. No doubt Lys Theron lived there now.

There was a private elevator down the right hall that went straight to the top. If Nassos hadn't changed his six-digit birthday code on the keypad, Takis would be able to go on up. Otherwise he'd have to phone her from downstairs. His pulse raced at the thought of seeing her again.

The code hadn't changed. After the doors opened, he stepped inside for the short ride and entered the outer hallway when it stopped. But he needed to alert her he was here. Even if it was presumptuous, when he explained how he'd gained access to the elevator, he hoped she'd understand.

Takis had just pressed the digits of the phone number written on the envelope she'd given him when the door to the penthouse opened. He received a surprise because instead of Lys Theron standing there, the stylish black-haired woman he'd seen at the older man's funeral emerged without her veil.

She glared at him. "No one is permitted up here. Who are you?"

"I'm sorry to have alarmed you," he murmured. "I was just calling Kyria Theron to let her know I was out here."

The attractive woman scrutinized him. "This isn't her apartment."

What?

"How did you get up here?"

Takis would have to proceed carefully. "I'm the new co-owner of the hotel." After many talks with his partners in the last week, that's what he was saying right now, but it was subject to change depending on many things.

"What's your name?" she murmured.

"Takis Manolis."

Her eyes widened. "Lys told me."

He nodded. "I saw you at the church on the day of

Nassos's funeral." This had to be the widow. "You must be Kyria Rodino."

"Yes. I was married to Nassos for twenty-four years and heard your name mentioned with fondness for the last twelve of them."

The revelation stunned him. "He was instrumental in changing my life. I'll never forget him."

Her eyes glistened over. "Neither will I."

Takis had a hard time taking it all in. "I'm very sorry for your loss. Please forgive me. I thought Kyria Theron lived here. Do you know where I can find her?"

"She has her own suite at the hotel. I have to leave and will ride down in the elevator with you."

Takis had made a big mistake coming up here.

Once they reached the hotel foyer, he thanked her for her help and the two of them parted company. He walked into the main lounge where he could be private and rang her number.

Before long he heard, "Kyrie Manolis?" She sounded surprised. "I wondered when I might hear from you."

"I just arrived at the hotel and am in the lounge. We have to talk." Before any more time passed he needed to explain that he'd trespassed earlier and had alarmed Nassos's former wife. "When will it be convenient for you?"

"I'll be right down."

"Efharisto."

Within two minutes the dark-blonde woman he'd come to see walked toward him dressed in a storm-gray crewneck sweater with long sleeves and a matching skirt. Some Cretan women in mourning wore darker clothes, if not black, for a long time.

Yet even garbed in somber colors, the feminine curves of her figure and the long legs he admired couldn't be hidden. She not only ignited his senses, but those of every male within her radius.

Takis had the additional advantage of being able to stare into those violet eyes at close range. When he'd been inside the church, he'd thought no eyes could be that color. At the time he'd assumed the sun shining through the stained glass had to have been responsible.

But the hotel lounge was no church. If anything, their color bordered on purple and mesmerized him almost as much as the enticing curve of her mouth. He wondered how many men had known its taste and had run their hands through hair as luscious as swirling caramel cream.

"It's nice to see you again, Kyrie Manolis."

"I've been looking forward to talking to you too. Since we're co-owners, I'd rather you called me Takis."

"So you've decided."

"Yes. Do you mind if I call you Lys?"

"I'd prefer it. If you'll come with me, we'll go to my suite to talk. Until the situation is settled and made official, I'd prefer us to meet in private rather than Nassos's office so we don't have to make explanations to anyone."

"You took the words out of my mouth."

They walked to the bank of elevators and took the next empty one that carried them to the third floor. He followed her to the end of the hall where she opened the door to a small foyer. It led into a typical hotel suite sitting room. Nothing special here, nothing that told him about her personality.

"There's a guest bathroom down that hall. If you'd like to freshen up, I'll call the kitchen and ask for lunch to be served. Anything special you would like?"

"Why don't you surprise me?" He watched her disappear before he left the room. When he returned, he found her seated in one of the chairs around the coffee table with the phone in her hand.

Her gaze wandered over him as he sat down. He enjoyed the sensation far too much and castigated himself. "Danae just called to tell me she met you outside the penthouse door looking for me. I'm curious. How *did* you gain access to the private elevator?"

He leaned forward with his hands clasped between this legs. "When I worked here for a year, I was given the code to take VIPs to the penthouse for Nassos."

A genuine smile broke out on her beautiful face. "You knew his birthday code."

"I'm afraid I couldn't resist finding out if it still worked, but I caught Kyria Rodino off guard. For that, I'm sorry."

"That's my fault. When I told you I lived at the hotel, I failed to be more specific. It wasn't until Nassos separated from Danae that he moved to the penthouse."

"I had no right to do what I did."

"I'm sure Danae was more amused than offended once you introduced yourself. It's something Nassos might have pulled if he'd been in your shoes. He had an impish side and indicated you were clever."

"If you translate that, it means I went where angels feared to tread far too often." The gentle chuckle that came out of her coincided with the rap on the door to the suite. Takis got up first. "I'll get it."

After tipping the employee, he carried their tray of food into the sitting room and put it on the coffee table. He removed the covers on *horiatiki* salad and Greek club sandwiches filled with lamb while she poured the coffee for them.

They both sat back to eat. She appeared hungry too. He swallowed his second half in no time. "This is an excellent lunch. Kudos to the chef."

"You can tell Eduardo yourself."

Takis glanced at her over his coffee cup. "My attorney examined the legal work and it is quite clear that Nassos didn't give either of us a choice. We're stuck for six months. How do you feel about that?"

She averted her eyes. "I don't have a right to feel much of anything. As I told you earlier, it's possible he didn't want me to be the sole owner for fear I might make bad decisions. The one man he felt he could trust was you, so I can understand why he made certain you would be there to help me if I got into trouble."

Nice as that compliment sounded, he didn't buy it. "*Have* you gotten into trouble in the past?"

His question seemed to unsettle her. She put her coffee cup on the table. "Not in business, but he didn't always approve of the men I've dated."

That had been the one thing on his mind since he'd

seen her in the church. If she was in a relationship now, he should be happy about it.

No doubt Nassos hadn't liked any male who tried to get too close to her. He'd probably had a man in mind for her, but only when the time was right. By becoming her guardian, he'd taken his responsibility seriously.

"Though I can't imagine it, is it possible he didn't want you to fall for someone who wanted more than your love?" A man would have to be blind not to want a relationship with her if he could. The fact that she was the owner of one of the most famous hotels in Greece would make a man heady if he could have both.

She sat back in the chair. "He couldn't have known that he would die this early in his life."

"No," he muttered. "No man knows that."

"But I wouldn't put it past him to have worried that I might make a bad emotional decision because of some man, even at the age of sixty or seventy."

"If Nassos had a fear that you could put the welfare of the hotel at risk no matter your age, he would never have willed half of it to you. I'm convinced your personal happiness was all that concerned him."

"Coming from you, that means a lot."

What Takis still hadn't worked out yet was why Nassos had made *him* co-owner. His partners had tried to disabuse him of the notion that when Nassos had made out his will, he'd seen Takis as the needy boy from Crete.

He still didn't want his father to know he'd inherited it from Nassos. He feared his parent wouldn't understand and would wonder what Takis had done to deserve such a gift.

Her features grew animated and she got to her feet to pour herself another cup of coffee. “Now that you’re here, I have a proposition for you.”

The course of their conversation intrigued him. “Go ahead.”

“When six months have passed, Nassos said we could do whatever we wanted with the hotel. I’ll be honest and tell you up front that I’d like to buy your half. I’ll be twenty-seven by then and will have come into the inheritance from my father. Whatever price you set, I’ll be able to meet it.”

Takis hadn’t been expecting a proposition like that. Her own father’s inheritance would make her independently wealthy. There was no question she’d be able to buy him out. In half a year’s time this unwanted situation could be turned around and he’d be done with it.

“On the face of it I like the idea. Since you worked with Nassos, then he would have taught you how to invest your money wisely.”

Her eyes lit up, reaching his insides. “I’d like to think that’s true. Takis…if it suits you, I’ll continue to run the hotel, leaving you free to go back to your other businesses.” If she was eager to see the last of him, he had news for her. “But if you want to be here full-time in a hands-on capacity to honor Nassos’s wishes, then we’ll work things out any way you’d like.”

Hands-on?

Not only was she gorgeous, she was too good to be true. He hadn’t known what to expect, but it wasn’t this amenable woman whose only agenda he could see was to eventually own the hotel outright. If she had an ulterior motive somewhere, he hadn't detected it yet.

When she'd told him at the *castello* they were co-owners, hadn't Takis wanted to be free of Nassos's gift?

He got to his feet, troubled because she was seducing him without even trying. Not since losing his girlfriend had he felt such emotion. But this was much stronger because he was no longer an eighteen-year-old boy.

"You've made this insanely easy for me in every way. Why don't we meet tomorrow morning at the Villa Kerasia outside the city? The quiet, small back room of the dining area will help us to keep a low profile while we talk business and discuss where we go from here."

"That sounds good to me," she answered without taking a breath. "Before you leave, I wanted you to know that within the week the penthouse will be empty. You can use it, decorate it, do whatever you want."

"Thank you. But when I'm in Crete, I stay with my family."

Her eyes went suspiciously bright. "Of course. Tylissos isn't that far from here. How lucky you are to have family to come home to. I envy you."

"I *am* fortunate," he admitted, but his thoughts were on her. She'd just lost Nassos and would be vulnerable for a long time. Takis didn't want to feel any emotions where she was concerned, but to his chagrin she'd aroused much more in him than the urge to comfort her. "Thank you for lunch. I'll let myself out and see you in the morning. How does eight thirty sound to you?"

"Perfect."

So was she. Tomorrow he'd be with her again. It was the only reason he could leave the hotel at all.

CHAPTER FOUR

LYS AWAKENED EARLY the next morning. She'd been restless during the night, otherwise her comforter wouldn't be on the floor at the side of her bed. The unexpected advent of Takis Manolis in her life had shaken her world.

The fact that he would be co-owner of the hotel with her for the next six months wasn't nearly as disconcerting as the man himself. He was a Cretan Adonis who'd gotten under her skin and had turned her insides to mush the first time she'd laid eyes on him. She wished to heaven she weren't excited to be meeting him for breakfast, but she couldn't turn off those hormones working madly inside her body.

There was nothing professional about her feelings for him. She had no idea how she was going to be able to work with him and not reveal how susceptible she was to his male charisma. No woman alive could be indifferent to him. Somehow she needed to be the exception. But she feared that it would be an impossible task.

Once she'd showered and washed her hair, Lys changed her mind five times about what to wear, something she never did, which proved he was in her head. She eventually settled on pleated navy pants with a navy blouse edged in navy lace and matching sweater.

Not only would she continue to wear dark colors to honor Nassos's memory, but she refused to dress in order to attract Takis's attention. Other women probably did it on a regular basis. But his appeal had affected her so greatly, it was embarrassing. She had no idea how long Danae would wear black before returning to her normal wardrobe. Lys would follow her example.

Once she'd brushed her hair and put on a soft pink lipstick, she left the hotel driving one of their service vans so she wouldn't be recognized by the paparazzi. She headed out of town under an overcast sky to the little settlement of Vlahiana southwest of Heraklion. She took in the beauty of the hills and vineyards rolling in the distance. Several villages clung to the hillsides, beckoning her toward them.

Takis had lived on Crete until he was eighteen and probably knew every inch of it. She was pleased he'd wanted them to meet at the small country inn hidden away where there wouldn't be any press around.

Nassos had once brought her and Danae here, explaining about the building that had been completely restored with ancient stones, a perfect blend with the near-white bleached wood. The artist in him had liked what had been done to it. She didn't wonder that Takis had chosen this same place to talk.

To her surprise, she saw his tall, well-honed physique walking toward her as she pulled up in the small parking area. He could have no way of knowing what she'd worn, but he'd dressed in charcoal-colored trousers and a navy sport shirt open at the neck, looking marvelous.

"We match," he said after opening the van door for her. As she got out, the scent of the soap he'd used in the shower assailed her senses. Her arm brushed against his chest by accident. The slight contact sent a thrill of excitement through her body. "I've already ordered our breakfast. It's waiting out on the back patio for us."

It turned out they had the area to themselves. The trellis roof above them dripped with shocking red bougainvillea. He helped her to sit at the small round table before he took a seat opposite her. The sight of so many delicious-looking items told her he was a typical Cretan who loved his food. There were sausages, smoked pork, eggs with *staka*, cream cheese pie and coffee.

She bit into a piece of pie. "If I ate this way every morning, pretty soon I wouldn't be able to get through the doors to the office."

"That will never be your problem, and I happen to think it's much nicer to eat while we talk business."

"I won't argue with you there." Her awareness of him made it difficult to keep her eyes off him while he devoured his food.

As he drank his coffee, he asked, "Were you running the hotel singlehandedly before Nassos died?"

"Pretty much, along with the general manager. Nassos spent most of his time watching over his other investments, which are now Danae's. But there's no question Nassos kept his eagle eye on everything. Since he's been gone, I've continued to do things the same way, but I'll admit I worry that I'm missing something."

"Do the staff know you're the new owner?"

"No. I'm sure they think that Nassos gave the hotel to Danae even though he divorced her. I know the manager assumes as much."

His piercing gaze stared directly into hers. "How do you feel about having to share the business with me?"

She sat back in the chair. "To be honest, when the attorney gave me Nassos's letter and I read what was inside, I almost went into shock. But by the time I flew to Italy, I'd managed to calm down."

"Your anger didn't show."

"I never felt anger. Not at all. If anything I felt hurt for Danae, who should have inherited the hotel. They met years ago while she'd been working at another hotel. She would be a natural to run everything, but he was too blind to see what he was doing."

He lowered his coffee cup. "You didn't expect to inherit?"

She frowned. "I didn't expect him to die, but I know what you meant to say. I had no expectations. I imagined that in time I'd meet a man, get married and years from now lose Nassos. Instead, he's gone and he has made you co-owner. That's all I know. But to answer your question, no, I'm not angry."

"What did you mean he was too blind?"

Lys shouldn't have said what she did. Now he'd dig until he got the answer he wanted. At this point it didn't matter if he knew the truth. In fact it would be better if it did.

"Tell you what. If you've finished eating, why don't we go to the hotel?" She was enjoying this time with him far too much. “If I show you the letter Nassos instructed the attorney to give to me, then you’ll understand and won’t have so many questions. I wish I had brought it with me. Did you bring a car?”

“No. I came in a taxi from home.”

“Then I’ll drive us back to town and we can talk in my sitting room at the hotel. Would it bother you if I’m behind the wheel?”

His half smile gave her a fluttery feeling in her chest. “I’m looking forward to it.” He put some bills on the table before helping her up. It had been a long time since she’d been with a man, let alone have one to help her into the van.

The thrill of being with him was like nothing she’d ever experienced. She wished they were going off and not coming back. A silly thought, but one that told her she was in serious trouble where Takis was concerned.

Before long she pulled into the private parking space in the hotel garage and they rode the elevator to her floor. They’d done this before when she’d welcomed him inside her room. After telling him he was welcome to freshen up, she went into the bedroom to get the letter out of the side table drawer.

Once she’d made a detour to her own bathroom, she entered the sitting room and handed it to him before subsiding in one of the upholstered chairs around the coffee table. She’d never invited a man into her hotel room before. But with Takis, everything was feeling so natural.

Takis felt her eyes on him as he opened it to read. Within seconds he couldn’t believe what Nassos had written to her. Near the end of it came the part where Takis's name was mentioned.

> Before you take possession, you must give the sealed envelope to Takis Manolis. You've heard me and Danae talk about him often enough. When he came to Crete periodically, we'd discuss business on my yacht, where we could be private.
>
> You'll know where to find him when the time comes. The two of you will share ownership for six months. After that time period, you'll both be free to make any decisions you want.
>
> By the time you read this, he's probably married with children and grandchildren too. I've thought of him as the son I never had.

The son Nassos never had?

"What's wrong, Takis? You've gone pale."

He must have read the whole letter half a dozen times before he realized he wasn't alone in the room. His head swung around. Takis had gotten it all wrong. He could throw the idea of pity out the window. Nassos *had* looked at him as a son. More than that, he'd looked on Lysette, his French nickname for her, as his daughter.

This letter explaining the reason for the Rodino divorce helped him understand why Lys had been hurt for Danae's sake. It showed his love for Lys and hinted of the affection and regard Nassos had felt for him.

Takis sucked in his breath. Nothing about the hotelier's actions where Takis was concerned had been the way he'd thought!

His friends had tried to convince him that the gift of the hotel had been Nassos's way of honoring him for making a success of his life. They'd been right. But without this letter, he'd have gone on threshing around for reasons that had no basis in truth.

He handed it back to her. "Thank you for letting me read it." His voice throbbed. "It's a gift I didn't expect. Because of your generosity I was allowed to see into Nassos's mind. Bless you for that, or I might have gone through the rest of my life being…unsettled."

Those heavenly purple eyes played over his face in confusion. "Why?"

"It's a long story."

"I'd like to hear it. Won't you sit down?"

He couldn't. Takis was too wired. If anyone deserved to know what had been going on inside him, she did. Her honesty and willingness to share something so private humbled him.

"Let me just say I thought Nassos pitied me because of my poor background."

She got to her feet. "I'm sure he did. The grandfather who raised him was ill and so poor, Nassos had to sell the fish he caught from a rowboat so they could live."

Takis's head reared. "I didn't know that."

"I'm not surprised. It pained him to talk about it. My own father's parents died in a ferry accident and a near-destitute aunt took him in, but sadly she too died early. My father and Nassos joined forces and started catching fish to sell so they wouldn't starve."

What she'd just told Takis blew his mind.

"No doubt when he discovered you were working at the hotel and showed such amazing promise after coming from a similar background as himself, he was glad to help you. He was always kind to people.

"If he'd known he was going to die this soon, I have no doubt that he would have given the hotel to you outright. He knew I'd be coming into my inheritance soon and would be able to make my way in the world just fine."

The more she talked, the more ashamed Takis felt for being so far off the mark. These revelations changed everything for him. He cleared his throat. "Do you like running the hotel?"

"Yes, but I haven't known anything else. When I flew to Italy to find you, I thought I might have to track you all the way to New York. My mother's best friend still lives on Long Island. When she came to the funeral, she invited me to stay with her for a while. I've toyed with the idea that if you wanted to work here and be by your family, I'd find a different kind of job in New York."

The thought of her not being here in Crete disturbed him more than a little bit. "You think I need breathing room?"

She cocked her head. "I don't know. *Do* you?"

What Takis needed was to put his priorities in order. His family took precedence over every consideration. Nassos's gift had opened up a way for him to have a legitimate reason to be on Crete for the next six months. But it was vital that as co-owner, she be the visible owner on duty while he was the invisible co-owner who helped behind the scenes.

"I'm going to share something I've never shared

with anyone but my two best friends and business partners. Except for visits to my family, I've been gone from Crete for eleven years. On my last visit here when I attended Nassos's funeral, my mother begged me to come home for good."

"That sounds like a loving mother," Lys said softly. Her genuineness made him believe she was truly happy for him.

"But they've never asked me for anything, or wanted anything from me, whether it be financial or something else. Now I'm worried about them and their health. Maybe I'm wrong about that. Nevertheless I'm planning to sell my hotels in New York and move here permanently to be near them all the time."

"I suspect they've been hoping for that for years."

"If that's true, I'm the last to know." Lys was easy to talk to. She made it comfortable for him, but the warning bells were going off that he was getting in over his head.

"Then you should move here and find out. It would be perfect for you and me. While you run the hotel and live around your parents, I can leave. If I find a new career in New York, then I might not want to buy out your half. In that case, when the six months are up, I'd rather you invested my half of the money from the hotel. Nassos's trust in you is good enough for me."

"I'm flattered that you have more faith in me than I do." But he shook his head, not liking that idea for any reason. Takis didn't want her to leave. It stunned him how strongly attracted he was to her. She was in his blood and he hadn't even kissed her yet. But that day was coming.

"In truth I don't want or need another hotel. The last thing I want is for anyone to know I'm co- owner. Yet for another half year that's the way it has to be and I plan to live out the rest of my life here. So unless your heart is set on going to New York, I'd prefer it if you would call the staff together and tell them you're the new owner of the hotel."

She got to her feet. "But that isn't the truth."

How strange that a few weeks ago he hadn't wanted this gift. Yet in just a short period of time everything had changed. Takis knew himself well and wondered if he could fallen in love with her in such a short space of time. He was overjoyed that for the next six months they'd be forced to remain joined at the hip so to speak.

"No one else needs to know that. I'll explain to Kyrie Pappas why I don't want any mention of me as the co-owner."

Her arched brows knit together. "I don't understand. You're being so mysterious."

"My family must never know my name is tied to the hotel."

She moved closer. "Why?"

"Because I'm a Manolis and there's only room for one Manolis hotel owner on Crete."

A long silence ensued. "You mean your father." She'd read his mind.

"If he knew the kind of gift Nassos had deeded to me—the kind only a father would give to his son—it would hurt him in a way you couldn't comprehend."

"Are you so sure about that?"

"Not entirely, but I love my father."

Tears filled her eyes. "I loved mine too. It's the

only reason I went to Crete with Nassos at the age of seventeen when I didn't want to."

"That had to have been very hard."

"It was in the beginning. I had to leave my friends and school, everything I knew. What I didn't know at the time was that in honoring Baba's wishes, I would learn to love Nassos. He gave me a new life and protected me because he understood a father's love and wanted to honor his best friend's wishes. I get the honor aspect, Takis."

Lys Theron was amazing. "Do you have any idea how grateful I am that you told no one about the will and came all the way to Italy to talk to me in person? Because of you, the secret is still safe."

She studied him for a long time. "I'll keep it. You're worried that if your father knew the truth, he would believe you had a much greater friendship with Nassos than he'd been led to believe. I can see why you think it could ruin your relationship for life."

How did someone so young get to be so wise? "I'm afraid it could," Takis whispered.

"I think you're wrong about it, but no one will ever know from me. I'll talk to Danae so she understands how serious this is to keep absolutely quiet."

No matter his feelings for her, he felt he could trust Lys with his life. "Thank you. But this brings us to our immediate problem. We'll have to conduct business without anyone suspecting the real reason we're together at all."

"What are you suggesting?"

"I've been giving it a lot of thought. When I leave you in a minute, I'm headed straight to the airport. I need to fly back to Milan and talk to my partners.

Among other things I'll have to make preparations to sell my hotel chain in New York and will probably be gone at least a week. When I come back, I'll have a proposition for you."

"Proposition?" she questioned.

"What goes around, comes around," he teased, reminding her of their conversation yesterday when she'd made one to him.

"Aren't you going to give me a hint?" The corner of her sensual mouth lifted, sending a burst of desire through him.

"Not yet. Certain things have to fit into place first."

"You're talking about the hotel in Milan. Do you plan to remain part owner?"

"Possibly." But that wasn't what he had on his mind while she filled his vision to the exclusion of all else. He had plans for them and knew in his gut that she wasn't involved with another man. Otherwise he would have to come up with another idea, but nothing had the appeal of the one he had his heart set on.

"Would you like a ride to the airport? I have an errand to run anyway."

Nothing she'd said could have made him happier. He still wanted to talk to her. "I'd appreciate it."

"I'll just ring Giorgos to let him know my agenda."

"That name isn't familiar to me. What happened to the other manager Nassos relied on in the past?"

"Yannis? He had to retire because his knee operations didn't work out well. He was hard to replace."

"I'm sorry to hear that. Is Giorgos a good manager?"

"Six months ago Nassos hired him as a favor for a close friend, but he had one reservation."

"What was that?"

"He was recently divorced, but he decided to give him a chance."

"Why would that matter?"

"I asked Nassos the same thing. He said it was just a feeling he had that Giorgos might not be able to concentrate on the job, but only time would tell. After the letter Nassos left for me revealing his torment over divorcing Danae, I suppose his concerns about Giorgos made sense. The man moved here from Athens, where he'd been a hotel manager with an excellent reference."

Interesting. "How do you like him so far?"

"I think he's very good at what he does."

"But?"

"I can tell he's lonely."

"Why do you say that?"

"Whenever I start to leave the office, he wants to talk for a while."

Takis struggled not to smile. "Is he attractive?"

"So-so."

"Does he have children?"

"No."

"How old is he?"

"Thirtyish I believe."

A dangerous age. Giorgos must have thought he'd died and arrived in the elysian fields when he discovered Lys on the premises.

While she made the phone call, the proposition he intended to put to her had grown legs.

CHAPTER FIVE

WHEN HER PHONE RANG, Lys had been out on the patio of Danae's villa talking with her about Takis and his fragile relationship with his father. She checked the caller ID before clicking on. "Yes, Giorgos?"

"I don't mean to intrude on your day off, but there was a man at the front desk asking for you a few minutes ago. He didn't leave his name. I told him I'd schedule an appointment, but I needed information first. All he said was that you would know who he was and he'd be back later."

Lys shot to her feet out of breath. *Takis?* But surely he would have phoned her if he'd flown to Crete! He'd been gone a week, but it had felt like a month. Seven days away from him had proven to her how much he had come to mean to her, feelings that went soul deep.

"Did you hear what I said? Do you want security when you return?"

She'd forgotten Giorgos was on the phone. "Was this man threatening in some way?"

"No. But he had an attitude that sounded too familiar and possessive for my liking."

If anyone sounded possessive it was Giorgos, whose observation surprised her. "Thank you for the warning, but I'm not worried. I'll be back at the hotel later."

After hanging up she told Danae what happened. The older woman cocked her head. "Who else could it be but Takis? Aside from Nassos, he's the most exciting man I've *almost* ever bumped into."

Lys chuckled.

"The man's charm is lethal. I have no doubt it rattled Giorgos, who, according to Nassos, was interested in you from the moment he came to work."

"You're kidding—"

This time it was Danae who laughed. "When Nassos realized Giorgos was invisible to you, he stopped worrying that he'd hired him."

"I had no idea I was that transparent."

"There were two or three men you dated that gave us concern because you seemed so swayed by them. We felt you were too young and we ran interference for your sake. But it was when you started seeing Kasmos Loukos, whose father owns the Loukos Shipping lines in Macedonia, we grew very nervous.

"That spoiled young man had already been seen with too many wealthy celebrities. Nassos knew Kasmos was shopping around for the best female prospect to build on his father's fortune. When we saw the way he went about seducing you, we were fearful you might really be in love with him. The problem was, you were an adult. We couldn't do anything about it, and only hoped you could see through him before it was too late."

"Which I did. One night he started talking to me about Nassos, asking questions that were none of his business. That's when a light went on and I remembered all the lessons you'd tried to teach me. I was no longer blinded and told him I didn't want to see him anymore. You should have seen his face—"

"Thank goodness that relationship didn't last! I'm afraid neither Nassos nor I ever thought you'd met your match. Speaking of which, I think you'd better take the helicopter back to the hotel so you can meet up with this mystery man before you die of curiosity."

Heat crept into her cheeks. "I'm not dying," Lys muttered.

"You could have fooled me." She reached for her phone. "I'll alert the pilot."

Lys checked her watch. Ten after one. She'd been here a long time. The two of them were closer than ever. They were family and needed each other while they mourned their loss. No longer did Lys want to go to New York except for a visit to the Farrells'. Her life was here. Takis was here and not going anywhere. *Joy.*

She walked over to hug her. "Have a lovely evening with Stella. Don't get up. I'll see myself out."

"Let me know how this ends."

"You know I will. Love you."

After leaving the villa, she walked out to the pad and climbed on board the helicopter. Within fifteen minutes the pilot landed on top of the Rodino Hotel. She took the elevator to the third floor and freshened up in her suite. With the blood pounding in her ears, she went down to the lobby.

If Takis was here and waiting in the lounge, he'd see her. But since he still hadn't phoned her, she began to think it must have been some other man. Lys couldn't think who that would be unless it was a high-tech salesperson not wanting to go through Giorgos to reach her.

Magda, one of the personnel on duty at the desk, waved her over. "Giorgos told me to watch for you. I'll get him." The woman hurried off before Lys could tell her not to bother.

A second later he came out of his office and walked toward the counter where she was standing. At the same time, she felt two hands slide around her waist from behind.

"Forgive me," Takis whispered. "I have my reason for doing this."

The intimacy brought a small gasp to her lips. She whirled around, meeting those intense hazel eyes that were devouring her.

"Don't look now, but Giorgos is having a meltdown," he murmured. She wouldn't have understood what he meant if she hadn't just had a certain conversation with Danae about the manager. Their mouths were mere centimeters apart. His warm breath on her lips excited her so much, she forgot that she was clinging to his arms. "I'll answer your questions later. Come with me first. We're going for a ride."

Her heart nearly ran away with her as he kept an arm around her shoulders and they left the hotel. Instead of walking her to a taxi, he helped her into a black, middle-of-the-line Acura parked in the registration check-in line. Leon, one of the staff members outside, stared at the two of them in surprise.

Takis started up the engine and darted into the heavy main street traffic in front of the resort. When she could find her voice she said, "This smells brand new."

He flashed her a smilc. "I just drove it off the lot. I'm here for the next six months and need transportation." His choice of car made total sense considering the modest income of his family.

"My driving must have frightened you more than I realized."

"Are you saying you would have agreed to be my chauffeur day and night? If so, we'll drive back to the car dealership and turn it in."

Lys laughed gently while he drove them along the harbor road to the Venetian Fortress of Koules. He pulled into a parking space where they could watch the boats.

After shutting off the engine, he turned to her, stretching his arm along the back of the seat. "I owe you an explanation. Thank you for going along with me back there."

"I take it you wanted to make a statement. So why did you do it?"

"In order for us to be together so no one knows the underpinnings of our relationship, I'm proposing we do something shocking. How would you feel about getting engaged to me?"

Engaged?

Lys looked away, literally stunned by what he'd just said.

"Hear me out before you tell me how outrageous I'm being. It could be the one thing that will make it easier to help us achieve our main goal."

"What do you mean?"

"Don't you agree the most important one is for us to get through the next six months honoring Nassos's wishes?"

Her pulse had started to race. “That goes without saying.”

“An engagement will give us the perfect cover. While you run the hotel, I’ll spend real time with my family. When I whisk you away for a little personal time together, or spend time in your hotel room, no one will know I’m helping you behind the scenes.”

Lys struggled to sit still. Nassos had told her Takis was a genius with vision, but this proposition went beyond the boundaries of her imagination. The thought of being engaged to him robbed her of breath.

“The only way the manager will understand why you and I are spending time together and not become suspicious is *if* he thinks we’re romantically involved. I was simply setting the scene.”

A thrill of alarm passed through her body. “There’s no doubt you accomplished your objective a few minutes ago,” she said in a tremulous voice.

“It had to be convincing. Tell me something. When you flew to Italy, did the staff know you were leaving the country?”

“Only Giorgos, but I didn’t tell him where and let him assume what he wanted.”

“That’s perfect. Just now it didn’t hurt for him and other members of the staff to see us meet in the lobby and assume we have a history away from Crete. When we walked out of the hotel with my arm around you, it no doubt created a new wave of gossip.”

“You *know* it did.” Being that close to him practically gave her a heart attack.

“If we’re engaged, it’ll be about you and me for a change. I’m aware the old gossip came close to crucifying you. An engagement would put an end to it.”

"I can't imagine anything more wonderful than changing that particular conversation." She took an extra breath. "I'll admit it was awful for Danae too."

He studied her for a moment. "Neither of you deserved this. It pains me for both of you. The new gossip you and I create will cause people to see you in a new light. With a ring on your finger from me, the old news will be forgotten."

She closed her eyes tightly. He was making it sound possible and that increased her nervousness. If this proposal had come from his heart, she'd be in heaven. But it hadn't, and she needed to remember that.

"Lys?" he prodded.

"Can you tell me what you've decided to do about your other businesses?"

"I'm already in negotiations to sell my chain of hotels in New York and invest the money. After talking it over with my partners, I'm going to stay committed to them. The *castello* hotel-restaurant will be the only asset I own and I'll fly to Milan when necessary."

"I'm sure they'll be happy about that." Her voice shook from emotions sweeping through her. "Do your parents know what you've done?"

He nodded. "I've told them I've come home for good and want to help out at the family hotel. My father hasn't said anything about that yet. Lukios has indicated I'm not needed. He explained they would have to let someone else go who must keep their job. I understood that and told him I'd be happy to do some advertising around Crete to bring in more clients."

"What did he say?"

"He shook his head and left the living room with

the excuse that he was needed at the front desk and we'd talk later."

"I'm sorry, but these are early days. Your mother must be ecstatic!"

"I think she's still in shock that I haven't gone back to Italy yet."

"You'll have to give your family time before everyone accepts the fact that you're home permanently. But you have to know she's thrilled, and she's the one to work on. After all, your mother was the one who begged you to come home permanently. In the meantime, you can offer to do little things for her."

Takis studied her intently. "You're a very intuitive woman, so I'm going to take your advice. A few more days and they might be more receptive to the idea of my helping around the hotel. Maybe I'll be able to break my parents down enough so they'll start confiding in me."

Lys moistened her lips nervously. "I'm sure things will get better for you, but I'm afraid you haven't thought out your proposition carefully enough where I'm concerned."

"What do you mean?"

"If you were to tell them we're engaged, it could make things a lot worse for you. I've been in the news recently. Have you thought they might not approve of me?"

His brows furrowed. "If you're the woman I've chosen, they won't say anything no matter their personal feelings. I know that if my mother heard your whole story, she'd be thrilled. Besides, deep down she's had a fear I'd end up with some foreigner and as you're half Cretan, she'll be overjoyed."

"I *am* part foreigner," Lys murmured. "How would you explain our meeting?"

"That's simple. We met at the *castello* hotel in Italy while you were on vacation a while ago. It was love at first sight and we've been together ever since."

His words sank deep in her psyche. It might not have been love at first sight, but a powerful emotion had shaken her to the core when he'd walked in his office to find her there. That emotion continued to grow stronger until she knew he was the man she'd been waiting for all her adult life.

Lys looked away from him. "How will you explain it when we break up in six months and call off the engagement?"

"I don't know. Right now I'm trying to navigate through new waters because of what Nassos has done to us. This situation could have happened forty years from now, but it didn't. You and I are both vulnerable for a variety of reasons and we need to think this through carefully if we're going to do it right."

"I agree."

"Isn't it interesting to realize Nassos had no way of knowing that he'd done me a favor when he deeded me half the hotel. It has forced me to come home and try to make a difference for my family, something I should have done a long time ago."

Lys could feel his pain. "I'm sorry you have the worry of their health on your mind."

"I've been living with it for a while. Maybe I've been wrong and misread what I thought about mother. Just because she has aged a little doesn't mean she's ill."

"That's probably all it is."

"Cesare has accused me of leaping to conclusions. Still, if one of them is ill, I need to find that out. But they're so closed up, it'll take time to pry them open if they're keeping a secret from me. Nothing else is as important to me right now."

"I can relate," her voice trembled. "After Nassos hit his head, he pretended that everything was fine, but I could tell he wasn't himself and it gnawed at me. So I can understand how disturbed you are by your mother's plea that you move back here."

He flicked her an all-encompassing glance. "No matter what, it's my worry. The decision of our getting engaged is up to you. If I see one problem, it's how Danae would feel about it. If neither of you is comfortable with the idea, then we'll figure out another way to proceed."

After Lys's conversation at the villa with Danae earlier in the day, she had no clue how the other woman would react over such an unorthodox idea. But you couldn't compare Takis in the same breath with any other man. Even Danae had admitted as much.

"I—I don't know what Danae will say…" Her voice faltered.

"I realize you love and respect her, and you are uncertain with good reason. Even if Danae could see some value in it, she would probably tell you no. Six months of being engaged to me will prevent you from meeting a man you might want to marry. It will rob you of an important chunk of time out of your life."

"And yours!"

"Let's not worry about that. What matters most to me is to be back with my family where I'm able to make a contribution any way I can and still be a sounding board for you without anyone knowing."

Lys was so confused she couldn't think straight. He'd brought up some valid points that went straight to the heart of their individual dilemmas. But she needed to sort out her thoughts and would have to talk to Danae.

He sat back and turned on the engine. "I need to get home, so I'm going to drive you back to the hotel. I'm in no hurry for a decision. There's no deadline. I'll leave it up to you to contact me when you want to discuss hotel business."

Before long he pulled up in front of the hotel. Lys could tell he was anxious to leave. "We'll talk soon, Takis. Take care."

"Just a minute." He leaned across and kissed her briefly on the mouth. She couldn't believe what had just happened. "I needed that," he whispered before she opened the door and got out.

Her heart thudding, she rushed past Leon without acknowledging him. Her only desire was to get to her room where she could react to his kiss in private. After what he'd just done, the thought of a fake engagement to Takis had caused her heart to pound to a feverish pitch. She feared she was already running a temperature. When she could gather her wits, Lys would phone Danae. They needed to talk.

Takis drove to Tylissos, still savoring the taste of Lys, whose succulent mouth was a revelation. He'd never be the same again.

Before long he stopped by the children's hospital. After phoning his mother to find out if she needed him to do any errands for her, he discovered that Kori had taken Cassia to the doctor because of another asthma attack. It meant she'd been forced to leave her part-time work at the restaurant. Takis told his mother he'd look in on them.

He found his older sister holding his niece in her arms while she recovered after the medication they'd given her.

"Tak-Tak," his little niece cried when she saw him enter the room and held out her arms. Takis gathered her to him and gave her a gentle hug, kissing her neck.

"Do you feel better now?"

"*Nay.* Go home."

Takis looked at his sister, who had the same dark auburn hair as her daughter, the color of cassia cinnamon. "Did the doctor say she could leave?"

"Yes, but I have to wait until Deimos goes off shift to pick us up."

"But that won't be until nine thirty tonight. Tell you what. I'm going to slip out and buy an infant seat for my car. Then I'll drive you to work."

"You have a car?"

"I bought one this morning. I need transportation now that I'm back for good."

She stared hard at him. "You're really going to live here again?"

He nodded. "I never planned to be gone this long. Now that I'm home, I'm staying put." Just being here to help his sister let him know he'd done the right thing to come back to Greece for good.

Takis handed a protesting Cassia to her mother. "This won't take me long. When I get back, I'll run you by the restaurant and take her to the hotel with me." His mother tended Cassia when Kori had to go to work.

Her face looked tired but her light gray eyes lit up. "Are you sure?"

"There's nothing I'd love more." He leaned over to give them both a kiss on the cheek. "See you in a few minutes."

Takis hurried out of the hospital and drove to a local store, where he bought a rear-facing and two forward-facing car seats. That way he could take all his nieces and nephews to the park at once.

Within a half hour he was back and had fastened Cassia in her new seat. He would put in the other seats when he had the time. Kori sat next to him while he drove her to the Vrakas restaurant, where Deimos cooked traditional Cretan cuisine.

"Don't worry about anything. I'll take good care of her."

"I know that. She loves you. So do I." Her eyes filled with tears. "Thank you. I'm so glad you've come home." Her love meant everything to Takis.

After she hurried inside, he chatted with Cassia during the short ride to the old Manolis Hotel. He pulled around the back next to his father's truck. Lukios's car wasn't here, which meant he'd gone to his house a block away. Both his brother and sister lived nearby.

"Come on, sweetheart." He lifted her out of the seat and entered the private back door where his parents had lived in their own apartment since their marriage. "Mama? Look who I've got with me!" His mother came running from the kitchen into the living room. "She's breathing just fine now."

"Ah!" She pulled Cassia into her arms. "Come with me and I'll give you some grape juice." Grapes grew in profusion on this part of Crete.

"Tak-Tak!" his niece called to him, not wanting to be parted from him. He smiled because she couldn't say the *is* part yet. He grinned at his mother, who laughed.

"I'm right behind you, Cassia."

While his father was busy with hotel business, he had his mother to himself in the kitchen. She put a plate of his favorite homemade *dakos* on the table, a combination of rusk, feta cheese, olives and tomatoes. Cassia sat in the high chair drinking her juice while he devoured six of them without taking a breath and finished off the moussaka.

Afterward he held Cassia and read to her from a bundle of children's books he'd brought her on his last trip home. She had a favorite called *Am I Small?* He had to read it to her over and over again.

The little Greek girl in the story asked every animal she met if she was small. It had a surprise ending. Cassia couldn't wait for it. Neither could Takis, who was totally entertained by her responses.

At quarter to ten, Kori ran into the apartment and found her daughter asleep in his arms. She thanked him with a hug and hurried out to the car where Deimos was waiting for them.

Takis turned out lights and went to bed in the guest room he used whenever he came home for a visit. However, now that he was back for good, he needed to figure out where to live. Tomorrow he'd look around the neighborhood and find a house like his brother's and Kori's, close to the hotel.

Takis took a long time to get to sleep, knowing the nub of his restlessness had to do with a certain female who'd come to live in his heart. They weren't engaged yet, but the way he was feeling, he didn't know how he was going to keep his desire for her to himself much longer. Earlier in the car he'd kissed her, but it hadn't lasted long enough and he'd been forced to restrain himself.

The next morning, he installed the other two car seats before visiting a Realtor in the village. By late afternoon he'd finally been shown a small Cretan stone house he liked with a beautiful flowering almond tree. It had been up for sale close to a year and was two blocks away from the hotel. The place suited him with two bedrooms upstairs and a little terrace over the lower main rooms covered in vines.

Takis stood in the kitchen while they talked about the need to paint the interior and upgrade the plumbing. The house would do for him and not stand out. While he and the Realtor finished up the negotiations, his cell phone rang. One check of the caller ID caused his adrenaline to kick in. He swiped to accept the call.

"Lys?"

"I'm glad you answered." She sounded a little out of breath. "Can you talk?"

"In a few minutes I'll be free for the rest of the evening."

"I just flew back from Kasos." She'd been with Danae. "How soon can you meet me at my suite?" The fact that she wanted to see him right away might not be good news, but he refused to think that way.

"I have a better idea. I'll pick you up in front of

the hotel in a half hour. There's something I want to show you. We'll talk then."

"All right. I'll be ready."

He hung up and thanked the Realtor, who drove them back to his office. The older man handed him the keys to the house. Takis walked outside to his car with a sense of satisfaction that he was now a homeowner on Crete, the land of his ancestors.

En route to Heraklion, he stopped for some takeout of his favorite foods; rosemary-flavored fried snails, *Sfaki* pies and a Greek raki liqueur made from grapes. He liked the idea of sharing his first meal in his own home with Lys where they could be alone.

Before long he reached the hotel. Lys stood out from everyone when he pulled up in front. Her black blouse and dark gray skirt made the perfect foil for the tawny gold hair he was dying to run his hands through. He leaned across and opened the door for her.

"Hi!" Lys climbed in the front, bringing her flowery fragrance with her. "Umm. Something smells good," she remarked as he drove away and headed out of town.

"I'm hungry and thought we could eat after we reach our destination."

"Where are we going?"

"To Tylissos. I bought a house today and thought you might like to see it."

She made a strange sound in her throat. "Already?"

"My parents' apartment is small. They don't need another person underfoot while they tend my niece during the day. She naps on the bed I use while I'm here."

"How old is she?"

"Cassia is three. I'm crazy about her. The cute little thing has chronic asthma. Yesterday my sister had to take her to the hospital so the doctor could help her, but she's back home now."

"Oh, the poor darling."

"She handles it like there's nothing wrong. Now tell me about you. I take it you've had a talk with Danae."

"Yes."

The short one-syllable answer could mean anything. "Is it a good or bad sign that you can't look at me? Don't you know I'm fine with whatever you have to say?" At least that's what he was telling himself right this minute.

"After discussing everything with Danae, she surprised me so much I'm not sure what I am supposed to say."

He left that answer alone and drove into Tylissos and it wasn't long before he pulled up next to a house on the corner. "We've arrived."

While she got out, he reached for the bag of food on the backseat. After they walked to the front door, he put the key in the lock and opened it. "Welcome to my humble abode. I'm afraid we'll have to eat in the kitchen standing up."

Her chuckle reminded him not everyone had such a pleasant nature. So far there wasn't anything about her he didn't love. While she wandered around, he put their cartons of food on the counter next to the utensils.

After a minute, she came back and they started to eat. "Your house is charming, especially the terrace."

"Best seen at twilight." The house needed work from the main floor up.

"Takis—"

They both smiled in understanding. It felt right to be here with her like this. He'd never known such a moment of contentment and wanted to freeze it.

Once he'd poured the *raki* into plastic cups, he handed one to her. *"To our health,"* he said in Greek. They drank some before he asked her what Danae had said. She kept drinking. "Why are you so reticent to tell me?"

Her frown spoke volumes. "I wish I hadn't talked to her at all."

"Why?"

"Because she thinks an engagement could be a good idea for the reasons you suggested, but she says it doesn't go far enough."

"What does she mean?"

"Her blessing is contingent on us taking the engagement a step further, which makes this whole discussion ridiculous."

"How much further?"

She shook her head. "None of it matters."

"It does to me. Go on."

"I told Danae about everything you confided in me concerning your relationship with your family, especially your father. She was very sympathetic, but she's convinced they won't believe you're serious about living here for good unless we put a formal announcement of our engagement in the paper."

Elated with that response, he said, "I tend to agree with her."

Lys looked surprised. "That's not all," she murmured, not meeting his eyes.

"What's wrong?"

"She says we'll have to put a wedding date in the announcement, but the paper won't publish it if the date is longer than three months away. That's so soon!"

A strange sensation shot through Takis. If he believed in such things, he had the feeling Nassos had spoken through Danae. No one could sew up a deal like Nassos, covering all the bases. "What reason did she give?"

"I was raised in the Greek Orthodox church and so were you. She knows your parents are traditionalists. Because of the scandal that surrounded me after Nassos died, a promise of marriage to me in the writeup will show their friends and neighbors that you never believed the gossip about me.

"Danae said that in honoring me that way, they'll see you intend to be a good, loyal husband and they'll be happy you've come home for good. Every parent wants to see his or her child making plans to settle down and have a family. Anything less than a newspaper announcement with a wedding date won't carry the necessary weight."

The woman was brilliant. "Danae's right. Did she say anything else?"

After pacing the floor, she came to a halt. "Yes. After knowing your history, she says she likes you and approves of you for my husband. She knows Nassos would approve of you too."

That sounded exactly like something Nassos would have said in order to protect Lys. "I'm humbled by her opinion. She's a true Cretan. The more I think about it, the more I know she's right about everything she said. How do you feel about it?" The blood hammered in his ears while he waited for her answer.

"I—I didn't expect her to be so direct," she stammered.

"You still haven't answered my question. Does it upset you that I'm the first man Danae has ever approved of for you?"

Her knuckles turned white while her hands clenched the edge of the counter. "I'm not upset."

"Then why are you so tense?"

"We're not in love! We don't intend to actually get married—" Lys protested. "It would hurt your family too much to pretend something that won't happen. I told Danae as much, so we'll forget the whole idea of an engagement."

His eyes narrowed on her features. "I don't want to forget any of it. The idea of marrying you appeals to me more and more."

A quiet gasp escaped her lips. "Please be serious, Takis."

"I've never been more serious in my life. When I first suggested the idea of getting engaged, my main concern was to fit in with my family again and it seemed the perfect way to do it. But now I find that I want to be married, and Danae is right. Three months will be a perfect amount of time to grow close before we get married."

Color filled her cheeks. "We'd probably end up not being able to stand each other!"

Someone was on his side. Lys hadn't said no to the whole idea because she loved Danae and listened to her. "That's the whole point of an engagement, isn't it? To find out how we really feel? I know how I really feel at this moment."

In the next breath, he pulled her into his arms. After kissing her long and hard, he relinquished her mouth. "Do you think you could see yourself living in this house as my wife? I'd give you free reign to furnish it any way you like."

"Don't say any more," she cried softly and eased away from him. "You told me you want acceptance from your family. I can promise you that won't happen when they find out I'm the daughter of the man who gave you your first job in New York. I represent everything that took you away from them in the first place."

When he'd confided in her at his lowest ebb, she'd taken his pain to heart. Unfortunately, he'd done too good a job and needed to turn this around.

"Besides the fact that I left Crete of my own free will, keep in mind we didn't meet until a few weeks ago. When I tell them I've found the woman I want to marry, you have nothing to worry about."

CHAPTER SIX

THE WOMAN HE wanted to marry?

After the intensity of that kiss, Lys was dying to believe him. Deep in her heart she wanted marriage to Takis with every atom in her body, but she was too confused to think.

Astounded by the strength of her feelings, she said, "It's getting dark… I need to get back to the hotel."

Ignoring him, she put everything in the bag except the bottle of liqueur, which she left on the counter. They walked out of the house and Lys hurried to his car. As she put the bag in the backseat, Takis caught up with her and slid behind the wheel.

"On the way home I'll drive you past the Manolis Hotel. It looks like something Cassia would build with her blocks. Two for the bottom floor and one for the top."

Several turns brought them to the main street where the buildings sprang from the cement and had grown side by side. Because of his description, she picked it out immediately, painted in yellow with dark-brown-framed windows and matching tiles on the roof. A sign hung over the bottom right entrance.

He stopped in front, not pressing her to talk about

anything. During the last eleven years, she assumed nothing here had changed in all that time. She thought about the eighteen-year-old boy who'd wanted to help expand his father's hotel business. Instead, he'd ended up in New York thanks to Nassos and her father. Now he'd come full circle and was back for good.

"What are you thinking?"

She took a deep breath. "That you've accomplished miracles in your life."

His features took on a grim cast. "I'll take the one that hasn't happened yet."

She presumed he was talking about his relationship with his father. Her heart ached for what he was going through.

He started driving again and they headed for Heraklion. "Since you know where I'll be living and how I'm spending my time, I'll leave it up to you to decide when you want to get together to talk business."

Nassos couldn't have known his will would put them in such a difficult position. In Italy Takis had told Cesare he didn't want the hotel, let alone the complication of it being tied to Lys.

"Takis? Are you worried that if we don't get engaged, somehow word will reach your father that there's another reason you're tied to the hotel when we're seen together?"

"Anything's possible, but I'll deal with it by Skyping with you on the computer when you feel the need for a meeting."

"I still wouldn't do that in the office where Giorgos or one of the staff could walk in."

"Then we'll do it from your hotel room."

By the time he'd driven up in front of the hotel,

she was in torment. He got out and came around to open her door. "I'll be working on my house for the next week. If anything comes up, give me a call. *Kalinikta,* Lys."

"Good night," she whispered. "Thank you for the delicious food."

"You're welcome," he whispered against her lips before kissing her. Lys's attraction to him was overpowering. Obeying a blind need, she kissed him back again and again, relishing the slight rasp that sent tingles of desire through her body. After that, she found the strength to dash inside the hotel entrance to the elevators.

With pounding heart she reached her room, filled with unassuaged longings. After a minute when she had caught her breath, she called the front desk to find out if there were any messages for her. Thankful when she learned there was nothing pressing, she hung up and took a shower.

Lys had hoped to fall asleep watching TV, but she couldn't concentrate. Throughout the night she tossed and turned. Her fear that Takis's father would learn about Nassos's willed gift wouldn't leave her alone. Her mind relived what Danae had told her, that she approved of Takis and felt he'd make the right husband for her. Lys was so in love, she wanted him for her husband.

Takis hadn't asked for Nassos's gift. Who would have dreamed he would pass away this early in life? Nassos hadn't known the degree of fragility between Takis and his father, otherwise he wouldn't have put Takis in this situation. Nassos would have found another way to show his admiration.

When morning came, she felt like she hadn't slept at all and knew she had to see Takis again. He'd become her whole life! After eating breakfast in her room, she dressed in dark brown pleated pants with a matching-colored long-sleeved sweater.

Once she'd run a brush through her hair and had applied an apricot frost lipstick, she went down to the office to return phone calls and talk to some vendors. She texted Danae that she'd call her later in the day. Lys wasn't prepared to talk to her yet.

Around noon she told Giorgos she was leaving without giving him a reason and headed for the parking garage before he could detain her. Giorgos couldn't hide his frustration that she'd been avoiding him. Takis had planted a seed. Clearly it had taken root.

Once out on the road, she made several stops to buy souvlaki, fruit and soda. All the way to Takis's house she hoped she'd see his car parked outside. To her relief she did find the car there and parked behind it. Anxious to talk to him, she grabbed the sack of food and hurried to the front door. After knocking twice with no response, she tried the handle. To her surprise it opened.

"Takis?" she called out. "Are you here?" No answer. She crossed through to the kitchen and saw a couple of old wooden chairs and a card table. On the counter he'd left a coffee thermos. He must have gone somewhere. Maybe he'd gotten hungry and had walked to the hotel that was only a few blocks away.

She put the food on the table knowing he'd be back or he wouldn't have left the door unlocked. While she waited for him, she went up the small staircase to the second floor. Both tiny bedrooms were separated by a bathroom that needed work. And before she could prevent the thought from forming, she decided that one of the bedrooms would make a perfect nursery.

Each had a door that opened onto the terrace. You would need a railing if you brought children over here. In her mind's eye she could picture a lovely table with a colorful umbrella surrounded by chairs and pots of flowers.

Beyond the village the view looked out on the ancient Minoan site with its archaeological ruins, reminding her of the statue of King Minos on Takis's desk in Italy.

While she stood there near the edge, deep in thought, she saw a pickup truck turn the corner and pull up behind her car. All kinds of equipment filled the bed. Her pulse raced as she saw two men get out. The taller of the two, an Adonis dressed in jeans and a white T-shirt, looked up and waved to her.

"*Yassou*, Lys! I'll be in as soon as I unload the truck!"

"Let me help!"

Excited he'd come, she hurried downstairs and opened the front door. His brother—it couldn't be anyone else with those features—had red tinges in his dark blond hair. He brought in a ladder and some paint cans. Takis followed, carrying other paint equipment and drop cloths.

His eyes, that marvelous hazel green, played over her. "I'm glad you're here." His deep velvety voice wound its way through her body, igniting her senses. He put everything down in the living room. "Lukios?

I'd like you to meet Lys Theron. Lys? This is Lukios Manolis."

Takis had told her that Lukios hadn't been friendly the other day. Lys had hoped for his sake that his brother would warm up. It appeared they were getting along better now and that knowledge made her happy.

"You're the wonderful brother he's told me about. It's so nice to meet you. I've been anxious to meet Takis's family." She smiled and put out her hand.

The other man shook it. "How do you do," he said in a subdued voice. His eyes swerved back and forth at the two of them, trying to figure things out. She had no doubt he'd seen her in the news.

"I thought Takis might be hungry while he worked, so I brought lunch. It's in the kitchen. He has such a big appetite, I bought enough for half a dozen people. Please feel welcome to eat with us if you'd like."

He looked taken back. "Thank you. Have you known each other long?"

Without giving Takis a chance to answer, she said, "Quite a while. We met in Italy while I was on vacation. Those were your children in the photos I saw on his desk at work? Both yours and your sister, Kori's. They are adorable. Your parents must be crazy about their grandchildren."

"They are," he murmured.

"In case you didn't know yet, Takis asked me to marry him yesterday and brought me here to see where we're going to live."

Lukios blinked. "I had no idea."

"He surprised me too." She smiled at him. "Since he told me I could decorate it any way I want, I decided to start with a housewarming present by offering my services to help with the painting."

"How come *I'm* so lucky?" Takis interjected, as if they had no audience. His eyes gleamed.

She knew what her response had meant to him and heat swept through her body. By throwing herself into his suggestion for an engagement, she had no choice but to be a hundred percent committed and go all the way.

"This is such a cozy house, I'm anxious to see how we can bring it to life."

Takis moved closer. "All I brought with me today is the primer for the walls. After we've put it on, we'll go to the paint store and decide on the best color for the rooms."

Lys had really done it now! She'd taken him by complete surprise, but it hadn't thrown him. Nothing did. Takis was always several steps ahead no matter the situation. His responses since coming in the house had to have convinced his brother that their relationship was all but sealed.

"Come in the kitchen, Lukios. Let me serve you while you tell me about your family. What is your wife's name? I'm sure Takis told me, but I can't remember."

"It's Doris."

"That's it. I had a friend in school named Doris too! I understand your two children are older than Cassia."

He blinked, as if he were surprised she knew so much. "Paulos and Ava. They're four and five."

"What a blessing. I always wanted siblings, but

my mother died when I was little. My father never remarried, so it was just me."

"That must have been hard."

"Yes, but I had a father I adored."

While she served him on a paper plate, Takis helped himself and stayed in the background of the conversation. She took it that he didn't mind that she'd more or less taken over and was chatting away.

"Is Doris a stay-at-home mother?"

"No. She works with me at the hotel."

"How terrific for both of you." She handed him some tangerines.

He peeled one and ate the whole thing at once, reminding her of Takis's eating habits. "You think that's a good idea?"

Ah. He was coming to life. "If I loved my husband, I'd want to be with him as much as possible. She's a lucky woman." Poor Danae would have loved to work with Nassos like that…

Lukios darted Takis a glance, but she pretended not to notice. "Do you want a Pepsi? It's the only soda I could find."

"Thank you."

She turned to Takis. "What about you?"

"I'll drink one later. Why don't you sit and I'll wait on you?"

Their gazes met. "I'd love it."

After she finished eating, Lukios got up from his chair and put his empty plate on the table. "Thank you for the lunch. It was very nice to meet you, Kyria Theron."

"I'm thrilled I got to be introduced to you at last."

"It was my pleasure. Now I'm afraid I have to get *Baba*'s truck back to the hotel. Work is waiting."

Takis put down his soda. "I'll see you out, Lukios." He leaned over and kissed her cheek. "Don't go away," he whispered. "I'll be right back."

He walked out of the kitchen, leaving her trembling. She was a fool to be this happy when it wasn't a real engagement, but she couldn't help it. There was no one like Takis.

A few minutes later Takis came back in the kitchen and found Lys cleaning up. "You're a sight I never expected to see in here after leaving you in front of the hotel last evening."

She looked up at him. "I'm sure you didn't. But I couldn't sleep during the night because of worry over your secret getting out. I remembered back to that day in your office in Italy. When you saw the deed, the shock on your face stunned me."

He stared at her. *It wasn't just the deed, Lys Theron.*

"Later, after your return to Heraklion, we talked about what Nassos had done by giving you co-ownership of the hotel. That's when I realized why you worried it could be damaging to your relationship with your father if he knew."

"I shouldn't have said anything to you about that."

"I'm glad you did. I—I want you to be able to preserve that precious bond with your father," she stammered from emotion. "I loved mine so much."

He leaned against the doorjamb with his strong arms folded. "So you've decided to be the sacrificial lamb."

"I don't think of my decision that way and hope you don't either."

"Be honest. You'd do anything for Nassos and Danae."

She threw her head back. "I guess I would."

And now she was willing to help preserve his father's love by entering into an engagement of convenience. If Lys knew the depth of Takis's feelings for her, would she admit she couldn't live without him either and toss the pretense away? He cocked his head. "You realize my brother swallowed your act so completely, he gave me a hug for luck before getting in the truck."

Luck? Her heart leaped. "He isn't the hugging type?" she teased.

"After what I told you about him, you know he isn't. The last time it happened, my girlfriend had just died."

"Oh, Takis—how awful that must have been. Is it still too hard to talk about?"

"No. I remember there was pain, but I don't feel it anymore."

"What happened to her?"

"I was working at the hotel in Heraklion the day Gaia took a bus trip with her friends. It was the high school's year-end retreat. They went to the Samaria Gorge."

"I've heard of it but have never been there," Lys murmured.

"It's a place in the White Mountains where it's possible to hike down along the gorge floor past streams, wild goats, deserted settlements and steep cliffs. The plan was for them to reach the village of Agia Roumeli and take a boat back to the bus for the return trip to Tylissos.

"The tragedy occurred when a tourist drifted across the road and hit the bus, causing it to roll over and down the side of the gorge. There were thirty students on the bus. Three of them died. One of them was Gaia."

She buried her face in her hands. "I'm so sorry."

"Her death prompted me to accept Nassos's offer to leave for the States and go to work for the man whom I now know was your father. After her funeral, the move to New York helped me get over it."

Lys nodded and wiped her eyes. "Had you been close for a long time?"

"From the age of fifteen."

"How terrible." She shook her head. "Does her family still live here?"

"Yes."

"Do you visit them?"

"Only once, the first time I came back to be with my parents. They didn't need to see me as a reminder. One look at the framed picture of her on the end table was enough to prevent me from dropping in on them again."

"What about the latest woman in your life now? Will news of your engagement hurt her?"

He strolled toward her. "I've had several short-lived relationships, none of them earthshaking, as the Americans have a way of saying. For the last three years I've been consumed with earning a living and haven't allowed any serious entanglements to get in the way."

Her purple gaze fused with his. "And there you

were, minding your own business at the *castello* when destiny dropped in to change your life yet again."

Obeying a strong impulse, he put his hands on her shoulders. Takis could feel her heartbeat through her soft cashmere sweater.

"I watched you walk out of the church at the funeral and thought you were the most beautiful woman I'd ever seen in my life. If I hadn't had to catch a plane for Athens right then, I would have gone to the cemetery in order to meet you and learn your name."

"I had no idea," she murmured.

"You'll never know my wonder when I entered my office and discovered the daughter of Kristos Theron standing in front of Nassos's photograph with tears in her eyes. That was my first shock, followed by another one in the form of the deed that bound you and me together in an almost mystical way. Today I received a third shock to find you here waiting for me."

"I shouldn't have come in, but you left the door unlocked. I hope you didn't mind."

"Mind?" His hands slid to her upper arms and squeezed them. "To convince Lukios is half the battle. You did something for me in front of my brother I couldn't have done for myself. After my years abroad, he's in shock I've found my soul mate in Crete, when he didn't think it was possible."

Takis hadn't thought it could ever happen either.

"Had you mentioned me to him before today?"

"Never."

"What about your sister?"

"She's always on my side. Just so you know, when I walked him out to the truck, he brought up nothing about you. If he recognized you from the newspaper, he didn't mention it. That should tell you a lot."

Her eyes glistened with moisture. "Then I'm glad."

"Glad enough to come with me and get your engagement ring? When I introduce you to my parents, I want it on your finger."

He could see her throat working. "I thought you were going to paint today."

"I'm getting things ready, but will have to wait until tomorrow morning. The water and electricity won't be turned on until then. Since we've eaten, let's drive into Heraklion."

Without her saying anything, she walked with him to his car. After they headed for the city she turned to him. "You mustn't buy me anything that stands out."

"I've already bought it."

A slight gasp escaped her throat.

He smiled. "The ring *does* have unique significance, but don't worry. It's not a ten-carat blue-white diamond from Tiffany's worth three million dollars."

"When did you get it?"

"The day I suggested the engagement. Once I visualize an idea, I act on it. I'm afraid it's the way I'm made."

"You're one amazing man."

"Amazing as in crazy, insane, exasperating? What?"

"All three and more."

He chuckled. "I don't want to hear the rest. Admit you like me a little."

She looked away.

"Why don't you pull out your phone and we'll compose an engagement announcement for the newspaper. The sooner it gets in, the better."

"Danae will want to check it over first." She pressed the note app. He watched her get started. "I think it should begin with something like Kyria Danae Rodino is pleased to announce the engagement of Lys Theron to Takis Manolis, son of Nikanor and—" She paused and turned to him. "What's your mother's name?"

"Hestia."

"Goddess of the hearth. What a lovely name." She typed it in and finished with, "Son of Nikanor and Hestia Manolis of Tylissos, Crete."

His hands gripped the steering wheel a little tighter. "You need to add Lys Theron, daughter of Kristos and Anna Theron."

A small cry escaped. "I didn't know you knew my mother's name."

"Someone at the hotel told me after I started working there. As for the rest of the announcement, we can figure out the June date after you talk to Danae. Then end it with saying that the wedding will take place in the Greek Orthodox church in Heraklion."

"Which one were your parents married in?"

"Agios Titos. That's where we'll take our vows."

He was living for it.

CHAPTER SEVEN

TAKIS DROVE TO a specialty shop called Basil. It was located next to the Archaeological Museum of Heraklion that sold Minoan replicas the tourists could afford. He parked the car and walked her inside.

"I love this place! When I first came to Crete, Danae brought me in here every time we took visiting friends of theirs through the museum. We'd always buy a few trinkets."

He guided her past clusters of people to the counter where he asked one of the clerks to get the owner. "Basil is holding a ring for me." Takis couldn't wait to slide it on her finger. He wanted her in his arms and his life forever.

"A moment, please."

"Look at this, Takis!" Lys walked over to a fresco hanging on the wall representing a Minoan prince. He stood in his horse-drawn chariot holding the reins. A warrior on the road handed him a drink from a golden cup. "I've seen this in the museum. It's a splendid replica. Can't you see it hanging over your fireplace?"

"Don't you mean ours?"

"Yes. This is all still new to me."

He hugged her around the waist. Her interest intrigued him. "Why do you like it so much?"

"The plain with those trees where he's riding reminds me of the view from your terrace. Danae once took me out to the Tylissos archaeological site not far from your village. You have Cretan blood in your veins and live in a Cretan historical spot that's over seven thousand years old."

He smiled. "You were born in New York, which dates back ten thousand years."

"Except that I'm half-Cretan and I don't have part Native American blood. My mother was American through and through. Somehow it doesn't seem the same."

A chuckle escaped his lips, enjoying their conversation more than she would ever know. *"Touché."* He gave her a brief kiss on the mouth, unable to resist tasting her whenever he could.

"Kyrie Manolis!" He turned around to see the owner come up to him.

"*Kalispera*, Basil."

The older man stared in wonder at Lys like most men did, unable to help it. "You've brought your beautiful fiancée. Now I understand your choice of stone. Come with me."

Takis guided her over to another counter. Basil went around behind. On the glass he set a small gold box with a *B* on it and took off the lid. Takis heard her sharp intake of breath when the owner handed the ring to Lys.

"This is incredible." Her voice shook.

Takis had hoped for that reaction.

"It's a replica of old Minoan jewelry," Basil explained.

"I know. I've seen one like it in the museum."

"Look closely. The three-quarter-inch band is intricately linked by twelve layers of tiny gold ropes, some braided, some mesh. The middle one represents the snake of the snake goddess, known for being gracious, sophisticated and intelligent.

"This ring would be identical to the one you saw in the museum, but your fiancé wanted a cut glass purple stone instead of the red garnet in the center. Put it on and we'll see if it fits."

After she slid it on to her ring finger, her eyes flew to Takis. He'd never seen them glow before. "This is too much. Thank you." She kissed him on the side of his jaw.

Basil laughed. "If the ring was authentic, he would be paying over five million euros at auction. But the beauty of shopping with Basil is that it didn't cost that much."

"It looks like the real thing."

"My artisans are highly qualified. Does it mean you are pleased?"

"How could I not be?" she told him.

Takis kissed her, uncaring that they had an audience. Color suffused her cheeks.

"Wear it in joy, *despinis.*"

Takis pocketed the box. "Before we leave, I'll buy the fresco on the wall over there." He pulled out some bills and left them on the counter.

"Put your money away. I have more of those in the back room. This will be my early wedding present for you. You two are so much in love, I think you must get married soon. One of my clerks will wrap it."

After Basil walked away, Lys looked up at Takis. "Will your family believe you didn't spend a lot of money on this?"

"They'll *know* I didn't when I tell Kori it came from Basil's. She shops here every so often because it isn't expensive. If anything, she'll tell me a snake ring isn't at all romantic. She'll pity you for getting engaged to a man whose mind is steeped in Cretan history."

"Then she'll be surprised when I tell her my Cretan father immersed me in the culture too."

As Takis marveled over his feelings for her, Basil hurried over to them with the wrapped fresco. "Here you are."

Takis thanked him and they all shook hands. Then he walked her out to the parking lot and put it in the backseat.

"I think we need to celebrate our engagement. Where would you like to go before we drive back to the house?"

"I need to phone Danae before we do anything else. Do you mind?"

"Why would I? We're not in any hurry."

He listened while she made the call. After a short conversation, she hung up. "She'd like us to fly to the villa for dinner. How do you feel about that?"

"It's perfect. We can go over the final draft of our announcement with her."

"She'll alert the pilot that we're on our way."

"Good." Full of adrenaline, he drove them to the hotel.

"You can park in my spot. I'll show you."

Leon had seen them together enough to wave him on through. Takis helped her out of the car and locked it. After putting his arm around her shoulders, they walked to the bank of elevators. The feel of her body brushing against his side lit him on fire.

When they passed Giorgos in the main hallway, the other man said, "Lys—you've a dozen messages on your desk."

"Any emergencies?"

"No."

"Then I'll get to them later. Thanks."

Before long they climbed in the helicopter and headed for the island. Lys kept examining the ring. All of a sudden she flashed him a glance. "You were right when you said this would have unique significance."

His brows lifted. "You think Danae will approve?"

"She'll probably tell you she can see why Nassos found you such an amazing young man."

Within a half hour they'd arrived at the fabulous villa, a place that reflected the personality of the famous hotelier. Danae had a feast prepared with some of Lys's favorite fish dishes. As they walked through to the dining room the housekeeper was pouring them snifters of Metaxa, a smooth Greek brandy Takis loved.

Danae stood at the head of the table. "Before we eat, I'd like to make a toast to the two of you. May this engagement smooth the path with your family and take away some of the sadness in Lys's heart."

Amen.

"Wait! I have a surprise." She went over to the

sideboard and brought Lys a gift wrapped in plain paper.

"What's this?"

"I found it in the bottom drawer of Nassos's dresser while I was cleaning out the penthouse. When I opened it, I remembered. After Kristos's funeral, Nassos brought this back to give you one day for a special occasion. It was a small painting of Kasos Island that he once gave your mom." Danae smiled at Lys. "I think this is the perfect occasion now that you're wearing Takis's ring."

Takis could tell Lys's hands were trembling as she undid the paper. "Oh, Danae." Tears spilled down her cheeks. "This is so wonderful. I'll always cherish it."

Danae had just given Takis another reason to like the woman Nassos had married.

Lys quickly wrapped it up and put it on the empty chair next to her. "Thank you, Danae."

"Consider that it came from Nassos, who was born here too."

"I'm so touched he kept it all this time."

"He loved you." Her gaze flicked to Takis, after glancing at Lys's hand. "In my opinion you couldn't have chosen a more perfect ring for Lys, who was fascinated with Minoan culture from the time she first came to live with us."

"I could tell that," Takis said after taking another drink of brandy. "She was so taken with one of the frescoes at Basil's, I bought it for her."

Danae's glance fell on Lys. "I bet it was the prince in the chariot."

"Danae—"

The older woman kept right on talking. "Lys

wasn't so different from little girls everywhere, but she was never one to buy posters of the latest rock stars to hang on her bedroom wall. A Cretan warrior was her idea of perfection."

Two hours later they flew back to the hotel. To her relief, Danae hadn't expounded anymore on the fresco. She could have told Takis that Lys had taken one look at the prince years ago when they'd seen the real fresco in the museum, and had fallen in love on sight. The fact that he bore a strong resemblance to Takis was something she knew Danae would tease her about quite mercilessly the next time they were alone.

Only now did Lys remember Takis saying he'd tell his parents it was love at first sight after meeting her. But there was one difference.

Lys *had* fallen in love with him. For real.

She knew it to the very core of her being. From here on out she had to be careful he didn't find out how she really felt about him.

This engagement was on slippery ground because he was acting like a man in love who wanted to marry her. During dinner he'd shown excitement over the June 4 wedding date Danae had suggested. Lys would be the greatest fool alive if she started to believe that she might be able to have what she desired most in the secret recess of her heart.

At ten thirty they got out of the helicopter and headed for the elevator. Takis held the door so it wouldn't close. "Why don't I come by for you in the morning? We'll stop to eat somewhere on the way to my house. Your car will be safe parked outside tonight."

"I'm not worried about that." He noticed her clutching the gift in her arm. "What time were you thinking?"

"Since you're running the hotel, you need to take care of those phone calls Giorgos told you about. So why don't you call me when you're ready and I'll come for you."

"All right."

He allowed the doors to close and they rode to the third floor, where he walked her to her room. Lys was so afraid that he might want to come in and she would let him, she was totally thrown when he told her he needed to get going. After giving her a quick kiss on the cheek, he turned away and strode down the hall to the elevator.

She felt totally bereft. *You idiot, Lys!*

After entering her suite, she put the gift on the coffee table and left to go downstairs. Lys was too wound up to go to bed yet. When she entered the office she found Giorgos still at the front desk talking with Chloe, who helped run the counter. The second he saw Lys, he followed to her office. That habit of his was getting on her nerves.

She sat down in her swivel chair. "I'm surprised you're still here. Where's Magda?" She and another staff member served as assistant managers on alternating nights.

"I got a phone call that she's sick, so I stayed."

Lys was afraid she knew why. "That was good of you, but I'm here now so you can leave."

"Sometimes I don't feel like going back to an empty flat."

How well she knew that. "Tell me the truth. Do you wish you were home in Athens?"

"No," he answered almost angrily and moved closer to her desk.

"I hope you're telling me the truth. Now that I've taken ownership of the hotel, it's important to me that everyone is happy."

His eyes widened. "This hotel is *your* inheritance?"

"That's right."

She could see her revelation had completely thrown him.

"But you're so young—" *Whoa.* "I thought—"

"You thought Kyrie Rodino would have willed it to his ex-wife," she interjected. "That would have been a natural assumption. What else is troubling you?"

He hunched his shoulders. "Who's the mystery man?"

Lys decided it was time to set him straight and douse his hopes there could be anything between the two of them. She held out her left hand. He eyed it as if in disbelief.

"You can be the first on the staff to learn Takis Manolis asked me to marry him." What she would give if she could believe he truly did love her…

Giorgos's head jerked up. "How soon?"

"Aren't you going to congratulate me?"

"Of course," he muttered, then darted her a speculative glance. "I take it he knows you're the owner."

What was Giorgos thinking? Instead of answering him she said, "Thank you for going the extra mile to cover tonight, but you look tired. After putting in a full day's work already, you need to go home. I've let work pile up here and need to dig in. Good night, Giorgos."

Instead of indulging him further, Lys started scrolling through her messages until he left her office. After a half hour, she had cleared most of her work and after telling Chloe to call her if there was a problem, she went back to her suite to get some sleep. Not that it was possible with this incredible ring on her finger.

Takis phoned her Wednesday morning while she was drinking coffee in her room. "*Kalimera*, Lys."

Her heart thumped just to hear his deep voice. "How are you?"

"I'll be better when I see you later. At breakfast I told my parents I'd like them to meet you. They want us to come over to the hotel at two when business is slow."

Startled, she slid off the bed. "You mean today?"

"It surprised me too. My brother must have said favorable things about you. More than ever I'm convinced Danae was right about the engagement. My parents truly are anxious to see me settled." But they didn't know why Takis had asked her to marry him. "I'm leaving it up to you when you want me to come for you."

She glanced at her watch. "Where are you right now?"

"In my car on the way to the house. The water and electricity are supposed to have been turned on. I want to get over there and check things out."

"Then you have enough on your mind. I'm going to get ready and I'll take a taxi to your house."

"Lys—"

"No argument. I'll bring sandwiches and salad from the hotel kitchen." She rang off before he could try to reason with her.

Without wasting time, she called the front desk to let them know she was leaving the hotel. After hanging up, she showered, then washed and blow-dried her hair.

She didn't have to worry over what to wear and reached for her simple black gown she could dress up or down. It had sleeves to the elbow and a round neck. She wore tiny gold earrings and sensible black high heels.

When she was ready, she called the kitchen and gave them instructions. One of the waiters was to meet her at the hotel utility van in the garage with the food. Next she phoned the hotel florist. After telling them what she wanted, she asked that one of the employees bring the vase of flowers to the van and set it on the floor. After retrieving the flowers, she drove out to Tylissos.

It wasn't until she pulled up behind the two cars parked at the side of Takis's house that she realized there'd been a car behind her. She'd noticed it on the highway after leaving Heraklion, but it passed her by as she turned off the engine.

But seeing a hard-muscled Takis walk toward her drove every thought out of her mind and she trembled with excitement. Dressed in a casual cream-colored polo shirt and tan trousers, he was so striking, her breath caught.

"I've brought flowers," she said after he came

around to open the door. "I hope your mother will like them."

"It's a perfect gift."

"A woman can't resist flowers."

"I'll remember that." The way he eyed her made her pulse leap.

"They're on the floor in back."

He retrieved them while she brought the food and followed him into the house. But halfway through the living room she stopped because her eyes had caught sight of the fresco he'd rested on the mantel of the fireplace. The colors stood out, emphasizing the drabness of the room that needed a complete makeover.

He could see where she was looking. "I've been studying the fresco and think we need to pick one of the background colors that would look good on the walls."

She darted him a glance. "Do you have a favorite?"

"Yes, but I'd be interested to hear what you like."

"Well, I've loved this fresco for a long time and already know the one I'd use."

"In that case let's take it to the store and match the paint we want. I'll put these things in the kitchen and we'll eat later."

As she watched him disappear, Lys imagined that deep down he was anxious about introducing her to his parents and needed to keep busy. That was fine with her because her angst about being favorably received was shooting through the roof.

They went out to his car with the fresco and drove into the village. The thirtyish female clerk inside the store had them sit at a table. She couldn't seem to take her eyes off Takis even though she could see Lys wore an engagement ring.

After admiring the artwork, the woman set it on a chair before bringing in a dozen color strips for them to look through, but she addressed her remarks to Takis.

Though Lys knew Takis wouldn't be marrying her if Nassos hadn't given him half the hotel, she planned to help him redo his house. She adored him and wanted to help make it as beautiful as possible. This was where he planned to live until he died, so it had to be right.

His gaze fused with hers. "Let's pick our favorite color and see how close we come."

Being with Takis like this made every moment an exhilarating one. Among the various colors, her eye went to the pastel green shades until she found the perfect match in the fresco.

She would have reached for it, but Takis's hand was quicker. He lifted a certain strip off the table and glanced at her. "I knew exactly what I was looking for. Now it's your turn. Choose the one you prefer."

Lys couldn't believe it. "You're holding it. Soft sage is my choice too."

"You're teasing me."

"No."

The smile left his eyes. "I'm beginning to think we're dealing with something here beyond our control."

A little shiver raced through her. "I admit this is amazing."

"That was so easy, I'm afraid to ask what other colors you're thinking of for the rest of the house."

"How about these for the walls in the kitchen?" She picked up the Minoan red and canary yellow strips.

He looked astonished. "You've been reading my mind."

"The borders on the fresco influenced me."

Takis kissed her neck before getting up to talk to the clerk. He couldn't have done anything to please Lys more just then. She made a silent choice of pale blue for one of the bedrooms upstairs, but didn't say anything. Perhaps they'd make that decision later.

"I'll be happy to help you with anything else you need." The woman smiled into Takis's eyes and couldn't have been more obvious. Lys was glad to leave.

Again she thought she saw the same car she'd noticed earlier, but it disappeared around the next corner. After what she'd been through while the police were investigating the reason for Nassos's death, she was probably being paranoid.

CHAPTER EIGHT

SOON THEY DROVE back to the house with the paint. While Lys carried the bags into the living room, Takis brought in the fresco and set it back on the mantel. "Shall we eat? I'm starving."

Lys chuckled. "Aren't you always?"

They walked into the kitchen, where he'd put the wrapped vase of flowers in the sink earlier. She set the food on the table and they sat down to eat.

Halfway through a second sandwich he smiled at her. "We'll set up our computers to the hotel's mainframe. Giorgos won't be the wiser when we use this house to discuss business while we transform this place. Have you told him we're engaged?"

"Last night I showed him my ring."

Takis's eyes glittered with amusement. "It's the best thing that could have happened to him. He took one look at you and fell hard. I feel sorry for him because there's only one of you."

"Speaking of problems, maybe I should go alone to the paint store next time."

"Why?"

She laughed. "You do that so well."

"What?" He stared at her.

"Pretend you don't know that woman can't wait to see you again."

His mouth curved sensuously. "You noticed."

"Even blind, I would have been able to tell."

"Now you know what I put up with whenever you're with me. We both know Giorgos is already a lost cause. As for Basil, I've done business with him from time to time and have never known him to give anything away. But he was so besotted with my fiancée and her violet eyes, he lost his head."

She scoffed. "I thought he did it because he cares for you. More and more I'm convinced that's the way Nassos felt about you upon a first meeting, not to mention the manager, who was so impressed, he introduced you to Nassos twelve years ago."

He sucked in his breath. "Why do I feel I'm being set up for something?"

"Why don't you believe you're a wonderful son worth loving?"

They finished eating in silence before he started to clean up. "Thank you for bringing lunch." She felt his eyes on her. "We should leave for my parents' in a few minutes. If you need to freshen up, the water is on now. Don't worry. I cleaned the downstairs bathroom. This house has stood vacant for a long time."

"I thought as much."

She got up and discovered it next to the area for a washer and dryer down the little hall off the kitchen. There was a lot of work to be done, but Lys found she couldn't wait to help.

When she came out, he stood in the kitchen waiting for her. The realization of what they were about to do frightened her. "Takis? What if they can't accept me?"

"We've been over this before—they will adore you. Are you saying you want to back out?" His voice sounded too quiet.

"No, but I'm nervous."

His hands reached out and he drew her against him. "Perhaps now would be the best time to put the seal on our relationship." When his compelling mouth closed over hers, she'd been halfway out of breath in anticipation. The shocking hunger in his kiss robbed her of the rest and she clung to him in a wine-dark rapture.

There was no thought of holding back on her part. Her desire for him was so great, she had no idea how long they stood there clinging to each other, trying without success to satisfy wants and needs that had been kept in check until now.

"I've wanted you from the moment I saw you," he murmured, kissing every inch of her face and throat. "The desire we feel for each other is real. Don't tell me it isn't."

"I won't," she whispered, incapable of saying anything else.

Again he swept her away in another kiss that went on and on. His mouth was doing miraculous things to her. She couldn't bear the thought of this moment ending, but Takis had more control than she did and finally lifted his mouth from hers. His breathing had grown shallow too. "Much as I'm enjoying this, we're going to be late if we don't leave now."

She couldn't think, let alone talk, and was embarrassed for him to witness the state of her intoxication.

Needing to do something concrete, she pulled out of his arms and reached for the vase of flowers. After grabbing her purse, she headed for the living room.

He opened the front door and helped her out to his car. She hid her flushed face from him as much as she could for the short drive to the Manolis hotel. To her surprise he drove down an alley behind the buildings, parked by his parents' truck and came around to help her out.

"Are you ready?" he murmured.

She clung to the vase. What a question when her legs were wobbling! His kiss had changed her concept of what went on between a man and a woman now that she was so deeply in love with this fantastic man.

Of course she'd been kissed before and had enjoyed it, but she'd never gone to bed with the men she'd dated. During Nassos's talks with her about men and marriage, she'd learned that he expected her to wait until her wedding night. Maybe if she'd fallen in love with one of those men, she might not have been able to resist. But it hadn't happened and now she knew why after Takis had aroused her passion.

Suddenly the back door opened. Lys recognized his mother, who'd passed on her reddish dark-blond hair to Lukios. She cried Takis's name and reached out to hug him. But it was his same startling hazel eyes that fastened on Lys.

"Mama? This is my fiancée, Lys Theron. She's the light of my life." The words came out smooth as silk and sounded so truthful, it shook her to the foundations.

Lys looked for signs that she was upset or disappointed, but instead she let go of Takis to hug her, flowers and all. They were both the same medium height. "This is a great day. Welcome to the family."

The unexpected warmth brought tears to Lys's eyes. "Thank you, Hestia. Takis has talked about his angel *mama* so much, I feel I know you already." In that moment Lys shared an unexpected glance with Takis. From the intense look in his eyes, she'd said the right thing to his mother.

"She's brought you flowers. Shall we go inside and unwrap them?"

Hestia wiped her eyes. "Come on. Your father is in the living room waiting for you."

Nikanor Manolis. The man for whom this charade was all about.

Takis grasped her hand and took her through the kitchen to the living room.

Lys saw immediately that he took after his father in height and features. The older man with salt-and-pepper hair stood in front of the fireplace dressed in dark pants and a white shirt.

"*Baba?* I would like you to meet the woman I'm going to marry." Hearing those words almost gave her a heart attack. "Lys Theron, this is my father, Nikanor."

She shook his hand. "How do you do, Kyrie Manolis. It's an honor."

He gave her a speculative glance. "Lukios tells us you two met in Italy."

"Yes. I was on a short vacation."

"You love my son?"

After everything Takis had told her about his father, she guessed she wasn't surprised he would ask a blunt question like that. But Lys could hardly think for the blood pounding in her ears. "From the first moment I met him, I couldn't help it." She didn't dare look at Takis right then. To her surprise his father kissed her on both cheeks, putting his stamp of approval on the news.

"Look what she brought us!" Hestia came in the room carrying the vase of pink roses and lavender daisies, breaking the tension. "They are so beautiful!" She set them on the coffee table.

"I'm glad you like them. Those colors are perfect together."

"I think so too. Sit down. I've made tea."

Takis led her over to the couch and squeezed her hand, revealing his emotions. In a minute his mother came back with a tray of tea and *kourambiedes* to serve everyone.

"What are your plans?" his father asked.

"We've set the date for June fourth, provided that's a convenient time for you and Mama. It's not a holiday. The engagement announcement is ready to be given to the newspaper."

His father looked at Lys. His brows lifted the same way Takis's sometimes did. "Tell us about your family."

She'd been ready for that question. "My mother was an American, born on Long Island, who died when I was little. My father was working in New York, but he was from Kasos Island here in Crete. In his will he specified that he wanted his best friend to be my guardian should he die before I turned eighteen. That best friend was Nassos Rodino, who died very recently.

"He and his wife, Danae, raised me from the age

of seventeen after my father was killed in a plane accident. She's the only person I have left and still lives on Kasos. Contrary to what the media reported after his death, we love each other as mother and daughter and will always mourn Nassos's passing. He was like a father to me."

"We're sorry for your loss."

"Thank you. Danae met Takis for the first time the other night. When she learned he planned to live here for good and work at his family's hotel, she gave us her blessing. To be truthful, she never liked the men I dated. I'm pretty sure it's because they weren't from Crete."

Takis shot her a look of surprise.

"All along both she and Nassos insisted that one day I marry a Cretan who honors his family," Lys added on a burst of inspiration. It was only the truth.

The older man's gray eyes lit up before he turned to Takis. "That's what you want to do, my son? Work here at the hotel now that you're home for good?"

Lys's eyes closed tightly, waiting for the answer that would change Takis's world.

"It's what I want, *Baba*."

"Then so be it."

She knew those words had to be the sweetest Takis had ever heard.

"Hestia? They want to be married June fourth."

"I heard."

"In the Agios Titos church," Takis supplied.

"Ah. That's where we were married." Her face beamed. "How soon will it go in the paper?"

"We'll submit it tomorrow. It will probably show up the next day. We plan to see the priest next week."

His father nodded in what seemed like total satisfaction.

"When I'm not busy working for you, *Baba*, I'll be busy fixing up the old Andropolis house. You know the one that has stood vacant for close to a year. Besides paint, it needs new flooring and plumbing."

"You're good at those jobs."

A compliment from his father must be doing wonders for him, but Lys didn't dare look at him and instead munched on one of his mother's fantastic walnut cookies.

"We will have everyone for dinner Friday night to celebrate. Our whole family together."

If his mother had a serious illness, Lys couldn't tell. Nothing seemed wrong with Takis's father either. All she knew was that this get-together had to have left their son overjoyed.

Hestia moved over by Lys to examine the ring. "It doesn't surprise me he gave you the snake ring. My Takis was always immersed in our Minoan culture."

"I'm fascinated by it too. When he picked it up at Basil's, he also bought a replica of a fresco from the museum I admired. We're going to hang it over the fireplace and use those colors to decorate. You'll have to come and see it."

"I'll bring Kori and Doris with me."

"I'm looking forward to meeting them and the children."

"Everyone will be excited to get to know you. They love Takis and won't be able to wait to see his house."

"Takis will have to put up a railing on the upstairs terrace first so they won't fall."

"I'll take care of it before they come!" he spoke up,

as if they were an old married couple. She shouldn't have been surprised that he was listening.

Lys was getting in deeper and deeper. She loved him so much, but if he didn't love her just as intensely… While he kissed his father, Lys stood up, taking one more cookie from the plate. "These are so good, Hestia, I want the recipe."

"I'll give it to you."

In a moment Takis reached her side. "Mama, Lys and I need to leave so you two can get back to work. I'll be over for breakfast tomorrow and we'll talk hotel business."

She walked them out of the room and through the kitchen to the back of the hotel where the cars were parked. "Where do you live, Lys?"

"Since I started working in the accounts department of the Rodino Hotel four years ago, I've lived in a room there, but I've gone home to the island on weekends."

"Will you continue to work there when you're married?"

"I—I don't know." She hesitated. "Takis and I still have many things to talk about."

"Amen to that." He'd come up behind them. "We'll see you on Friday, Mama." He kissed her before helping Lys get in his car.

Hestia stood there smiling and waved as they drove down the alley to the next street.

"Your parents are wonderful," Lys murmured when they'd turned the corner.

He didn't respond. She turned her head toward him, waiting for him to say something. But he just kept driving until they arrived back at his house. Worried that something was wrong, she got out of the car and hurried toward the front door. In seconds, he'd unlocked it so they could go inside.

When it closed behind them, she felt his hands on her shoulders. He whirled her around. She couldn't understand the white ring outlining his mouth.

"Takis—" Her heart was thudding. "What did I do to make you this upset?"

"I'm not upset." He gave her a little shake. "Don't you know what you did back there was so miraculous, I'm afraid I'm dreaming."

Relief filled her system. "What do you mean?"

"You really don't get it, do you? You've charmed my parents so completely, you've made it possible for me to get in their good graces again."

She shook her head. "I didn't do anything. Can't you see how much they adore you?"

"That's your doing. You make me look good."

"What a ridiculous thing to say!"

"Ridiculous or not, you have my undying gratitude." His hands ran up and down her arms, bringing her against his hard male body. "Damn—we don't have a couch, let alone a bed, so I can't kiss you the way I want."

"It's probably a good thing there's no furniture."

"You don't really mean that." His deep grating voice sent waves of desire through her body. "I could eat you alive standing right here and know you feel the same way."

She took a deep breath. "I admit I've been strongly attracted to you from the beginning, Takis."

His gaze poured over her features relentlessly. "Have you ever been to bed with a man?"

"Would it matter to you if I had?"

"Yes," he bit out.

"Why? You've had intimate relations with other women."

A pained look crossed over his face. "I'm jealous of any man who has ever made love to you. I'd rather be the only one who knew that kind of joy."

"That works for women too."

"Are you admitting you're jealous of my past relationships?"

"Not jealous. But I do want to know about the one you had with your girlfriend in high school."

"We didn't sleep together, Lys. I was trying to honor her until we could be married."

Tears clogged her throat. "She was a very lucky woman to be loved by you. If the accident hadn't happened, you would never have left Crete and would probably be married with children by now."

"But destiny had something else in mind for me, and I'm in the battle of my life to regain what I lost."

She struggled to understand. "Tell me exactly what it is you think you lost. Your parents are thrilled you've come home and your father wants you working with him again."

His chest rose and fell visibly. "Because you're going to be at my side."

"You honestly believe it took *me* to make this happen today? If that's true, then I feel sorry for you."

Lines marred his striking features. "How else to explain why they want to tell the whole family Friday night?"

"How about accepting the fact that you're their son and they love you? Do you need more than that?

For so long you've been telling yourself that you're an unworthy son, you couldn't see what was in their eyes today. Why don't you just sit down with your father and tell him all the feelings in your heart?"

"My friend Cesare has asked me the same question."

"Then listen to him! Your fear has brought you to a standstill. For a man as outstanding and remarkable as you are, I find it inconceivable you're in such terrible pain. A simple conversation with your father could change the way you look at life." She lowered her head. "In a way, you remind me of Nassos."

Takis's head reared back. "What do you mean?"

"Remember the letter he wrote to me? Just think what might have happened if he'd gone to Danae and had admitted he'd been wrong to divorce her and wanted her back. But his fear that he might not be forgiven wouldn't let him do that and he died unexpectedly, never knowing how much she loved him and wanted to get back with him."

His brows furrowed. "How does that have anything to do with me?"

"It has everything to do with you. You're afraid to talk to your father for fear you'll hear him say he can never forgive you for leaving Crete. But the point is, he might say something else quite different to you.

"Just think, Takis. After my talk with Danae, I realized she would have told Nassos she wanted him back, but he never gave her a chance. It's so sad that it's too late for them. Please don't let it be too late for you and your father."

She kissed his firm jaw. "Now I'm going to leave and get back to the hotel. I've let work go too long.

When you're ready to start applying the primer, I'll come and help."

As she started out the door he said, "You still haven't told me if you've been to bed with a man."

She paused and turned to him. "Shall we make a deal? When you decide to have that talk with your father, then I'll tell you all the secret details of my intimate life with men."

"Was it true what you said about your boyfriends not being from Crete?"

"Yes."

"How many were there?"

"I only had three serious ones. All of them were born in other parts of Greece, the sons of wealthy parents who came to Crete for vacations and stayed at the hotel. I knew Nassos and Danae weren't impressed with any of them."

Her words brought a smile of satisfaction to his arresting features.

"By the way, I love your parents."

The next morning Takis made arrangements for a Skype conference call with his partners. He'd set up his computer in the kitchen while the guys sat at the computer in Cesare's office at the *castello*.

"You're looking good, amico." This from Cesare.

"It's great seeing you guys again."

"Before we hear your news, we have some of our own," Vincenzo exclaimed.

"Good or bad?"

"Definitely good. My cousin Dimi is going to marry Filippa in June at her church in Florence. They made the decision last evening, but want to keep it low-key with only family and close friends. You're invited, of course, if you can make it. We'll text you the time and address of the church."

Takis's mind leaped ahead. He would take Lys with him so his friends could meet her. Cesare had seen her, but it wasn't the same thing as talking to her. "I'm very happy for him. Dimi deserves it."

"Being that Filippa is Gemma's best friend, my wife is beyond thrilled. But now we want to know what's going on with you."

"Quite a lot actually. The sale of my hotels in New York has gone through. Furthermore I've bought myself a house two blocks from my parents' hotel in Tylissos and now have internet."

"You sound good."

"I am. Two days ago Lys Theron and I got officially engaged. Our announcement went in the newspaper today. I'm emailing you a copy of it as we speak."

After total silence, Cesare let out an ear-piercing whistle. "You're actually getting married?"

"We decided it was the best way to keep news about Nassos's will a secret. By implying that Lys and I are in a romantic relationship ending in marriage, no one will know or suspect I'm co-owner of the Rodino Hotel. She has informed the staff that she's the new owner."

Vincenzo leaned forward. "So what will you do? Get divorced after the six months' stipulation concerning hotel ownership has passed?"

"There'll be no divorce."

"Is she on board with all this?"

Takis had been waiting for Vincenzo's astute question, which meant his friend had been thinking hard about the things Takis hadn't explained. "I intend our marriage to last forever."

Cesare cocked his head. "The Takis I know wouldn't publicly announce his engagement to be married unless he wanted it more than anything else in this world."

"In the beginning I suggested the engagement in order to protect the relationship with my father. But I've fallen in love and yes, a life with her is what I want more than anything else in this world."

After a silence, "I take it you didn't have that conversation with him after all."

First Cesare, then Lys, now Cesare again. "I'm handling all I can for the moment. Any problems I need to know about business on your end?"

"Sofia, your assistant, might be getting married soon and will have to move back to Geneva," Vincenzo interjected. "That means we'll be needing to find a new person to replace her. Got anyone in mind?"

"Let me talk to her first. In the meantime I'll send Dimi a text to congratulate him."

"He'll like that."

"I know you guys are busy so I'll let you go."

"What's the hurry?"

"I'm waiting for a man to come and help me install a railing for the upstairs terrace on my house. You can't believe what a disaster this place is."

"Then we won't keep you. Ciao, Takis."

"Ciao, guys. It's always good to talk to you."

He ended the session and got back to work, purposely keeping their conference short. He knew they were worried about him and the rushed engagement. But he didn't want to let them delve into his psyche too deeply until Lys admitted that she was crazy in love with him too.

Once the wrought iron railing had been installed, he swept the stone tiles. Before long a truck from the local furniture store delivered a full-size swing with a canopy he'd ordered online.

The workers carried it upstairs to the terrace. They also brought up a round glass-topped table set in wrought iron with an umbrella and six matching chairs. There was also a matching side table he put next to the swing. Until the interior of the house was done, the terrace would be his hideaway with Lys. In the evening, the neighbors wouldn't be able to see them entwined.

After the men left, he phoned Lys. "How soon can the owner of the hotel come to my house this evening? I would pick you up, but I want to finish getting the primer paint on the walls by tonight. There's a surprise waiting."

"That sounds exciting. I'll be there as soon as I can with dinner." Click.

She did that a lot, cut him off so he wouldn't argue, but he found he liked everything she did. He was in love. The kind that went soul deep. One day soon he would get her to admit she couldn't live without him either.

CHAPTER NINE

AS LYS PULLED the van behind Takis's car at seven, she saw the surprise he'd mentioned. An attractive wrought iron railing with a motif of grapes and leaves had been installed on the terrace. He got things done so fast it was scary.

When she went inside, she was astounded to see Takis had put the primer on everywhere. It looked like a new house already!

She heard him call to her. "Come on up and bring the food!"

Lys needed no urging to dash upstairs. "Oh, Takis—this is fabulous!" she cried when she walked out on the terrace. It was even better than what she had imagined earlier.

He relieved her of the bags and put them on the table. She ran over to the swing and sat in the middle. "I love it!"

Takis followed her down so he was half lying on top of her. "So do I." He devoured her mouth until she was breathless. "I've been waiting for this since the moment I bought the house."

With his rock-hard legs tangled around hers and their bodies trying to merge, Lys had never known such euphoria. He was male perfection and she couldn't get enough of him. They lost track of time in their need to communicate.

"What if someone sees us?" she asked after coming up for breath.

"They won't. It's dark now, so I can do what I want." He bit her lobe gently.

"*Takis*—not here—"

"Are you afraid for us to make love?" He teased, kissing her throat.

"I thought that was what we were doing."

His deep laugh rumbled through her. "You say you had three boyfriends?"

She hid her face in his neck. "I did, but—"

"But it wasn't like this?"

Lys trembled. "We should eat. The food will be cold."

"Not until you tell me the truth. You've never been to bed with a man. Admit it."

"You're right. I haven't."

He kissed her with such tenderness, she couldn't believe it. "You have no idea how that changes my whole world."

"Why?"

"Nassos did the perfect job of protecting you so you could wear white to your wedding. Until we're married, I promise to honor his wishes for you."

She couldn't wait to lie in bed with him all night while they loved each other into oblivion. But what if he didn't love her the same way?

He kissed her lips once more. "You're so quiet. What's wrong?"

"Nothing," she muttered. Lys should never have admitted the truth.

"I think my fiancée is hungry."

"I think it's the other way around."

He gave her another deep kiss before standing up. "Come on." He reached for her hands. "Let's sit at our new table to eat."

After he'd set everything up he said, "I had a conference call with my partners this morning and there's news. We've been invited to Dimi Gagliardi's wedding in June. I don't know the exact date yet. He's Vincenzo's only cousin and one of my favorite people.

"He's marrying the best friend of Vincenzo's wife, Gemma, Filippa. We'll be flying to Florence for the ceremony."

"That sounds exciting."

He darted her a searching glance. "Now we have more important things to talk about. Next Tuesday evening the priest would like to meet us at the church."

Would he talk to the priest if he didn't love her? If he didn't want to marry her? She had to believe he meant what he said, but it was hard. "I think I'd better go. When I left the office, I still had some work to do."

He wiped his mouth. "In that case I'll follow you back to Heraklion and help you."

"I thought you didn't want to be seen."

"That was before our wedding announcement went in the newspaper. No one will think anything except that I'm so crazy about you, I can't stay away from you. For personal reasons, I want to make sure you get home safely. You're the most important person in my life."

No, she wasn't! Takis's father took priority, which was the reason they were in this situation now. Lys got up from the table and helped clean it off before going inside and down the stairs. Only a few minutes later, she had left the house and climbed into the van.

"Drive safely." He leaned in to kiss her hungrily. His touch caused her to melt before she turned on the engine and headed for Heraklion. Takis drove right behind her. At the hotel she parked the van and Takis parked in the empty space next to hers that Nassos had once used.

With his arm around her shoulders they took the elevator to the main floor and walked to her office. Along the way he kept her so close, anyone seeing them would assume they were lovers. By now the staff already knew.

Magda smiled her greeting before they disappeared down the hall to Lys's office. Takis walked her inside and pulled her into his arms. "I've got to have this before we do anything else."

She saw the blaze of desire in his eyes before he covered her mouth with his own, giving her a kiss that couldn't disguise his need. The slightest contact with him set her on fire and she found herself responding, helpless to do otherwise.

"We need a swing in here too," he whispered, kissing her eyes, nose, virtually every feature until he captured her mouth once more. "I'll arrange to have one sent from the store."

"*Takis—*" Lys finally found the strength to ease away from him. "I thought you wanted to help me work."

"I lied. Now that we're engaged, I don't want to be apart from you. I want you with me day and night."

"Please don't say that."

He caught her face in his hands. "Why? Because you know you want the same thing?"

"This is all happening so fast!"

His eyes gleamed like lasers. "That's not true. I saw you at the funeral and was determined to meet you the next time I came to Crete no matter what I had to do. Can you deny you felt something for me in my office in Italy?" he demanded before devouring her again.

Something in his tone convinced her he wasn't lying about his feelings. They'd both felt the chemistry between them when she'd flown to Milan. But a strong physical attraction didn't mean he loved her the way she loved him. Once they were married and he'd been reconciled with his father in his own mind, how would he feel then?

But for Lys, she'd never be able to love another man again. There was no one who came close to Takis. If their marriage didn't work out, she'd be like Danae and live a single life. With the money from her father, she could buy a place on Kasos near Danae. They could travel together, work on philanthropic projects together. But at this point the thought of Takis not being in her life was impossible to imagine.

"Lys?"

Startled, she tore her lips from Takis and turned her head to see Magda in the doorway.

"Sorry to intrude, but we have a problem."

"What is it? You can speak in front of my fiancé. Let me introduce you to Takis Manolis."

"It's very nice to meet you, Kyrie Manolis. Congratulations on your engagement."

"Thank you, Magda. I'm afraid you'll be seeing me around here a lot. I have a hard time staying away from Lys."

The other woman smiled before looking at Lys. "The finance minister Elias Simon from Athens has just checked in and was led to believe he could have the penthouse suite for the rest of the week."

Lys shook her head. "I can't imagine how that happened since we've never let guests sleep there. When Kyrie Rodino was alive, he used it for VIP meetings, nothing else. Tell the minister we'll put him in the Persephone suite."

"Will you tell him?" Her eyes pleaded with Lys, who understood her nervousness. Kyrie Simon had a forbidding presence.

"I'll take care of it."

"Thank you."

After she hurried away, Lys turned to Takis. "I'll be right back."

"I'll come with you."

The minute the two of them walked out to the front desk, the finance minister took one look and burst out, "Takis—"

"Elias—" The men shook hands.

"What are you doing here instead of New York? On business again?"

"I've moved back to Crete for good and got engaged." Takis grabbed Lys around the waist. "I'd like you to meet my gorgeous fiancée, Lys Theron, the former ward of Nassos Rodino. Now that he has passed away, she owns the hotel."

The other man's dark eyes fastened on her in male admiration and they shook hands.

"I envy you, Takis. If I were thirty years younger..."

"I'm a very lucky man."

"That certainly goes without saying," he said, smiling at her.

"Kyrie Simon? I'm sorry that there was a misunderstanding about the penthouse. It's not a guest room, but we'd love you to stay in the Persephone suite."

"No problem."

"Magda will check you in. Now if you will excuse me, I have some work to attend to back in my office."

"Of course. That gives me time to chat with Takis. You realize you're going to marry one of the most important men in the country. Has he shown you the hospital he built and funds in Tylissos? It provides such invaluable free medical care for the patients. There's another one being built in Athens as we speak. He's a remarkable man."

What?

"I'll tell you later," Takis said in an aside and kissed her cheek.

She went down the hall and sat down at her desk, but she couldn't concentrate on a thing. He'd built a hospital here? Another one was going up in Athens? How long had that been going on?

While she was alone, she phoned Danae, who was still awake. After catching her up on the latest news, she asked the older woman what she knew about a hospital in Tylissos that had been built and was free to the patrons.

"Only that it's a children's hospital for those parents who can't afford big medical expenses. Stella told me about it last year and wished the government would build one here in Heraklion."

Lys was stunned. "The government has nothing to do with it. I just found out tonight that Takis is the one who had it built and pays for everything."

A long silence ensued. "*Your* Takis?"

If only he were… She gripped the phone tighter. "Tonight Kyrie Simon, the minister of finance from Athens, checked into the hotel. He saw Takis. They appear to know each other well and it slipped out during their conversation."

"Your fiancé is a dark horse in many ways. What a lovely thing to find out about the man you're going to marry. If Nassos were still alive, he'd be bursting with pride."

"The man who should be overjoyed is his father, but I'm sure he doesn't know anything about all the great things his son has accomplished. It kills me that Takis lives with this terrible pain. I love him so much, Danae." They spoke a little longer before she hung up.

After another minute, Takis came back in her office. Her gaze fused with his. "I just got off the phone with Danae. Why haven't you told me about these hospitals?"

He stood in front of her with his legs slightly apart, so handsome, so masculine, she couldn't look away. "I would have gotten around to it."

"You told me your niece had to go to the hospital for an asthma attack. You had it built for *her*."

"For all children with medical problems whose parents struggle to make a decent living."

She shook her head. "But no one knows you were the one."

"I want it that way."

"Even your parents?"

"Especially them."

"But these hospitals aren't hotels. Your mother and father would be so thrilled and proud if they knew what you've done. And you're building another one?"

"I'd rather remain anonymous."

"Takis—they deserve to know more about your life!"

"They didn't deserve to be abandoned by their son."

Lys got to her feet, upset by his comment. "What can I say to convince you that they love you and never thought any such thing?"

His brows furrowed. "You can't. I'm sorry Elias let that information slip."

"I'm not. Don't you know how proud I am of you?"

"Thank you for that. But I know I can trust you not to say anything when we go to the family party tomorrow evening."

They weren't getting anywhere with this conversation. She took a deep breath. "Thank you for helping Magda out of a difficult situation. You've won her devotion." Takis had a rare potent male charm that had made mincemeat of Lys.

"It was my pleasure. Elias can be very intimidating. That's why he's in his particular position. Between us I think he makes the president of the country nervous."

Lys chuckled. "By tomorrow morning Magda will tell everyone that my fiancé is on first-name terms with a top-level Greek government official. You'll have elevated me to new heights in our staff's opinion."

His eyes narrowed on her mouth, sending darts of awareness through her. "Didn't you know it's the other way around? Elias insists on being invited to our wedding. He has a worse case on you than Basil. I didn't think that was possible."

She chuckled despite her out-of-control desire for him. "Don't be silly."

"Do you still have work to do, or shall I walk you to your hotel room?"

Lys wanted to be alone with him. She was bursting with feelings she was dying to share. "I'd like that." She grabbed her purse and left the room, turning out the light. They nodded to Magda and walked down the hall to the elevator. By the time they reached her suite, her heart was jumping all over the place.

Lys unlocked the door. "Come in."

"I'm afraid I can't."

She swung around in surprise. "Do you have to go right now?"

"Yes." Lines darkened his face.

"Why? Is something wrong at home?"

"No. The only problem is the way I feel about you. If I come in now, I'll make you my wife tonight and forget the ceremony. As it is, if I thought you'd say yes, I'd ask the priest to marry us in three weeks instead of three months' time."

Those words brought her close to a faint.

"Think about it and give me your answer tomorrow when I come to get you." In the next breath, he walked down the hall to the elevator, leaving her totally bereft.

She didn't want him to go. "Takis?"

He turned.

"Please don't leave yet."

"You'd better think hard about what you're asking. If I cross over your threshold, I won't leave till morning. Is that what you want after everything Nassos did to protect you from moments like this?"

For once in her life she was going to be honest and throw caution aside. "Yes."

"Why?"

"Because—because I need you and don't want to be alone tonight."

He moved closer, causing her heart to leap. "I need you too, but that's not a good enough reason to break all the rules."

"We've already broken several."

"But not the most important one."

"In my office earlier you said you wanted to be with me day and night."

"I do, once we're married."

His moral strength astonished her. "Nassos is no longer alive."

"Which leaves me to watch out for you. Weren't you the one who told me he probably gave me half ownership of the hotel to help keep you from making a mistake?"

"He didn't mean the kind of mistake we're talking about right now and you know it!" Her cheeks had grown warm. "You're going to make me say it, aren't you."

"Say what?" he murmured. "That you love me? That you can't live without me?"

The blood pounded in her ears. "You're a man who didn't plan to marry right away. I wonder what you'd do if I said those words to you."

His eyes gleamed an intense green. "Why don't we find out?"

He was toying with her, not helping her out. If he truly loved her, he wouldn't be so cruel. "To hear them would scare the living daylights out of you."

Takis cocked his head. "If you don't say them, we'll never know."

You're a fool, Lys. He was the most aggravating, incredible, beautiful man alive. "So you're really going to leave."

"It's your call. I dare you to sleep tonight, *agape mou*."

Two words that meant beloved. *Was* she his beloved?

"*Kalinikta*, Lys."

"Good night!" she snapped at him in English.

She heard his chuckle clear down the hall until he disappeared. He was driving her crazy.

Takis, feeling pure joy, headed for the garage to get his car.

After saying good-night to Elias, he'd waited another couple of minutes outside Lys's office until she'd hung up from her phone call. He hadn't meant to eavesdrop, but it had been clear she'd been talking to Danae. That's when he'd heard the truth come from her own lips.

I love him so much.

Tomorrow evening they'd be with family and the

answers to all questions would come straight from their hearts. There'd be no deception, no regrets.

Early Friday morning Lys's phone rang. Excited because she knew who it was, she reached for her cell on the bedside table. "Takis?"

"No, Lys. It's Danae."

She sat up in bed. "What's wrong? You sound worried."

"If you haven't seen a newspaper or turned on television, then don't."

Alarmed by her words, Lys slid off the bed and got to her feet. "Tell me."

"The paparazzi have taken pictures of you and Takis together. One of the write-ups reads: 'Lys Theron, heiress to the Rodino fortune, sets her sights on marrying billionaire New York hotelier Takis Manolis. Is there nothing this gold digger won't do for money?'"

Lys's thoughts reeled. Though she'd been used to this kind of coverage after Nassos's death, she hadn't imagined that it would continue. How had the press discovered their relationship? Could it have been that car she had seen following her a couple of times. It must have been! But what concerned her was the impact it would have on Takis's parents.

"Thank you for telling me. I love you and am indebted to you. Now I've got to phone Takis and warn him in case he hasn't seen the paper yet." She hung up and rang him. *Pick up. Please pick up.*

To her chagrin the call went to his voice messaging. She left the message for him to call her immediately. Without hesitation, Lys took a quick shower and got dressed in a black sweater and skirt. Once she was ready, she hurried to the garage for her car.

Maybe he was painting and had turned off his phone. All she knew was that she had to find him. If the paparazzi were still following her, she didn't care. What mattered was tonight's get-together with Takis's family.

They would have seen or read this new barrage of sensationalizing information linking the two of them. Her desire to protect him from any pain had her pressing hard on the accelerator all the way to Tylissos.

Lys spotted his car at the house before she pulled up behind it. After getting out she ran to the door and knocked. When there was no answer, she tried opening it, but he'd locked it.

"Takis?" she cried out and knocked harder.

Maybe he was over at his parents' hotel. If Danae had seen the news, there was no doubt he'd seen it too. Possibly his brother might have come over to the house to talk to him and they were out somewhere. Or maybe he'd driven Takis over to the hotel.

She simply didn't know, but she intended to find out and dashed to her car. It didn't take long to reach the hotel. She parked near the front entrance and hurried inside. An attractive dark-haired woman manned the front desk.

"May I help you?"

Lys took a deep breath. "My name is Lys Theron. I need to speak to Takis Manolis. Is he here by any chance?"

"You're Lys!"

"Yes."

"I'm Doris, Lukios's wife."

"Oh—I'm so happy to meet you."

"We're all very excited about tonight."

If Takis's sister-in-law had seen the news this morning, she was hiding her reaction to it well.

"So am I, but I need to find Takis. Do you have any idea where he might be? I went over to the house and his car is there, but he didn't answer the door."

"Let me check with Hestia. She'll know." Lys waited while she made a phone call. When Doris hung up she said, "After breakfast he went to the village with his father and hasn't come back yet. If you'll wait just a minute, she's going to phone him and find out when he'll be back."

Lys held back her groan. "Thank you." The poor darling was probably trying to defend her reputation the best way he could, but it didn't look good.

Doris's phone rang and she picked up. Their conversation didn't last long before she clicked off. "They may be gone for a while. Hestia would like you to come back to their apartment. She wants to talk to you. Their door is at the end of the left hall."

"I appreciate your help, Doris."

Shaking inside as well as out, she headed for the apartment where Takis had been born and grew up. Hestia met her at the door with a hug and asked her to come into the living room. Wonderful smells from the kitchen filled the room.

"I'm sorry to come by now when I know you're preparing for this evening, but I need to see Takis as soon as possible."

His mother eyed her with concern. "Something's wrong. What is it?"

She sat on the couch, folding her arms against her waist. "I wish I could tell you."

"If it's about the latest tabloid gossip, I pay no attention to it."

Lys let out a slight gasp. "Then you know what was in the paper this morning."

"Takis mentioned it at breakfast before he and his father left the hotel together."

"I went over to his house, but he's not there. I—I'm so afraid."

"What is it?" she asked in such a kind voice, Lys had to fight the tears that threatened. "He asked me to marry him, but I fear I'm not the right kind of woman for him. That's what I need to tell him so we can call off this engagement party."

"My son has never done anything he didn't want to do. He wants you for his wife."

"But gossip follows me wherever I go and it will rub off on him. I'd do anything to protect him and your family."

"Tell me something truthfully. Do you love him?"

Her question brought the tears rolling down her cheeks. "Desperately, but he loves you and your husband with all his heart. He's been so traumatized all these years for hurting you by leaving Crete, the last thing he needs now is to marry a woman who will bring more hurt to you."

His mother shook her head. "What hurt are you talking about?"

Lys wiped her eyes. "He carries this terrible guilt that he abandoned you when he left for New York. He can't forgive himself for it."

"Oh, my dear—" She came over to the couch and

put her arm around Lys. "By the time Takis was a year old, his father and I knew he was different than the other two. He insisted on exploring his world and needed more to make him happy. When his girlfriend died, we knew he had to find his life and were thrilled that Kyrie Rodino gave him that opportunity."

"You were?" Lys cried. "Honestly?"

"Of course. We're so proud of what he's done and accomplished."

Lys couldn't comprehend it. "Then he's the last person to know. He's been afraid that he's let you down and can never win your approval. And he's worried that there's—" She stopped herself before she said something she shouldn't.

"That there's what?" Hestia prodded.

"If I tell you, I'm afraid he'll never forgive me."

"Of course he will."

"H-He's afraid either you or your husband are seriously ill," her voice faltered. "He thinks that's why you asked him to come home for good."

His mother lifted her hands in the air. "We're in the best health we can be at our age."

"Oh, thank heaven!" Lys half sobbed.

"Where would he get an idea like that?"

"Because you asked him to come home. He thought there had to be a vital reason."

"There was. There is. We love him, and we miss him. We figured he'd made enough money on his hotels that he could come back and do something else amazing here in Crete."

"He has done that!" Lys jumped to her feet. "You know the children's hospital where your granddaughter had to go the other day?"

Hestia nodded.

"Takis had that hospital built and funds it completely." At this point tears spilled down his mother's cheeks. "He's building another one in Athens."

"Our dear son," she whispered.

"Please, Kyria Manolis. Let him know how you feel. Tell him you're both healthy. Reassure him you wanted him to find his way in the world. He needs to know how much you love him so he'll be whole. But he doesn't need a woman with my reputation ruining his life. Forgive me, but I don't dare marry him." She removed her ring and handed it to Hestia. "Please give this to him. Now I have to go."

Hestia called to her, but she dashed out of the apartment to her car. The tears continued to gush as she drove toward Heraklion. Her phone rang, but she didn't answer it. When she reached the hotel, she parked the car and rushed to her suite.

Once inside, she ran sobbing to her bedroom and buried her face in the pillow. When her phone rang again, she refused to answer it in case it was Takis. If he knew what she'd done by confiding in his mother, then he might never want to speak to her again.

Takis was surprised when his mother met him and his father at the back door of the apartment. "I'm so glad you're home! Your fiancée has been trying to reach you."

"I know. I tried to call her back, but she hasn't answered yet."

"I'm not sure she's going to."

He frowned and followed her inside to the kitchen. "What do you mean?"

She glanced at his father. “Both of you need to sit down so we can talk.”

Takis lounged against the counter, unable to sit until he knew what was going on.

“Lys came by the hotel earlier looking for you.”

Takis groaned aloud. “We went into the village to pick up the bedroom furniture you ordered and set it up at the house. I wanted it to be a surprise for her.”

His mother nodded. “While you were busy, we had a very informative talk about many things including the children’s hospitals you’ve been building. I’ll tell you everything, but first I want you to know you’re the luckiest man on earth to have found a woman who loves you so much.”

“She admitted that to you?” Takis was stunned.

“You’d be shocked what she told me.” In the next breath she related their whole conversation, leaving nothing out. After she’d finished, his father spoke first.

He stared at Takis through eyes that glistened with tears. “Your mother and I have loved you since the day you were born. We were so afraid for you after Gaia’s death, we rejoiced when Kyrie Nassos opened a new door for you. We didn’t want to say or do anything to discourage you from leaving, and we’ve never regretted that decision. You have no idea how proud we are of you.”

Takis couldn’t believe what he was hearing. Cesare had been right about everything. As for Lys…

“We’re not ready for the grave yet, son. We expect to enjoy years of life with you and the wonderful woman who loves you enough to have confided in your mother.”

Takis was so overcome with emotion, he could only hug them for a long time. After clearing his throat, he said, “Since Lys was so honest, I have something important to tell you too. You may not love me so much when you hear what I’ve done. It’s about the reason we’re engaged. Nassos left a will.”

Once his whole confession was out, silence filled the room. His father walked over and clapped him on the shoulder.

“I only have one thing to say. The fact that Kyrie Nassos thought so much of you he would give you half his hotel tells me and your mother that you’re the finest, most honorable Manolis we’ve ever known. I think all that’s left to say now is that you go find your fiancée and thank her for making this family closer than ever.”

His mother smiled. “I already love her.” She reached in her apron pocket and pulled out the engagement ring. Takis was aghast Lys had taken it off. “Give it back to her with our love.”

Takis’s heart was running away with him. He looked at his father. “Will you drive me home so I can get my car? I need to go after her before she decides to do something crazy like leave the country.”

“Where would she go?”

“To a friend of her mother’s in New York. If that’s her plan, I’ve got to stop her.”

Takis broke all speed records driving into Heraklion. It was a miracle he wasn’t pulled over. To his relief, her car was still in its space when he parked his Acura. But she could have called for a limo. There wasn’t a moment to lose.

He hurried to her suite and knocked on the door. When she didn't answer, he phoned her. Still no response. Without a second to lose, he raced to the front office. Magda was on duty.

"Have you seen Lys this afternoon?"

"No."

"She hasn't left the hotel?"

"Not that I know of. Let me check with the manager." She came right back. "No one has heard from her."

"Then I need a card key to her room. I'm worried about her. We're due at our engagement party."

Magda seemed hesitant.

"Tell you what. Will you come with me and let me in?"

"Yes." She grabbed a card key. Then she turned to the other woman manning the desk and said she'd be right back. Together they hurried to the third floor.

Magda knocked on Lys's door and called out to her. After no response, she used the card key to let them inside.

"Lys?" Takis called her name. "It's Takis. Are you ill?"

"What are you doing inside my suite?" sounded a familiar voice in an unfamiliar tone. He could rule out sickness. Her voice sounded strong.

Relief flooded his system that she hadn't gone anywhere yet. He thanked Magda. "I'll take care of this now. I promise you're not in any trouble."

"I'll have to take your word for that."

After she left, he started down the hall. "I'm coming in the bedroom, so if you're not decent, you'd better hide under the covers."

"I'm dressed if that's what you mean."

He moved inside. She looked adorable sitting on the side of her bed in a pink robe and bare feet, her face splotchy from crying.

Her purple eyes stared accusingly at him. "How did you get in here?"

"I'm part owner of the hotel, remember?" He sat down on a side chair.

"Nobody knows that."

"Magda let me in."

"Of course she did once you used your charm on her. She should be fired!"

"On the contrary, she passed the most important test for me by functioning in a crisis."

"What crisis?"

"I couldn't find you anywhere. After the talk with my mother, I feared you might be in here too ill to respond. In my opinion we should make Magda general manager if Giorgos ever leaves."

Lys lowered her head. "Then your mother told you everything."

Takis loved this woman with every atom of his body. "Yes."

She got to her feet. "The headline in the paper has probably ruined everything you've tried to do where your father is concerned. For all I know it already has."

"You couldn't be more wrong."

Lys paced the floor, then turned to him. "Why didn't you answer your phone this morning?"

"I was out shopping for our bedroom furniture with my father and turned it off."

Lys blinked. "You went with your father to do that?"

"Yes. It's tradition for the parents. He insisted and we had a lot of fun."

"Then it means he didn't see the paper this morning."

"True, but *I* did, and I told my parents about it at breakfast."

He heard her take a quick breath. "Did your mother tell you I've broken our engagement?"

"Yes." He reached in his pocket and pulled out the ring. "Here's the proof. It would have been nice if you'd told me first."

"I did try, but you weren't anywhere around."

"We've got all the time in the world now."

"You don't need an explanation. We both know we can't go on with this lie any longer. It's not fair to your parents who love you."

"What lie is that?"

"The only reason two people should get married is because they love each other. Your parents have to know the real reason we got engaged. But since you don't want them to know about the will, I can't go on with this deception."

"You don't have to. They know about it."

He could see her swallowing hard. "When did they find out?"

"I told them this afternoon."

She sank down on the end of the bed. "I don't understand."

Takis got to his feet. "I finally had the talk with them you urged me to have. You were right about everything and I was wrong. When I explained about the will, they told me they were thrilled Nassos thought enough of me to give me such a gift."

"Oh, Takis—" she cried, sounding overjoyed. "Then there are no more shadows? You're happy at last?"

"No. I'm still waiting for you to tell me if you love me. The other night you wanted me to stay with you. An admission of love would have brought me running to you."

She looked away from him. "You're being very unkind, Takis. After talking to your mother, you *know* I do."

"You do *what*?"

"Love you."

"When did you know?"

"In your office in Italy. But none of it matters because a love like mine needs to be reciprocated, which it isn't, so I wish you'd leave now."

"I can't do that because I love you more than life."

A gasp escaped her lips. She turned to him. "I don't believe you," she whispered.

"Do you honestly think I would have asked you to marry me if you hadn't turned my world inside out? I knew at the funeral you were the woman for me. The moment was surreal to watch my destiny walk past me. The feeling I had for you transcended the physical. How can you doubt it?"

"Because I'm afraid to believe it."

He reached for her left hand and slid the ring back on her finger. Then he cupped her beautiful face in his hands. "I can understand that fear. You lost your parents and Nassos. But you're never going to lose me. We're going to get married and raise a family."

She wrapped her arms around his neck. The love-light in her eyes blinded him. "I love you so much I don't think I can contain it."

"I don't want you to try." Driven by desire, he picked up his bride-to-be and carried her over to the bed, following her down on the mattress. "If you had any idea how long I've been waiting to love you like this. Give me your mouth, my love."

Her passionate response was a revelation to Takis, but they'd no sooner started kissing each other than her cell rang, followed by a loud knock on the hotel room door.

He was slow to relinquish her luscious mouth. "I'll get the door while you answer the phone."

When he hurried down the hall and opened it, he discovered Danae standing in the hallway, the phone in her hand.

A smile broke out on her face. "I'm relieved you're the reason Lys hasn't answered her phone."

He reciprocated with a smile of his own. "I'm relieved it's you instead of the manager. Come in. She'll be thrilled to see you."

Danae kissed him on the cheek. "Liar," she whispered.

Lys came hurrying into the living room and gave Danae a hug. "I'm sorry I didn't answer the phone earlier."

"That's all right. I'm thinking you two need to move up the wedding date. How about three weeks from now? Check with your parents. We'll have the reception on Kasos."

Takis had never known this kind of happiness.

"You're a woman after my own heart, Danae. Since you're here, I'm going to leave."

Lys darted him a beseeching glance. "Do you have to go?"

This was like déjà vu. Luckily Danae had interrupted them, preventing him from breaking his vow not to make love to her before the wedding.

"Yes." She knew the reason why. "I'll be back later to take you and Danae to our engagement party." He gave her a brief kiss on the mouth before letting himself out.

CHAPTER TEN

Three weeks later

THE DAY BEFORE the wedding, Takis's close friends flew in from Milan. While the men met together, Gemma, Vincenzo's wife, and Filippa, Dimi's fiancée, came to Lys's hotel room to talk. Lys was delighted to get acquainted with the two women, who were best friends and so important in Takis's life.

It was clear to her they were all going to become close, especially when Gemma announced that she was pregnant.

"Does Vincenzo know?"

She smiled at Lys. "Oh, yes, and now he's so excited and worried over my morning sickness, he never leaves me alone. The doctor gave me an antiemetic and now it's under control, but Vincenzo has been driving me crazy. If he behaves like this until the baby is born, I might lose my mind."

"No, you won't," Filippa quipped. "He won't allow it."

Lys couldn't stop laughing. "Do you think your doctor will let you go on in your position as executive pastry chef?"

"I've already talked to my ob about that. He's monitoring me carefully and will tell me when it's time to quit. Vincenzo and I have already talked to Cesare, who is in the process of looking for a replacement."

"I don't know," Lys murmured. "Takis says you walk on water."

"She does," Dimi's fiancée concurred.

Gemma grinned. "Stop it, you two. There are plenty of great cooks out there and there's still plenty of time." She eyed Lys. "I'm so excited for you and Takis. He's the most gorgeous, wonderful man. He'll move mountains for you because it's the way he's made."

"I knew that about him before we even met and was halfway in love with him sight unseen."

"You really never met him when he was working in New York?" Filippa couldn't believe it.

"No. I was a sixteen-year-old high school student when he first started working for my father and I was hardly ever at the hotel. A year later my father died and Nassos brought me to Crete."

"Takis's story is an incredible one. So is yours," Gemma murmured. "I'm so glad you'll be spending some time at the *castello* after your honeymoon. Takis loves it there."

Gemma nodded. "We can't wait to all be together. The men have missed him more than you can imagine, Lys. You have to promise you'll fly to Milan often or life won't be the same around the place."

"It's true," Filippa said with a smile. "Dimi looks upon him as a brother. They're all so close."

"I think it's very touching," Lys murmured.

"In case you didn't know, that man can't wait to

marry you. Dimi says if he has to wait one more day, he's not going to make it."

"I feel the same way."

"We can tell." Gemma chuckled. "Since we've been given our specific instructions, we'd better hurry out to the limo to meet the men."

"They're taking us to lunch," Filippa informed Lys. "We don't dare be late or Vincenzo will come charging in here to find out what's wrong with Gemma."

Laughter broke out as they made their way down to the lobby. Lys hadn't known what it was like to have a sibling. Now she felt she'd acquired several for life.

The next day Lys stood before the black-robed priest dressed in floor-length white silk and lace. She carried a sheaf of purple roses that matched the genuine purple sapphire earrings Takis had given her as a prewedding gift.

During their midmorning wedding ceremony at the flower-decked church in Heraklion, surrounded by their families and a few close friends, Lys was in a complete daze.

The sight of Takis, her tall Cretan prince in his dark blue suit and wedding crown, pushed everything else out of her mind. That picture of him would be engraved in her thudding heart forever. He was now her husband, the most wonderful, gorgeous man in the entire world!

As they were led in the walk around the table three times where they drank from the cup, signifying their journey through life together, she prayed you couldn't die of happiness. By keeping his vow to her, he'd made this sacred moment meaningful in a way nothing else could have done. But now that she was his wife, she couldn't wait to show him what he meant to her.

They would be spending time on the yacht Danae had offered them, but where they were headed was a secret. Every time she thought about their wedding night and being alone with him, waves of desire swept through her. Once they left the church, she was scarcely cognizant of their helicopter flight to Kasos for the reception.

Danae had outdone herself to make Takis's family and friends comfortable. She'd arranged for every one of them to stay overnight where they could swim and eat and enjoy this wedding holiday.

What delighted Lys most were the three children who adored their uncle Takis and hung around the two of them. The girls touched her dress and veil and asked dozens of questions.

Deep inside Lys hoped she'd get pregnant soon. When she saw how happy he was teasing them, playing with them, that day couldn't come soon enough. The second bedroom upstairs would make the perfect nursery when the time came and she knew the color she wanted.

In the midst of the excitement, Takis's father stood to make a toast. "I'm the proudest of men to see my last remarkable child married to a lovely woman who I hope will do her Cretan duty and provide us with more grandchildren." He'd read Lys's mind.

Takis gripped her hand and clung to it.

After Nikanor's toast, Dimi stood up. "I couldn't love Takis more if he were my own brother. I'm thrilled he married a woman I already love. Lys has accomplished something no one else could ever do by putting the light in his eyes that was missing."

"It's true," Takis whispered against her ear.

Lukios followed with a toast. "Guess what, Dimi? I *am* blood and couldn't be prouder of my remarkable brother, whose greatest achievement is sitting next to him. Welcome to the family, Lys."

She teared up while other toasts followed. Eventually Cesare raised his glass of champagne. "Here's to the groom, a man who kept his head even while he lost his heart. I was there at the *castello* the day he lost it and witnessed the earthshaking event with my own eyes."

Everyone roared, especially Takis, whose laughter told Lys it was a private joke between the two of them. She'd have to ask him about it later.

Then Vincenzo gave the final toast and lifted his glass. "Here's to the newest Manolis couple on Crete. Like my beloved wife and me, may they remain lovers for all of life and the hereafter."

"You can plan on it!" Takis declared without shame, causing everyone to laugh and clap. Then he pressed a kiss to her cheek. "It's time for you to change. We're taking a helicopter ride to the yacht. Hurry. I can't wait to get you alone."

Those words said in his deep voice charged her body and she left for her bedroom to put on the stylish new cream-colored suit she and Danae had picked for her. She pinned a purple rose corsage to the shoulder. It was heaven to be out of mourning at last. The sorrow of the past was gone. With Takis waiting for her, there was nothing but joy ahead.

Twenty minutes later everyone followed them outside to the helicopter. Twilight had crept over them. Lys hugged Danae, both of them shedding happy tears. "I have no doubt your parents and Nassos were looking on today."

A sob caught in her throat. "I think so too. I love you. Thank you for everything and for making his family and friends so welcome. We'll be back soon."

"You've married a very exciting man, Lys. I envy you for what's in store."

Lys watched Takis hug his family before he helped her climb on board and told the pilot they were ready. Earlier in the day their luggage had already been flown out.

Lys was thankful they didn't have to fly a long distance. She'd anticipated this moment too long to wait any longer. Before she knew it, they'd put down on the landing pad of the yacht. She practically leaped out of her seat, anxious to be alone with Takis who helped her out.

"Am I dreaming, darling?"

He stopped to kiss her thoroughly. "If you are, I'm in it with you. *Forever.*"

Their wedding night was about to begin. Now if her heart would stop running away with her, she might be able to breathe.

When they reached the outer doors of the master cabin, he swept her in his arms and carried her over the threshold. "At last," came his fierce whisper.

"*Takis—*"

His friends had prepared the suite to his specifications. The flower-laden room was lighted solely with candles. Bless Danae for confiding in him about Lys's fascination with the prince in the fresco. Not only had she told him there was a strong resemblance to Takis, but Lys had once said that in a fairy-tale world, she would love to be married to the prince.

Upon hearing that, Takis had made up his mind that on their wedding night, he'd treat her like a princess. He couldn't re-create a Minoan palace, but he would convince her she was the most precious thing in his life. As he lowered her to the floor, adrenaline gushed through his veins in anticipation of what was to come.

Her heart kicked her ribs hard as she looked around, leaving him to freshen up in the bathroom. She'd been on this yacht many times before, but rarely came in this room and had never seen it looking like this. Takis had transformed it into a bridal chamber fit for a queen. The perfume from the flowers was intoxicating. She walked over to smell the ones next to the bed.

"Takis?"

"I'm right here."

She turned to him and almost fainted. He looked so beautiful in the simple white terry cloth robe, she couldn't think, let alone talk. His eyes gleamed like green gemstones in the soft light.

He handed her an identical robe. Her knees came close to buckling. With hands that were trembling, she went in the en suite bathroom. After removing her clothes, she put it on.

Lys had known he had a creative side to his nature, but to go to this kind of trouble to please her endeared him to her in a brand new way. With her heart beating out of control, she walked back into the bedroom.

He stood at the side of the massive bed. "Come closer so I can look at the most beautiful bride in all Crete."

"Takis—"

"You're not frightened of this surely? Not after all we've been through."

"I—I don't know what I am," her voice faltered.

"You're my desirable wife, the compassionate-hearted woman I've wanted from the moment I first laid eyes on you. I don't deserve you, but I swear an oath that I'll love you forever. Come here to me, *agape mou.*"

She flew into his arms. He swung her around before lowering her to the bed. Their mouths met in frantic need and they began to feast on each other. One robe, then the other landed on the floor.

Their bodies came together in an explosion of love and desire. Lys hadn't known it could be like this. All night long they gave and received unimaginable rapture. "I love you so much, Takis. You just don't know..."

"Then you have some concept of how I feel. You're the light of my life, Lys. Love me, darling, and never stop."

They didn't stop. It wasn't till midmorning there was a loud knock on the cabin door.

Lys groaned and held him tighter. "Tell whoever it is to go away."

"If it wasn't for the fact that Cesare prepared our breakfast before leaving, I would. But he's sure to have given explicit instructions to make sure that we ate a perfect Cretan breakfast."

A chuckle escaped her lips. "And he knows how

hungry you are for every meal. I love him for that since I forgot all about feeding you."

He kissed a certain spot. "You've fed me the nectar of the gods, but it's true I still need mortal food and his creations are out of this world. In truth he should be the new cook for the restaurant after Gemma leaves."

"Have you told him that? Maybe he'd like to do it for a while."

"I'll have to run it by Vincenzo. Do you know Cesare had always said his mother was the best cook who ever lived?"

"That's a thought. We'll have to talk some more about it, but right now I know you're hungry. So am I." She kissed his hard jaw that needed a shave and let him go long enough to slide out of bed and put on her robe. "Stay there and I'll get it."

He lay back on the pillows, looking every inch the prince of her dreams. There wasn't enough she could do for him. "I love you desperately, Takis, and want to do everything I can to make you happy."

After kissing him passionately, she flew across the room. A staff member had left the tray with Cesare's breakfast beside the door. It was laden with every conceivable dish Takis would love. She carried it to their bed, where they could lounge and eat to their hearts' desire.

After eating as much as she could, she lay back. "You're right. I've never tasted better food in my life." She eyed her fabulous husband. "Would it hurt his feelings if you actually approached him with the idea of being the chef at the hotel in Milan?"

Takis put the tray on the floor, then pulled her back

in his arms. “Of course it wouldn’t,” he murmured against her throat. “After running his own chain of restaurants in New York, he’s been begged by restaurants around the world to be their executive chef. All he has to do is name his price.”

She covered his face with kisses. “But he wants to be with you and Vincenzo and Dimi. You four have an amazing relationship. I’d be jealous if I didn’t understand how it all started, and why.”

“We’re very close, but you will always come first.”

“Why did you laugh so hard when Cesare made his toast?”

“I was afraid you would ask.” He kissed her again. “After you left my office, he witnessed my meltdown. I couldn’t understand why Nassos had left me half a hotel.

“To make matters more complicated, I’d just met you after seeing you at the funeral. Since then you’d never been out of my thoughts and I knew in my soul *you* were the woman meant for me. But I didn’t want to be in love. At the height of my frustration, I threw the deed across the room, but it landed on Cesare’s chest.”

She burrowed her face in his neck, chuckling quietly. “Thank you for telling me. You have no idea how much I love you.” Her eyes filled. “It was the perfect wedding, wasn’t it?”

“Almost as perfect as you. Thank God for Danae giving me her blessing. And thank God for Nassos for bringing us together. If I didn’t know better, I could believe he had an inkling that he might not be on this earth long. Every time I think about his letter to you and the deed to me, I get a prickling down my spine.”

"So do I," she said in a shaken voice. "I—I can't imagine life without you now."

"Don't try. I'm planning to love you all day and night for the rest of our lives, Kyria Manolis."

She smiled and kissed him with fervor. "That's right. I *am* Mrs. Manolis, and I want a baby with you as soon as possible. The next time we go to the paint store to pick out the color for the nursery, *I* plan to be the one that woman deals with, not you. I want blue."

"I was thinking pink."

They kissed again. "For once we disagree."

"No. We'll simply build another couple of rooms on the rear of the house. I'd like to call our first daughter Lysette, in honor of Nassos. He brought us together, my love."

"That's so sweet." She covered his face with kisses. "Spoken like my unmatchable husband. I think our first boy should be Nikos Takis Manolis, in honor of your father and *you*!"

Takis's low chuckle melted her bones before he rolled her over and began kissing her into oblivion.

Much later they were served another exquisite meal. After they were replete, Takis lay on his side so they could look into each other's eyes. "I have an idea what we should do with the hotel in Heraklion."

"So do I. We'll keep it and run it together."

"Yes, and whichever one of our children shows an interest in running it, we'll let them have at it."

She traced his lips with her finger. "What if one of them wants to change it in unorthodox ways? How will you feel about that?"

He took a deep breath. "One thing is for sure. All of us will talk everything out together so there can be no chance for misinterpretation that can lead to years of uncertainty."

"Oh, I'm so glad you said that!" she cried. "No woman was ever so lucky. Come here, my husband, and let me love you like you've never been loved before. I might not let you out of this room for days."

"I'm going to hold you to that promise, you beautiful creature."

By the first of June the weather was actually hot in Florence, Italy. Lys had felt sick before they'd flown here and had welcomed the cool of Dimi's villa.

Either her symptoms meant she was coming down with the flu, or… *Was it possible she was pregnant this soon?* Gemma had confided that she'd had similar symptoms when she realized she was carrying Vincenzo's baby.

Before leaving for the church the next morning, Lys did a home pregnancy test. To her joy, it showed she was pregnant with Takis's baby. But she didn't want to tell him the news until after Dimi's wedding.

The festivities leading up to the big day and exquisite marriage ceremony had worn her out and after they left for Dimi's villa following the reception, she noticed the temperature hadn't cooled down.

For the moment, she longed to lie down in their room until their flight home tomorrow. But once they were in the limo, Takis told the chauffeur to drive them to the airport. She turned to her husband in alarm. "I thought we weren't leaving until tomorrow."

He flashed her his mysterious smile. "Don't worry. I made arrangements for our luggage to be put on the plane. We're taking a little twenty-four-hour detour to Milan before we go home. After our honeymoon on the yacht several months ago, I wanted us to enjoy another one in Milan, but decided to save this surprise until after Dimi's wedding."

She hated to tell him she wasn't feeling well and spoil his plans. "I—I didn't realize you have work to do at the *castello* this trip," her voice faltered. All she wanted was to get back to the villa and go to sleep in a cold room, but he'd been so wonderful to her, she couldn't dampen his happiness right now. With Dimi's marriage, he was on a high.

Takis kissed her. "This isn't for work. Humor me, *agape mou.*"

She loved him so much she would do it if it killed her.

Two hours later when they pulled up to the front entrance parking, he kissed her awake. "Come on, sleepyhead. We're here."

She tried her best to cooperate as they walked up the endless stairs leading to the main entrance. He hurried them inside and down the hall to the rear of the *castello,* where she had to face a winding stone staircase.

Her head began to swim as they ascended the medieval tower, and positive she wouldn't make it, she sagged against him.

"Are you all right? We're almost there."

"My darling husband—are you sure you don't hope I'll expire before we reach the top?"

The whole shadowy medieval stairway echoed with his laughter. "A few more minutes and all your fears will disappear."

When she reached the fortress-like door, he opened

it for her. "We've arrived where it will be my joy to wait upon my precious wife."

Her heart kicked her ribs hard as they walked over the threshold and he led her toward the bedroom. The tower suite was a vision of ducal elegance dating back several centuries. The light through the stained-glass windows covered the room in thousands of different colors and nearly took her breath away.

"Takis?"

"Go ahead and lie down on the bed. I'll be right back."

It was heaven to take off her suit and just sink onto the bed. She had no strength at this point. A minute later she heard him call to her and she opened her eyes.

Lys didn't know what to expect, but it wasn't to see the prince of her dreams come to life before her eyes. He looked so magnificent in the white tunic, and in the dimly lit room, Takis's eyes gleamed from his bronzed face.

In spite of how ill she felt, Lys's heart began to beat in time with the desire that thrummed through her veins and she tried to sit up, but he sank down on the massive bed next to her.

"Don't move. I want to look at my beautiful wife."

"Takis—"

"Since the moment you became my wife, since the moment I met you, I knew that you were the one person I needed, the one person I loved. I swore on our wedding night that I'd love you forever. And I intend to show you just how seriously I take that oath. Come here to me, darling."

But as he lowered his mouth to kiss her in frantic need, she had to turn away from him.

"Lys—are you all right?"

"I'm fine," she cried gently. "It's just that… I'm not feeling too good."

He smoothed his hand against her cheek. "I had no idea you felt ill. You should have told me."

"It's been coming on for a couple of days. I didn't want to say anything."

"I'm sending for the doctor." Anxiety had wiped the glow from his face and eyes. It reminded her of the way Vincenzo had looked at Gemma, who'd suffered serious morning sickness in the beginning of her pregnancy.

"No. It's all right. I don't need a doctor. I took a test."

"A test?" Takis looked at her expectantly.

"We're pregnant, darling, isn't it wonderful?"

For the second time in a minute the expression on his handsome face changed. This time to one of shock and joy. His hand slid to her belly. "Our baby…?" His voice of wonder reached the core of her being.

"I'll go to the doctor as soon as we get back to Tylissos. But as much as I want to make love to you right now, I can't."

Suddenly she rolled off the bed and hurried into the bathroom and was sick. He followed her in to help her.

"What can I do for you?"

She rinsed her mouth and face before turning to him with a faint smile. "I think you've already done it, big time." He helped her back to the bed. "But I do have one more favor."

"What is it? I'd do anything for you."

"Promise you won't make too much fuss."

"I promise I'll try to take this in my stride."

"Liar," she teased.

"I only want to take the best care of you and the baby," said Takis. "That's why I took you here."

"And it was a beautiful surprise to be brought here to the castello by my Cretan prince. I love you, Takis".

"And I love you too, Lys," said Takis, "I can't wait to spend the rest of my life with you, my love, my everlasting love."

* * * * *

WHISKED AWAY BY HER SICILIAN BOSS

REBECCA WINTERS

To all of you readers who have read my books
and let me know you enjoy them.

You'll never know what your kind, encouraging
words do to make this author's job a pure delight!

Thank you from the bottom of my heart.

CHAPTER ONE

Salon des Reines, Paris, France

THE CHAUFFEUR OF Le Comte Jean-Michel Ardois pulled the limousine up in front of the bridal salon on the Rue de L'Echelle. In the last two weeks Princess Tuccianna Falcone Leonardi of Sicily had been here with her mother three times for the bridal dress fitting. Each time they'd come, she'd made excuses to visit the bathroom in order to study the layout of the exclusive shop.

This morning was her final fitting to make sure everything was perfect for the wedding ceremony tomorrow. Only Tuccia had no intention of showing up for the elaborate nuptials arranged by her parents and Comte Ardois ten years ago in a horrifying, iron-clad betrothal forced upon her. She'd dreamed of her freedom forever. Now had come the moment for her escape.

Madame Dufy, the owner, welcomed them inside. After fussing over Tuccia and telling her how excited she was for her forthcoming marriage to the *comte*, she took them back to the dressing room befitting a queen.

"Delphine will be with you in just a moment with your gown. It's as exquisite as you are, Princess."

The second she left, Tuccia turned to her mother, the Marchesa di Trabia of Sicily. "I need to go to the restroom."

"Surely not!"

"I can't help it. You know how I get when I'm nervous."

"You are impossible, Tuccia!"

"If I don't go, it might happen in here."

Her mother's hands flew up in the air. "All right! But don't take too long. We have a long list of things that must be done today."

"I'll hurry, Mamma."

Yes, she'd hurry. Right out of the clutches of the *comte*!

She knew he planned to assign her a bodyguard the moment they were married and never let her out of his sight for the rest of their lives. After overhearing him discuss it with her parents, who'd said she needed a strong hand, she'd been planning how to disappear.

Tuccia opened the door and walked down the hall to the door of the bathroom. But she only went inside to leave her betrothal ring on the floor near the sink. Whoever found it could think what they wanted. After looking around to make sure no one had seen her, she rushed down another hallway straight out the back door of the shop.

From there it was only a short run down the alley used for delivery trucks to the street where she climbed in a taxi.

"Le Bourget Aeroport, *s'il vous plait.*"

Her heart refused to stop thudding as they drove

off. She looked behind her. No one had come running out of the alley chasing after her yet. Tuccia prayed all the way to the airport where she boarded an Eljet chartered for her under a fake name and paid for her by her aunt Bertina. Once it landed in Palermo, Sicily, she'd take a taxi to her aunt's palazzo.

Before long Tuccia's favorite person in the whole world would be offering her sanctuary. Her life would continue to depend on Bertina's help, or all was lost.

The next day, Milan, Italy

Dinner had concluded in the private dining room of the legendary fourteenth-century *castello*, the home of the former first Duc di Lombardi in Milan, Italy.

Vincenzo Gagliardi, the present-day *duc*, lifted his goblet with the insignia of the Gagliardi coat of arms. "*Buona fortuna* this trip, Cesare. Our business is depending on you. May you return with my wife's replacement soon. The baby will be here in two months. I want Gemma off her feet ASAP."

"Amen," Takis declared, raising his glass. "You're going to have to be quick, *amico*." He touched his goblet to Cesare's, and they sipped the local vintage Lombardia that Vincenzo had produced from the vast wine cellar for his send-off.

Cesare Donati eyed his two best friends with a smile. They'd been like brothers to him for more than a decade. Together they'd turned the former fortress palace of Vincenzo's family into the five-star Castello Supremo Hotel and Ristorante di Lombardi, Europe's most sought-after resort.

"I have a surprise for you. I'll be back in two days

with our new pastry chef. I told Gemma as much this morning."

"That soon?" they said in unison.

"It's been arranged for a while, so have no concerns."

His friends smiled in relief. For Cesare's contribution to their successful enterprise, he'd already found the perfect person to replace Gemma as the *castello*'s new executive pastry chef.

But he'd been keeping the identity of his choice a secret until he could present Ciro Fragala in person with one of his many specialties for their delectation.

Vincenzo's wife had learned to make Florentine pastry from her mother who'd cooked for the last *duc.* Though her cooking was perfection and drew the elite clientele that came to the *castello,* in Cesare's opinion the best cook in the world was his own Sicilian mother.

She'd learned from the nuns who made divine pastries and ran the orphanage where she'd been raised until she turned eighteen. On her say-so—and she would know better than anyone else—Cesare had done the necessary research on Signor Fragala, the pastry cook she'd declared to be the finest in all Sicily. After a visit to the Palermo restaurant with his mother two months ago, he'd agreed totally with her assessment.

Hiring Ciro meant sensational new desserts for their business enterprise in Milan. The two of them had met with the fifty-five-year-old widower several times in the last few weeks. The chef had said he would leap at the chance to work at the famous *castello* restaurant.

Since he didn't have children, it wouldn't be a problem to move. He'd given his notice and Cesare planned to fly him to Milan. The new chef would work well with their executive French chef at the *castello.* Most of all, the guys would be pleased by the man's amiable personality.

"We'll drive you to the airport," Vincenzo stated.

Cesare shook his head. "Thanks, but you've done enough by surprising me with this dinner. You've both got pregnant wives who've been generous enough to let us have this meal together. By now they'll be wondering where you are. The limo is waiting as we speak."

"Then we'll walk you out," Vincenzo murmured.

"Grazie."

He drained the rest of his wine and got to his feet. Reaching for the suitcase he'd left by the double doors, he moved ahead of them to the portrait-lined corridor of the former *ducs* with their legendary silvery eyes.

"Stay safe," Takis said as Cesare climbed in the rear of the limo.

"Always."

Vincenzo smiled. "We can't wait to meet this mystery paragon of pastry chefs." He patted Cesare's shoulder and shut the door before it drove away from the *castello.*

Two hours later, the Lombardi ducal jet arrived at Palermo International Airport, where another limousine waited for him on the tarmac. Cesare told the driver to take him to the posh Mondello borough. It was there he'd bought a villa in the famed *art nouveau* style for his mother and sister who was now married and lived in the city with her husband and their toddler.

He'd wanted nothing but the best for his wonderful mamma, Lina Donati.

She would never leave Palermo. After being raised by the nuns and learning how to cook from them, she'd started out working in a local restaurant after leaving the orphanage.

Her subsequent marriage was short-lived. Abandoned by her husband, she'd cooked her way through life to support their little family and had made a name for herself. Cesare believed she made the best food on earth. In her honor he'd had a state-of-the-art kitchen installed because he couldn't do enough for her.

Thanks to a bad back from being on her feet all the time, she now cooked exclusively for Bertina Spadaro, who wasn't a demanding employer. Cesare had begged her to retire. He would take care of her forever. But his mother said she couldn't imagine not having work to do and she loved Bertina. The aristocratic older sister of the Marchesa di Leonardi di Trabia had become her friend.

The Leonardi family descended from the royal Sicilian family of the commune of Trabia, thirty miles from Palermo, and could trace their roots back to the 1400s, when the land and castle were granted them by Frederick III. The present *marchese* and *marchesa* had established their own *palazzo* in the heart of Palermo.

Bertina and Lina had become fast friends over the years and were in each other's confidence. The rest of the time his mother spent with Cesare's family, or tended her spectacular herb garden.

The elite area of Mondello had everything: exclusive yachting clubs dotting its sandy beach, restaurants, shops and a marina with numerous yachts, including the *marchese*'s gleaming white royal yacht that stood out from the others.

Before buying the villa for her, Cesare, too, had been captivated as he'd walked through the sand of its private beach front, inhaling the air filled with the heady scent of orange blossoms and jasmine. Whenever he flew to Palermo, Cesare was reminded that with all its rich history, there was nowhere else in the world he found more fascinating.

But tonight as they drove into the ancient, colorful city, he was met with the strong smells of fish and spices that always brought back memories of his youth. There was a hint of the old Arab souks, taking him back to his childhood. As a boy, these streets with their subtle niches and labyrinths had been his backyard.

His father had been in the merchant marines, but ran off before Cesare was a year old, leaving his mother to work in a trattoria and support him and his older sister Isabella. They'd lived in the apartment above it in a rougher neighborhood of Palermo. Cesare's world had been filled with lots of purse snatchers, few showers that usually didn't work, grueling heat. Everything had been run-down and chaotic.

Since he'd been too young to remember his father, he didn't miss him, only the idea of him. Cesare had envied his friends who had fathers and taught them things. Early in life he'd felt embarrassed at times that he was the only one who went to mass unaccompanied while the other boys walked in the church with their own fathers.

As he grew up, the embarrassment went away, but he lacked the confidence he saw in his friends whose sense of belonging seemed to give them an extra layer of it.

Cesare couldn't comprehend a man abandoning his wife and children, never caring about them again. Sometimes in his teens he'd dreamed about meeting his father, but those dreams were unsatisfactory because his father always turned away from him. The dreams eventually stopped, but not the feeling that there was something lacking in him.

At the age of thirty, Cesare was living a different life. Thanks to the college mentor who'd taught him and his partners how to invest, his worth now figured in the billions. But the past could never be forgotten and had formed him into the man he'd become.

Over time he'd seen enough to decide romantic love was transitory at most. Of course there were exceptions, like his partners' marriages. But at this stage in his life Cesare wasn't that confident that he was marriage material. He hadn't witnessed two parents loving each other. So far he felt he was better off alone like his mother. With a sister and brother-in-law and their daughter Elana, Cesare was happy enough with the family he loved.

In fact he had all he needed, including the occasional relationship with a woman. There was no guarantee that one would stay with him if he did get married, or that it would last.

Or that he might not be more like his father than he thought...

From time to time that thought haunted him because he hadn't met a woman who meant everything to him. Maybe he'd subconsciously pushed them away so he didn't have to deal with commitment. Though he didn't want to bring up past pain to his mother, one of these days he would have a talk with her about the man who'd disappeared on their family, on *him.*

When the limo finally reached the villa, Cesare put his darker thoughts away and paid the driver before getting out. His mother was expecting him, and knew he'd be flying Ciro Fragala back to Milan with him the next day. But it was close to one o'clock. She always went to bed early.

He'd told her not to wait up and they'd talk in the morning before Ciro arrived at the villa in a limo Cesare had arranged for ahead of time. The man would be shipping his belongings to Milan and he'd stay in a room at the *castello* until he decided where he wanted to live.

Every time Cesare came to Palermo, he was charmed by the large ochre-colored villa spread over two floors with three beautiful terraces and a Mediterranean garden. The small pool was lined with glazed tiles of North African origin.

From the terrace off the dining room he was met with a glorious view of the Gulf front. It was a sight he'd always loved after climbing the bluff called Mount Pellegrino many times in his youth. From there he could imagine himself escaping the suffocating heat and madness of the city and sailing away to America. Incredibly that dream had come true.

Once he'd entered the foyer, he turned off the outside light and moved across the stone tiles of the villa in the dark to the kitchen with his suitcase. After setting it down, his first instinct was to grab himself a small bottle of his favorite *grappa digestivo* from the cabinet where he knew it was kept, then head upstairs to his suite with it. Before sleep, all he wanted was to take a few sips to remind him he was back in the land of his roots.

But as he turned to pick up his suitcase, he bumped into another body and heard a cry.

"Mamma?" He automatically hugged her to him. "*Mi dispiace tanto.* I didn't think you'd be up this late. Did I hurt you?"

That's when the bottle slipped from his hand and cracked on the floor. But the strong scent of the 60 proof alcohol wasn't nearly as shocking as the feel of the woman in his arms.

She wasn't built anything like his wiry brunette mother or her housekeeper who came in several times a week. In fact she was taller than both of them. To add to his surprise, the flowery scent from her hair and skin intoxicated him. It took him a second to gather his wits.

"Don't move. There's broken glass. I'll turn on the light." He let her go and walked to the doorway to flip the switch. Cesare was shocked yet again.

If he didn't know better, he would think he'd released a gorgeous enchanted princess from her bottle. Her stunning figure was swathed in a lemon silk robe. Thank heaven she was wearing sandals. Between her medium-length black curls and eyes gray as the morning mist off the ocean, his gaze managed to swallow her whole before he realized she looked familiar to him. He knew he'd seen her before but couldn't place her.

She stared back as if disbelieving before taking a few steps away from the wet mess on the stone flooring. A hand went to her throat. "You're Cesare," she murmured, sounding astonished.

"I'm afraid you've got me at a disadvantage, *signorina.*" Maybe he was in the middle of a fantastic dream, but so far he hadn't awakened. Quickly he walked over to the utility closet for a cloth and brush to pick up the glass and clean the floor.

"My name is Tuccia. I'm so sorry to have startled you."

Tuccia. An unusual name.

Tuccia. Short for… Princess Tuccianna of Sicilian nobililty?

Over the years there'd been photos of her in the newspapers from time to time, mostly stories about her escapades away from the royal *palazzo* where she got into trouble with friends and was seen partying in local clubs to the embarrassment of the royal household. But Cesare had never seen her up close.

The latest news in the Palermo press reported she was engaged to be married to some French *comte* who lived in Paris and was one of the wealthiest men in France.

No. It couldn't be, yet he realized it *was* she.

"I'm afraid I don't recognize it," he dissembled until he could work out why the daughter of the Marchese and Marchesa of the ancient Sicilian House of Trabia, was in his mother's villa.

"You probably wouldn't. It's not common."

She was trying to put Cesare off, but he intended to get to the bottom of this mystery. "Did Mamma hire you to be a new maid?"

She averted her eyes. "No. Signora Donati allowed me to stay with her for tonight." He frowned, not having known anything about this. Why hadn't his beloved mother told him what to expect when he arrived? "I—I thought I heard a noise, *signor*," she stammered, "but I didn't have time to turn on the light."

"No. We were both taken by surprise," he murmured, still reeling from the sensation of her incredible body clutched to his so she wouldn't fall.

Cesare had enjoyed various relationships with attractive women over the years, but he'd never gotten into anything serious. Yet the feel and sight of the beautiful young princess, whose face was like something out of Botticelli, had shaken him.

"I guess you know you have the most wonderful mother in the world," she gushed all of a sudden, breaking in on his private thoughts. He was amazed by her comment. It had sounded completely sincere.

He closed the utility door and turned to her, growing more curious by the second. "I do. How did you two meet?"

His question caused her to hesitate. "I think it would be better if you ask her. I'm truly sorry to have disturbed you and will say goodnight." She darted away, leaving him full of questions and standing there wide awake in the trail of her fragrance.

The princess, reputed to be a spoiled, headstrong handful, had elegance and manners. *Damn* if she didn't also have an unaffected charm that had worked its way beneath his skin.

He took a deep breath. Though Cesare didn't like waking his mother, he knew there'd be no sleep until he had answers. Before heading upstairs to her bedroom, he opened the cabinet for another bottle of *grappa.* All he found was a half-opened bottle of cooking sherry.

That's what he got for not turning on the light earlier. That and the memory of a moment in time he feared wasn't about to let him go.

With a pounding out-of-control heart, twenty-five-year-old Principessa Tuccianna Falcone Leonardi rushed to the guest room down the hall at the rear of the villa. She should never have made a trip to the kitchen, but needed something to drink. Lina had told her to help herself to anything, including the soda she kept on hand in the fridge.

Being crushed unexpectedly against a hard male body in the dark had come as such a huge surprise that her mind and body were still reeling. She could still feel the male power of him and smell the faint scent of the soap he'd used in the shower. The combination had completely disarmed her.

After he'd turned on the kitchen light, she'd had her first look at Lina's tall, incredibly attractive brown-haired son. Tuccia knew of him, but had no idea that Lina had given birth to the most striking man she'd ever seen in her life. Those deep blue eyes and his masculine potency had managed to make such an indelible impression her heart still kept turning over on itself.

"I didn't know there was a man in Palermo who looked like that," she whispered to herself. Tuccia was positive there wasn't another one in all Europe who could match him.

More than ever she was revolted at the thought of marrying her forty-year-old French fiancé who had only stared at her with lust. The fabulously wealthy Comte Jean-Michel Ardois, who would soon inherit the title after his ailing father passed away, was always trying to touch her, and lately more and more inappropriately.

On occasion she'd seen him be quite ruthless with the people who worked for the Ardois family. He was a cold, calculating man whom she could never love or bring herself to marry.

Her betrothal at the age of sixteen had been a political necessity arranged by her parents, the Marchese and Marchesa di Trabia, whose funds needed constant bolstering. Since that time she'd felt doomed to an existence she'd dreaded with every fiber of her being.

After careful planning, she'd seized the moment to run away twenty-four hours before the ceremony was to take place. Taking flight from the boutique, she'd flown back to her home in Sicily. Thanks to her Zia Bertina, her mother's widowed elder sister, she'd been given the help she needed to escape on that jet.

Bertina lived in her own palazzo in Palermo where she entertained close friends and loved Tuccia like the child she'd never been able to have. Tuccia's *zia* was a romantic who'd always been in sympathy with her niece's tragic situation, and had prevailed on her cook, Lina Donati, to let her hide at her villa overnight. In the meantime she was still trying to arrange transport for Tuccia to stay with a distant cousin living in Podgorica in Montenegro until the worst of the scandal had passed.

But Tuccia had placed her in a terrible position.

Bertina had continued living in the palazzo after her husband died, but she needed monetary help on occasion. Tuccia's *zio*, Pietro Spadaro, hadn't been a wealthy man. If Tuccia's parents got angry enough at Bertina, they could stop giving her extra money. They might throw her out of the only home she'd known since her marriage.

Worse, if they knew Bertina had involved a cousin in another country, let alone asked such a desperate favor of her adored cook to help solve Tuccia's problems, who knew how ugly the situation could get. If Bertina were forced to lose the palazzo and any extra money, she wouldn't be able to pay Lina for being her cook. Lina could be out of a job for harboring her. All of it would be her fault.

She couldn't believe her bad luck in running into Lina's son. Naturally he was going to wonder why she was here and question his mother. What she needed to do was get dressed and pack her bag so she'd be ready to steal from the villa at dawn before anyone was up.

Tuccia knew a full-scale search by Jean-Michel and her parents had been underway for her since she had disappeared from the salon. At least with her gone from Lina's villa, Bertina wouldn't be implicated.

She had saved enough money to take a bus and travel to Catania where she could get a job through a friend who would help her. If she were careful, she could subsist for a while. She didn't dare access her bank account even though its pitiful balance had never been big enough to pay for as much as an airline ticket.

Tuccia had no idea how long she would have to remain hidden. But even if it meant being disowned and disinherited, it didn't matter because she'd rather be dead than have to marry Jean-Michel. She was sickened at the thought of him taking her to bed, let alone living with him for a lifetime.

CHAPTER TWO

CESARE SAT AT the side of his mother's bed, still trying to comprehend what she'd just told him. "Apparently you and Princess Tuccianna have enjoyed a relationship you never told me about."

"Only since I started cooking for Bertina two years ago. Until tonight I'd been sworn to secrecy. She needs help desperately, Cesare."

He reached for her hand. "Don't you know what a terrible position this has put you in, Mamma? The authorities from two governments are looking everywhere for her. Her jilted fiancé could be dangerous. He has the kind of money and power that could crush you. If her parents found out you gave her shelter, your name could be ruined. You could lose your job with Bertina. They could make life miserable for you."

"It's Tuccia's life I'm worried about, not mine. You know how I feel about titles. It's a feudal system. No young woman should have to marry a man almost twice her age because of money and power. You can't imagine how frightened Bertina is for her niece. The *comte* will impose his will on her. She's very beautiful. And you know exactly what I'm talking about."

Cesare was afraid he did. He'd seen first-hand the

trouble that kind of will had created for Vincenzo and Vincenzo's cousin Dimi. The two had grown up together at the *castello* and had suffered through tragedy together because of overpowering parental dominance over both of them.

After Cesare had become close friends with the two royals he had learned their story, so he understood why the princess refused to be tied legally to a man who could do what he wanted to his young, helpless wife. Cesare was sickened by it himself, but his protective instincts had kicked in for his mother. He didn't want her to be a part of this and he got up from the bed.

"How long have you agreed to let her stay with you?"

"Until Bertina has worked out an escape plan to get her to a distant relative in Montenegro no one will trace."

He shook his head. "Of course they will! That's no plan," he bit out.

"I agree with you and I don't like any of it, either. But the princess is desperate. Bertina has told me that the father, Comte Ardois, was promiscuous and notoriously unfaithful over the years. She has it on good authority that his son Comte Jean-Michel is exactly the same way.

"He's had a mistress on the side for a long time. I can't bear that kind of life for her. Neither can she! Tuccia is like a lamb going to the slaughter. To me it's criminal!"

"What you're telling me sounds like a repeat of the stories Vincenzo told me about life at the *castello* growing up."

"So you do understand that Tuccia is a young sweet girl and needs to get far away from him while she still can."

"Yes, but not at your expense."

"Someone has to step up. If I lose my job because of this, I'll find another one. If that isn't possible, then I *will* let you take care of me. The point is, the *marchesa* and her husband have never been concerned about their daughter's feelings. They've spent their whole lives doing their royal duty and expect the same from Tuccia. The princess is alone in this. If Bertina hadn't chartered that jet for her so she could leave Paris, Tuccia would have been forced to walk down the aisle today and be married to a monster."

His hands went to his hips. "But now she has *you* involved."

"Because I want to be. I like Tuccia very much. If she were my daughter, I'd do whatever I could to save her from such a wretched life. You're the most brilliant, clever man I've ever known, *figlio mio.* If I asked for your help this one time, would you do it for your mamma?"

Her blue eyes beseeched him. She was serious! He could see it and feel it.

"What do you think I could do?"

"Fly her to Milan tomorrow on the Gagliardi ducal jet with Ciro. Help her find a place to stay in the city where no one will think to look for her. She won't be traced."

His eyes narrowed. "Is this the reason you let her stay here tonight? Because you knew I was flying in and planned to use me?"

"Yes," she answered with her usual refreshing honesty. "Have I ever asked you for a favor like this before? Time is of the essence."

"Mamma—" His head reared in exasperation.

She sat up straighter in the bed. "I don't see a problem. Tuccia's crisis takes priority. That girl needs to be far away from here by tomorrow. It won't hurt you to take her with you. Be sure she's wearing a disguise. Signor Fragala won't suspect who she is."

He stopped pacing. "He'll recognize her once we're on board."

"So you'll swear him to secrecy. If he can't be trusted, tell him you've changed your mind and won't let him have the coveted chef position after all. It's in *your* hands. Once you've settled her, you can take Ciro to the *castello* and get on with your business. Is that such a terrible thing to ask this one time?"

Cesare couldn't fathom that they were having this conversation at three in the morning. "There's no place she won't be recognized."

"Then take her to the *castello* with you. Smuggle her in a back entrance and hide her in one of the turret rooms for a few days. That will give her enough time to figure out a solid plan on her own. Besides being well-educated and well-traveled, she's a very intelligent girl and resourceful."

"And according to the papers, impossible," he added.

"If you knew the truth, you wouldn't judge her. Every time her name gets in the news, it's because she has tried to run away from her family. But she always gets caught and is brought back. Her parents cover it up by saying that she's an indulged, immature troublemaker. She's the loveliest girl I've ever known, and it's a tragedy how her life has been."

Such accolades for the princess shocked him. His mother wasn't about to relent on this. She was a fighter who had a heart of gold. That was how she'd made it through life.

"You'll help me to help her, won't you?"

Cesare loved and admired his mother more than any woman he'd ever known. After the hundreds of sacrifices she'd made for him and his sister growing up, how could he possibly turn her down?

Letting out a sigh he said, "Stop worrying. After Ciro arrives in the morning, I'll take her to Milan tomorrow with us." But not to the *castello.* He didn't want the guys to know what was going on.

"If you'll do that for me, I'll love you forever."

"I thought you already did," he teased.

Her eyes had filled with tears. "Oh, Cesare. My dear son. *Ti amo.*" She started to get out of bed, but her phone rang. Her eyes darted to his in alarm. "Maybe something's wrong with your sister or my little granddaughter—"

Cesare's body stiffened. A phone call in the middle of the night could mean anything. Probably it was Bertina calling his mother to tell her the police were on their way over to the villa looking for the princess.

She reached for the cell phone on her bedside table and checked the caller ID. "It says San Giovanni Hospital."

He stood stock-still while he waited to find out what was going on, but his mother did little talking. Once she hung up, she looked at him with haunted eyes.

"I'm afraid I have very bad news for you, Cesare."

"What do you mean?"

"Ciro was rushed to the hospital a few hours ago

with an infected lung and kidney. I thought he didn't seem well when I visited the restaurant a few days ago and assumed he had a cold.

"He must undergo an operation to drain off the fluid. The nurse said he had the presence of mind to ask the hospital to contact me before he lost consciousness."

"Santo Cielo," Cesare murmured in disbelief. This whole night had turned into a bad dream. "The poor devil."

"It's terrible."

"Get dressed and we'll drive to the hospital in your car. Since he's my responsibility, I'll tell the hospital and take care of his medical bills."

"Bless you. I'm getting ready now, but I'll visit him alone and be your go-between until he has recovered. Right now you've got to take care of the princess. The sooner, the better. That phone call could have been Bertina alerting me that the police were on Tuccia's trail. There's no time to lose."

There was no time for sleep, either, not while this situation continued. He walked to his suite to shower and change clothes for the flight back to Milan. Afterward he went downstairs to the kitchen to fix himself coffee. He found the delicious sweet rolls filled with ricotta and chocolate his mother always made for him when he came and ate several.

During his early morning feast, his mother joined him before leaving for the hospital. After she went out to her car, he contacted the pilot to let him know they'd be returning to Milan shortly, then he arranged for a limo to come to the villa. Now all he needed was for the princess to make an appearance.

* * *

It was six-thirty in the morning when Tuccia finished writing three letters at the desk in the guest bedroom. The first was her deepest apology to Jean-Michel, explaining why she couldn't marry him and had run away. They weren't in love with each other, and that was the only reason for two people to marry.

She put it in an envelope with his name and address on the front. When and where to mail it was the scary part and had to be considered carefully because her life depended on it.

Tuccia put the letter in her purse, then wrote two long thank-you letters to her *zia* and Lina. She signed them with love before leaving them on top of the dresser so Lina would be certain to see them. One of these days she would write to her parents, but that could wait.

After making the bed, she grabbed the small suitcase Bertina had loaned her and hurried through the villa to the kitchen for a piece of fruit. A ten-minute walk would take her to the shops where she could eat something more substantial and catch a bus.

"Where do you think you're going in that disguise?" a deep familiar male voice asked as she reached the foyer.

Her camouflage consisted of a scarf she'd tied around her head like a lot of local women did to cover their hair. She turned around to see the man she hadn't been able to erase from her thoughts, standing there in jeans and a jacket. He looked too marvelous to her this early in the morning.

"I wanted to slip out before your mother awakened

so I wouldn't disturb her. I left messages to thank her and my aunt."

"I'm sure she'll appreciate that, Principessa."

Of course he'd recognized her and had talked with Lina. Now he knew everything about her situation. She was so sorry he'd been dragged into her problem. "Your mother has been exceptionally kind to me. I'm embarrassed my *zia* asked for her assistance, and I'm ashamed I accepted it because it has placed her in danger."

"Mamma has a big heart. It sounds like Signora Spadaro does, too."

Tears glazed her eyes. "They're both strong, remarkable women, but they've done more than enough to help me. It's time I dealt with the mess I've created for myself."

She tried to open the door, but it wouldn't give. Tuccia looked over her shoulder. "Is there a trick to unlocking it?"

With a half smile that gave her heart a jolt, he activated the remote in his hand and the door swung open.

"Thank you." After a slight hesitation, she said, "It was a privilege to meet the famous son of Lina Donati. In case you didn't know it, she thinks the sun rises and sets with you."

Tuccia felt him follow her out the door into the balmy seventy-seven-degree air where a limousine had pulled in the drive. She put on her sunglasses. Apparently he was going somewhere. When she would have walked past it, he called to her.

"Mamma says you need to get out of Palermo immediately. If you'll climb in the limo, I have the means to make that happen."

His comment stopped her in her tracks. "You mustn't get involved in my problem. I'm already weighed down with guilt and couldn't handle any more."

He opened the rear door. "But I *am* involved. I don't believe I've ever helped a genuine princess in distress before and rather like the idea. Come on. You've been living dangerously since leaving Paris. Why stop now?"

His sense of humor caught her off guard and she chuckled in spite of the fear gripping her that this freedom couldn't last. Not wanting to hold things up, she climbed in. He set her suitcase on the bank of seats in front of them and sat next to her, pulling the door shut. His rock-hard limbs brushed against her jeans-clad legs. The contact sent a dart of awareness through her body.

She heard him tell the chauffeur to drive them to the airport. They drove through a breathtaking portion of Mondello to the main route leading out of the city. Tuccia had the sensation of being spirited away where nothing could hurt her.

It was a heavenly feeling she'd never experienced before. She'd sell her soul for it to last, but she knew this wonderful moment could only be enjoyed until they reached the airport.

"Where are we going?" she asked at last, alive to everything about this extraordinary man.

"To Milan."

"Where you work when you're not in New York."

"More importantly, it's where you'll be safe. I fear my mother has done far too much talking about me."

"That's because she loves you." Tuccia had heard about the spectacular *castello* restaurant he owned and ran with his business partners. His other business interests in New York City were legendary. "I can't imagine what it would be like to know that kind of love from my own parents."

"That's a lonely statement."

"Now *I'm* doing too much talking and sound so sorry for myself, I'm ashamed. But you have no idea what I'd give to erase the image the country has of me. I'm *not* the tempestuous, volatile woman everyone believes me to be. I just want to be free like other women to make the kind of life I want for myself."

"According to my mother, you've run away from a fate worse than death."

"Put that way it sounds ridiculous, doesn't it? Unfortunately it's true for me and I've dragged three innocent people into my personal disaster. I pray there won't be any repercussions for you," she half sobbed the words.

His hand grasped hers, sending a wave of warmth through her. "No one brought my mother and me kicking and screaming," he teased gently. "If I were in your shoes and betrothed to some odious *marchesa* twice my age, I can promise you I would flee to the other side of the universe where no one would ever find me."

Odious was the exact word to describe Jean-Michel.

The analogy was so ludicrous she found herself laughing. But it underlined the fact that Cesare Donati wasn't married. Tuccia couldn't help but wonder how many women must have flung themselves at him.

"That's better," he said before releasing her hand.

Soon they arrived at the airport and were driven to

the area where the private jets sat on the tarmac. The limo wound around and stopped next to one in silver and blue that stood out with a coat of arms depicting the Duc di Lombardi. A thrill of excitement passed through her to know she'd be flying to northern Italy with him. Just the two of them.

Once Cesare helped her out of the limo with her suitcase, the steward welcomed them aboard. He showed her to the elegant club compartment where she sat across from her protector as she thought of him. Pretty soon the Fasten Seat Belt light went on and she heard the scream of the engines as they taxied out to the runway.

After they'd taken off and achieved cruising speed, the light went off and the steward brought them breakfast trays. She found she was starving and ate everything, including a second cup of coffee to drink.

Cesare flashed her a searching glance. "How long has it been since you had a substantial meal?"

"My aunt kept trying to feed me after I arrived in Palermo, but I was so nervous I couldn't eat very much. Now I'm hungry."

"How did you manage your escape so perfectly when all of your other attempts have failed?"

"I can see my aunt has told your mother everything about my past." Tuccia heaved a sigh. "I've been planning this latest scheme since my first dress fitting two months ago. Yesterday morning I went to the dressmaker with my mother for the final wedding dress fitting.

"When Madame Dufy went to find the dressmaker and bring out my gown, I told my mother I needed to use the ladies' room and hurried down the hallway. As soon as no one was in sight, I shot out the back door of the salon. I knew there was a nearby *tête de taxi.* From there I was driven to the airport where Bertina had chartered a private jet for me ahead of time under a fake name. And here I am."

His gaze held hers. "That was a daring plan."

"I'm sure you think me selfish and cruel, but it was the only way to end the nightmare of my life. I've written a letter to Jean-Michel to apologize. It's all ready to be mailed except for a stamp."

"Where is it?"

"In my purse."

"May I see it?"

When she pulled it out, he walked over and took it from her. After examining the address, he put it in his pocket. "I'll make sure he gets it without the police being able to trace it."

"You must think me heartless and that I'm living up to all the falsehoods spread about me. Actually they're not all false. I do have a bad temper that erupts at times and I've gotten a lot of staff into trouble who were supposed to keep a close watch on me."

After a silence he said, "What I think doesn't matter." The Fasten Seat Belt light went on again. He strapped himself in. "We're descending to Milan. Very soon I'll take you to a place where you'll be hidden from the world and hopefully safe for another twenty-four hours. While you're figuring out what it is you would like to do with the rest of your life, I'll have to leave you, but I'll be back in a couple of days."

Her spirits plunged at that revelation. "Where are you going?"

"To Palermo."

"Again? I don't understand."

"I'm going to see the man I'd hired to be the *castello*'s new executive pastry chef."

Her brows met in a delicate frown. "Why didn't you visit with him before you brought me all this way first?"

The pilot set the jet down and it taxied to a stop. "Because he was rushed to the hospital during the night and couldn't come with me to start his new position. He was supposed to meet my partners today and get settled in."

"Oh, how terrible for him *and* you!"

"Since you needed to leave Palermo before the authorities caught up to you, I brought you instead."

The man continued to astound her. She shook her head. "I can't believe you would do that for me." Tuccia loved him already for his sacrifice.

His blue eyes darkened with an emotion she couldn't put her finger on. "Mamma said it was a matter of life and death. After learning how desperate you are to escape the life your parents and fiancé have orchestrated for you, I'm inclined to believe she was telling the truth."

His compassion filled her with feelings that threatened to overwhelm her. "Please—you don't have to send my letter to the *comte*. It's too much. I'll find a way to do it," she said in a throbbing voice he could probably feel.

"It's a simple thing that needs to be done so he'll call off his army. There's no one like you, and no question he wants you back. Needless to say, you're a royal prize he won't tolerate getting away from him."

Tuccia shivered because she felt he truly did understand the gravity of her desperate situation where Jean-Michel was involved.

A few minutes later another limousine drove them out of the city. They swept past farms and villas until they reached a small village at the base of a prominent hill. On the top she caught sight of a massive fortress. The ochre-toned structure with its towers and crenellated walls sprawled across the summit.

"That's the ancient Castello Di Lombardi," Cesare explained, "now a hotel *ristorante*."

The one he'd helped to make famous. Tuccia was eager to see it up close and thought they would drive up there. Instead he asked the driver to take them to a *pensione* in the village. Evidently he'd made arrangements for her ahead of time.

Just as he helped her out of the limo and told the driver to wait, the *padrona di casa* came out of another door. She greeted them and showed them inside the attractive apartment. After a few explanations she left. Cesare lowered Tuccia's suitcase to the floor and turned to her.

"You should be very comfortable here while I'm gone. I asked her to fill the cupboards and fridge with groceries to last several days. As you heard her say, if you need anything, just pick up the phone in the kitchen and she'll answer."

The last thing Tuccia wanted was for him to go, but she realized he was anxious to get back to Palermo and didn't dare keep him. What a terrible position he was in!

"I don't know how to thank you for all you've done for me. How can I make this up to you?"

He studied her features for a minute. "I've had two friends who helped me when I thought all was lost. It's nice to be on the giving end for a change."

She could feel her eyes smarting. "I don't deserve this."

"I remember telling them the same thing. A word of warning. Do you have a cell phone on you?"

"Yes."

"Don't use it for any reason and don't go walking in the village. The only person who knows you are here is the woman who let you in. She's a friend and will keep silent. When I return, we'll talk. Until then, try to relax, watch TV. *A presto*, Principessa."

"*Alla prossima*, Cesare." She followed him to the door and watched him drive away, causing her heart to act up until it actually hurt.

Once he was gone, Tuccia went back in the living room for her suitcase. Then she walked to the bedroom so full of emotions, she didn't know where to go with them. She didn't know another person in the world except her aunt who would make a sacrifice like this for her. Cesare Donati was the most incredible man she'd ever known.

While she was in the shower, her mind focused on the chef he'd hired for his fabulous *castello* restaurant. He had to be a spectacular cook. How sad he'd fallen ill at the very moment he was supposed to go to Milan with Cesare.

She wished she could help him in some way during the short interim while the chef was recovering. Cesare had been so good to her and she wanted to find a way to repay him. She'd much rather stay right here.

But of course the whole plan was to get her away from Jean-Michel and her parents.

You're losing your mind, Tuccia.

On his way back to the airport Cesare phoned his mother, wondering what kind of a mess she could be in if the police had already found out she'd been harboring Tuccia at the villa.

She picked up on the fourth ring. "Cesare—where are you?" she blurted before he could say anything.

"You'll be happy to know my mission has been accomplished. Are you alone?"

"Si."

"Good. Now I can tell you the princess has been installed in a safe place."

"*Grazie a Dio.* I can always count on you."

She didn't sound worried about the police yet. "I'm flying back to Palermo to be with you. If there are no complications, I should be there in about two hours. I'll come straight to the hospital. After we've talked to the doctor and done all we can do there, I'll take you out to eat and we'll have a long talk. How does that sound?"

"Wonderful, except that there's no point in your coming back unless you want me to help you find another pastry chef beyond Palermo. That could take months."

"What do you mean another chef? I don't understand. Ciro will get better with a treatment of antibiotics."

"I thought so, too, but *you're* not going to be happy when I tell you what I've just found out from the doctor. Ciro came close to dying during the night because he has developed a heart condition. The prognosis for a full recovery could be six months away."

"Incredibile!"

"I know how upset you must be to hear that news, Cesare. I'm so sorry. He's in the ICU and won't be able to talk to anyone for a few days. There'd be no point in your coming right now. You might as well turn around and stay at the *castello* until he's been given a private room and can have visitors. Then you can fly down and have a serious talk with him."

The situation had gone from bad to worse. "Thank you for watching over him. I'm indebted to you."

"Bless you for saving Tuccia's life. What will you do about the chef position now?"

Right now Cesare's concern over the princess had created the most stress for him. "That's not your problem. I'll just have to be the pastry chef myself and interview more applicants for the position. But let's agree that finding someone who knows how to make Sicilian desserts with an expertise close to his or yours will be an endeavor in futility."

"You make the best *cassatine* with almond paste in existence."

"I learned from you, but that was years ago."

"You never forget, but I'm desolate for you this has happened. What will Tuccia do? Did she talk to you about it during the flight?"

"Yes. She has a plan that might work." For a day maybe. "I'll think of something. Don't you worry about it. Have you told Bertina her niece is safe?"

"I drove to the palazzo to tell her in person and

give her Tuccia's letter before returning to the hospital. She was so relieved she broke down sobbing before burning it."

Good thinking on Bertina's part. "Have the police questioned her yet?"

"Yes. She told them she knew nothing."

"They'll be contacting anyone who is friends with her, especially her cook. You'll be receiving a visit soon. Don't talk to her on the phone."

"No worry. I'm at the hospital now and just finished reading Tuccia's sweet letter to me before burning it." He had a brilliant mother. "Thanks to your willingness to help the princess escape so fast, there's no evidence she was ever at the villa, and of course I know nothing." He chuckled in spite of his concern for her. "Stay in close touch with me."

"Haven't I always? Take care of yourself, Mamma."

"You, too. I'll talk to you later. *Dio di benedica*, Cesare."

After they hung up, he told the limo driver to take him to the main express mail outlet in Milan. Asking him to wait, he went in to have Tuccia's letter to the *comte* couriered overnight to Cesare's attorney. Rudy Goldman always spent this time of year at his retreat in Barbados. Inside the mailing envelope he put the following instructions.

Rudy.

Put a stamp on this and send it airmail immediately.

Many thanks,

Cesare.

His attorney was the soul of discretion and always did what he was told without question. When Cesare had addressed the mailing envelope, he paid the clerk who put it in the slot. Before long it would be on its way to Bridgetown. The *comte* needed to receive it ASAP. Cesare knew in his gut the other man would start a search for his fiancée.

She *was* a prize. No one knew that better than Cesare. His thoughts wandered. Not every man would be worthy of her love when she had an ancestry that had made her unique in the world. Certainly not Cesare, whose family tree might as well have half a trunk missing. What could a fatherless man bring to a marriage with a princess?

Depressed by his thoughts, he returned to the limo and told the driver to take him back to the *pensione.* It was the same apartment where Vincenzo's wife Gemma had once stayed when she'd come from Florence to the *castello* for an interview. The *padrona* could be trusted.

By the time the limo pulled up in front, Cesare had made up his mind to send Tuccia to the States in the morning. The police wouldn't find her there and he could put her out of his mind. She was on it too much already.

He got out to the pay the driver, then walked to the front door of her apartment and knocked loud enough for her to hear. "Tuccia? It's Cesare. May I come in?"

"You haven't left for Palermo yet?" she called out in surprise. "I'll be right there."

In less than a minute she opened the door in bare feet, dressed in the yellow silk robe she'd worn in the middle of the night. He could smell the peach shampoo she'd used to wash her hair. She had a brush in one hand and had been styling her naturally curly black hair.

The sight of such natural beauty would make any man go weak in the knees. Cesare was no exception. "I had a call from my mother and have been forced to change my plans."

"Uh-oh." Anxiety marred her features. He knew what she was thinking.

"Forgive me for making you stand there. Please come in."

Her faultless manners impressed him. "Thank you." He walked in the little living room off the kitchen.

She eyed him nervously. "Did the police interrogate her already? Is she in terrible trouble?" Tuccia put the hand not holding the brush to her heart. "Bertina should never have involved your mother and I shouldn't have listened to her."

"So far everything is all right. The police talked to your aunt who told them she knew nothing. I'm sure my mother will be next, but she'll have no information, either. They both received your letters."

"I'm so glad. Then why have you changed your plans? I don't understand. But before you tell me, let me get dressed. Please sit down. I'll only be a minute."

He chose the chair by the coffee table while she rushed to her bedroom. Cesare caught a fleeting glimpse of her long shapely legs beneath the flap of her robe before she disappeared. He was growing more enamored of her by the second.

How could it be that after all the years of working with attractive businesswomen, he found himself in trouble just being in her presence for a few hours total. Along with her attributes, her utter femininity blew him away. It was a good thing she'd be gone tomorrow so there'd be no temptation to spend any extra time with her.

CHAPTER THREE

IN NO TIME Tuccia reappeared wearing a pair of white slacks and sandals toned with a café-au-lait-and-white print short-sleeved top. She sat on the end of the couch with one leg tucked under her. "Tell me what's wrong."

"As you know, the Sicilian pastry chef I'd planned to hire is in the hospital. But there's no telling when he'll be well enough to work again. Mamma found out he has developed an unexpected heart condition. I had high hopes for him. With his exciting creations, he would have brought a new clientele to our *ristorante.* Except for my mother's cooking, there's no one to equal him."

Tuccia sat forward with a troubled look on her lovely face. "My *zia* says she's the most superb cook in all Sicily. That means she has to know what she is talking about. What will you do?"

"Since I'm in charge of the *ristorante* at the *castello,* I'm the only one who has the authority to fix the problem. In an emergency, there are times when you have to do it yourself."

Her eyes widened. "You mean *you're* going to be the pastry chef?"

"It'll be nothing new to me while I find someone else. But right now I'm concerned about you. Have you decided what you want to do with your life?"

A slow smile broke out on her face. "That was a trick question, right?"

The woman was getting to him. "Not at all. Since you never intended to follow through on the betrothal, what had you imagined you would be doing when you finally made your escape?"

Her smile faded. She looked away. "To be honest I only thought about how to subsist until my parents stopped looking for me and go from there."

Cesare had assumed as much. "If I hadn't offered you safe passage on the jet this morning, what was your exact plan when you reached Catania?"

"I was going to find temporary work in a greenhouse through an old school friend until I'm forced to move on for fear of being spotted."

He hadn't expected to hear that. "Are you a gardener with a knowledge of horticulture that would make you an asset at the greenhouse?"

"Of course not."

"Yet you're willing to prevail on the friend you mentioned to get a job there?"

"Yes. She works at the university and could help me find a position for a while. But because you told me not to use my phone, I haven't talked to her yet and wouldn't be able to until I reached Catania."

"Do you have an affinity for flowers?"

Her head flew back. "Have you forgotten I'm a princess who has no knowledge of anything practical? But I'm strong and could cart plants around in a wheelbarrow if I have to."

"I wasn't trying to insult you."

"I know," she half moaned. "You're being so good to me. I'm sorry I snapped."

"I think you're handling your desperate situation with amazing grace."

She shook her head. "But it's one I created and I don't deserve your kindness."

"Why do you say that? Everyone deserves help from time to time."

He heard a deep sigh. "I guess because my parents rarely showed any kindness to me while I was growing up."

"Did they hurt you physically?"

"Oh, no. Nothing like that. But their stifling, rigid rules made my life unbearable."

"Nevertheless it doesn't mean you're not deserving of kindness," he reminded her. "Just so you know, your letter to Jean-Michel has been dealt with in a way that won't be traced to you. He should be getting it in a few days, so you can put that worry out of your mind."

Her eyes filled with tears. "You're a saint."

"Hardly." He leaned toward her with his hands on his thighs. "I've given your precarious position a lot of thought. Your idea to go to Catania would only be a stopgap for a few days. I still think it would be best if you leave Europe tomorrow. I'll arrange it."

She shook her head. "I couldn't let you do that. You've done more than enough for me and have your own problem to solve right here."

"First things first, Tuccia. You need to get far away. New York would be the perfect place to get lost. With my contacts, I could set you up in your own apartment and they would help you find a job that you would like to do. No one would suspect you're the princess who disappeared. You'd be safe. That is what you want, isn't it?"

"You know it is, but I've been thinking about the chef who's in the hospital and how desperate you must be feeling right now. You saved my life by bringing me to Milan. Instead of putting you in an impossible position, I'd like to do something of value for you in return," she said in an aching voice.

She had a way of running over every roadblock. He sat back and studied her for a moment, intrigued. "What do you mean?"

"Why not teach me to be a pastry chef so I can work at your *ristorante* until he's well and can fly here. I'd do anything to help you if I could."

It took all his self-control not to laugh. To his shock, he had the strongest suspicion she was being completely serious. "Are you saying you know how to cook?"

A small sound escaped her throat. "No. I'm embarrassed to tell you I've never cooked anything from start to finish in my life, although I spent a lot of time in the palazzo kitchen growing up. The cooks were kind to me and let me watch. I washed lettuce and sometimes they'd let me beat egg whites or stir the gravy. Once in a while they'd allow me to sift the flour into the cake bowl before it was baked."

"Does that mean you didn't learn to cook at boarding school?"

She laughed outright. "You have a strange idea of what goes on there."

"Actually I *do* know, and was only teasing." Despite the impossibility of what she'd said, the more they talked, the more he found himself enjoying her company. Too much in fact.

"I'm relieved to hear it, Cesare. To be honest, that boarding school in France happened so long ago I've forgotten. All I know is, I was waited on. When my parents enrolled me at the University of Paris, I had to live with them in an apartment in St. Germain des Pres. Would it reassure you to know that I told my maid I could make my own tea and instant coffee in the microwave?"

He laughed at her sense of humor and her sparse knowledge in the cooking department. A princess with a classic education from the finest schools and universities in Europe, but to make a pastry... "Tuccia—"

"Please hear me out, Cesare," she cut him off before he could say anything else. "According to your mother, you could head any Cordon Bleu cooking school in the world. You could teach me. It would be like getting a college education of a different kind."

His eyes searched hers. She wasn't kidding. Princess Tuccianna had been known for doing some daring, outlandish things, but this idea had shocked him to the core.

"As intelligent and resourceful as you are, you don't know what would be entailed."

She sat forward. "My parents' cooks didn't know how to cook in the beginning, did they? They had to learn from someone," she reasoned. "Why couldn't I do the same thing under your expert tutelage? I'd work fast and it would free you up to get on with running all your businesses. My anonymity would be assured hidden behind the *castello* walls. Within six months, the chef you hired would be back."

Cesare no longer felt like laughing. This beautiful young woman was bargaining for her life. He had to give her credit for possessing the kind of guts he hadn't seen in most people.

When he didn't say anything, she blurted, "I've been thinking about what you asked me."

"What was that?"

"About what I wanted to do with my life. If you were to teach me how to make pastry, I would have learned a marketable skill. When Signor Fragala returns, I'd be able to use all that knowledge I'd learned from you. With a reference from you—provided you gave me a good one if I deserved it—I could find a position in any country."

He could hear her mind working. It was going like a house on fire. To his astonishment he was listening to her because she was making a strange kind of sense.

"After a half year in hiding, I'm positive my family will have disowned me so it wouldn't matter where I chose to live and work. I'd be a normal woman with a good job."

"You'll never be a normal woman, Principessa." his voice grated. Nor would he want her to be. He liked her exactly the way she was. "Can you honestly sit there and tell me the thought of being disowned doesn't pain you?"

She lowered her head. "I guess I don't know how I'd feel about it until it happened. But what I *do* know is that I'm *never* going to bow to my parents' wishes again. Hopefully before long Jean-Michel will have comforted himself with another mistress while he hunts for a new titled princess to marry."

Cesare rubbed the back of his neck, unable to believe he was actually toying with the idea of teaching her the rudiments. In a perfect world, if she did follow through and did learn how to cook, it would give her the independence she'd never known. It would allow her to earn money and she'd be free to make her own choices, something that had been denied her from birth.

At some point in time she'd decide to get in touch with her parents, or not. He couldn't believe he was allowing his thoughts to go this far.

Quiet reigned before she said, "I know what you're thinking. I don't have any money right now to pay you to teach me. But if I were a good student and could work at the *castello*, you wouldn't have to pay me any money. Not ever! I'm already indebted to you for your sacrifice. It would be my gift to you for saving my life."

The last was said in a trembling voice. It was the wobble that did it to him.

"Are you a fast learner?" Cesare knew she was grateful. He didn't want her to go on begging for the chance to repay him. Her willingness to take a risk of these proportions made her a breed apart from anyone he'd ever known.

She stared at him with those heavenly gray eyes. "I guess that depends on the subject matter, but I graduated with honors in European history."

"Congratulations, Tuccia. That's no small feat. But to make a pastry chef out of you… I don't know."

"You're right. It's too much to ask and I'd probably be a disaster."

He didn't like the discouraged tone of her voice and it made up his mind for him. "Maybe not."

A gasp escaped her lips. "You mean you're willing to entertain the idea?"

Her excitement put a stranglehold on him. "Let's just say I'll put you on probation for a few days and see how it goes."

"You're not teasing me?" she cried.

"No. I wouldn't do that. Not about this."

He could tell she was fighting tears. "When would I start?"

"As soon as we've eaten dinner."

"So soon? Aren't you exhausted after everything you've been through in the last twenty-four hours?"

Her question stunned him because her first thought had been for him. He could have asked the same of her after being on the run.

"Not at all." In fact he'd never been so wired in his life.

"Does that mean we're going up to the *castello* right now?"

He stood up. "No. This *pensione* is going to be your home, your school room and your lab. You'll do everything hands-on right here. After a few days I'll decide if I can turn you into the next executive pastry chef at the Castello Supremo Hotel and Ristorante di Lombardi. Otherwise I'll put you on the plane for New York."

Tuccia let out an incredulous cry of joy and she jumped to her feet. She rushed over to him and put a hand on his arm. The contact sent a shock through him. His awareness of her made it hard to breathe.

"You mean it? You're not joking? But you just said you weren't joking. I'm sorry, but I just can't believe you're willing to give me a chance."

"Everyone deserves a chance." He looked her in the eye, trying to get a grip on his emotions. "What fake name were you going to use when you applied for the greenhouse job in Catania?"

His question made her blink, and she let go of him. "Come on," he prodded her. "You've obviously had one in mind for a long time."

"Not the same one my *zia* used to charter that plane for me. I guess… Nedda Bottaro."

"Nedda? The heroine in the opera *Pagliacci*?"

"Yes. I love opera and *Pagliacci* is one of my favorites."

"But Nedda meets such a cruel end."

"I know. She and Carmen suffered the same fate. I always cry."

Cesare heard pain in her voice. "Why use the last name Bottaro?"

"It means a wine cask maker. There'd be no connection to any of my family names."

He nodded. "Wise decision. If I deem you a promising pupil, we'll go with both when I introduce you to my partners. I'll tell them I stole you from the finest *ristorante* in Palermo."

She rubbed her hands against womanly hips in a nervous gesture. "How soon will that happen?"

"Not for a while. I'll have to teach you a lot first, and quickly, too. After dinner we'll start with something simple. I'll take a taxi to the grocery store and get the needed ingredients. While I'm at it, I'll buy you a new Pay as You Go phone to reach me if you need to and program it. By the time you go to bed, you'll be able to make the recipe I have in mind in your sleep."

She paced the floor, then wheeled around in front of him. "If I can pass your tests, that means I'll be making desserts for hundreds of people a week."

"That's right. Kings, sheikhs, presidents of countries."

Her radiating smile illuminated those hidden places in his soul that had never seen light. That thought appeared to delight her.

"You'll have assistants to help you."

"But I don't look anything like a chef."

No. She didn't look like anyone else in the whole wide world. "You will after we dress you properly. When I bring my partners to the kitchen to introduce you, no one will ever guess you're Princess Tuccianna."

Her cheeks had grown becomingly flushed. "I want to be good enough to meet your standards. You'll never know what this means to me."

He was beginning to. While she stood there, Cesare phoned for a taxi. After he hung up, he turned to her. "I'm starving and am going out to pick up a meal for us after I shop. When I get back, we'll get started."

She followed him to the door. "If I can't do the job you need done, does this mean you'll have to be the head pastry chef at your own hotel?"

He liked it that she was a little worried about him. "Yes. My partner's wife, Gemma, can no longer handle the job this late in her pregnancy. I'd promised I would produce her replacement by tomorrow, but with Signor Fragala in the hospital, the job has now fallen on my shoulders. I'll have to let them know in the morning. That doesn't give me time to find anyone else with his credentials. It could take me several months."

"And I don't have *any*," she half moaned the words.

In an unconscious gesture he put a hand on her shoulder and kneaded it gently. "I'm not my mother's son for nothing. You've convinced me you want this job more than anything. By the time I'm through with you, I'm hoping you'll be able to write your own ticket as a pastry chef."

After a long pause he said, "At this point I've been wondering. Is the difficult, uncontrollable, incorrigible Principessa di Trabia of Palermo, Sicily, worth her salt? It would be fun to find out the truth. I'll be back soon."

Tuccia rested against the closed door with her arms folded. His touch had crept through her body like a fine wine, weakening her physically. Yet his final comment before he'd gone out the door had caused a sudden surge of adrenaline to attack her.

"Is the difficult, uncontrollable, incorrigible Principessa di Trabia of Palermo, Sicily, worth her salt?"

Cesare had said that to get a rise out of her. Without question he'd accomplished his objective.

Frightened and excited by the whole situation she'd created for herself, Tuccia turned on the TV in the corner to distract her for a little while. She grazed the channels with the remote and came across two stations giving the four o'clock news. The second she saw a news clip of herself and Jean-Michel flash on the screen, she felt sick and sank down on the couch.

"Authorities in France and Italy are asking for anyone to come forward who knows anything about the whereabouts of Princess Tuccianna of Sicily, the daughter of the Marchese and Marchesa di Trabia. She's the fiancée of the acting Comte Jean-Michel Ardois of the House of Ardois and prominent CEO of Ardois Munitions. Princess Tuccianna disappeared yesterday morning in Paris and hasn't been seen since.

"The famous couple were to have been married today. Speculation that she was kidnapped by some foreign government faction for ransom has not been counted out.

"According to police, the Marchesa had been waiting in the lounge for her daughter to change after the final fitting of her wedding gown at the exclusive bridal shop on the Rue de L'Echelle. But she never came out. The police found her betrothal ring and are suspicious that some employees working at the shop helped aid in the kidnapping and are now being detained.

"Both families are desperate for news of the beautiful dark-haired twenty-five-year-old princess. So far any sightings of her have turned out to be false. She speaks French, Spanish, English, Italian, Sicilian and is known to be an excellent swimmer and sailor who—"

Tuccia turned off the TV and buried her face in her hands, swamped by guilt for the terrible thing she'd done. At least Jean-Michel would get her letter soon, but in the meantime innocent people were being questioned and detained. Hundreds of policemen in two countries were searching for her. She'd endangered her aunt and Cesare's mother. But she couldn't go back to that life. She just couldn't.

Jean-Michel wanted to marry a woman with a title, preferably a young one who'd give him children and not cause him trouble. Her parents wanted a son-in-law with a fortune that would never run out. No love was involved. Tuccia was a pawn and always had been. It was a fact of life that she'd been born to royalty.

It truly wasn't fair to Cesare, who'd been forced to come to her rescue this morning, flying her with him on the ducal jet no less. Knowing the huge risk of aiding a fugitive—that's what she was at this point—a lesser man might never have done such a favor, not even for his own mother.

To add to her crime, Tuccia had proposed an idea to save both their skins. But it was so audacious *and* dangerous if anyone were to find out who she was. For Cesare to be willing to go along with her idea made him a prince among men as far as she was concerned.

He had a reputation for being brilliant. She'd known that about Lina's son long before she'd ever met him. But she hadn't counted on him being so incredibly handsome, too. Working with him, she would fast lose her objectivity. How could she possibly concentrate on what she was doing while she was in his presence? If there was such a thing as love at first sight, she'd fallen victim to it.

By working with him, there was no doubt she'd be learning from a master. It would be an honor to be the student of a man famous on two continents for his business acumen as a restaurateur. He'd built an enviable empire of restaurants in New York.

Part of her wanted to show him she *was* worth her salt. But what if she failed? She'd passed lots of tests in her life, but none would be more important than this one now that she'd made the commitment.

While she was sorting through her tortured thoughts she heard a knock on the door. Tuccia rushed to let him in. He was loaded with three big sacks of food and carried them into the kitchen.

She shut the door behind him. "It looks like you bought out the store."

"Several stores to be exact." He washed his hands in the sink. "The risotto with veal looked good at the deli. I picked up some rustic wheat bread and a bottle of Chardonnay Piemonte to go with it."

"Wonderful. I'm hungry, too." She peeked in the sacks and found their dinner, which she put on the round kitchen table. Their gazes fused. "I take it the other two sacks contain enough pastry ingredients to feed a small army."

"You're partially right. The rest are provisions for you to take with you in case you change your mind before the evening is over."

Her spirits plunged. "What do you mean?"

"While I've been gone, you've had time to reconsider what we've talked about. After we've eaten, I'll be happy to take you to the train station if that's your wish. The standard service leaves at quarter to nine for Sicily. There'll be no amenities. You'll have to sit up in your seat all night. But you'll be like dozens of passengers with little money and melt into the crowd."

He pulled wine glasses from the cupboard and poured some for them, but what he'd just said to her had shocked her.

CHAPTER FOUR

TUCCIA STOOD THERE with her hands on her hips. "You honestly expected that I would change my mind while you were gone? That I didn't mean any of the things I said?"

"It would be understandable," he said, sounding so reasonable she wanted to scream.

"Naturally you have every right to believe I'm not up to the task. No one would believe it."

"I have faith in you, but I want to give you the freedom to back out of this if you think you might have spoken too hastily."

As they sat down to eat, he handed her a copy of the *Il Giorno* newspaper to read. She came face-to-face with a two-month-old picture of her and Jean-Michel attending the opera in Paris. The headline read, *Sicilian Princess still missing.*

"You've done a good job of disappearing, Tuccia. So good I believe you have an excellent chance to reach Catania unobserved with your disguise. I had no right to suggest you go to New York. You're a grown woman and can make your decisions. It's time you were allowed to function without interference from anyone."

He ate a second helping of veal. The minutes were ticking away. Maybe he was wishing she would leave for Catania, then he'd never have to give her another thought in his life.

Her appalling selfishness sickened her. She couldn't help but wonder if he was disgusted with the overindulged princess who'd created an international incident. He'd have every right!

It was miraculous he'd let his mother talk him into bringing her to Milan, except that Tuccia's aunt was a force to contend with. Because his mother worked for Bertina, she probably didn't know how to say no to her.

Unable to handle her own ugly thoughts any longer, she got to her feet and clung to the back of the chair. He looked at her while he finished off the bread.

"Cesare?" she began.

"Yes?"

"When I was at your mother's last night, I was frightened out of my wits at what I'd done to escape my prison. Terrified would be a better word. That is until this morning, when you snatched me away from the jaws of death at great risk. I know that sounds dramatic, but that's how it felt to me and still does."

"I have no doubt of it."

She struggled to say the rest. "You've saved my life. If you're really willing to teach me how to make pastry, and you think I can learn, I'd like to try. I want to help you honor your commitment to your partners who are depending on you. I haven't changed my mind about any of it. But if the police don't find me first, I can only pray your friends won't discover I'm a fraud who has made a mess of everything for you."

The blue of his eyes darkened as they stared at her out of dark-fringed lashes. The male beauty of the man caused her to feel desire for him even to the palms of her hands.

"I believe you. No matter how you see yourself, Tuccia, in my opinion you're the bravest woman I ever met and I believe you can take the challenge head-on," he said in a husky tone. "What brought you to this decision?"

After the unexpected compliment, Tuccia had difficulty swallowing. "I couldn't let you get away with thinking I'm not worth my salt."

There was a gleam in his eyes. "I'm impressed by your willingness to put yourself in the hands of a stranger."

"That part is easy, Cesare. Because I've been friends with your mother, you haven't been a stranger to me, even if we didn't meet until last night." She was embarrassed because she could hear the throb in her voice. All it had taken was meeting him to be crazy about him.

He got to his feet and started clearing the table. "She likes you enough to have begged me to help you escape. That shows the strength of your friendship. It's good enough for me."

"I'm just sorry I'm the clay you have to work with to try and make a pastry cook out of me. But I swear I'll work my hardest for you."

"You've convinced me. Shall we get busy?"

"Yes. What will we make first?"

"The most clamored-for dessert in Sicily. I'm sure you've eaten virgin breasts before."

Tuccia should have been ready for that one, but it

was so unexpected heat scorched her cheeks. She went over to the sink to wash her hands. "You can't be a Sicilian without having eaten those cakes. But when I was little, the cook at the palazzo was offended by their name so she called them nun buns."

A chuckle escaped his lips. "They have several names. Mamma grew up in an orphanage run by the nuns," he continued. "They were known for being great cooks and made those special delicacies for which they're famous. She taught me everything she learned from them. Tonight we'll get started on the first of three different kinds."

"I didn't know there was more than one."

"You'd be surprised at the varieties."

She knew he was talking about the cakes, but her blush deepened anyway.

"Some of the ingredients have to be refrigerated before completing them, but we'll finish everything before you have to go bed. In a few days' time we'll present them to my partners as your specialty when I introduce you. A bite into them and they'll believe they'd been transported to heaven."

Laughter peeled out of her. "I hope you're right!"

His laughter filled the kitchen. "Why don't you sit down and we'll go over the recipe. It's known only to my mother and me." He walked over to one of the sacks and pulled out a notebook and pen. She shouldn't have been surprised all that knowledge was etched in his brain.

"Shall I write it down while you dictate?" she asked as he handed her the items.

"I think that would be best for you. To read your own writing rather than try to figure out mine will save you time in the long run. That notebook is going to be your bible. Don't ever lose it. Are you ready?"

"Yes," she said in a tentative voice.

Last night Tuccia had appeared to Cesare like a fantastic female apparition that had made him think maybe he was hallucinating. This evening she wasn't just a heavenly face and body. In the last eighteen hours she'd taken on substance and exhibited a keen intellect that had been growing on him by the minute.

In her desperation to remain hidden from the world for a while, she'd begged him to teach her. He knew she was frightened. This woman, who'd been raised to be a princess, was running on faith.

Right now she reminded him of a young child, submissive and obedient to her parent. Cesare was humbled by her determination to grab the lifeline he'd thrown her. He'd brought the newspaper with him to help remind her that anything—even learning how to cook pastry—was better than being forced to go back to her old life.

"The first item you'll be making is called *pasta frolla* for the shells. These are the ingredients: four cups of flour, one cup of granulated sugar, two sticks of sweet butter, one tablespoon of honey, five medium egg yolks, lightly beaten, and lemon zest. After you've kneaded it and put it in the fridge for an hour, you'll make the ricotta cream filling. That requires one cup of sugar, two pounds of ricotta, orange zest, cinnamon powder, one drop of vanilla, a quarter pound of candied citron and chocolate shavings to taste. Lemon glacé will be the final step that includes one and a half cups of granulated sugar, a quarter cup of lemon juice, and a sprinkle of raspberries. I realize this sounds like a lot, but it's straightforward. You'll like forming the shells. Are you with me so far?"

She looked up with a faint smile. "Yes. I can't wait to find out if I share your optimism."

Her response was encouraging. "Come on. We'll get started on the dough. While you find us a bowl in the cupboard, I'll put the first set of ingredients on the table."

He oversaw everything, but made her do all the work. She added the ingredients, making little mistakes, but soon she'd formed it into a ball.

"Okay. Now knead it."

"I know how to do that from watching the cook." But once she got started, the dough kept sticking to her fingers. "This is impossible!" she cried in frustration.

Cesare burst into laughter. "Wash your hands, and then dust them with flour before trying it again."

"But that will wash half the dough away."

"No problem."

"That's what you say," she mumbled, but did his bidding and started over with the kneading. "This is much better." She finally lifted her head and smiled. "Thank you."

"You're welcome. Now pat it into a disk and wrap it in wax paper. An hour in the fridge and it will be ready to shape into tart shells. While the dough is getting cold, you'll start making the filling."

Three hours and three tries later she'd produced a pan of tarts she was willing to let him taste. After she'd decorated them with the lemon glacé, she designed the tops in an artful way with raspberries and chocolate shavings.

With a hand he could tell was trembling, she put one on a dish and handed it to him. “Will you be the first to sample my *pièce de resistance*?”

Cesare knew what this moment meant to her and he bit into it. She’d followed the recipe to the letter. He found no fault with the taste or texture and was so proud of her effort after three tries that he wanted to sweep her in his arms. Instead he kissed her hot cheek.

“Congratulations, Tuccia. My partners will tell you these tarts are perfect.” He swallowed the whole thing and had to be careful not to swallow her, too.

“Thank you. I know they’re anything but. The shells are still uneven and in this batch I put a little too much cinnamon in the filling when I tasted it.”

“The fact that you know what you can improve on makes you an excellent cook already. How does it feel to have made a masterpiece created by the nuns?”

She took a deep breath. “If these tarts meet your exacting criteria, it’s because you were my teacher. To answer your specific question, after I got over being nervous with you standing there watching me, I had more fun than I would have expected.”

“Good. I’m glad to hear it.”

“It amazes me that I’ve eaten desserts of every kind all my life and never paid attention to the intricacies that go into the preparation. That’s what frightens me. This was just one dessert. When I think of the dozen others I have to learn how to make, I feel totally inadequate.”

“Keep in mind that all it takes is one step at a

time. I'll wrap up your pan of mounds and take them with me."

"Why?"

"I want my partners to try them." He heard her groan. "After the dishes are done, I'll say good-night."

While he called for a limo, he watched how hard she worked to clean up the flour on the table and floor, let alone her clothes. She'd proved she was worth her salt, but this had only been her first lesson. Another few days of this and the last thing she would tell him was that it was fun.

He had to give her full marks for putting the kitchen back together with little help from him. "You've done a great job, Tuccia. I'll be back in the morning and we'll talk about what's going to happen. I hope you get a good sleep."

She walked him to the front door. "I'll never be able to thank you enough for shielding me and giving me this chance."

"I'm equally grateful and impressed that you're willing to try something so different from the world you've come from to help me. Who knows? We may pull this off yet."

She flashed him a tired smile. "'May' being the operative word. *Bona notti*," she called to him.

On Cesare's way to the *castello*, her parting words resonated inside him. She'd said good-night to him in Sicilian, using the Palermo dialect. It reminded him of the language he used with his own family, making him feel more connected to the princess.

That was bad. He couldn't afford to have intimate thoughts about her, but that was a joke because he could still feel her body pressed against his in his mother's kitchen. That was a moment he couldn't forget if he wanted to, even if she'd just run away from her fiancé.

Cesare had offered to help her so she could gain her independence. He hadn't done it to take advantage of her. The last thing he intended was to come on to her. If he did that, he'd be every bit as bad as the lecherous *comte* Cesare's mother had described.

You are just as bad, Donati.

By the time the limo dropped him off around the back of the *castello*, he realized he had to tell his partners the truth about her. If they couldn't handle it—and he was pretty sure they couldn't—he would understand. So would Tuccia. Even though he hadn't been around her long, he knew she'd pretend it was all right.

It was five to ten when he stole through the passageway to the back stairs not used by the hotel clientele. Halfway to his room on the second floor in the private section, he ran into Takis coming down the stairs from the turret bedroom he and Lys used when they were in Milan. They had their own home in Crete and flew back and forth.

"Cesare—You're back! We didn't expect to see you until tomorrow. What have you got there?"

"You'd be surprised."

Takis frowned. "What's going on?"

"I had a slight change in plans. Where are you headed?"

"To the kitchen." Takis smiled. "Lys had a sudden craving for ice cream."

"So it's true about pregnant women."

"*Si.* One day it'll be your turn to find out."

A sudden vision of a pregnant Tuccia in her yellow silk robe flashed through Cesare's mind, disturbing him.

"*Eh, amico.* What's wrong?"

Diavolo. What wasn't? "Everything's fine."

"The hell it is." Takis could read him like a book.

"Your wife needs you. Is Vincenzo here or in Lake Como with Gemma?"

"In order for us to be together tomorrow and meet the new cook, they never left for home."

"*Perfetto.* See you two in the morning."

Not wanting to prolong this any longer, Cesare bounded up the rest of the stairs. When he reached his suite, he put the tray of tarts on the coffee table and went in the other room to take a shower.

Later, after throwing on a robe, he phoned his mother and found out the police had been by the villa asking questions about Tuccia.

"I said I didn't know what they were talking about. I'd been at the hospital all day and told them to check the nursing station at San Giovanni if they needed verification. That was enough for them and they left. I'm positive they won't be back."

"*Grazie al cielo.*"

"Bertina is overjoyed no one can find her niece."

It might interest his mother to know Cesare's relief was just as great. The more he thought about Tuccia's detestable royal engagement, the happier he was that he'd played a part in her escape. As for the rest… "I take it Ciro is still in the ICU."

"Oh, yes. The nurse told me she would call me

when they moved him to a private room so I could visit."

"That's good."

"Tell me how you are. How's Tuccia?"

"We're both fine." He'd told Takis the same thing. Fine covered a lot of territory, good and bad. "Don't worry about anything. Get some sleep, Mamma. That's what I'm going to do."

Not wanting to answer any more questions, he hung up wondering if he'd be able to get any while he was torn apart by thoughts of Tuccia and what would be the best thing for her. Now that he'd agreed to help her, he had to see this through one way or the other. But he couldn't seem to stop from touching her. Earlier tonight he'd kissed her.

Cesare was about to turn out the overhead light when there was a knock on the door. Instinct told him it was Takis. He crossed the room and opened it to discover both him and Vincenzo standing at the threshold.

"Shouldn't you two be with your wives?"

Vincenzo's silvery stare had a way of pinning you in place. "We think you need us more."

"I'd hoped to have this conversation in the morning."

Takis shook his head. "Let's talk now or none of us will get any sleep."

How true. But the fear that his partners might not be on board with his plan to train Tuccia had been bothering him. Deep inside lurked another fear that if she left Milan to do something else, she wouldn't tell him where she'd gone and he might never see her again.

"Come in." They walked in his sitting room and sat down. He paced for a minute before coming to a stop. "I don't want to keep you up all night, so here's the bottom line. The person I'd hired for our *ristorante* is in the hospital in Palermo as we speak."

In the next breath Cesare explained everything that had happened from the moment he'd arrived at his mother's villa until now. He told them about Ciro's sudden illness and Tuccia's plight.

"I took her to the *pensione* where Gemma stayed. She's safe there for the time being. During the flight I came up with a solution to both problems."

In the next breath he told them of his idea to turn her into the temporary new pastry cook for the *castello* until Ciro was well. He only left two things out; the fact that she'd been the one who'd begged *him* for the job, and his intense attraction to the *principessa.* Cesare had never burned for a woman like this in his life.

"Hearing about her disappearance is like a dose of déjà vu for me," Vincenzo commented.

Cesare nodded. "When Mamma admitted why she was hiding Tuccia, I could understand. It took me back to that morning in New York when you told me and Takis about your escape from your father at eighteen years of age. She's twenty-five, but still in much the same situation as you were back then."

"That was a horrific time. I can well imagine what Princess Tuccianna is going through right now."

"But she's my responsibility, not yours. Tonight on the way up here I decided I had to be out of my mind to think up such a ridiculous plan." She'd been so desperate, he hadn't been able to find the strength to turn her down. “On the jet she talked about another plan she had in mind to stay in hiding. I don’t doubt it would work for a while.

“Once she’s gone I’ll be acting pastry chef while I search for the right person to replace Gemma. I can only hope Ciro might recover much sooner than the doctor estimated.”

Without commenting, Takis eyed the covered pan on the coffee table. “Are you going to let us taste her first endeavor?”

“I was just going to ask the same thing,” Vincenzo commented.

“There’s no point. I’m not willing to drag you two into this mess.”

“Why don’t you let us decide.”

“No, Takis.” He shook his head. “All we would need is for the press to find out she’s working within the walls of the *castello.* We’d be charged for obstructing a police investigation. I’d face an additional charge for flying her here. It would cause an international scandal that could ruin our business.”

At this point Vincenzo had gotten to his feet. “Not showing up for her wedding would be a disappointment to her fiancé and parents, but it isn’t a crime. As far as I can see, no crime has been committed by anyone. She turned to her aunt for assistance. That woman called on your mother who enlisted your help. The police don’t know that.”

“Vincenzo’s right,” Takis chimed in. “Besides, Tuccia is over twenty-one and is welcome here as a staff worker. If she wore a disguise and used a fake name, it’s not our fault we didn’t recognize her.”

"Thanks, guys, but the police wouldn't see any of it that way."

"How are they going to find out?"

Cesare rubbed the back of his neck in frustration. "I don't know, but you can be sure there'll be a leak somewhere."

Takis looked up at Cesare. "Mind if we find out what a good teacher you are?"

"Go ahead. She's never cooked anything in her life, but she followed Mamma's sacred recipe for Sicilian nun buns to the letter." He uncovered the pan so they could take one.

Both men started eating and didn't stop until half of the decorated mounds were gone. Tuccia could have received no greater compliment.

Vincenzo lifted his head. "You swear you didn't cook these yourself?"

"I stood over her shoulder. That's all."

"She really made these on her own?" Takis looked astounded.

Cesare nodded. "It took her three tries. She even cleaned up the mess in the kitchen afterwards."

"Do you think this was a one-time accident, or is the princess the proverbial diamond in the rough?"

"I'd like to see her make half a dozen Sicilian desserts at the *pensione* before I could answer that question, Takis. Today it was fear that drove her. She'd do anything to stay hidden. But to master the art of fine pastry making and love to do it is a gift only a few people possess. Within a few days she could hate it.

"As for her working here as the pastry chef, it would mean dealing with the kitchen assistants. I have no idea how she would handle them under pressure. For all of those reasons I'm going to tell her this won't work."

"Not so fast," Vincenzo interjected. "Before you say or do anything, why don't I ask Gemma to visit her tomorrow? Let her lay out what a day in the kitchen would be like for Tuccia. She'd be able to ask my wife questions about the routine and the personalities she would have to deal with."

"But Vincenzo—Gemma learned from her mother and studied pastry making for ten years at the finest school in Florence. She would laugh in disbelief at such a ludicrous idea."

Vincenzo shook his head. "We've all heard the news about the princess who ran away. No one would be more understanding than my wife who saw first-hand what went on between my father and me years ago. Takis and I agree those nun buns the princess made were divine. I think it's worth going to the trouble to give her a chance. I know Gemma will feel the same way."

"You don't want her on her feet at this late date in her pregnancy. Neither do I."

"Cooking for hours every day is entirely different than having a serious talk with Tuccia."

Takis nodded. "He's got a point, Cesare."

"I don't know. I have a lot to think about. Tomorrow when I go down to the *pensione*, I'll probably discover she wants to leave. Whatever is decided, I'll let you know. I guess you realize I'm indebted to you two for being the best friends any man could ever have. Now go to bed. That's an order."

Both men stole the rest of the mounds from the pan before walking out the door.

Cesare tossed and turned all night, too eager to see her again to sleep. Early the next morning he got dressed and left the *castello* in his hard-top sports car parked around the rear. He took the empty pan with him.

When he reached the village, he stopped at a *trattoria* for takeout: breakfast for two. To his dismay he realized that he was so excited at the prospect of seeing her again he couldn't think about anything else. Though it had only been a few days, Tuccia had taken up space in his mind and heart.

He'd known desire for women and had enjoyed several short-term relationships, but they'd always stopped short of marriage because some crucial element had been missing. That was what he'd always told himself. But this was different because so far Tuccia appealed to him on every level and had already colored his world.

He reached the *pensione* at eight and got out of the car. After knocking on the door, he expected her to answer in tears and be anxious to get to the train station.

CHAPTER FIVE

LAST NIGHT TUCCIA had wished Cesare had stayed. But if she'd asked him not to go, she would have given him the wrong idea. She had a problem because she knew she'd fallen in love with him and was more attracted to him with every passing minute. When the limo pulled away, she'd closed and locked the door, fearing she wouldn't get to sleep for a long time.

At four this morning, an exhausted Tuccia had turned off her watch alarm and got out of bed to do her homework. It was one thing to cook while Cesare had stood there directing her every step. The trick was to do it while he wasn't watching.

She knew there were enough ingredients for her to make one more batch of the tarts on her own. But with no big shallow pan, she'd had to improvise with two small round pans with higher sides she'd found in the cupboard. As a result, she still had half the batter to cook.

If she failed miserably, then she'd be the first to ask him to drive her to the train station. It would be the last thing he would ever have to do for her. Before she threw herself at him, she realized it would be better if she never saw him again.

Tuccia had thought her initial physical attraction to him would fade, but the opposite had happened. His underlying goodness as a human being had opened her eyes to the other qualities in his nature that had nothing to do with his striking male looks. Everything about him from his intellect to his humor stimulated her. So much, in fact, that she was breathless as she waited to see him again today.

The knock on the door came sooner than she had expected, sending her pulse racing as if she had a sickness. She put down the cup she'd been using to add the final lemon glaze to the tarts she'd made. There were still three to be coated and decorated.

After wiping her hands on a towel, she hurried to answer the door, knowing flour still dusted part of the same blouse she'd worn last evening. There was even some on her forearms.

When she opened it, their eyes met for a quiet moment. His were smiling, if there was such a thing. She got a fluttering in her chest as his gaze wandered over her.

"I bet you didn't know there's flour on the tip of your nose." Before she could blink, he removed it with his thumb. His touch sent an electricity-like spark through her body. "If I don't miss my guess, I would say you've already been hard at work this morning."

She was worried yet excited to show him. "Come in and find out."

Cesare walked through to the kitchen with another bag of food and the empty pan. He put them both on the counter and pulled a phone out of his pocket.

"This is for you. All programmed." He put it at the end of the counter.

Tuccia thanked him, but she had no idea where the batch of tarts he'd left with had ended up. She didn't think she wanted to know.

Without asking her permission, Cesare took a finished product from one of the small round pans. He examined it first. Then he bit into it. An anxious Tuccia waited while he took another bite and another, until it was all gone. *Uh-oh. Here it comes.*

"Why are you closing your eyes?" he asked in a quiet voice.

"I don't know. So I can handle the bad verdict better?"

"On your fourth try, you've achieved perfection. The cinnamon balance is just right. As for the shapes, my mother wouldn't know them from her own. If I didn't have a knowledge of your upbringing, I'd think you came out of the same nunnery." This time he brushed her mouth with his own.

She opened her eyes, trying to contain her joy. "Thank you, Cesare, but you don't have to overdo it."

He ignored her comment. "I'm even more impressed you found something else to cook them in. This apartment is ill-equipped for a chef. When Mamma told me you were resourceful, I don't believe that even she understood the scope of your abilities."

Tuccia scoffed. "She was only quoting my *zia* who thinks I can do no wrong. She and my *zio* wanted babies so much. What they got was me when my parents didn't know what to do with me. Bertina was the one bright light in my existence."

"As you still are in hers," he came back, seemingly deep in thought. "Otherwise she wouldn't have risked everything to help you." His blue gaze swerved to hers, sending more darts of awareness through her body. "That includes using my mother who happens to have the same favorable opinion of you."

"I'll never be able to thank her enough for what she's done. But right this minute I want the honest answer to one question. After talking to your partners, should I be getting ready to leave for Catania?"

He lounged his rock-hard body against the edge of the counter with his arms folded. "I'd like *your* honest answer to another question first. Why did you get up at the crack of dawn and go to all the effort of making another batch when you could have stayed asleep?"

She took a deep breath. "Because I needed to find out for myself if I was capable of following that recipe on my own."

"Which you've demonstrated beyond all doubt. Would it interest you to know my partners devoured the tarts you made?"

"No, they didn't," she said with an embarrassed chuckle.

"One bite told them everything they needed to know. They stuffed themselves and took the few uneaten mounds with them when they left my room."

"Now you're just trying to make me feel good because…because that's the kind of man you are," she said, her voice faltering.

"You don't have to compliment me back." Yes, she did. She owed him her life right now. "Let me prove it to you."

Tuccia watched him pull out his cell phone and make a call to Vincenzo, the present Duc di Lombardi. They talked for a few moments before he hung up.

"Vincenzo's wife, Gemma, will be arriving within

the hour. Shall we eat the breakfast I brought now? Then I'll clean up the kitchen while you get ready for our guest."

A slight gasp escaped her lips. "Why would she be coming here?"

He reached for the bag of food and set it on the table. "You've passed your first test by baking a dessert the *castello ristorante* would be proud to serve. But this is only the beginning if you decide to accept the daunting challenge facing you."

She averted her eyes. "You're right. It's so daunting, I'm terrified."

"Be frank with Gemma and see what happens."

"What's she like?"

"Only a few years older than you and one of the nicest, kindest women I've ever known."

"Besides being a master pastry chef."

He nodded. "A chef who's about to become a mother. She can't wait for their baby to arrive and is anxious to let someone else take on her former mantle."

"Which no doubt *you* will be doing before the day is out, Cesare. Please forgive me if I skip breakfast. That was very kind of you to bring it, but I'm afraid I can't eat anything right now."

She rushed to the bedroom to take a shower and change into jeans and a knit top. Tuccia had only packed a few understated clothes at Bertina's because she knew she would have to travel light on her trip to Catania and didn't dare stand out.

After being sheltered at Lina Donati's villa for one night, she could never have known she would end up here in Milan to face a situation undreamed of.

Be frank with Gemma.

Tuccia interpreted that to mean she must put the princess part of herself aside. For once she had to dig down to her core and decide if she thought she could pull this off.

This could all end in a second if she asked Cesare to call Vincenzo back and tell him not to bring his wife to the *pensione.* Within a few minutes Tuccia could be driven to the train.

That would leave Cesare to take on the exclusive role of executive pastry chef until he found someone else exceptional, or until Signor Fragala recovered.

But for Tuccia, it would mean never seeing him again. Her heart told her she couldn't handle that. He'd become too important to her.

Sucking in her breath, she reached for the brush to style her curls. Once she'd applied some light makeup and lipstick, she left the bedroom to face what was coming.

Cesare walked outside when he saw Vincenzo's Mercedes pull up in front. While his friend came around from the other side, Cesare helped a blonde, very pregnant Gemma out of the front seat and kissed her cheek. "Thanks for coming."

"It's my privilege. How *à propos* that the princess is staying here in the same apartment I did."

"I thought it the safest place to conceal her."

"You've found the perfect spot tucked out of the way. It takes me back to those first days when I left the *pensione* to meet you for the first time. I was shaking in my boots to be interviewed by the internationally famous restaurateur owner of the Castello Supremo Hotel and Ristorante di Lombardi."

"I would never have known it, Gemma. When you told me your mother's pastry would always be the best, I felt an immediate affinity to you since I felt the same way about my mother's Sicilian cooking. Your desserts were divine."

She kissed his cheek. "Little did I know I would come face to face with Vincenzo when I thought he'd disappeared from my life forever."

Her husband put his arm around her nonexistent waist. "None of us will forget that day. I too thought I'd lost the love of my life. *Grazie a Dio* we found each other."

While his friend chose that moment to kiss Gemma thoroughly, Cesare went back inside the apartment. Tuccia had come in the small living room looking so appealing he'd have liked to do the same thing to her. He was in serious trouble because he knew he couldn't hold back much longer in showing her how he felt.

"They're coming," he said, after answering the question in her misty gray eyes, which were more noticeable because of her black fringed lashes and black hair. She had the most remarkable coloring and light olive complexion. With her oval face and alluring mouth, she looked so irresistible he had to force himself to look away or he'd make her uncomfortable.

He heard the others file inside. "Princess Tuccianna, allow me to present two of my dearest and closest friends, Vincenzo Gagliardi, the Duc di Lombardi, and his wife Gemma."

"It's a real honor for me." Tuccia shook their hands.

"We're the ones honored, Princess," Vincenzo declared. Cesare could tell his friend was bowled over by her beauty, a feat that didn't happen often.

"Please, just call me Tuccia. Won't you sit down? I feel a fraud inviting you into this *pensione* Cesare not only found for me, but is paying for until I can reimburse him."

Cesare noted she was always grace itself. The spoiled princess as reported in the news wasn't the same person he'd pulled against his body a few nights ago for fear she would fall.

"Your desperate situation has called for drastic measures. I had a similar experience in my late teens and was anxious for any help I could get." Leave it to Vincenzo to make her feel comfortable.

"Nevertheless I've put all of you in a dangerous position simply by being here and want you to know I'm ready to leave after we've talked."

Gemma got up from the couch. Cesare noticed that she was a little slower these days. "Tuccia? Before there's any talk like that, why don't you and I go in the kitchen where we can be private and let the guys talk business in here."

Cesare nodded. "That's a good idea." He watched Tuccia follow Gemma into the kitchen. She might be nervous now, but before long she'd realize she couldn't be in better hands than Gemma's. His gaze swerved to his friend.

"How does your wife really feel about this?" he asked in a quiet voice.

"She ate one of the tarts I took back to our room. When she'd finished, she said, 'I know this was Cesare's recipe, but if Tuccia can make all his Sicilian desserts as exquisite as these, the *castello* is going to gain a new following.'"

"That's high praise, Vincenzo."

"Gemma is nothing if not truthful."

"If by any chance this works out, I'll insist Tuccia live here and make each dessert in the kitchen first. It will help her feel confident before she leaves for the *castello* every morning to manage her assistants. But I'm afraid that without the right disguise, someone will recognize her and the police will descend."

Vincenzo flashed him a subtle smile. "Meeting her explains a lot. She's a genuine knockout, Cesare. Gemma will be hard-pressed to come up with something that hides her beauty."

"Tell me about it."

"I don't think I have to, *amico*."

No. And the second Takis laid eyes on her, Cesare was in for it. "Was there anything on the morning news I should be concerned about yet?"

"Nothing. The police are at a standstill. Her parents have offered ten million euros for the person who finds her."

"Only ten for their precious daughter?" he bit out in disgust.

"No doubt the *comte*'s reward will be forthcoming before the day is out."

Cesare looked over his shoulder at Tuccia who was deep in conversation with Gemma. "I wonder how much he'd be willing to pay for her safe return. But it won't matter when he gets her letter explaining why she ran away." Cesare confided that he'd couriered it to his attorney in Barbados who would send it on.

"That was excellent thinking."

"She's been suffering terrible guilt."

"Understandable."

"But that part is done. When I arrived here this morning and saw that she'd already been up three hours making the recipe again, I knew for a fact that no amount of money would ever induce her to go back to him."

Vincenzo's brows lifted. "How did she do?"

"Hold on. I'll show you."

Cesare got up and walked into the kitchen. "*Scusa*, ladies." He plucked one of the round pans off the counter and took it into Vincenzo.

His friend reached for an iced tart and ate it in two bites before nodding in satisfaction. "After Gemma and I leave here, we'll drive into Milan and take the rest of these to my cousin and his wife to taste. Dimi will be in shock when we tell him what has happened."

"*Who* will be in shock, *mia cara?*" Gemma had just come back in the living room with Tuccia. Both men stood up.

"I thought we'd visit Dimi before we go back to the *castello* and let them sample Tuccia's nun buns. Did you get your business done?"

"We're off to a good start, aren't we, Tuccia?"

"Your wife has encouraged me to give it a try for which I'm very grateful." The relief on her face was tangible.

"Meraviglioso!" Vincenzo picked up the pan and helped his wife out the door to his car. Cesare knew how happy his friend was that someone else was going to be doing the work Gemma had done for so long.

He shut the door and turned to the woman who was transforming his life in ways he couldn't have imagined days ago. "I'm sure you have a great deal to discuss with me."

She nodded. "Thankfully Gemma is going to work two more days while I keep cooking desserts here at the apartment. Then it'll be my first day in the *castello* kitchen. She'll acquaint me with everything and stay long enough to introduce me to the staff before I'm on my own."

"You won't be alone. I'll be there in the background until you get your bearings. But tell me what it is that concerns Gemma the most?"

"A disguise for me, especially for my hair."

Her crowning glory was a dead giveaway. "Why don't you freshen up. Then we'll drive to the uniform shop in Milan used by the kitchen help. We'll find something that works. You'll have to wear your scarf and sunglasses."

"It'll be wonderful to get out for a little while." He could imagine. "I'll hurry."

After she disappeared, he reached in the fridge for a soda. Their shopping spree would include a stop to the grocery store. Once that was done they'd pick up some takeout and bring it back to the apartment for a meal. Toward evening they'd get busy working on a couple of new desserts. He loved being alone with her.

Tuccia hurried out to his sports car. Once again she had that sensation of being spirited away where nothing could hurt her. But this time she wanted Cesare to be more than her protector. Though he'd kissed her several times, she wanted… She wanted the impossible.

He drove them into Milan with expertise and parked

in front of a shop labeled Uniforme di Oggi. "Remember to keep your head mostly down."

"I will."

She couldn't get over the huge selection of chef apparel at the back. While she was taking it all in, Cesare seemed to know exactly what he wanted.

"Here. Try this on."

Cesare handed her a short-sleeved white lab coat that fell above the knee. After she put it on, he shook his head. "It needs to be larger to cover a T-shirt and chef's pants." He handed her a coat two sizes bigger. She tried it on.

"That will do fine. We'll take six of them. Now for six sets of pants and T-shirts that fit. Everything white."

Once she'd pulled the clothes off the racks and handed them to the clerk, they walked over to the counter to look at the chef hats and beanies of all kinds. Again, Cesare already had something in mind and reached for the traditional white floppy hat.

He handed it to Tuccia. "Go in the changing room and try it on where no one will see you. If it's not the right fit, call outside the door to me and I'll get the right one." They walked down the little hall. "Don't get any ideas about slipping out the back way, or you'll be on your own, Principessa." He said it with a slow smile that sent a river of warmth through her body.

Once inside, she removed her scarf and tried on the hat. It was too big. She told him as much. He returned in a minute with a smaller version. This one was just right. It would keep her hair snug inside and prevent any strands from slipping.

She put the scarf and glasses back on before emerging. “This one is the right size.”

“Good. We’ll take six of them.”

He walked her over to the counter and before long they left the shop for his car with her new clothes. Talk about fun. Being with Cesare like this was turning out to be the happiest day of her life. To know the two of them would be working together for months and months was her idea of heaven. She didn’t care how hard she had to work.

He drove her around to another store featuring eye glasses. “Stay in the car. I’ll be right back.”

With his brown hair and tall male physique, he made every man walking along the street look pathetic in comparison. When he came out of the store a few minutes later and flashed her a smile, she couldn’t breathe. He handed her a bag with several sets of eye glasses for her to choose from.

“I have an idea,” he announced. They’d already left the city for the village. “I’ll pick up a meal and ask Takis to join us. My other partner needs to meet you. When he walks in the apartment, I want you to be wearing a complete chef’s outfit. Of course he knows what you look like. If you can pass his inspection, then we’ll know we have a chance that your identity will remain a secret.”

“It *has* to,” she whispered.

For a second time in several days Cesare reached for her hand and squeezed it. “This is going to work, Tuccia.” She got the feeling he wanted this to work as much as she did. Soon they reached the grocery store and he let go of her. “I’ll try not to be too long.” He turned on the radio. “In case you want to listen.”

While he was gone taking his warmth with him, she moved the tuner and heard the top-of-the-hour news. Her disappearance was still the lead story and a reward was being offered for help in finding her.

How odd that she felt so removed from the princess they were describing. In just a few days she felt like she'd turned into someone else. People were walking around the village and here she was, right in the middle of them with no one the wiser.

Cesare's energy was something to behold. He came back to the car loaded with more groceries and their dinner. She smiled at him. "That was fast. I'm sorry I couldn't be of help." She would adore shopping for groceries with him. Anything where they could be together.

He started the car. "One day all this will be behind you. Let's go home. I gave Takis a call. He'll be here at five which doesn't give you much time to work on your disguise."

"I have an idea about what to do with my hair. If I pull on a nylon stocking first, it will help keep it in place."

"That ought to work. Do we need to buy you some nylons?"

"No. I have a pair with me. Do you think it will be all right if I wear my leather sandals?"

"If they're comfortable, I don't see why not."

When they reached the *pensione*, she got out and helped carry in the bags. "I'll put the clothes in my bedroom."

"Don't come out until you've morphed into a chef. I admit I can't wait to see what you look like."

Neither could Tuccia. After a quick shower she put

on a pair of white semi-baggy drawstring pants. Next came the short-sleeved crew neck T-shirt. Now for the tricky part. She took off the scarf and rummaged in the dresser drawer for a stocking.

She fit it around her head so no hair could escape and pinned it to the crown. After grabbing a chef's hat and sack of eye glasses, she dashed in the bathroom. First she pulled out a pair of the clear lenses with neutral brown frames. Very professional looking. They fit over her ears just fine. Then she put on the hat, slanting the floppy part. The whole thing actually worked. She didn't recognize herself.

Tuccia normally wore a melon colored lipstick. She decided that wouldn't do and wiped off all traces. Pleased with the effect, she went back in the bedroom and pulled on the lab coat. It had pockets and seven buttons down the front opening, leaving the top of the T-shirt exposed. Her figure was non-existent, but that was the whole point.

Still dressed in her sandals, she felt ready for the fashion show. With pounding heart she tiptoed in the living room and found Cesare putting the groceries away. He'd laid the table for their dinner.

"*Signor?* May I have your attention, *per favore*?"

He wheeled around with a sack of flour in his hand. But when he saw her, it dropped to the counter, reminding her of the night in his mother's kitchen. She burst into laughter at the shock on his painfully handsome face.

She moved into the kitchen. "Perhaps you don't recognize me. I'm the new executive pastry chef at the Castello Supremo Hotel Ristorante in Milan, Italy. I can see by your expression that I've achieved a certain amount of success in that department, *signor*."

Loving this, Tuccia turned around like a model on a runway. "If you'll take a closer look, you'll see the detail of the stitching on the pockets of this stunning creation." His eyes played everywhere, as if trying to figure out where she'd gone.

"Pay attention to the large puffy hat, the latest in chic chef wear. This designer was chosen by the world famous five-star restaurateur Cesare Donati. He features nothing but the best in his kitchens, whether here or in New York. It's the greatest privilege I've ever known to be working for him."

His hand rubbed his chest as if he were in a trance. "I saw you go into the bedroom a little while ago," he began in a deep voice. "But I still can't believe it's you underneath all that white."

"Then you think I'll do?"

A knock on the door prevented him from responding. "Come on in, Takis."

Tuccia watched his dark-blond partner walk inside and shut it. Here was another incredibly attractive man who she'd been told had come from the island of Crete. His hazel eyes narrowed on her before he turned to Cesare. "I thought you said that Princess Tuccianna would be here."

"Did you hear that?" Cesare asked her.

"Yes. If the *signori* will excuse me, I'll tell her your guest has arrived for dinner."

She darted back to the bedroom so excited, she had trouble taking off all of her disguise. In a few minutes she returned to the living room with her hair brushed and lipstick on her mouth, wearing the same clothes she'd worn to town with Cesare.

His eyes pierced hers. "Princess Tuccianna, may I present my friend and partner, Takis Manolis."

"I've heard a great deal about you, Signor Manolis. It's a real pleasure to meet you."

He looked taken back. "It *was* you dressed as a chef." A grin broke out on his face. "After knowing what you look like, I would never have guessed. I'm honored to meet you." He shook her hand warmly.

"Even though I'm a wanted fugitive who's putting all of you in jeopardy?"

"Last night Cesare filled us in on the details. After I ate half of those nun buns you made, I told him I believe you'll make an excellent chef. And now that I've seen you in your uniform, I'm convinced no one will recognize you."

"I agree the transformation was miraculous," Cesare murmured. She couldn't wait to hear more about it once they were alone. "Let's eat, shall we? I'm afraid all the shopping we did has worn me out and I'm ravenous."

They sat at the kitchen table where Cesare treated them to scallops, beef *tagliati*, parmesan aubergine and pasta *con le sarde.* Tuccia could hardly believe she was sitting here with these two amazing men, chatting and enjoying the take-out food as if she didn't have a worry in the world. She'd entered into another realm of existence and never wanted to be anywhere else.

"Gemma told me her meeting with you went very well."

"She's a lovely person who answered a lot of questions for me."

"I'll tell you something honestly. She's convinced your Sicilian pastries will create a new sensation with our clientele."

Tuccia put her wine glass down. "You mean Cesare's."

"In time they'll become yours, too."

Takis had a charm almost as lethal as Cesare's. "One dessert does not make a chef, but I'm going to do my very best not to let you down. This evening Cesare will be assigning me a new recipe to cook."

"That's right." Cesare smiled at her. *"Cassateddi."*

She took a deep breath. "Those half-moon-shaped pastries were a favorite of mine growing up, but I never dreamed I'd learn how to make them."

"I loved them, too. So will Takis and Vincenzo. But they're only the beginning. Tomorrow you'll be making *testa di turco*, followed by *sfingi di San Giuseppe, casstelle di Sant'Agata* and Sicilian chocolate torte."

Cesare had just done an excellent job of frightening her to death.

"I think you're overwhelming her, *amico."*

She leaned toward Takis. "His mother told me he drove her crazy growing up. No matter what she cooked, she'd find some of it missing the second she turned around," Tuccia confided.

Immediately Takis burst into rich male laughter. But Cesare didn't join in.

Too soon their visitor announced that he had to leave and said good-night. She was sorry to see him go because she'd gotten a little carried away with her out-of-school tale where Cesare was concerned. She'd been having too good a time and feared she'd crossed an unmarked boundary in their relationship.

While Cesare walked him out to his car, she hurriedly cleaned up the kitchen. When he came inside, she was already seated at the table with her bible, ready to write down the recipe for what she hoped would turn out to be a worthy *chef d'oeuvre.*

He washed and dried his hands, then he sat down, eyeing her with an intensity that made her squirm. "Tuccia," he began, "I—"

"I know what you're going to say," she broke in on him. "I apologize for saying something so personal in front of your friend. It was wrong of me to overstep like that. I promise it won't happen again."

His brows met in a frown. "I wasn't going to say anything of the sort. Before Takis drove off, he told me you were as sensational as your nun buns and we should keep you at all costs. Takis would never say anything like that unless he meant it."

She looked down because emotion had caused her eyes to smart.

"Before you interrupted me, I was going to tell you the disguise is perfect. I have no doubt you'll be a new trendsetter for the kitchen assistants. They'll take one look at you and want to be just like you, but they'll fail because there's only one Princess Tuccianna."

Tuccia was afraid her cheeks were on fire. She wanted him to forget she was a princess. She wanted him to see her as a woman he could love heart and soul. Looking up she said, "That's absurd, but thank you. Don't you think we should get started on the *cassateddi*? I'll need half the night to make it several times."

Those blue eyes narrowed on her features. "I thought *I* was the slave driver around here."

"Would you rather leave and come back tomorrow morning? I'd understand if you have another engagement."

"I have no plans to meet another woman."

Maybe not tonight. But it didn't mean there wasn't someone who loved him and was waiting anxiously to be with him. She couldn't bear the thought and was ridiculously jealous of any woman he'd been with.

"You're wrong, you know, Tuccia."

"What do you mean?"

"I can read your mind. There's no room in my life for any woman until the *castello*'s new pastry chef can create masterpieces without my help."

Just like that he'd drawn a sharp line in the sand. Meaning she shouldn't get any ideas about him for herself?

She sucked in her breath. "Since I'd hate to see you deprived of that kind of pleasure too long because of me, I'll work day and night to achieve that goal." She tapped the notebook with her pen. "I'm ready when you are."

CHAPTER SIX

TWO HOURS LATER Tuccia was in tears. She'd turned out two batches of half-moon shells filled with cream, but they'd been failures. Cesare had tried to eat one and it had fallen apart because she hadn't shaped it right. He had to eat it in pieces. She had to smother a moan watching him.

"The taste of this is superb."

"That doesn't count when its misshape falls apart before reaching your mouth. I tried to execute your directions to the letter, but I couldn't seem to get it right." She dried her eyes with a towel, but they kept falling. "This will never do. I'm going to make the recipe again."

He reached for the towel and wiped her cheeks. "We don't want your tears falling into your next attempt." His comment made her laugh and he kissed both her cheeks before she got started again on a third batch.

His pride in her work ethic kept growing while she took pains to crimp the edges just right. Another hour passed before he tested a sample of her latest work. "I find no fault in this presentation or the taste."

"Thank you," she murmured, but he could tell she still wasn't happy.

Cesare had no doubt that when he left the apartment, she'd make up another batch. Her fighting spirit was a trait he admired more than she would ever know. He stood against the doorjamb and watched while she put the third tray of shells inside the fridge.

"Did Gemma tell you about Maurice Troudeau, our executive chef?"

A corner of her delectable mouth lifted. "She said the key with him was to praise his work often and ask for help once in a while, even if you don't need it. I used that technique on Auguste Senlis, the most difficult history professor at the Sorbonne, and it worked."

Of course it did, but he wasn't smitten because of her smarts. No man anywhere who came into her sphere could remain unaffected. Takis and Vincenzo were a case in point.

"If I have a concern, it's because your French is too perfect. You're a princess on the run who speaks it fluently. Unfortunately you can't afford to speak it with him at all. When I introduce you, you'll be known as Nedda Bottaro from Sicily who speaks Sicilian with a Palermo dialect. Your knowledge of English is too minimal to count on. That's it."

"I understand."

He was sure she did. "Have you thought of a backstory? The staff will ask and you'll have to be ready."

"Yes. I was born in the back room of a bordello in Trapani and never knew my father. My mother didn't, either."

Cesare was having trouble holding back his laughter.

"When I was old enough to be of use, she gave me to the woman next door who was a cook and needed a helper. I never went to school. After my mother died of an infection, I ran away to Palermo and did all kinds of jobs until I prevailed on a baker to let me work for him. I liked that work best and stayed there until I was discovered by you!" Her gray eyes stared straight into his. "What do you think?"

At this minute he didn't dare tell her what he thought or felt. He was in love with her. "I have one suggestion. At least say that you went to school once in a while. Your intelligence shines through in everything you say and do."

"So does yours. Thank you for tonight's cooking lesson. I'll see you in the morning."

If she had any idea he would rather stay with her all night and every night, she'd fly out the door. "Tuccia? Before I leave, let's go in the living room and talk for a minute about something serious. You've been cooped up here for several days, no doubt missing a few friends to talk to."

Cesare went in the other room first so she'd follow. They both sat down. He took a chair and she the couch. "I know you've run away from your parents, but deep down this has to be torturous for you."

She curled up against the side. "If I told you the truth, I'm afraid you might think me a person with no natural affection."

He steadied himself. "Explain that."

"I know you're supposed to love your parents. I suppose I do in a philosophical way, but it's Zia Bertina I've always turned to. She was the mother I needed. My own was cold and my father was always a stranger to me. When I think of them, I get an empty feeling inside. With a mother like yours, I know you can't comprehend it."

Cesare shifted in the chair. "You're right." He had no words.

"I don't tell you this so you'll feel sorry for me, but only to explain that I've lived with this situation for twenty-five years. Your concern for my feelings has touched me very much, but you needn't worry yourself on my account because I have to stay secluded. As long as I have my *zia* who has loved me all my life, I'm happy."

He sucked in his breath. "But it's still not too late for you to leave Milan and do what you want, whether in Catania or elsewhere. You should be able to embark on a new life, work at something that interests you and make new friends."

"Find a lover *I've* chosen?" she added in a voice that made her sound much older.

He closed his eyes for a moment. "Why not?"

"I never wanted the fiancé I can't stand, let alone some lover, followed by another and then another that goes on and on like a revolving door. We royals are known for it. To be honest I can't think of anything worse."

Neither could Cesare.

"Right now there's just one thing on my mind. To prove that I can make a success of something truly important, not only to me, but to you and your partners. Your *ristorante* is without a pastry chef. If I could pull this off, nothing would make me happier."

Her earnestness crept through him, causing his throat to swell. "I believe you mean that."

She nodded. "I've surprised myself. Do you know what a shock it is to discover that I *like* such painstaking work? Who would have thought I'd find it a challenge to crimp the edges of those half moons so they were just right? But if you think there's still too much danger, or that it's really not going to work, then please tell me now and I'll leave whenever you say."

Humbled by an inner purity in her, Cesare got up from the chair. When he'd suggested they come in the living room for a little talk, he never expected to feel his heart torn apart by the confessions of a girl whose parents hadn't been able to show her how precious she was.

The backstory she'd concocted for the staff could only have come from a princess who'd been born with every advantage under the sun except love.

"Rest assured we need you right here, Tuccia." He leaned over to kiss her lips briefly, unable to help himself. But if she'd wanted to respond, he didn't give her the chance and stood up. "Stay where you are. You look too comfortable to move. I'll let myself out and see you in the morning with breakfast and more groceries."

After a detour to the kitchen for one of the pans of *cassateddi* to share with his friends, he left for the *castello* a different man than the one he'd been four hours ago.

On the drive home, Cesare pulled out his cell to call his mother. He was glad to hear that his sister was there visiting with her husband and baby. They all chatted for a few minutes until Isabella got off the line.

"Now we can talk about important matters, Cesare. I have to tell you Bertina is out of her mind with worry."

"Let her know I just came from being with Tuccia. She sends her love and wants to assure her *zia* all is well. She would phone, but knows the police have tapped the lines."

"I'm sure of it. Tuccia is really all right?"

"Would I tell you otherwise?"

"No, *figlio mio*. I trust you with my life."

"That's nice to hear. Does Bertina have any more news about the search?"

"The police are baffled. Their bungling has enraged her sister and brother-in-law. Bertina's sources tell her that Jean-Michel is so overcome he has remained incommunicado to the media. There's been no ransom note and they fear for her welfare."

"I have something to tell you, Mamma." In the next breath he told her about the letter being sent to Jean-Michel. "Once he receives it, everything will change."

"It can't get to him soon enough!"

"I agree." In the meantime Tuccia would hear the worst when she turned on her TV. "I hope Bertina is putting on the show of her life to prove how grief-stricken she is."

"If I didn't know the truth, I'd be convinced she's in the depths of despair. I've decided she could have been a great actress."

Superb acting appeared to run in the royal family. Tuccia's fashion show earlier this evening had stunned him close to speechless.

"One more thing you should know, Cesare. Bertina says Tuccia's parents are truly distraught over the situation and she can tell this experience has caused them to realize it's their fault that she's run away. They are beside themselves with worry and she senses a softening."

"That's wonderful news, Mamma." When he could, he'd relay that message to Tuccia. "Tell me about Ciro."

"If there are no more complications, he'll be taken to a private room tomorrow."

"We'll hope for the best. I have to hang up now, but I'll call you soon. *Bona notti*, Mamma."

It was ten after one in the afternoon and Tuccia still hadn't finished cooking this latest recipe. She let out a moan. "These *sfingi di San Giuseppe* balls are all wobbly. I can't make them even."

Cesare chuckled. Nothing seemed to bother him. The man had arrived early that morning in jeans and a silky claret-colored open-necked sport shirt looking devilishly gorgeous. There ought to be a law against it.

She hadn't slept all night remembering the taste of his mouth on hers. He wouldn't have kissed her if he didn't have feelings for her. It was the reason she'd been a mess after he'd left the apartment the night before. Since then she'd been reliving that moment and wanted to repeat the experience. But this time she wouldn't let him go.

"They're supposed to look like that."

"No, they're not! What am I doing wrong?"

"Nothing. When they're fried, their centers will hollow out so you can fill them."

She shot him a glance. "You promise?"

"I swear it. Have you put out the toweling?"

"It's right here on the counter next to the stove."

"Have you checked the temperature of the olive oil?"

"Yes. The thermometer says it's ready."

"Then get started. Remember not to let the ball plop, but don't be afraid of it."

Tuccia began the laborious process of cooking and draining. They smelled good and everything was going fine until the last one. It fell off the spoon too fast and some drops of oil splashed on her wrist. She cried out in surprise.

Cesare was there so fast he had her hand under the cold water before she could think. "Keep it there for a few minutes," he said while he removed the oil and turned off the burner.

"I tried to be careful, but I was clumsy."

"I defy anyone cooking with oil for the first time to escape with no burns."

While the water was still running he examined the three small welts on her skin. "These will hurt, but I have a remedy my mother used that works well."

She couldn't feel the pain, not while their bodies were so close and he was touching her. "Thank you," she said in a tremulous voice before lifting her head.

His eyes searched hers before his free hand caressed the side of her face. "I'm sorry you got burned," he whispered.

Tuccia felt his breath on her lips. Her heart felt like it was going to pump right out of her chest. Driven by her love for him, she pressed her mouth to his, daring to let him know she wanted more. "It's nothing," she whispered, then quickly turned to put her hand under the water once more.

He moved away from her. "I'll run to the *farmacia* and be right back." Cesare was out the door before she could think. It was just as well. If he'd stayed close to her a second longer, she would have made a complete fool of herself and thrown her arms around his neck.

She'd never known the white-hot heat of desire for a man until now. To experience its power for herself was life-changing. The few guys at college she'd flirted with in class had meant nothing more than a little experimentation that couldn't go anywhere.

Though she'd always planned to run away before she had to marry Jean-Michel, she never expected to find loving fulfillment with one man. Tuccia hadn't believed such a thing was possible. First she had to *find* the right man, and he had to find *her*.

But when she heard the door open and Cesare walked back in the apartment with a small sack in his hand, she knew beyond a shadow of a doubt she was looking at the right man. The *only* man for her. She felt it in the marrow of her bones.

Tuccia turned off the water and waited. He walked over to the counter and pulled from a shelf the bottle of honey she'd used in one of the recipes. Next, he opened the sack and drew out some gauze pads and a small box of plasters.

Without looking at her he covered the gauze with honey and said, "Put out your arm and we'll get rid of that pain."

Tuccia did his bidding. Within a minute he'd covered the three welts with the gooey gauze pads and secured them with a plaster. She marveled at his dexterity. "I had no idea honey could be used like this."

"It has dozens of restorative elements."

"Thank you, Cesare. I'm very lucky to have a boss who's a doctor, too."

He smiled a smile that sent her pulse off the charts. "You should be feeling relief soon."

"That's good because I need to poke a hole in those balls and fill them with the ricotta cream I've made."

Cesare darted her a glance. "All of it will keep. Before you do any more cooking, I thought we'd pick up lunch and have a picnic. It will give those burns a chance to settle down."

"A picnic? I'd love it! When I think about it, I haven't been on one of those since I was a little girl. My *zia* would take me to the park and we'd feed the birds. I'll grab the things I need and meet you at the car."

She dashed into the bedroom for her scarf. When she'd put it on, she slid her sunglasses in place and hurried out of the apartment. Cesare, the striking, quintessential Sicilian male, was there to help her in and they drove off.

For once in her life, what was happening to her wasn't a dream her mind had concocted while she'd been asleep. She was wide awake. This was real. Her feelings were real and she wanted to shout to the world that she was madly in love with him.

He stopped at a local deli for takeout and they headed toward Milan. Before long he turned onto the grounds of the Giardino Della Guastalla. "These gardens are five hundred years old," he explained. "I know the perfect spot where we can be alone. Maybe we'll be able to feed a few birds the remnants of our lunch. Do you mind sitting on the grass?"

"To be out in nature is exactly what this warm day calls for."

He parked and they walked to a lush spot beneath a giant oak tree. The freedom to be out here alone with Cesare made her giddy. After removing her sunglasses, she lay down in the grass on her stomach and rested her head against her arms.

"Careful of those burns," he said, sitting down next to her.

She squinted up at him. "Honestly? I forgot I was hurting. Your honey has worked miracles."

"I'm glad." Cesare opened up the cartons. She turned on her side and leaned on one elbow while they ate shrimps and pasta salad with little forks. He opened a bottle of red wine and poured it into cups. She drank some and munched on a French bread roll.

"I feel sinful lying here."

Blue eyes full of amusement roved over her. "Because you're with me instead of your former fiancé?"

"No." She smiled. "Because I'm with someone I care about to the exclusion of anyone else," she said before it was too late to stop her thoughts from becoming verbal.

He drank the rest of his wine. "Surely there've been some men you've liked who have tried to have a secret relationship with you?"

"I was always under surveillance, Cesare." She looked at him through veiled eyes. "As you know, there are different levels of liking without much emotional involvement. I liked some of the guys in my classes, but didn't have the freedom to do anything about it. But to actually care for someone means having the time to explore feelings that touch on the deeper elements of the human heart."

Realizing she'd said too much, Tuccia sat up and wound her arms around her upraised knees. "I'm afraid I've embarrassed you when I didn't mean to."

Cesare leaned closer. "Why would I be embarrassed to be paid a compliment like that?"

She put her sunglasses back on. "You always know the right thing to say, so I'll never see what's really going on inside you. But I'm thankful for this moment out of time to enjoy the company of a man revered by his mother and his friends. No men from my world can claim that distinction."

"Do you mind if I ask you a question about Jean-Michel?"

"Of course not."

"When your marriage was arranged, had you already met him?"

"No. My parents gave one of their many parties at our palazzo and insisted I attend. I was only sixteen and had refused to go because I couldn't bear to be around grownups. But this time my father came to my room carrying a long dress. He said he would wait while I put it on. It was humiliating to be walked from my apartment to the grand ballroom like I was a baby.

"He led me through their usual set of guests to my mother. She was standing next to a man twice my age I didn't recognize and didn't like on sight. He was shorter than my father and overdressed, reminding me of a peacock. I shrank from his dark eyes where the lids remain at half mast like some French men's.

"My father introduced me to Jean-Michel Ardois, the son of Comte Ardois of Paris. He wasn't Sicilian, another huge strike against him. The man kissed my hand and slid a ring with a crest on my finger. While I stood there in shock, my father announced our engagement."

Tuccia smiled at the man who'd become the center of her universe. "Aren't you sorry you asked?"

His expression had sobered. "I want to know everything about you. Where's the betrothal ring now?"

"I'm sure it has been returned to Jean-Michel. I left it on the floor of the ladies' room at the salon."

He studied her features. "How often did you have to spend time with him?"

"Twice a year I endured a visit from him at my parents' palazzo until my father enrolled me at the University of Paris. He said I would have to learn French in order to be the *comte*'s wife. Once my parents took an apartment there, I had to go to the ballet or the opera with him every few months. Several times we went horseback riding on the Ardois estate. Our desultory conversations were worse than waiting for a train that never seems to come."

Cesare drank more wine. "You're not only articulate, you paint haunting pictures. Tell me more."

It was wonderful being able to open her thoughts and heart to him. "The first time we went out alone, I made up my mind I would run away before the marriage on my twenty-fifth birthday. If I could have disappeared the night of the betrothal, I would have. But I was never left alone until that morning at the salon for my dress fitting,"

"Literally never?" He sounded incredulous.

"Never. My parents accused me of being a willful child and didn't trust me. Someone was always watching me, even when I stayed with Zia Bertina."

A strange sound came out of him. "Did he ever try to take advantage of you?"

"Yes. I was so disgusted I slapped his face hard and pushed him off me. It left a red mark that probably branded him for several hours."

"Did he try to accost you every time you were together?"

She could tell Cesare's dislike for Jean-Michel was growing more intense. "No. I don't think he dared for fear I'd do something worse. Instead he bided his time until he had legal power over me. *Grazie a Dio* that never happened."

On that note she got to her feet and put the cartons back in the bag with the rest of the wine. To her surprise he stood up and put his arms around her from behind. "I thank God it didn't happen to you, either." He kissed her neck.

Tuccia could have died of happiness right there, but a group of people were walking by. Cesare had seen them, too, because he let go of her.

"We—we need to get going so I can finish the *sfingi* and start the *testa di turco*," she stammered. Before he could say anything else she added, "My arm is so much better I can hardly believe it, so you don't have to worry that I can't work anymore today, Dr. Donati."

His quiet laughter hid whatever he was really thinking. Together they walked to the car. He gave her arm a squeeze before helping her get in. She'd wanted him to crush her against him and tell her he was in love with her, too.

Unfortunately this interlude was over, but it was yet another one with him she'd always treasure. The memories were stacking up and her love for him was exploding.

CHAPTER SEVEN

WHEN THE LAST batch of *testa di turcos* were finished and decorated, Cesare proclaimed them perfect and announced he was leaving. One more day tomorrow to guide Tuccia through two more recipes and then this private time with her was over.

He would no longer have a legitimate reason to come to the *pensione.* From that point on their business would have to be conducted at the *castello* kitchen. A limo could take her back and forth. After today he realized he couldn't afford to be in such close quarters with her. Her burns had given him a reason to touch her, something he should never have done.

To see her lying there in the grass while he wanted to get down there with her and kiss them into oblivion had almost killed him. Another time like that and he'd have to act on his desire. If those people hadn't walked by while he was kissing her neck, he would have pulled her back down and shown her how he felt.

But he'd picked up enough on hearing her talk about her life with her parents to realize how lonely, how empty her life had been. Being forced to think about marriage at the age of sixteen *was* criminal, as his mother had said. Cesare refused to be the man who came along at the most vulnerable time in her life and took away her chance to be emotionally free.

Today at the park he *knew* she wanted him. But she deserved marriage. That was the only way Cesare would make love to her. She would have to be his legal wife, but the situation with Jean-Michel wasn't yet resolved. And deep down inside, he didn't feel worthy of her.

"Cesare?" His head jerked around. "I guess you didn't hear me. Who is the person who prints the menus for the guests? How far ahead do I have to get the names of the desserts to that person?"

"Don't worry about that yet. Gemma's pastries will be served until next Monday." He was impressed she'd been thinking that far ahead.

Tuccia bit her lip. "What about the ingredients that come to the kitchen from town? Am I in charge of ordering them, or do I coordinate with Maurice? There's so much I don't know."

"How could you have learned everything in a few days?" Her ability to consider all the ramifications of her new job astounded him. "I'll be there to answer your questions.

"Right now we're concentrating on your feeling good about the half-dozen desserts you're mastering. That way you'll have confidence talking to your assistants and giving them instructions on how to prepare what you've planned. I promise things will fall into place. Now I have to leave."

She walked him to the door. "I can't tell you how nice it was to eat at the park this afternoon. If you're tired of my thanking you, then you'll just have to get used to it."

"That works both ways. You're helping me so I don't have to go back to doing a chef's job I gave up a long time ago. We're even."

Tuccia shook her head. "No, we're not." She clung to the open door. "How long were you a chef?"

"From the moment I arrived in New York. The pay put me through part of college. I took out a loan to buy a small restaurant that was going under and called it Mamma's. People love Sicilian food and pretty soon I'd made enough money to buy another restaurant."

She let out a sigh. "And history was made. It explains why you're such an expert teacher. Your mother must have been so proud of you to leave Sicily and put your stamp on the world. *I'm* proud of you, Cesare. Does your father have any idea what an outstanding son he has?"

No one had ever asked him that. Her sweetness was getting to him. He rubbed the back of his neck. "I don't even know if he's alive. When he left my mother, she never saw or heard from him again."

"What a tragedy for him. Your father missed out on the whole point of life. I'd love to meet him and tell him what a fantastic son he has."

Cesare cleared his throat. "I thought the same thing about your parents when you told me about your emptiness."

A shadow crossed over her stunning features. "Forget me."

That would be impossible.

Donati. If you stay here talking to her any longer, you're a fool.

"I spoke with my mother earlier. She said your parents are genuinely upset over your disappearance. I was glad to hear it. Bertina sees a fissure in the ice where they are concerned. I just thought you should know."

Her eyes clouded over. "That's pretty hard to believe."

"I don't think she would have said anything if she didn't think it were true." He kissed her temple. "See you in the morning. I'll make breakfast when I get here. Same time?"

She nodded, causing her black curls to shimmer. He longed to plunge his fingers into that silky mass and devour her.

Without lingering any longer, he walked out to the car and drove away without looking back. Needing a distraction, he turned on the radio and found a twenty-four-hour news station. But he didn't hear anything about her case until he'd pulled into the parking area of his favorite sports bar in the village.

That's when he learned that Interpol was now involved to coordinate police cooperation throughout Europe in order to find the princess.

After shutting off the engine, he went inside and ordered, a pale lager from a Lombardi brewery both he and Takis enjoyed. While he waited for the waiter to bring some appetizers, he phoned Vincenzo. His friend wouldn't be taking Gemma to their home in Lake Como until next week. Cesare needed some advice and no one had a better head.

He reached Vincenzo's voice mail and asked him to call him when he could. Once he'd finished his lager, he headed for the *castello* and let himself in his private office off the lobby. While he did some work on the computer that had been piling up, his friend returned the call and Cesare talked to him about Tuccia's disappearance.

"Tonight I heard that Interpol is now involved. It's getting ugly. Tuccia has sent Jean-Michel a letter of apology. He should be getting it soon. But part of me wants to urge her to get in touch with him right away and settle this thing quietly with him and her parents. The press could then be informed that she's safe and they've called off their marriage."

A long silence ensued. "In a perfect world, Cesare. But I was born in her *imperfect* one. She's done something uncommonly courageous. It's just my opinion, but I think she needs to see it through on her own inspiration, come what may. That's what *I* did with no regrets."

It was the "come what may" part that made Cesare shudder. He couldn't ignore what she'd told him at the park about her caged life, but he valued Vincenzo's judgment. "Thanks for listening. I appreciate it."

"We've been through a lot together, *amico*. Are you going to be all right?"

"I'll have to be, won't I."

He hung up. There'd be little sleep for him tonight. Instead of going up to his room, he began printing off copies of the recipes she'd been following under his supervision. When the time came, she would have to hand them to her assistants.

Dozens of other tasks needed to be taken care of. Why not now while adrenaline surged through his veins over the cruelty Tuccia had endured this far in her life. She'd been robbed of a normal existence. If he didn't have responsibilities, he'd disappear with her to some hidden spot on the other side of the globe and love her without worrying about anything else.

This morning Tuccia had got up at five-thirty to finish her surprise for Cesare and make some rolls. She'd started their breakfast before she'd gone to bed and hoped he'd love it. He'd done so much for her that she wanted to do this small thing to repay him. Today would be their last for working together alone.

In the past when she'd gone out on the royal yacht with her parents and their friends in the summer, one of the aspects she looked forward to was the Sicilian breakfast served on board. Curious to know how *granita* was made, she'd prevailed on the cook to show her.

When the mixture of sugar, water and almond paste was melted, then frozen, stirred, mashed, frozen, stirred, mashed and frozen many times until it came out looking like snow, it was served in a goblet. Eaten with a yeast brioche, it tasted like heaven. The cook also made fruit *granitas* topped with whipping cream, but she'd preferred the almond and dipped her roll in it.

From the window over the sink she saw Cesare arrive. It was ten to eight. He was early! Every time he came to the apartment, excitement exploded inside her. Thank goodness she'd set the table ahead of time and had made coffee. She'd even designed a menu for him, describing what he would be eating. She folded and propped it where his plate would go.

Though she wanted to fling the door open and run into his arms, she steeled herself to wait until he knocked before answering the door. The second he walked in wearing a dark blue polo shirt and white trousers, he paused. His gaze zeroed in on her.

"Something smells wonderful."

Somebody *looked* wonderful.

"I'm glad. Welcome to Tuccia's, Signor Donati!" She made a sweep with the arm that had fresh honey gauze pads taped over her burns. They wouldn't be necessary after today. "If you'll come in and find a seat, I'll be your server."

She watched him walk in the kitchen and sit down to examine the menu. His head reared. He stared at her with a stunned expression. *"Granita di mandorle?"*

"Si, signor."

Delighted with his reaction, she rushed to pour their coffee. She'd already put sugar on the table because he liked a lot of it. Then she pulled two filled snifters out of the small freezer compartment. After putting them on a plate with a warm roll, she set them on the table and sat down.

Tuccia had already tasted it and knew it was good. Not as good as the cook on the yacht had made it, but she was proud of it. Out of the corner of her eye she watched Cesare take his first few bites, wishing he were her husband so they could do this every morning.

Pretty soon he was dipping his roll into the concoction the way she always did. Halfway through his meal, he ran out of roll and reached for her hand across the table.

"You told me you didn't know how to cook anything except to make instant coffee and tea in the microwave."

"I forgot about this. I love it so much I begged the cook on my parents' yacht to teach me how."

He released her fingers. "It's superb...just the right taste and consistency. You must have been up all night."

"I wanted to treat *you* for a change. It was worth it."

He seemed taken back. "My mother's version isn't as good as this one. We're going to be serving your rendition for one of our nightly desserts starting next week."

She moaned. "It's so much work!"

His deep laughter filled the kitchen. "That's what the assistants are for. I have a gut feeling our fame for fine Sicilian cuisine is going to spread and we'll be inundated with too many would-be guests to accommodate."

He got up from the table and brought back a plate with more rolls. Having finished off the flavored ice, he devoured the rest of them in no time at all. "These are delicious by the way. You're such a fast learner it's breathtaking. I'm convinced you could do anything at all if you put your mind to it."

"I think you're flattering me into giving you another serving of *granita.* I made enough if you want more now."

"I'll definitely want some later." He sat back in the chair. "Tell me. Would you rather lie down for the rest of the morning and catch up on some much-needed sleep? Later on this afternoon I'll come back and we'll work on the chocolate torte. Once you've made it, we won't have to worry about your cooking anything new for a few days."

"I'd rather do it now if you don't mind. Then I'll be able to relax enough to face tomorrow."

"So be it. Let's get started. I'll clear the table while you find your bible."

"It's on the shelf." She got up to reach for it and saw Cesare put the menu in his trouser pocket. If that meant what she hoped it meant, all the hard work and loss of sleep had been worth it.

Later, while she was icing her next five-layer creation, Cesare's cell phone rang. She kept working while he walked in the living room. He didn't come back to the kitchen for at least fifteen minutes. She couldn't read his expression.

"Is everything all right?"

He lounged against the wall with his hands in his pockets. "Ciro took a turn for the worse during the night and has ended back up in the ICU."

"His heart?"

"Yes."

"How sad." She waited to hear more. "What else is wrong? I know it's something serious."

"I'd rather not have to tell you this, but you have the right to know."

"What is it?" Her voice shook.

"My mother had just arrived at Bertina's palazzo to prepare meals this morning when the police showed up without notice and took her to police headquarters for further questioning."

Tuccia put a hand to her mouth.

"Mamma returned to the villa to phone me. The police know that Bertina is the person you've always turned to and that she was the one who chartered the jet for you. Naturally they believe she knows where you are hiding."

"Of course."

"Just remember your aunt is a strong woman who loves you very much. She says your parents have softened a great deal and went to the station with her to lend their support."

"You're kidding—"

"No. I really do think they are suffering over what they did to you. Mamma and I agree she'll be able to handle an interrogation. The police don't have evidence of any kind. Bertina doesn't know where you are, only that you're safe. The police won't be able to hold her."

"The situation is growing unbearable. I could end all the pain for Bertina by just going home."

In the next breath Cesare walked over and put his hands on her shoulders. He looked into her eyes. "That's not going to be necessary. Once Jean-Michel gets your letter, he'll tell the police and the princess hunt will be over. But if you feel strongly about this, I'll fly you to Palermo today to see your aunt."

"I know you would, but I couldn't let you down now."

"Forget about me."

"You're too wonderful to be real." She buried her face in her hands. "I wish I knew what to do. I don't want my *zia* to suffer, but I've made a commitment to you. Hearing the bad news about Ciro only makes things worse."

Cesare pulled her against him and wrapped his arms around her. "I have an idea that will make the most sense. Let's wait another day until I hear from my mother. Hopefully your fiancé will have gotten your letter. Nothing may be as bad as you're imagining."

His tenderness was too much. Tuccia broke down sobbing quietly against his chest, unable to stop. "Forgive me for soaking your shirt. I'm a disaster and you shouldn't have to put up with me for another second."

"What if I want to."

When she tried to pull away, he lowered his head and started kissing her wet face until his mouth covered hers. It all happened so naturally that her lips opened. In another second she experienced the full intensity of a kiss that thrilled her to the very depths of her being.

"Cesare—" she cried, so completely besotted she started kissing him back with a passion she didn't know herself capable of. For this fabulous man to be loving her like this brought a rush of joy to her heart she could hardly contain.

"Forgive me if I've been needing this," he whispered in a shaken voice. "You have no idea how you've affected me. Tuccia—" He drew her so close there was no air between them. "Tell me to stop."

"I can't. I want you to go on kissing me and never stop." Once again they were devouring each other. The more she clung to him, the more she realized she'd never be able to appease this growing hunger for him. He'd come into her life and changed it forever.

She wanted him with her whole heart and soul, but if he was only kissing her in order to comfort her, then she had to do something to turn this around. All he needed now was to have to worry about being stuck with a fugitive who was desperate for love and attention and had begged him to let her remain here and work for him.

It was up to her to see this for what it was and not get carried away. Deep down she was fearful he saw her in that light. How could he not? She broke their kiss and wheeled out of his arms. It took all her strength to turn and face him head-on, knowing her cheeks were flushed and her lips swollen.

Tuccia had to prove that he could count on her. "I—I'm afraid we both got carried away," she stammered. "You're a very attractive man. I'm shocked you're not married yet. Any woman could lose her head with you. I'm no exception. I've thought about what you said. It would be best to give the situation another twenty-four hours before I make any kind of decision that could impact both of us."

"I was hoping you'd say that."

She could believe it. The man was depending on her to keep her head at this point. Needing to stay busy, she cut a piece of torte and handed it to him on a plate with a fork. "Try this and tell me what you think."

Please just do it, Cesare.

He did her bidding, eating half of it before putting the plate on the table. "You pass with flying colors, Tuccia."

"It was your recipe." Relief swamped her. "You don't think I need to make it again right now to improve it?"

"No." His eyes had narrowed on her mouth. Her heart felt like it was running away with her. "The torte is exquisite."

"Then do you mind if I lie down for a little while?"

One brow lifted. "I was about to suggest it. You need sleep. I'll come by at five with a meal and we'll talk over what's going to happen tomorrow."

"Thank you for understanding." She took a quick breath. "Thank you for everything."

"Try not to worry too much, Tuccia."

"That would be impossible."

He looked like he was going to say something, then thought the better of it. The moment he walked out of the apartment, she locked the door, then ran to the bedroom and flung herself on the bed in agony. After fleeing from a man she'd despised, she'd run straight into a man she adored.

Tuccia wondered if she dared tell him exactly what she felt, that she loved him and wanted to be his wife. Maybe that was what she would do the next time they were together. No more holding back.

At ten to five, Cesare, showered, shaved, and wearing a tan summer suit, walked in the *castello* kitchen. He nodded to Maurice before packing a bag of *fettuccini Alfredo* with chicken to go. Nothing else was needed. Tuccia had cooked rolls and cake that morning. There was still a half bottle of Chardonnay waiting to be enjoyed with another snifter of her fabulous *granita.*

Princess Tuccianna was so full of surprises he decided there wasn't anything she couldn't do. One taste of her mouth and he knew he wanted to go on tasting it for the rest of his life. When she'd surrendered herself to him, he'd experienced ecstasy like nothing he'd ever known and had come close to having a heart attack.

He'd sensed he was in deep water the first night he'd caught her in his arms in his mother's kitchen. But since then his feelings for her had escalated to such a degree his life had been irrevocably changed.

She was in his heart, in his blood, but that wasn't enough. Cesare wanted her in his life day and night. He wanted her in his bed. He wanted babies with her.

He wanted everything that he'd feared would never happen because he hadn't believed love would come to him.

Yet now that he'd found this extraordinary woman, he feared it was too soon to tie her down with his own needs. For years her parents had exerted too much pressure on her to conform to their demands, and she'd run away.

After the ecstasy of their kiss, Cesare wanted to marry her and never let her go. But Cesare sensed that would be the wrong thing to do. She needed time to develop her sense of self first.

The greatest gift he could give her would be to hold back and allow her to become the incredible person he knew her to be. As long as she worked for him, he could keep her close to him until the time came when he had to tell her how he felt.

On his way out of the kitchen he walked over to Gemma who was setting up for the evening crowd. It was a good thing tonight would be her last night as pastry cook. Her baby would be coming before long. She needed rest.

"Tuccia and I will be here at nine in the morning."

"I'll be watching for you. Is she nervous?"

"She doesn't show it."

Gemma smiled at him. "What about you, Cesare?"

"I know she's going to be fine."

"With you helping her, she couldn't possibly go wrong."

If Gemma had seen him kissing Tuccia earlier as if his life depended on it—which it did—she would probably have told him to slow down. He kissed Gemma's cheek and left the *castello* for his car.

On the way down to the village he turned on the five o'clock news. Following the latest world events he learned there'd been a break in the case involving Princess Tuccianna's disappearance. But the police weren't revealing the details yet. That had to mean the letter had reached Jean-Michel.

Pleased by the new development, he turned it off and pulled up in front of the *pensione.* Tuccia must have seen him arrive because she opened the door for him, appearing to have gotten some rest.

This evening she wore the same print blouse and pants from a few nights ago. Her wardrobe didn't consist of more than three or four changes of clothes. The apartment's washer and dryer had been a necessity, but he intended to rectify the situation and take her shopping.

She eyed the bag he carried. "More goodies?"

"Maurice's version of *fettuccini.*"

"I can't wait to try it. Then I can compliment him on it tomorrow. Come in." Tuccia closed the door and followed him into the kitchen. She'd cleaned it spotless and had set the table. The TV was on in the living room. "I've been listening to the news."

"So have I," he stated and reached for some plates to serve their dinner. "We both know what that new development in your case means. By now Jean-Michel will have called off the search. Within the next few hours he'll make some kind of statement to the press. In the meantime I'm sure your aunt is going to be fine, otherwise I would have heard from my mother by now."

"I pray you're right."

"Even so, the letter provides proof that you're alive.

Therefore your family will have to hire private detectives to look for you if they are still intent on finding you. According to Bertina, they're hoping you'll come home because they love you. So I'd say tonight is a time for celebration!"

He reached for the Chardonnay and poured it into glasses before putting them on the table. "Where are your delicious rolls?"

"There were four left. I put them in the microwave and will warm them up."

When they finally sat down at the table, he raised his wine glass. "Before we eat, I'd like to make a toast." Her gray eyes sparkled as she lifted hers. "To the princess who overnight has turned into a pastry cook *par excellence*."

"I'm going to try." They touched glasses and sipped their wine. "Now I'd like to make one." She raised her glass again, staring straight into his eyes. "To her teacher, a man who is without equal."

Cesare wished it were true.

Everything she said and did had such impact he didn't know where to go with his feelings without betraying them. But he'd made himself a promise to keep things professional for a while longer. She, too, was behaving as if their soul-destroying kiss that morning had changed nothing.

But they both knew that it had.

All he could do was clink her glass and drink more wine.

"Hmm," she said after tasting the *fettuccini*. "This is exceptional. I can see why Maurice was hired."

"We've been very happy with him." Cesare ate another of her rolls. "It's a balmy night out. After we finish dinner, would you like to go for a drive while we talk about tomorrow?"

"You must be reading my mind. I was afraid to ask."

She'd probably be shocked if she knew what was going through his. He'd rather take her in the other room and dance with her. Unfortunately if he did that, they would end up in the bedroom and not come back out for days. So much for him following his own advice to put those thoughts out of his mind.

He took a deep breath. "I thought I'd show you around the *castello* estate to get you acquainted. You'll enjoy seeing the swans on the lake."

"Ooh. How beautiful."

"It's quite a sight on a moonlit night, though the moon won't be out for several hours. When we return, I'll finish off the *granita* and another slice of torte."

After they finished eating and had cleared the table, they walked outside and took off in the car. Tuccia turned to him in her seat. "I've wanted to see the fortress up close. It has such a rich history. I can hardly believe that Vincenzo's family home has been turned into a hotel and restaurant."

"Vincenzo's father and uncle squandered everything and the estate was seized by the government to be sold to the highest bidder. Vincenzo asked me and Takis if we wanted to pool our assets and buy it with him."

"When was this?"

"The three of us were in New York at the time. He had the idea to turn it into the business proposition it is today. That way he could preserve his family legacy and do something honorable for the region. I thought it a fantastic idea. So did Takis."

"Bravo for Vincenzo," she exclaimed. "I can understand that happening in a family as power-hungry as his. It's the only reason my parents made sure early in my life that they would have a son-in-law with a fortune. That would be their insurance to keep them living their lavish lifestyle to the end of their days."

Her words caused Cesare's stomach muscles to clench. He drove them to the summit and took the road that wound behind the *castello*.

"This place is massive."

"You're right."

Two sets of guests from the hotel were out walking. He drove the car past them until they reached the lake much further away. She rolled down her window. "It's so lovely and peaceful, but I don't see any swans."

"They're probably hiding in the rushes, but they'll come out." Cesare turned off the engine and turned toward her. "Tomorrow will be here before you know it. Gemma is ready to ease many of your concerns. But I'd like to know what is worrying you most and relieve you if I can."

Tuccia shook her head. "Do you know what I wish? That I could have been a normal person you'd hired at one of your restaurants in New York. Think how much I could have learned from you."

He had news for her. If she'd come into his life back then, they'd be married by now. He wouldn't have hesitated asking her. "Instead you're learning to be a pastry chef here."

"But it isn't fair to you," her voice cracked.

"Tuccia..."

"It's true. You're playing a dangerous game in order to protect me, Cesare. I honestly don't know what Jean-Michel would do if he caught up to you."

Cesare smiled. "I'm afraid you should be worried what I'd do to him if I had the opportunity."

"You don't mean that."

"Try me. What can he do except rage?"

"I suppose you're right."

"All I know is, your mother should never have asked you to help me."

He slid his arm along the back of the seat. "Aside from the fact that I met you at her house in the middle of the night, she didn't have anything to do with my decision to fly you here."

She stirred in the seat. "How can you say that?"

"Because I've had to live with Vincenzo and Gemma's story for many years. The night my mother told me about *your* situation, the horror of their history came back to haunt me. For you to be forced to undergo a betrothal at your age was not only feudal, it was criminal."

"Zia Bertina said the same thing many times. That's why she agreed to help me escape. I'll love her forever for what she did for me."

"The emotional damage to you was as bad as anything physical," Cesare spoke his mind. "When Mamma asked if I would help you leave Palermo, I didn't have to think about it and was determined to help you any way I could. That hasn't changed for me. Does that answer your question?"

Once more she hid her face in her hands, but she nodded.

He ruffled one of her curls with his fingers. "You

said you wished you were a normal girl I'd hired to work in one of my restaurants in New York. In truth it's exactly what I've done, but this restaurant happens to be in Milan. Shall we put all the angst of the past aside and concentrate on tomorrow? You're my new pastry chef who's going to be running the show."

She finally lifted her head. "I intend to make you proud. Maybe you should take me back to the apartment. I rested a little today, but I didn't sleep. If I go to bed now, I'll be in much better shape by morning. Another time I'll come out here and watch for the swans."

Tuccia's resilience was something to behold.

"There'll be many opportunities." Cesare started the engine and he drove them back to the *pensione.* When they arrived, he walked her to the door.

Don't touch her, Donati.

If he made that mistake, he would never leave her apartment. "I'll be by for you at eight. We'll have a working breakfast with Gemma."

"I'll be ready. Thank you for the dinner and the tour, Cesare. *Dormi bene.*"

"*E tu.*"

Giving in to unassuaged longings, he pulled her in his arms, kissing her long and hard.

He walked back to his car aware of a new fear attacking him. How would he handle it if he asked her to marry him and she turned him down?

CHAPTER EIGHT

CESARE WOULD BE by for her in a few minutes. Tuccia stood in front of the bathroom mirror in full chef regalia. She peered through her glasses. No lipstick. Not a hair in sight. No perfume, either. Gemma had told her not to wear any, but she could use a non-scented lotion.

"This is your big day. If you're recognized by someone on the kitchen staff, then it's all over. Until then you're going to do whatever it takes to prove worthy of Cesare's faith in you."

Last night he'd pulled her in his arms and kissed her as she'd hoped. Now she was longing for the day when that happened again. Tuccia had felt his touch in every fiber of her being. She'd ached for him until she was afraid she'd never get to sleep. To her relief a miracle did happen, but only because she'd been up most of the night before.

She walked through the apartment to gather her purse and bible. This place had become her home. Hers and Cesare's. She'd never known such happiness. While she stood looking out the window, she saw his car pull up. Would her heart always palpitate with a frenzy when he came near?

Not wanting to keep him waiting, she walked outside and climbed in before he could help her. His eyes were alive as they wandered from her floppy hat and down her body clothed in white to the sensible walking shoes she'd drawn out of her suitcase. She could tell he was thinking about what she really looked like under her disguise and it sent her pulse racing.

"*Bon jornu,* Signor Donati," she said in Sicilian.

"Chef Bottaro. I've been searching a long time for you." The way he'd said it in such a husky tone gave her hope that he was letting her know he loved her. With a smile, he started the car and they took off. "There are many things I want to discuss with you, not the least of which is how you're feeling this morning."

"Like I've climbed to the top of Mount Pellegrino. There's no going back and I'm looking down at a roiling ocean, terrified to make my first jump."

Something flickered in the depths of his eyes, intriguing her. "You sound like you've done that sort of thing before."

She nodded. "When I was a lot younger and hadn't been put on as tight a leash."

His mouth tightened. "I used to climb that cliff regularly before I left for New York."

"All those ships going out to sea," she mused. "Lucky you that you could leave and fulfill your destiny."

They'd reached the summit, but this time he took another road leading around the back of the *castello* where she saw a sign that said "Staff Parking Only." He pulled to a stop and shut off the engine. Turning to her, he clasped her hand and entwined his fingers with hers.

"In case you didn't realize it yet, today you're about to fulfill yours." He leaned closer. "This is for luck, even if you don't need it." To her surprise he gave her a long hungry kiss on the lips that sent a surge of warmth through her body.

She started to kiss him back, but he eased away too soon, leaving her bereft. Then he levered himself from the driver's seat. After coming around to help her out, Cesare used a remote to let them in the rear entrance and walked her down a hall with several offices. He knocked on the last door. "Gemma?"

"Oh, good. You're here!" She opened it. But the second she saw Tuccia, she let out a small gasp. "Am I having a hallucination, or is it really you?"

Cesare gave Gemma a hug. "Allow me to introduce Nedda Bottaro, the new Sicilian executive pastry chef who's going to set a trend."

"I'll say you are." Gemma in turn gave Tuccia a hug. "I would never have known you," she whispered. "You look more sensational than Maurice, who's always immaculately turned out in the latest *haute couture* style for the well-dressed chef. When he sees you, he'll be speechless."

"Is that good or bad?"

"Definitely good after he finds his voice. Come in the office which is now going to be yours and have some breakfast I had brought in. Then we'll all go to the kitchen and I'll introduce you to everyone."

They sat down to eat and talk. Later, as Gemma was showing her what she kept in the desk drawers, Vincenzo unexpectedly appeared at the door. "Excuse me for interrupting, *cara*, but I knew you would all want to see this morning's headlines. The police have called off the search for you, Tuccia."

She almost fainted from the news. So Cesare had been right. The letter had reached Jean-Michel.

Vincenzo thrust the newspaper in her hands, but in her dazed state, she turned to Cesare. "You're the reason this has happened so fast. I'm almost afraid to believe it. Will you please read what it says?"

"If that's what you want." He put down his coffee cup. "*Sicilian Princess No Longer Missing* is the headline. Le Comte Jean-Michel Ardois of Paris has released the following information to the press: 'Princess Tuccianna Falcone Leonardi, daughter of the Marchese and Machesa di Trabia of Sicily, has sent him a letter offering her deepest apologies for having disappeared the day before their marriage and causing grief to him and his family. In her letter to the *comte*, she says that throughout their betrothal, it became clear that they weren't suited for each other. She thought about it for a long time and was convinced that they both needed to find someone else in order to be fulfilled. At the last minute she decided she had to run away to spare both of them a lifetime of unhappiness because the only reason two people marry should be for love.'"

Tuccia heard a nuance in Cesare's voice that told her he was touched by her words.

"She lives in hope he'll forgive her and that one day soon he'll find a wonderful woman deserving of his love. The princess wishes him the very best in the future and hopes that in time she too will find happiness for herself."

He broke off talking. The room had gone quiet.

At this point Cesare's gaze flicked to hers. Emotion had darkened his eyes to a deep blue color. If he but knew it, Tuccia had already found her happiness. The most wonderful man on earth stood just a few feet away from her.

Vincenzo took the newspaper from him and finished reading the article, but he too sounded emotionally affected as he read the rest. "'Her parents, the Marchese and Marchesa di Trabia, have told the press they won't give up searching for their beloved daughter. She's their only child and they're praying she's safe and will want to come home soon.'"

Tuccia lowered her head. "It's hard to believe my parents would say those words. Up to now they've thought of me as the willful, unrepentant daughter who deserves to be punished. But if Cesare's mother is to be believed, my *zia* says they are sorry for what has happened. I hardly know what to think."

"Let's be thankful you've accomplished the most important thing," Cesare murmured, sounding more subdued than she'd ever heard him. "The *comte* isn't going to come looking for you now."

She lifted her head. "You're right. It would be too humiliating for him. I really do wish him well. But it's not so easy to forgive my parents."

Vincenzo wore a sober expression. "I relate to your feelings completely, Tuccianna. That's why you'll continue to work here in that disguise and we'll do everything possible to protect you until you know it's safe."

She got up from the chair. "Thank you so much," she whispered. Tuccia needed time to comprehend all this news.

Vincenzo smiled. "I defy anyone to know it's you hiding under all that white."

"When I look in the mirror, I surprise myself," she quipped. "Thanks again to all of you for helping me. I owe you a debt of gratitude I'll never be able to repay in this life."

She looked at Gemma. "If you don't mind, I'm so keyed up with this being my first day I'd like to meet the kitchen staff and get this part of it over with."

Gemma chuckled. "It'll be my pleasure. Let's go."

Tuccia stepped past Cesare. The four of them left the office and walked down another hall to the huge, state-of-the-art kitchen filled with a dozen assistants in aprons and beanies.

Her heart almost failed her to think she was going to be the pastry chef here. At the far end she saw a man in a tall chef's hat who was busy talking to Takis. Everyone was here. Her big day had arrived.

Help.

"Come on," Gemma urged. "I'll introduce you to the head man first."

Tuccia followed her.

"Maurice Troudeau? I'd like you to meet my replacement, Nedda Bottaro."

The middle-aged French chef gave Tuccia a blank stare. Obviously he didn't know what to make of her.

She took the initiative. In her heaviest Sicilian accent she said, "It's my honor to meet you, Signor. Thanks to Signor Donati, last evening I was treated to your *fettuccini Alfredo*, which I confess is the best I have ever eaten. I'm sure the herb you put in it is a secret I would never ask you to reveal.

"But I can tell you it's just one of the reasons your

reputation has spread all the way to the tip of Sicily where I come from. They think they make the best *fettuccini Alfredo*. Not true." She swiped the backs of her fingers under her chin in a typical gesture of her Palermitan heritage to make her point.

The Frenchman eyed Gemma. "So you brought us a real Siciliana."

"To our delight, Cesare found her."

Tuccia spoke up. "It's a great honor for me. I know I'm going to need your help if you're willing, Signor Troudeau."

His gaze swerved back to her. "You can call me Maurice."

She was excited to have made that tiny breakthrough. "*Grazie*, Maurice. Please forgive the interruption when I know you are so busy. I, too, must get myself organized."

Opening her arms, she put her palms out in front, a Sicilian gesture to indicate there was much to do. When she turned, she almost walked into Cesare.

He'd seen her gestures and his blue eyes twinkled as if to say she was doing everything right.

By now Gemma had asked the pastry assistants to assemble around them. One by one Tuccia was introduced to the six of them. Three men and three women from Spain, Crete, France and Italy. After she'd chatted with each of them for a few minutes about their backgrounds and experience, she got down to the crux of what she'd planned to say ahead of time.

"Call me Nedda. We're going to be making Sicilian desserts from my part of the world. Such a change from the delectable Florentine desserts created by Signora Gagliardi. Everything will be different at first, but she says you are all experts so I'm happy to be working with you. Some day I'll tell you my story, but not this morning.

"Don't be afraid to ask me any questions you want. Signor Donati says we should work together like one happy family. I agree. Of course there will be little squabbles from time to time, but that it is to be expected. *Si?*"

"Si!" they said in a collective voice.

"He's going to give you the recipes we'll be making for the next few weeks. I'd like you to study them. *Pignolata, cassata, biancomangiare, cannoli*—so many you'll be counting them in your sleep like the proverbial sheep." Except that she hadn't made them yet and had a lot of homework to do first. Cesare had printed them out for her.

Everyone laughed.

"Tomorrow we will begin." She nodded to Cesare. "Go ahead, *signor*, while I get acquainted with this kitchen. I don't like working in such a large space and will probably want to move some things around."

Vincenzo and Takis talked with Cesare for a few minutes, then left.

While Gemma gave Tuccia a two-hour tour of her new world, she felt Cesare's gaze on her the entire time. Eventually the three of them ended back up in the office.

A tired-looking Gemma smiled at her. "I never saw anything so amazing in my life as the way you made the kitchen your own. When you rattled off all those desserts, you sounded as if you'd been making them all your life." Ha!

"I've eaten them all my life, if that counts," Tuccia interjected with a smile.

"Maurice is so dazzled by the Siciliana I don't think he'll ever be the same again."

"Neither will the assistants," Cesare stated. "Everyone was mesmerized beyond their ability to talk, including me. What do you say I drive you back to the *pensione*, and we'll let Gemma have her freedom."

"Of course," Tuccia exclaimed. "I can't thank you enough, but I know you need to rest."

"I'll admit I can't wait to go upstairs and lie down. But I also have to admit I'm envious of the experience you're about to have, Tuccia. With Cesare's help you really are going to turn into an outstanding chef. I just hope you won't have to leave us prematurely."

"That's the last thing I want."

"Amen," Cesare murmured. "Shall we go?"

After thanking Gemma and giving her a hug, they walked out to the car and left for the village. Tuccia felt Cesare's gaze on her. "You're very quiet all of a sudden. You must be as hungry as I am. It's after three."

"That's not it. I was thinking about the latest news. Jean-Michel will probably demand recompense from my parents for his pain. And how do I know if my parents really are sorry?"

"Time will tell. But that isn't all you need to be worried about." He'd pulled up in front of the deli.

Her head jerked around. "What do you mean?"

"You're going to have to watch out for Mario and Manoussos, the two assistants who aren't married yet. Both seem to be besotted by you."

"That's ridiculous."

"I overhead them talking in the pantry about who was going to bed the *squisita* Siciliana first."

She scoffed. "You made that up."

"I wish I had. Little do they know they'll never be able to get you alone, not when I bring you to the *castello* every morning, and take you home every night."

Tuccia loved the possessive ring she'd detected in his voice.

"Even though there are strict rules about the staff having relationships, they'll try everything in their power to persuade you to go out for lunch with them. After one success, they won't stop."

"Cesare—I don't pl—"

"I know what I'm talking about," he cut her off, "because the types in my restaurants in New York are no different when it comes to a beautiful woman. Don't say you weren't warned." He reached for the door handle. "I'll be right back."

He actually sounded upset, but that was because he felt totally responsible for her safety at this point. That meant physically and other ways, too. They'd shared a moment of intense passion, but to her chagrin she knew Cesare would never take advantage of her. Furthermore he wouldn't allow anyone else to, either.

If he only knew what was in her heart, he wouldn't give a thought to what he'd overheard. But it thrilled her to think that on his watch, he might not like the idea that she could get interested in a man she found attractive.

Manoussos, the assistant from Crete, had a rather dashing appeal in his own way. Kind of like a younger Takis. While her mind was still mulling over their conversation, Cesare came back to the car with their food and drove them to the apartment.

"Excuse me while I change out of these clothes. I'll be right back."

It was wonderful to discard the hat and stocking. Now her head could breathe. After removing her uniform and shoes, she put on jeans and a top. Once she'd run the brush through her curls, she hurried back to the kitchen. Cesare had already laid out their meal and poured the red wine they'd opened the other day.

"I can see you've bought enough *polenta* and *cotoletta alla Milanese* for half a dozen people."

"I'm partial to both."

She would have to remember that considering he was a connoisseur of fine food. After a few bites she agreed the ribs were delicious. "But I'm afraid that for me the grilled *polenta* is an acquired taste."

"Long ago it was considered the food of the poor, but I loved it when I first moved to Milan."

"My friend in Catania loves it, too. She said it reminds her of the porridge she ate when she was studying in England. I miss talking to her. She wouldn't believe it if she knew what I've been doing."

He drank the rest of his wine and sat back in the chair. "Today has marked a drastic change in your life. After nine years, you're no longer engaged to be married, releasing you from your prison. Even better, you're employed with a vitally important job and benefits."

"All because of you," she blurted.

"You don't need to keep thanking me, Tuccia." He'd turned serious all of a sudden. She hardly knew what to think. "This job is going to run your life for a while.

To make it a little easier, you're going to have to take breaks in order to handle the stress. It's time we talk about a schedule for you."

"All right."

"Basically you come to work at eight-thirty and can leave by three o'clock Monday through Friday. You'll alternate being on duty Saturday or Sunday evening twice a month from six to nine. Not to cook, but to make certain things are running smoothly."

She thought about it for a minute. "If there are problems, then I need to improvise. Is that what you're saying?"

"Should there be any issues, I'll be there to help."

"I see. But who spells you off?"

He raked a hand through his hair. "We're not talking about me."

She shouldn't have asked. Cesare was in a strange mood.

"Gemma and I worked out a schedule where she had two weekends off a month and Maurice the other two. I believe it's still the best way to arrange your time. When you're off, Maurice will handle any difficulties that come up."

"That sounds more than fair. Does it mean that you'll be taking those same weekends off?"

"Yes. That's how it has worked in the past so I can fly to New York and get my business done there."

The knowledge that he'd be gone at the same time she had two days to fill on her own private agenda was more than disappointing news. It was awful. Tuccia was so used to being with him she couldn't imagine him being so far away. To think that a week ago they hadn't even met. Now…

"Do you know how to drive, Tuccia?"

His question surprised her. "Yes. My *zia* taught me how. But I don't have a license because my parents never allowed me to have a car. Why do you ask?"

Frown lines formed around his eyes. "Always assuming you'll wear your disguise, I was going to let you use my car when I'm not in Milan. Under the circumstances, I'll make an arrangement with the limousine service so a driver will be on call for you at any time, day or night, when I'm not available. You need freedom to do the things you want and have to do."

No one in the whole world was more thoughtful than Cesare. *No one.* But in his odd frame of mind, she chose not to tell him that he didn't have to do that for her.

"Thank you. I'm very grateful for your generosity. But what would you think if we altered the daily routine a little?"

"In what way?"

"If you picked me up in the mornings, we could talk about the day ahead of me. But at three o'clock I could go home in the limo with another recipe you wanted me to make. I could get the groceries needed and do my errands. Then I'd make the dessert. When it was done, you could come by to test it. It will free up your time. What do you think?"

"It's your decision."

"I see."

If she dared, she'd ask if she could fly to New York with him. She'd traveled all over Europe under supervision, but she'd never been in New York before. Tuccia would love to see the original Mamma's, and where he'd lived before he'd put the *castello ristorante* on the map.

"Just so you know, your first weekend off will be in two weeks, starting when three o'clock rolls around on Friday afternoon. Do you have other questions for me right now?"

Too many, especially one about how she would fill her time while he was away, but anything she wanted to ask him wasn't about her schedule and she feared he didn't want to hear it.

"No. Between you and Gemma, I'm feeling much more confident about everything."

"You were brilliant today."

"The credit goes to my teacher."

A strange silence followed before he suddenly got up from the table. "I'm afraid I have to go, but I'll be by for you at eight in the morning."

"Could you do one more favor first and buy the ingredients I need to make the pastries I've never prepared? I'll start practicing on a couple of the recipes before I go to bed."

He smiled. "I'll be right back." Twenty minutes later he returned with the items needed.

"Thank you so much, Cesare. Now don't let me keep you any longer."

He was probably so sick of teaching her how to cook his recipes he couldn't wait for some breathing space. It was only five in the afternoon and there wasn't a thing she could do about it. He'd done his duty, now he was out of there.

"Thank you for lunch," she said after following him to the door with her heart dragging on the tiles.

He gave her a heartbreaking smile, but didn't try to hold her or kiss her. "I promise, no more *polenta.*"

"It was good for me to try it. I'm a cook now and need to be open to new taste experiences from the expert himself."

"You're becoming a very fine pastry cook," he corrected her.

"*Arrivederci*, Cesare."

He nodded before getting in his car and took off like a rocket.

Trying to pull herself together, she walked back in the kitchen to clean everything up. While she worked, Cesare's words rang in her ears.

Today has marked a drastic change in your life.

No kidding. Her teacher had done his job.

She remembered something else he'd told her days ago.

There's no room in my life for any woman until the castello*'s new pastry chef can create masterpieces without my help.*

That day had come. Though they were Cesare's masterpieces, he'd decided it was time to push his needy fledgling out of the nest.

You're on your own, Tuccia. You'd better get used to it fast.

CHAPTER NINE

TUCCIA COULDN'T BELIEVE how fast the next week flew by. It didn't take her long to get into a rhythm. So far the camaraderie with her assistants was building. They were remarkably trained and skilled, hoping to become a chef at a great restaurant one day themselves.

The two guys who constantly flirted with her made the day fun, but she could never take either one of them seriously despite Cesare's reminders to be careful not to lead them on. She loved it that he was always around in the background, watching everything without being obvious about it.

Tuccia still felt a fraud at having been promoted to executive pastry chef status in a week. But the others had no idea how it had happened. With Cesare her mentor, she'd been hyper-glided into the coveted position, one that was saving her life.

Maurice liked to tease her about her Sicilian ways. Things were coming along. In truth she liked having an important reason to get up in the morning and go to work. She liked cooking! With every new dessert, she needed less help to figure it out and perfect it.

On Thursday, just before quitting time, Cesare

came in while she was testing the results of her assistants' creations in the ricotta cheesecake department. Each cook had put his or her initials on a piece of tape on the side of the pan. "This particular cake is lacking two essential ingredients that were included in the recipes I passed out." She knew who had made it. "Why don't we ask Signor Donati to tell you what they are?"

Manoussos no longer looked happy as she cut Cesare a piece and walked over to give it to him with a fork. Their gazes met in silent amusement. He started to eat. Tuccia was loving every second of this. Cesare finally put the empty plate down on the counter.

"Signorina Bottaro is right. I don't detect the strong flavor of chocolate or amaretto."

"You see," she exclaimed. "The secret of this cheesecake is to crumble amaretto cookies into the crust, and add two extra tablespoons of chocolate. Leave out either of these ingredients and it will taste like all the mediocre cheesecakes you've ever eaten."

"It was my mistake," Manoussos spoke up. "I was playing a little joke to see if you could tell. But I didn't realize Signor Donati would be doing the testing. I'm very sorry."

"I'm glad you did it and I forgive you," Tuccia said with a smile. "Now perhaps you'll take me seriously and understand the *castello ristorante* doesn't do mediocre!" She stared at all of them. "That's it for today. See you bright and early in the morning."

Cesare broke into laughter after they'd walked out to his car. "He's still upset that he can't get anywhere with you. I have it in my heart to feel sorry for him because he'll never get the chance."

That made two people who were upset because Tuccia wasn't getting anywhere with Cesare and she was in pain over it.

She loved him to the bottom of her soul. They could be together all night every night if that was what he wanted. But maybe she needed to face the cold hard fact that he didn't feel the same way about her. She didn't want to believe it, not when she was so deeply in love with him.

During the second week of her being in charge of her crew in the *castello* kitchen, Cesare had come by the apartment after work to test the chocolate *setevelli torta*, a nine-layer cake he'd taught her how to make. When he tested the end result, he told her it tasted like the food of the gods.

She smiled and thanked him. "Such praise makes a girl's head swell." In horrible pain because he wasn't being more demonstrative in an intimate way, she had to do something to end it. "Since I'm thrilled I've passed your exacting test, please feel free to leave and enjoy the rest of your evening."

For once he looked taken back. Was it shock, or could it possibly be disappointment that she'd brushed him off so fast and he didn't like it? She got excited to think it might be the latter.

"Why do I get the feeling you want me to go?"

"It's not that. If you must know, I've made plans for tonight and I don't want to put them off. The limo will be here soon."

"To do what?" he asked in a controlled voice.

Oh, Cesare—tell me what's going on inside you.

"To do some important clothes shopping in Milan."

"You could have asked me at any time. I would have taken you."

"I know you would, but I'm no longer like the inflight helpless woman who developed an embarrassing crush on her protector during those first few days." There! She'd said it to disabuse him of any notion that he needed to worry about her any longer.

From the look of his tautened mouth, she'd found her mark. It encouraged her to go on and finish making her point. "That fairy tale has ended now that you've given me the tools to help myself. Since the police are no longer looking for me, I want to get out on my own."

"Tuccia—it's probably not a good idea for you to walk alone at the shops this time of evening. It'll be dark soon. A beautiful woman is a target for unsavory types."

"But it's what I've been wanting to do, and any woman is a target for a pickpocket. I can defend myself and I'll take my chances. To be a normal person without a bodyguard following me around sounds like heaven."

His jaw hardened. "Is that what I've become to you?"

She folded her arms, tamping down her elation that he was upset. "I'm going to forget you asked me that question. It's not worthy of you. I was referring to the security my parents hired to keep me watched day and night. Cesare—I need my freedom. Is it so inconceivable that I would want you to have yours and get on with your life the way it was before we met?"

The lids of his eyes had lowered so she couldn't read their expression.

"In fact as long as we're having this conversation, I want you to know that the salary you've put in the bank account for me will remain untouched until I've paid back every cent I owe you. Wait—" she said when he started to protest.

"I don't want to be beholden to you or anyone. Because of your incredible generosity, I've been given an option that opens many doors to my future when I no longer work here."

"You're planning on leaving us soon?" His voice sounded almost wintry.

His reaction was more than she could have asked for. If by some miracle he'd fallen in love with her, too, then she had to do something to get him to break down and tell her how he felt.

"I would never do that to you. But yesterday you told me you heard from your mother and received wonderful news. Ciro is starting to make progress. It's possible he'll be well enough to work again in a couple of months rather than six. You have to be so relieved if he's able to come back much sooner than expected."

Ignoring her comment he said, "Do you wish you could get out of our agreement sooner?" He wasn't letting this go. She prayed it was a good sign.

"No." She shook her head. "Every day I'm here I learn something new and valuable. There isn't a cook in Europe who wouldn't sell his or her soul to be the executive pastry chef in a restaurant as renowned as yours. Don't you think I know that? Until Ciro is ready to come to work, I'll do everything I can to justify your faith in me."

He stood at the door, ready to leave. "Would you rather I didn't pick you up in the mornings?"

She hadn't expected that question, but she'd done it to herself and had to live with it. "I love being picked up. Who wouldn't? But I'm sure it isn't always convenient for you. All you have to do is phone me if something comes up and I'll send for the limo." Tuccia moved closer to him. "Do you want to know what my greatest concern is?"

"I don't have to guess," he muttered. "You're talking about your aunt."

"Actually I'm not as worried now. But I'm thinking about you and the risk you took to talk your partners into helping me in the first place."

"I didn't have to go that far," he bit out. "When they heard about your situation and ate that batch of tarts you made, they wanted to protect you."

"Nevertheless I wish I could do something important for you to pay you back."

"You are," he said in a gravelly voice. "Talk among the staff is growing that your desserts have already resulted in rave reviews from our latest guests. In fact several of the top food magazines, including *Buon Appetito*, already want an interview with the new pastry chef."

"That's nice to hear, but I can't take any credit for it. The people they need to talk to are you and your mother."

He cocked his head. "Would it interest you to know that the top dessert so far is your *granita*? Maurice says it's perfection."

Tuccia adored Cesare for saying that. She loved him so terribly she was going to blurt it out if he didn't leave in the next few seconds. "Then the credit for that goes to the chef on my parents' yacht."

"Not everyone can follow a recipe the way you've done and improve it. Why won't you take credit for what you're doing?"

She averted her eyes.

A sound of exasperation came out of him. "I can see I'm not going to get the answer I'm looking for from you."

Nor I from you, my darling.

"Enjoy your evening out, but be careful. Unless there's an emergency, I'll be by at eight in the morning." He opened the door.

"Cesare?" She was dying inside.

He turned around so fast it startled her. "*Si*?"

"Would you mind answering a question for me?"

"Have I ever?"

Oh, dear, but she was determined to ask him anyway. "I was just wondering if you would consider taking me to New York with you on my first weekend off. To see it with you would mean everything to me."

"I'm afraid that would be out of the question. I have too much business and couldn't show you around."

His rejection was swift and true, cutting her to the very marrow of her bones. Tuccia would never make that mistake again. "I just thought I'd ask. I hope you have a lovely night without any worries for a change."

"That'll be the day," he ground out, "but I appreciate the thought."

It was the hardest thing she'd ever done to keep a smile on her face and pretend he hadn't destroyed her with those words. But somehow she managed to maintain her poise until he drove off.

Now that he was gone, she knew what she had to do. After he'd left and she could no longer hear the engine, Tuccia called for a taxi rather than the limo service Cesare had arranged for her to use. She didn't want her whereabouts this evening to be traced.

When it drew up to the apartment, she walked outside and exchanged greetings with the *padrona* before she got in. Once she shut the door, she asked the driver to take her to the airport and drop her off at the main terminal.

Then she sat back and contemplated what she had to do. If Cesare had been willing to take her to New York, everything would have been different. But with that dream gone, she needed to follow through on a plan growing in the back of her mind.

Before long the limo pulled up to the drop-off area. She paid the driver and got out, waving him on. Then she walked through the crowds to the ticketing counter and booked a round trip ticket from Milan to Palermo. Bless her *zia* for slipping her a little money in case of an emergency. Bertina must have been psychic!

She would leave next Friday after work, the beginning of her first weekend off, and return Sunday evening. The police weren't looking for her so she didn't worry about being spotted. If by chance any detectives her parents had hired did see her name on a passenger list and alert her parents, she'd have to deal with it then.

As soon as she'd booked both two-hour flights and had paid cash, she got another taxi and headed right back to the *pensione.* Relieved that she'd finally done something about an impossible situation, she prepared for bed and climbed under the covers.

Her plan was to take a taxi to Bertina's palazzo. Tuccia couldn't bear to put her *zia* through any more grief. They needed to talk face-to-face about everything. She needed the woman who'd been like a mother to her growing up, before she faced her parents.

Without doing that, she could never embrace the newfound independence Cesare had tried to give her at great risk to him. Whatever happened, it was time to take total charge of her life.

On the next Friday afternoon at three o'clock sharp, Cesare said good-night to Tuccia and watched her leave the *castello* in the limousine. He decided to give her an hour after she got back to her apartment before he made a surprise appearance at her door. She believed he was leaving for New York. That was what he'd wanted her to think.

Surely she knew why he'd told her she couldn't come with him when she'd asked him. She had to know he was madly in love with her.

For the last week he'd been functioning on automatic pilot and knew it couldn't go on until he got Tuccia alone. His plan was to whisk her away in his car to Lago di Garda. Italy's largest lake was situated two hours away from Milan by car. He'd booked a romantic hideaway near the picturesque town of Salo where they wouldn't be disturbed.

In three weeks she'd become his whole world and he wouldn't rest until they'd talked everything out and he'd told her what was in his heart.

He let Vincenzo know he was leaving. After he cleared the decks with Maurice, his work was finished here. Cesare showered and packed a bag. With everything done, he took off in his car for the *pensione.*

When he walked to her door and knocked, he felt an adrenaline rush impossible to contain. "Tuccia? It's Cesare." He waited and listened, but didn't hear anything. "Tuccia?" He knocked hard. "I have to talk to you."

Nothing.

Had she already gone somewhere in the limo?

He got back in his car and called the limo service. The dispatcher told him she'd rung for a car to pick her up at the *castello* at three o'clock, but she hadn't requested another limo. Cesare thanked him and hung up, not liking the vibe he was getting.

His next thought was that she must have gone for a walk in the village. Rather than try looking for her, he called her cell phone, but she didn't answer. If she was inside the apartment, he couldn't imagine her not picking up when she saw the caller ID.

Growing more anxious, he phoned the *padrona* and asked if she'd seen Tuccia. The older woman said the last time she saw her was yesterday when she came home still wearing her chef's outfit.

"Will you do me a favor and let yourself inside to find out if she's too ill to answer the door?"

"*Naturalmente.* I will call you right back."

Cesare watched her leave her apartment and enter Tuccia's. Suddenly she reappeared at the entrance and waved for him to come in. At this point he broke out in a cold sweat fearing what he would find.

He jumped out of the car and rushed inside, dreading to think what he might find. But instead of Tuccia passed out on the floor or ill in her bed, the *padrona* handed him a sheet of paper. He could see it was lined and had come from Tuccia's bible.

"I found this on the table, *signor.* She left this for you. I will go now."

"Grazie," he murmured, feeling gutted.

After the door closed, he read what she'd written.

In case someone from the castello *tries to reach me and can't, I've gone to my* zia *in Palermo for the weekend.*

His eyes closed tightly. He squeezed the note into a ball. Pain almost debilitated him. She had to have taken a plane because a train or bus would never have gotten her there in time. Cesare knew how terrible she felt for her aunt, but he hadn't expected Tuccia to fly into the hornet's nest this soon.

Blackness had descended on him. After locking her front door, he took off for the airport in his car. The first thing he did en route was phone the pilot and alert him he needed to fly to Palermo ASAP. Next he called his mother, but she didn't answer and it went to her voice mail.

He left the message that he'd be in Palermo tonight and needed to talk to her the second he got there. Cesare had come to the low ebb of his life. He couldn't lose Tuccia.

When the taxi drove up to the gates of the palazzo at quarter to ten that night, Tuccia paid the driver and jumped out. She ran into Paolo. Her aunt's groundskeeper looked shocked when he recognized her, and he let her through.

She put a finger to her lips. "Shh. I want to surprise my *zia.* How is she, Paolo?"

"Very, very sad and missing you. Praise the angels you have come back."

Tuccia kissed his ruddy cheek and darted up the long flower-lined walkway to the main entrance. She tugged on the door pull and waited for Adona to answer. The housekeeper never went to bed until late.

After a minute she could hear someone talking on the inside and then the door opened.

The second Adona saw her, she put her hands to her mouth in shock. "Ah! Ah! Principessa!" she cried and called out to Bertina. Her booming voice must have reached the second floor because suddenly there was Tuccia's *zia* hurrying down the staircase in her robe with her dark hair undone, to find out what was going on.

Tuccia put down her suitcase and ran toward her. They met at the bottom step. She flung her arms around the woman who'd made her life worth living.

"Mia cara ragazza." Bertina kissed her over and over again while the tears ran down her cheeks. "I've been afraid I might never see you again. My prayers have been answered."

"So have mine," Tuccia cried, kissing her cheeks once more. "I've missed you more than you will ever know. Let's go up to your room so you can get back in bed and we'll talk in comfort."

"Do you need anything? Something to eat? Drink?"

"No. I just got off the plane and had a meal in flight. The only thing I need is to have a long, long talk with you about so many things."

With their arms hooked, they climbed the staircase where she'd rushed up and down so many times growing up. She could have found Bertina's boudoir wearing a blindfold. The room smelled like her lemon perfume, bringing back so many memories.

"Come on. I want you to get back in bed. You've had a great shock. I'll sit right here beside you and we'll catch up. Shall I ask Adona to bring you some tea?"

"No, no. I don't want to bother her."

Tuccia helped her off with her robe and puffed the pillows. Then her *zia* leaned back and pulled up the covers. "I just want to look at my beautiful daughter for a little while. You *are* my daughter, even if my sister gave birth to you."

"You already know how I feel about you." She kissed her forehead. "Ever since I ran away, I've worried about you until I've been ill over it."

"I've been all right. Over the last few days I've had several long talks with your mother who is suffering over what has happened. We're not sisters for nothing, and I know she has a sorrow in her heart until she can make peace with you."

"Then it's true what you told Lina?"

"Of course. She and your father, though he doesn't show it, were frightened when they thought you'd been kidnapped. It was one of those life-changing experiences for them. I don't believe they're the same people from before."

"So you believe what was printed in the newspaper?"

"Yes. They miss you and want you to come home. I'm convinced of it."

Tuccia stared into her eyes. "I want to believe it."

"I think that if you call them and have a talk, you'll find they're full of regrets, especially for the cruel betrothal forced on you, and they want a fresh start. You don't have to do it, of course."

"No. I want to do it, Zia. That's why I'm here."

She clapped her hands. "My prayers have been answered."

"Mine, too. If it hadn't been for Cesare's mother keeping him informed so he could tell me how you are, I would have lost my mind."

"Lina has become my close friend and has been a great blessing in my life."

Tuccia held her hand. "You have no idea *how* great, Zia."

Bertina heard the inflection in her voice. "Tell me what you mean."

"Do you know where I've been for the last three weeks?"

"No. I only know her son flew you to Milan so you could get away."

"There's so much to tell you I don't know where to start."

"At the beginning!" Bertina squeezed Tuccia's hand hard, causing her to chuckle. "Do you know that even though you've had to live through such a terrible ordeal, you seem happy. I don't think it's just because you're free of that deplorable engagement. I detect a glow about you."

"You do?"

"Yes. Your eyes are alive, like you've come out of a deep sleep. What's going on?"

"Did Lina tell you that the chef her son had hired

for the *castello ristorante* had gone to the hospital the same night she let me stay at her villa?"

"Oh, yes. We've both been to visit him at the hospital." Tuccia didn't know that.

"But she hasn't told you anything else?"

"Only that he found a place for you to stay in Milan."

"At a *pensione* in a village at the base of the *castello*."

"So you didn't have to leave Milan. It sounds like he was very good to you."

She took a big breath. "I'm afraid good doesn't begin to cover what he has done for me. What I'm about to tell you is going to come as a huge shock."

Bertina looked at her in that amazing way she had of reading between the lines. Tuccia had never been able to keep secrets from her, not that she'd wanted to. "Why do I get the feeling that the devilishly handsome Cesare Donati is more involved in all this than I had imagined?"

She bit her lip. "I'm in love with him, Zia! Wildly, passionately in love."

Her brows lifted. "Have you been living with him?"

"Not in the way you mean. I *wish* he'd asked me to live with him."

"Tuccianna—"

"That may sound terrible to you, but it's how I feel. We've been together every day and I've never known such joy in my life."

Bertina nodded. "Is he in love with you, too?"

She looked down. "I don't know. I think he is—I pray he is."

"You mean he hasn't told you?"

"No."

"Nor you him?"

"I couldn't! Our relationship hasn't been like that. One night he started kissing me and I thought I would die from happiness, but since then he hasn't tried to make love to me. I'm still trying to figure out why. I think he loves me, but—"

"You only think?" the older woman laughed.

"Unless I don't understand men and have been reading everything wrong."

"Why don't you start again, slowly, and give me a minute-by-minute explanation of what you've been up to that has turned you into a different person? Don't withhold any details. Together we just might figure everything out."

"I want to do that, but first I need to talk to my parents."

"Why don't I call them and tell them to come over here now."

"You think they'll come this late?"

Bertina shook her head. "If you only knew how much they've missed you, you wouldn't have to ask that question."

While Tuccia sat there trembling, she listened to the brief conversation. When her *zia* hung up, she said, "They're coming this instant. Why don't you freshen up and meet them at the door?"

"Will you come down with me?"

"No, my darling girl. This is a conversation you need to have with them alone. It's been twenty-five years in coming."

After going the bedroom she always used here, Tuccia hurried downstairs and waited until she heard the bell pull outside the door. When she opened it and saw her parents standing there, she was stunned by the rush of emotions that bombarded her.

"Tuccianna—" her mother cried and ran to embrace her. "You've come back. I was so afraid we would never see you again." They hugged for a long time.

After they broke apart, she looked at her father. "Papa?"

"Figlia mia." Tears poured down his cheeks. For the first time she could remember, he reached out and hugged her so hard she could barely breathe, but she didn't care. "Forgive us," he cried and broke down sobbing.

"Let's all go in the salon," she said, putting her arms through both of theirs. Once in the other room they sat down on the couch. She pulled up a chair so she could be close and look at them. Gone were the severe expressions of two people who'd been so rigid.

"I'm the one who's sorry for doing something so terrible, for frightening you and embarrassing you and Jean-Michel. But I couldn't marry him. I just couldn't!"

Her mother nodded. "I knew that the moment you'd disappeared from the bridal shop. I don't think I'll ever get over the shame of forcing you into an engagement that ruined your life for years. Bertina made us see how wrong we've been."

"We didn't mean to hurt you, Tuccianna," her father murmured in the saddest voice she'd ever heard. "While you've been gone, we've learned some things about Jean-Michel that let us know he would never have made you a good husband. You don't ever have to worry about him again. We've been so blind. How can we make this up to you?"

"By accepting me for who I am, and accepting the most wonderful man on earth whom I hope to marry."

"You've met someone?" her mother cried.

"Yes. Cesare Donati. I'm terribly in love with him. He came to my rescue the day I ran away. We've been together ever since. Let me tell you about him. About us."

For the next little while she related her experiences, leaving nothing out. "I'm now the executive pastry chef at the *castello* in Milan. I can't wait for you to meet him. You already know his wonderful mother."

"We do?"

"Yes, Mamma. She's Zia Bertina's cook."

Her father's eyes widened. "Lina Donati?"

She nodded. "Bertina asked her to hide me at her villa that first night, and I bumped into Cesare. It was love at first sight for me. But I don't know what's going to happen now." Tuccia knew he'd tried to be so careful with her to honor her because that was the way he was made. But she needed to know why he wouldn't take her to New York. They had to talk.

"We want you to be happy, Tuccia," her father declared.

"That's all we want." Her mother had broken down in tears again. "Will you let us be a part of your lives?"

Overjoyed to hear that question, she flew off the chair and embraced both of them.

CHAPTER TEN

THIS TIME WHEN Cesare arrived at the villa near midnight, his mother was up to greet him. They hugged before he followed her into the kitchen. She'd made his favorite *tarelli* lemon biscuits and her own version of espresso.

"I was at the hospital when I got your message and hurried home. You'll be pleased to know Ciro is making amazing strides. I think he might be released from the hospital sooner than anyone expected."

Cesare let out a deep sigh. "That news couldn't come at a better time." He had plans for him and Tuccia.

"It's clear you have something serious to say to me, Cesare. Tell me what has happened for you to show up like this late at night in such a frantic state."

They sat around the kitchen table while he drank his coffee. "I'm afraid you're going to be shocked when I tell you. I'm in love with Tuccia Leonardi."

She leaned forward on the table and eyed him seriously. "I've been wondering when you would finally tell me about what you did with her. What's wrong?"

"She left Milan without telling me. I'm terrified I might have lost her. If the worst has happened, I don't know how I'm going to live without her. Mamma, how did you handle it when Papa left you? I can't comprehend it."

His mother reached for his hand. "Where did that question come from?"

"I guess from the time I heard you crying in the bedroom when I was six. You were looking at his picture."

She squeezed his fingers before letting him go. "You thought I was crying about him. I wish I'd known. I could have saved you years of grief."

"What do you mean?"

"My tears over him had been shed long before he ever left. He didn't want marriage or responsibility. When I realized how unhappy we both were living together, I asked him to leave."

Cesare frowned. "You asked him?"

"Yes."

"So he didn't just walk out?"

"No. But I knew he wanted to and so I gave him his freedom. The day you saw me in tears, I was crying because he never did come back to see you and Isabella. You deserved a wonderful father and I could only be your mother. But I thank God every day he was your father because I have the two most wonderful children on earth. Now tell me why you think you've lost her?"

"Tuccia's my life, but when I went to her apartment earlier today, she'd gone. There was a note that said she'd flown here to see Bertina."

"Does she know how you feel about her?"

"Not in so many words."

"Because she's a princess?"

"I don't know. Maybe I've felt I wasn't good enough for her."

"Nonsense! My brilliant son. You're as blind as a bat where the *principessa* is concerned. Now let's really talk."

He sucked in his breath. "There's a lot you don't know. Without telling me, Tuccia flew here on her own."

His mother eyed him curiously. "How come you know so much about what the princess does? What have you been keeping from me?"

"A lot."

She smiled in that irritating way that said she'd already figured everything out. "You fell in love with her when you whisked her away to Milan without Ciro on board."

"I'm afraid I did more than that." He had her complete attention now.

"What man with blood in his veins wouldn't have done the same thing? Bertina and I have often said it's sinful how beautiful she is. Her parents did a cruel thing forcing that betrothal on her, but it has protected her. Until *I* interfered," she added. "So what did you do?"

"I made her the pastry chef at the *castello* in order to hide her."

A laugh escaped. "You mean a kitchen helper."

"No. She's the chef who has replaced Ciro and has been for two weeks."

"With your partners' approval?"

"Yes."

"Did she even know how to cook?"

"Not when she started."

"I presume you've been teaching her everything you know."

He nodded. "Except for an exceptional *gratina* she'd learned how to make years ago by watching the cook on her parents' yacht."

"I told you she was resourceful. I take it you've forgiven me for asking you to help her get away."

Cesare sat back in the chair. "I want to marry her, Mamma."

"At last you've found a woman who's your equal."

"But—"

"But nothing! Do you imagine for one single second she would have begged you to teach her if she weren't halfway in love with you by the time you arrived in Milan? She's known her own mind for years. When she met the man meant for her, she did whatever she could to get you to fall in love with her."

That was what he'd wanted to believe. "She's beyond wonderful."

"I know, and I can't tell you how delighted I am."

"In that case, I need a big favor from you. Will you call Bertina right now? Tell her I found out Tuccia is with her. Ask them to come for breakfast first thing in the morning. Tell her this has to do with Tuccia's parents and it's absolutely vital. But don't let her know I'm here. I'll do the rest."

He waited while she reached for the phone and made the call. "Bertina?" she said, putting it on speaker. "Forgive me for disturbing you this late, but this is an emergency. I've had word that Tuccia is with you."

"Oh, Lina—she arrived earlier tonight. I'm so happy I think I'm dreaming!"

"I can only imagine your joy at seeing her again. But before anything else happens, you must bring her to my villa first thing in the morning."

"Why? What's wrong?"

"There's something of great significance going on you don't know about. We have to talk, Bertina. I wouldn't ask this of you if I weren't frightened for both of you."

"After all you did for me, of course we'll be there."

Cesare's mother smiled at him in in relief. "Good. I'm looking forward to seeing Tuccia again."

"There's so much I have to tell you. We'll come early."

The second she hung up, Cesare shot out of the chair and walked around to hug her.

At eight in the morning, Tuccia and her aunt left the palazzo in a limo. Once again she found herself being driven through the streets to Mondello, one of the poshest areas of the city.

Before Tuccia had gone to bed in the suite she always used, Bertina had phoned to tell her about the conversation with Cesare's mother. She'd insisted she had some news they needed to hear.

Her heart thumped with sickening speed. The only way anyone knew she'd flown to Palermo tonight was through Cesare. But that meant he'd had to go to her apartment and find the note she'd left. Since he didn't have a key, he would have been forced to ask the *padrona* for help if he thought something was wrong. Why had he bothered?

She'd thought he'd flown to New York after they'd said goodbye. Evidently he'd dropped by the *pensione* before leaving for the airport. There'd been a phone call from him while she'd been on her way to the airport in the taxi, but she'd turned her phone off. Though she could have answered it—had wanted to respond—she was trying to keep her distance.

Had he phoned his mother because he was worried her parents would try to prevent her from returning to Milan? Surely he knew she would never allow that to happen. Tuccia had made a contract with him, one she would never break. How could he think she wouldn't return on Sunday night to fulfill her obligations?

But maybe he still saw her as a young woman who'd been so sheltered she'd be unable to stand on her own once she faced her parents. That was crazy. All she wanted in life was to be his wife. Nothing else could ever satisfy her.

"We're here, Tuccianna."

"I'm nervous, Zia. What do you imagine Lina needs to tell us that's so important?"

"I don't know, but I trust her with my life."

Just the way Tuccia trusted her son.

They got out of the limo and walked to the villa entrance. When the door opened, Tuccia expected to see Lina. Instead she let out a gasp and came close to a faint. *"Cesare—"*

His blue gaze traveled over her, missing nothing. "Won't you both come in? It's good to see you, Bertina." He kissed her on both cheeks. "Mamma is waiting for you in the kitchen where she has breakfast ready. Tuccia and I will join you in a few minutes, but first we have some unfinished business to talk over."

Bertina had been to the villa many times before

and walked down the hallway to the kitchen without needing directions.

Tuccia stayed where she was, glued to the spot. "What are you doing here? I thought you'd flown to New York."

"That's what I wanted you to think while I worked out a plan to take you away to a place where we could be private. But when I got to the apartment, you'd gone.

Like a fool I've given you too much time and space, but that's over. Come on. We need to be alone."

To her joy he reached for her hand and walked her up the stairs. She followed him down a hallway to what had to be his suite. After he shut the door, he lounged against it and grasped her upper arms.

"Let's get something straight right now. I only flew after you for one reason. It's the only reason I took you to Milan in the beginning. Since running into a princess in a yellow robe three weeks ago, it's the reason why I've been turned inside out and upside down. I'm in love with you, Tuccia, but you already know that. The question is, are you in love with me?"

"Oh, Cesare—" She couldn't believe what she was hearing. "How can you even ask me that? I'd fallen in love with you by the time the ducal jet landed at Milan airport. You're all I think or live for. I need you more than you will ever know."

They both moaned as he pulled her against him and he started kissing her the way he'd done at the apartment. Tuccia lost track of time as she tried to show him how much he meant to her. His mouth was doing such incredible things to her she burned with desire for him. To her joy she no longer had to hold back. He loved her!

Somehow they ended up on his bed where they began to devour each other. After three weeks of starvation, she realized she had absolutely no self-control, but she didn't care. This incredible man loved her and was making her feel immortal.

Yet Cesare was the one to call a halt before they got too carried away. He slowly relinquished her mouth and looked down at her. His eyes burned with love for her. "We're not alone in this villa and there are two people waiting for us to join them."

"I know."

"Before we go down, I have something else to say. I want to marry you as soon as possible."

"I want that, too."

"We'll make it work and live at the apartment until Ciro can come to the *castello*."

"I love the apartment. To me it's been like our little home. I'd be happy living with you there forever."

"I've felt the same way. Though I haven't dared touch you and you know why, cooking and eating together have been the highlights of my life."

"Mine, too."

"I need to meet your parents and tell them our intentions while we're here in Palermo."

"They already know my intentions."

"So you've seen them already?"

"Yes. I was with them tonight at Bertina's. It's true that they've become different people. We hugged and kissed and they can't wait to meet the man I told them I planned to marry. I'm free to live my own life and

I love you for helping me find the courage to face them."

He kissed her mouth. "I love you so much I can't live without you."

"I've been waiting to hear you say that!" she cried for joy.

"You're an amazing, loving woman. If it's all right with you, we'll go see them together so I can ask for your hand."

"They're old-fashioned and will love it."

He held her tighter. "If I have you, I have everything."

"I love you, Cesare. Way too much." She kissed each masculine feature of his striking face before kissing his mouth over and over again.

"There's something else we have to talk about. I'm anxious to plan our wedding. It needs to take place as soon as possible, or I won't be able to stand it," he whispered.

"It's all I've thought about since I met you."

"By some miracle I've found the woman for me."

"I feel the same way about you and can't belong to you soon enough."

"Two weeks from this weekend is your next time off. Our marriage can take place then. I would like Gemma and Vincenzo to be there, but I doubt they'll be able to. Still, I'm not waiting any longer to make you my wife.

"Depending on your parents' wishes, we'll have it performed in my church here, or in yours. We'll return to Milan Sunday night and take a honeymoon later after Ciro is back at the *castello*."

She ran her hands through his hair. "We'll have to

make as many arrangements as we can while we're here, but I don't want a big wedding. Just a few family friends."

"I love the way you think because I'd prefer a quiet wedding too, Tuccia." He gave her a long hungry kiss. "Now much as I don't want to leave this room, I think we'd better go downstairs to the kitchen. My mother and Bertina are dying to know what has been going on."

"I'm pretty sure they know exactly." She kissed his hard jaw, loving the taste and feel of him.

"It'll be fun to make their day."

She laughed. "I know it will."

They had trouble letting each other go. When she got up from the bed, she felt positively dizzy. "I need to fix myself first." She opened her purse and got out her styling brush.

Cesare took it from her and started running it through her curls. "I've been wanting to do this forever. But don't put on any lipstick yet. I need another kiss from you before I can go anywhere."

She threw her arms around his neck and kissed him so passionately that they wove in place. "I've ached to do this since we went to the park. I almost pulled you down and begged you to make love to me. Every time you said good-night to me and walked out without holding me in your arms, I could hardly bear it."

"In two weeks we won't ever have to suffer again. We'll be together day and night."

"By night I'll be Signora Donati. By day I'll be Nedda Bottaro."

He shook his head. "Once we've said our vows, you'll be my wife in the kitchen, too, and you'll wear whatever clothes you feel like wearing. Manoussos will be in pain when he finds out the truth."

They left the room and started down the stairs. "No he won't. You're being silly."

"Trust me. I'm a man and I know these things."

She turned to him when they reached the foyer. "Oh—I know you're a man. The most wonderful man who ever lived. Kiss me again, Cesare."

Ten days later, while Tuccia was checking the last of the desserts for the evening meal, Cesare reappeared after being gone most of her work day. Every time she sensed his presence, her heart almost burst out of her chest.

It was almost three o'clock. She'd never known him to be away from the kitchen this long. He walked over to her with a gleam in his eyes. "I'd squeeze your waist if I could find it," he teased.

Tuccia chuckled. She'd been so happy since their return from Palermo, she felt like she'd been floating. Her parents were both so impressed with Cesare that they'd given the two of them their blessing and hadn't found fault with anything. Not now that she'd come home to them.

The wedding at her family's church would be going ahead on Saturday. That day couldn't come soon enough for Tuccia.

"Guess who's in labor and has been in the hospital since eight this morning?"

"Gemma? Oh, I'm so excited for her! How's Vincenzo?"

"A complete wreck. The doctor told him it could take a long time because it's her first baby. I stayed with him as long as I could. Now Dimi and his wife are there. Takis and Lys are on their way from Crete on the jet. I'll drive you home to change and then we'll go over to the hospital."

Before long she said good-night to everyone. Cesare gathered some sandwiches in a bag and hustled her out of the kitchen to the car. When they reached the apartment, she got out of her uniform and changed into a skirt and blouse in record time.

"You look fabulous. Three more days before our world changes." He gave her a long, hungry kiss, then they left for the hospital in Milan. Everyone had gathered round in the hospital lounge. They talked about the coming wedding. It was going to be a very small morning ceremony of twenty people with a brunch afterward at the palazzo of Tuccia's parents.

Afterward she and Cesare planned to fly to Milan and spend Saturday night and Sunday at Lago di Garda before returning to their apartment. That was the place where he'd planned to take her the evening he'd come by the apartment and had found her gone. So much had happened since that night.

While they were chatting, a nurse walked toward them. "Signor Gagliardi says for you to come. If you'll follow me."

Cesare grasped her hand and they walked through the swinging doors to the second room down the hall. When they entered the room, Tuccia's breath caught. There was Gemma holding a baby in her arms with a cap of black hair. She was beaming. An exhausted-looking Vincenzo sat next to her. Both were examining their new arrival.

The proud father looked up at them. "Come all the

way in and meet our baby. We've decided to call him Nico. He's seven pounds six ounces and measures twenty-two inches long. Though he came two weeks early, the pediatrician says he's perfect."

"Felicitazioni!" sounded their cry. "A new Duc di Lombardi has graced our world."

Soon they left the hospital. She kissed Cesare's cheek. "That's a perfect family."

He reached for her hand. "That's what we're going to have, Tuccia."

"I know we're not even married yet, but already I want your baby."

"There's one promise I'll make to you. I'll do my best to get you pregnant."

"I'll do my best to get pregnant," Tuccia gave a happy sigh. "Everything has worked out because of you, Cesare."

His hand slid to her thigh. "I don't think you have any idea how much I love you."

Her heart was too full to talk. All she could do was cover his hand with her own.

"Takis seems to be handling his wife's pregnancy well," he said, "but he can be inscrutable at times. I would imagine that deep down he's holding his breath until she delivers."

After they reached the apartment and he took her inside, he pulled her down on the couch so they half lay together. "I've made a decision about something and wanted to talk it over with you."

"What is it?" But being this close, she couldn't resist kissing him again and again.

"I'm going to sell all my business interests in New York and invest the profits. I don't want to have to fly there anymore and leave you. Our life is here. We always have a place to stay at the *castello*, and at the villa when we visit my mother. But I'd like to think about a home of our own in Palermo."

"I'm so glad you said that. It's what I want. Our own place. It doesn't have to be big. Just large enough to hold two or three children. I want us to have a normal life."

"I want the same thing. You know Takis has worked things out so he can be here part of the time. The rest of the time he spends with Lys at their home in Crete. And Vincenzo lives in a villa on Lake Como with Gemma. There's no reason we can't do the same thing and fly back and forth when it's necessary."

"I think you've just made me the happiest bride-to-be in the whole world. Please don't go home tonight. Stay with me."

He hugged her tighter. "I'd like to take you in the bedroom, lock the door and throw away the key forever. Don't tempt me. Just three more days to wait, *amore mio.* We're almost there."

CHAPTER ELEVEN

CESARE STOOD AT the front of the church in Palermo with Dimi and Takis. They all wore dark blue dress suits and ties with a white rose in the lapels. He'd put the rings in his pocket. Even though Vincenzo couldn't make it, this made four times that they'd celebrated each other's weddings.

Six weeks ago, if anyone had told him he'd be married to the love of his life this morning, he would have laughed in disbelief. He kept looking at the back of the church, waiting for Tuccia to enter on the arm of her father.

The *marchesa* and her sister Bertina sat together by Cesare's mother. Behind them sat Isabella and her husband, Tomaso. They'd left the baby with Tomaso's mother. Filippa, Dimi's wife, and Lys sat by each other. The few other guests were the close friends of Tuccia's parents.

She'd insisted on keeping their wedding as low key as possible. Her life growing up had been filled with too many bad memories. She'd begged for simplicity and a non-princess wedding. Cesare had seen to her wishes.

As he wondered if something had gone wrong, he

saw the priest out of the corner of his eye. Behind him walked Tuccia on her father's arm. She looked a vision in a full-length white silk wedding dress. The lace mantilla covering her gorgeous black curls was a sight he'd never forget. She held a bouquet of white roses from her aunt's garden.

The priest had agreed to perform their short ceremony in Sicilian.

"Cesare Donati, please take Princess Tuccianna Falcone Leonardi by the hand and repeat after me."

Their eyes met before he grasped it. The love and trust in those gray orbs melted him on the spot. Thus began the age-old ritual that took on indescribable meaning to him as he kept looking at the woman who'd agreed to marry him. There was no person more precious to him.

They exchanged vows and rings.

"I now pronounce you man and wife. In the name of the Father, the Son and the Holy Spirit."

The priest didn't have to tell him to kiss his bride. Cesare gathered her in his arms and embraced her. Her hunger for him matched his. They were on fire for each other. If he could run away with her now, he would, but they had one more celebration to get through.

Holding her hand tightly, he walked her down the aisle to the foyer where everyone hugged and congratulated them. Afterward they went outside to get in the limos that drove them to her parents' palazzo for their wedding brunch on the east patio.

While they ate, Tuccia's father made an announcement. "Unbeknownst to Tuccianna and her new husband, I've made arrangements for them to have a small honeymoon aboard our yacht, so they won't be flying back to Milan for a few days."

Cesare's heart leaped. They wouldn't have to endure a flight. At least not for a couple of days.

At that juncture Takis rose to his feet. "No man should have to worry about getting back to work right away. Maurice knows about your marriage and has agreed to run the kitchen until the Siciliana gets back. He told me to tell you he's looking forward to seeing the new Signora Donati without your uniform and that floppy chef's hat."

Everyone laughed, but Tuccia's face went crimson. Cesare loved it.

"How soon can we leave?" he whispered near her ear.

"As soon as I change. I'll be right back."

She gave him a wife's kiss to torture him and hurried through the rooms to the upstairs. Once she'd gotten out of her wedding dress, she put on a pale pink summer suit and strappy high heels. Grabbing the case she'd packed earlier, she hurried back down. More hugs and kisses ensued.

But his impatience was too great. He put his arm around her shoulders, waved goodbye to everyone and they rushed outside to get in the limo. What an amazing experience to be headed for the dock in Mondello and go aboard the royal yacht.

Cesare had seen it out in the harbor many times along with the other yachts after he'd hiked the bluff. When he'd been younger all his thoughts had been intent on leaving for New York to make his way in the world. Little did he dream that his great adventure would bring him right back home, right to this yacht where his new wife had learned to make *granita.*

The deck steward showed them to the master bedroom below deck. Once he left them alone Cesare picked Tuccia up in his arms and twirled her around. "Finally I have you all to myself the way I've dreamed."

"I've had the same dreams. Love me, Cesare." Her voice shook.

"As if you need to ask me." He carried her to the bed and followed her down. They started to kiss, one after another until there was no beginning and no end. "I'm so hungry for you, I'm afraid I'll eat you alive."

"I'm afraid you won't," she cried, feverish with longing.

"*Amata.* You're so beautiful I can hardly breathe. My adorable, precious, beloved wife."

Those words were still part of her euphoria when she woke up during the night. They'd made love for hours, only to fall asleep, then start the whole heavenly process over again when they came awake.

She'd tried to imagine what it would be like to really love a man. But nothing could have prepared her for the kind of love showered on her by her new husband. There were no words to describe the ecstasy that had her clinging to him throughout the night.

At one point her rapture was so great she wept.

"What is it?" he cried.

"I was just thinking. What if I hadn't run away? What if your mother hadn't let me stay overnight? I might have missed *you.*" She moaned.

He buried his face in her neck. "Don't even think about it."

"I can't help it. I'm too happy, Cesare. No woman could ever be as happy as I am."

"You're supposed to be when you've found the right person to love. *Ti amo*, Tuccia. This is only the beginning."

Two years later, the Castello di Lombardi

Tuccia followed little Cesare around on the grass behind the *castello* near the ruins of the fourteenth-century church. Their little brown-haired son had just turned a year old, but was still unsteady on his feet. Filippa and Dimi's little dark-haired boy, Dizo, was just two months older, but handled himself with amazing agility. Her gaze followed two year-old Nico around. He was Vincenzo's clone.

Cesare came up behind her and put his arms around her waist, nuzzling her neck. "It's hilarious out here with all the children running around on the grass. Look how Nico runs after Zoe. She's the image of her mother."

"Lys is a beauty, and I can tell Zoe is going to be a heartbreaker, too, when she grows up," Tuccia said, eyeing the two-year-old with a smile.

"I think she has already stolen Nico's heart."

Tuccia turned around and gave her husband a long, passionate kiss. "Wouldn't it be amazing if they grew up loving each other?"

"You mean like Gemma and Vincenzo? It wouldn't surprise me."

"I love having a birthday picnic for all of them. Maurice and Ciro have really outdone themselves for this celebration."

"He doesn't make pastry as good as yours, my love."

"Of course he does, Cesare. Doesn't Gemma have the best ideas? This is so fun! Uh-oh. Cesare fell down."

He kissed her cheek. "I'll go get him."

Tuccia joined the women sitting on the blanket while she watched her gorgeous husband run after their son. As far as she was concerned, this was heaven.

The men were tending the children to give the women a break. All the women except Tuccia were pregnant again. Gemma was seven months along with a girl this time.

"Is Vincenzo as freaked out this time around?" Lys wanted to know.

"He's not nearly as bad as he was the first time."

"Thank heaven," Filippa exclaimed. They all laughed.

Gemma raised herself up on one elbow. "Do you know what's really strange? To be out here on the same grass where I played as a little girl with Vincenzo and Dimi. Sometimes they had sword fights."

"Who won?" Filippa wanted to know.

"They were both pretty fierce and equally matched. One time when it was Vincenzo's birthday, my mother made a little cake for him and I brought it out to him."

Tuccia smiled. "Did you always love him?"

"Always."

"And soon you were making cakes."

"And then I met Filippa at cooking school."

Tuccia stretched out. "I can't believe how lucky I was to meet Cesare. I fell so hard for him I actually learned how to make his mother's pastry in order to be near him."

"Are you taking my name in vain again?" a deep familiar voice sounded behind her. The girls chuckled.

She rolled over and looked up at him holding their son. "Afraid so. We were just saying how lucky we are to be married to such remarkable men."

Cesare's smile melted her on the spot. "Funny. The guys and I were just having the same conversation about the superb women in our lives. It all happened one morning in Vincenzo's New York apartment when he asked if Takis and I wanted to go into business with him and Dimi across the water." He stared into her eyes. "And here we are. Life truly is more fantastic and wonderful than fiction."

"I agree, Cesare." *I love you*, Tuccia mouthed the words before getting to her feet. "Come on. Let's go back to the hotel room and put little Cesare down for a nap. I want some alone time with my husband."

They hurried inside the *castello* to the private wing on the second floor. After putting their sleepy boy down, they went in their bedroom. Tuccia started to take off her clothes, unable to wait until she held Cesare in her arms.

He removed his faster and within seconds he pulled her down on the bed. *"Bellissima?"* he whispered against her lips. "Do you still love me as much as you did when we got married?"

She heard a hint of anxiety his voice.

"My darling husband, how can you even ask me that?" Except that she *did* know why. His mother had confided in her about his father. "Listen to me." She leaned over him, cupping his face in her hands.

"You're stuck with me forever. I'm never going anywhere. You're my whole life! It began the moment you crushed me in your arms. I've never told you this before, but I'm telling you now. That magical night, I felt like you'd imprinted yourself on my heart and soul. When you turned on the lights, there stood the most gorgeous man my eyes had ever beheld."

Cesare kissed her until they were both out of breath. "It was a magical night. You looked like an enchanted princess escaping her bottle."

"That's how it felt, and there you were. I love you, Cesare. Never doubt it for an instant."

"Never again, *amorada.* Never again."

* * * * *